WOMAN'S HOUR
BOOK OF
SHORT STORIES

VOLUME II

WOMAN'S HOUR BOOK OF SHORT STORIES

VOLUME II

Selected and introduced by Pat McLoughlin

BBC BOOKS

A BBC Radio Collection double cassette
containing readings of a selection
of these stories is also available.

Short Story Index
<u>1989-1993</u>

Published by BBC Books
a division of BBC Enterprises Limited
80 Wood Lane, London W12 0TT
First published 1992
Stories © Individual copyright holders
Copyright © in this selection BBC Books 1992

Reprinted 1992

ISBN 0 563 36389 4

Set in 11/13pt Garamond by Ace Filmsetting Ltd, Frome
Printed and bound in Great Britain by Clays Ltd, St Ives Plc
Cover printed by Clays Ltd. St Ives Plc

CONTENTS

———— ◆ ————

ACKNOWLEDGEMENTS

———— ◆ ————

We are grateful to the following for permission to reproduce copyright material:

Virago Press for 'Her Mother' by Anjana Appachana; Jonathan Cape Ltd for 'Unearthing Suite' by Margaret Atwood. First published in *Bluebeard's Egg*; Gerald Duckworth & Co Ltd for 'Somewhere More Central' by Beryl Bainbridge from *Mum & Mr Armitage: Selected Stories of Beryl Bainbridge*; Oxford University Press for 'The Kiss' by Winifred Beechey, © Winifred Beechey, 1991. First published in *The Reluctant Samaritan: Tales of Old Age*; Jonathan Cape Ltd and the Estate of Elizabeth Bowen for 'Maria' by Elizabeth Bowen from *The Collected Short Stories of Elizabeth Bowen*; Rogers, Coleridge and White Ltd for 'A Model Daughter' by Clare Boylan, © Clare Boylan. First published by Hamish Hamilton Ltd in *Concerning Virgins*; John Johnson Ltd for 'Night in Paris' by Patrice Chaplin; Hamish Hamilton Ltd for 'Another Marvellous Thing' by Laurie Colwin from *Another Marvellous Thing*; Fourth Estate Ltd for 'How Slattery Tricked His Mother Into Touching Him' by Nina Fitzpatrick from *Fables of the Irish Intelligentsia*, © Nina Fitzpatrick, 1991; David Higham Associates Ltd for 'Swan' by Jane Gardam. First published by Hamish Hamilton Ltd in *Showing the Flag*; Curtis Brown Ltd for 'To Uncle, With Love' by Rumer Godden from *Swans and Turtles*; The Society of Authors and Miss Rosamond Lehmann for 'The Gypsy's Baby' by Rosamond Lehmann; Murray Pollinger on behalf of Penelope Lively for 'Clara's Day' by Penelope Lively; William Heinemann Ltd for 'Violets and Strawberries in the Snow' by Shena Mackay. First published in *Dreams of Dead Women's Handbags*; Curtis Brown Ltd on behalf of Deborah Moggach for 'Some Day My Prince Will Come' by Deborah Moggach from *Smile and Other Stories*; Chatto & Windus Ltd for 'Wigtime' by Alice Munro from *Friend of My Youth*; Peter Owen Ltd, London for 'There's a War On' by Cora Sandel from *The Silken Thread: Stories and Sketches*; Chatto & Windus Ltd and the Executors of the Estate of Sylvia Townsend Warner for 'A View of Exmoor' by Sylvia Townsend Warner from *One Thing Leading To Another*; Virago Press for 'The Saint' by Antonia White from *Strangers*.

INTRODUCTION

———— ♦ ————

The success of the first *Woman's Hour Book of Short Stories*, published in 1990, and increasing enthusiasm for the short story as a good read, have made this second anthology possible. Spoilt for choice as ever – oh how to whittle down the ever-increasing total of distinguished stories broadcast on *Woman's Hour* over the years – I once again decided on a theme which would help this distillation. The use of such a theme in the first anthology (the varying aspects of 'love') seemed to enhance its appeal, and I hope that this time the common denominator of 'the younger generation' will prove equally attractive.

I am also glad to introduce a detail suggested by a reader of the first volume – and a regular listener to the programme. She commented that she would have liked to have been reminded of the performers who read the stories on the air. This seems a valuable suggestion on two counts: one is that no matter how well-written a story is, its virtues can be lost on the air if it not brought skilfully to life by the storyteller. Secondly, this anthology, like the first one, is complemented by a Radio Collection cassette featuring twelve of the stories, where those skilful interpretations are most vividly demonstrated. I have not included the names in this introduction but you will find them, plus the original transmission dates on *Woman's Hour*, at the end of each story.

And so to the stories themselves, nineteen in all, and divided fairly evenly between well-known and less well-known names.

Some of the well-known ones have already featured in the first anthology. I feel it would have been perverse to exclude such very different yet equally brilliant writers as Elizabeth Bowen and Shena Mackay, purely on the grounds of an earlier appearance; but however familiar the writer I have, as before, aimed for less well-known examples of their work. I have tried, too, to balance the moods and I hope that within these pages you will find stories to make you laugh and cry.

The best writers of course do both, as the first storyteller in this collection fully demonstrates. And how else to kick off 'the Younger Generation' than with the birth of a baby? The baby is in fact 'Another Marvellous Thing', which is both the title and the penultimate story in American writer Laurie Colwin's interconnected series (published in 1987) about the progress of an affair. It is conducted between two very ill-sorted protagonists – Francis Clemens, an urbanely polite and elegant older man (the very encapsulation of American East Coast sophistication), and Billy Delielle, a cranky, tough-minded but tender-hearted young woman. A witty, perceptive account of the affair (and the other 'marvellous thing') is given in 'My Mistress', the opening story of the series – which appeared in the first *Woman's Hour* anthology. In 'Another Marvellous Thing' itself, it is more than a year since Billy ended the affair. In this story Francis makes only a very brief and unwitting appearance when the taxi carrying the heavily-pregnant Billy home from a baby shower, stops at a red light, and there he is – the man who for two years had been her lover.

Seeing him, she reflects again on the surprising fact that two such unlikely people had been in love – 'as brilliant as a painted bunting. He was also, in marked contrast to Billy, beautifully dressed. He loved opera, cocktail parties, and lunches. They did not agree about economic theory, either'. And as the cab pulls away – 'It was amazing that someone who had been so close to her did not know that she was having a baby'. Now she is awaiting the birth of her husband Grey's child. The preliminaries nor the birth itself are straightforward, but still Billy's mordant wit manages to break through – 'I knew we never should have had sexual intercourse'. When their son is born he is underweight, and has to spend the first weeks of his life in the Infant Intensive Care Unit. For Billy it has uncomfortable echoes. 'This is like having an affair with a married man. You love the person but can only see him at certain times.'

The second baby in this collection appears in 'There's a War On' from *The Silken Thread* by Cora Sandel (published 1986). Cora Sandel, who died in 1974, was Norwegian, but her cosmopolitan life – she married a Swedish sculptor and lived in France and Italy – is reflected in her writing. Like many European writers, Cora Sandel is not as well-known outside her own country as she deserves to be. She is better known for her novels – particularly her *Alberta* trilogy – but her shorter works, on the evidence of this collection, fully deserve the comparison that's been made between her and Colette, whose books she translated into Norwegian. And on the subject of translators, Cora Sandel seems to have been particularly well-served by Elizabeth Rokkan.

Cora Sandel's life (1880–1974) straddled some of the most dramatic years in European history. It included two world wars and 'There's a War On' takes place in a cellar during the bombardment of Paris in the First World War. Three-weeks-old Bernard has been born into a world far from the affluence and security of Billy Delielle's little son. His parents are 'two irresponsible young artists from Scandinavia, who hadn't the good sense to get back home in time, and were even more lacking in sense when they went and acquired Bernard in the middle of all this'. But 'a child is a child' and Bernard and his fate preoccupy the other inhabitants of the cellar, who, night after night, take refuge there. For, not to put too fine a point upon it – 'Bernard is starving'. Finally it is 'thin little Madame Mialon' who hardly ever speaks, who comes up with an unexpected solution.

In this second anthology from stories broadcast on *Woman's Hour*, I thought it would be an extra enrichment to include one of novella-length. This feeling was strengthened by the knowledge that in 1988 we had broadcast a superb one – *The Gypsy's Baby* by Rosamond Lehmann; and this third baby (although an off-stage one, very much a catalyst in the plot) takes us neatly into family life in general.

Rosamond Lehmann (1901–90) was predominantly a novelist, rather than a short story writer, and novels such as *Invitation to the Waltz* (1932), *The Weather in the Streets* (1936) and *The Ballad and the Source* (1944) are, like *The Gypsy's Baby* (1946), highly autobiographical. *The Gypsy's Baby* in fact features two very different families, polarised at opposite ends of the British class structure. The Ellisons are undoubtedly Rosamond Lehmann's own family – privileged, upper middle class, but with a highly-developed social conscience. And then there are the prolific Wyatts who live in squalor in the back lane behind the Ellisons' garden.

Already uneasily aware of each other, the two families are brought into closer contact when the Ellisons' Dandie Dinmont dog kills the Wyatts' cat. 'Your grey dog got our Fluff. We don't like 'im no more.' But it is not just the loss of Fluff that the Wyatts have to contend with, as we witness through the eyes of Rebecca Ellison (like her creator, the second child and middle daughter of a family of four) – it is the disintegration of the Wyatt family itself. In many ways it is a heartbreaking story, but it has humour and optimism too.

The narrator in Deborah Moggach's 'Some Day My Prince Will Come' (published in her anthology *Smile* in 1987) has two children, five-year-old Tilly, who is something of an *enfant terrible*, and Adam, just three. Her husband is a man made irritable by time and too much do-it-yourself every weekend, although there are intimations that things have never been that marvellous between them. Her sense of regretful might-have-been, is heightened when, one Saturday afternoon, to get the children from under her husband's feet ('I peeled off their Plasticine from Martin's hammer before he saw it'), she takes them to *Snow White* at the local cinema, and there sees an old flame. Up on the screen, the Prince, romantic love epitomised, kneels down to kiss Snow White to life. 'When did Martin last kiss me? Properly. Or when, indeed, did I last kiss him? . . . Did your character change when you had children? Mine did.'

Deborah Moggach, the mother of two children herself, speaks from heartfelt experience. Sylvia Townsend Warner (1893–1978) was unmarried and childless, and the product of an age when children were more expected to fit in with the vagaries of the family they found themselves in, rather than change it. Described as a novelist, poet and letter writer of unique wit and sympathy, she has equally been recognised as a brilliant writer of short stories that range from 'the hilarious to the melancholy'. She wrote several featuring the Finch family, which are definitely at the hilarious end of her writing, particularly 'A View of Exmoor' (published in *One Thing Leading To Another* in 1984, and in her *Selected Stories* in 1988). The Finches, somewhat exotically dressed, following their relation Arminella Blount's wedding ('Cordelia and Clara in their bridesmaids' dresses copied from the Gainsborough portrait of an earlier Arminella Blount in the Character of Flora') get lost on Exmoor. '"Father," said Cordelia, "we've been through this village before. Don't you think we had better ask?"' But never mind, it gives the deliciously dithery Mrs Finch ('in green moiré') the opportunity to recount an extraordinary event once witnessed on Exmoor by Aunt Harriet and Uncle Lionel.

With Shena Mackay's beautifully titled 'Violets and Strawberries in the Snow' (from *Dreams of Dead Women's Handbags*, published in 1987), we return abruptly to the bleak realities of modern life. Yet the author's skilful handling of three young girls visiting their father in a mental hospital on Christmas Day, makes it a lyrical, moving and, yes, even funny experience. Douglas, the father, is 'a casualty of alcohol', surrounded in hospital by other derelicts of life. 'Just because a person hears voices in her head,' a woman cries, 'it doesn't give anyone the right to stop them being with their kids on Christmas Day.' Yet Douglas would have done anything to prevent his daughters visiting him. 'He was so proud of them', and they 'had so much cause to be ashamed of him'. They came in 'like children, he thought, in a fairytale, sent by their cruel stepmother up the mountainside to find violets and strawberries in the snow'.

Rumer Godden's 'To Uncle, With Love' (published in *Swans and Turtles* in 1968) is more directly about Christmas itself, and an altogether cosier and more secure one, in a comfortable middle-class household just after the First World War. Rumer Godden, born in 1907, would have been a child then, and much of her writing (*The River, The Greengage Summer, The Battle of the Villa Fiorita*), like Rosamond Lehmann's, is autobiographical, reflecting a family very like her own.

Successful, too, as a writer of children's books, she seems particularly attuned to the small but all-important crises of childhood, which occur in even the most sympathetic of families – 'In our family Christmas was a thoroughly kept festival and brought an adamantine necessity of present-giving that was hard on us four small girls'. It was not an age that believed in over indulging children with material goods – 'pocket-money was only ninepence a week', and this made Christmas a particular challenge. 'For weeks we toiled at bookmarkers, penwipers, raffia table-napkin rings, calendars. The Uncles were particularly difficult.' This was especially true of their elegant Uncle Edward. 'How could we give him a lead pencil, a packet of drawing-pins, a cake of cheap soap?' One Christmas the storyteller finds a surprisingly luxurious answer on a threepenny bookstall, but it sends a hidden shockwave far into the future.

The dilemma of what to give for Christmas is resolved in a different way in Patrice Chaplin's 'Night in Paris' (published in *Best Short Stories 1988*, edited by Giles Gordon and David Hughes). Lucy is eleven when, in 1950, her Aunt Ethel sends her a bottle of perfume for Christmas. 'It was called "Night In Paris" and was packaged in a blue box with an Eiffel Tower and a half moon on the front.' Patrice Chaplin is a prolific and wide-ranging writer – she has published more than ten novels, over a dozen plays for the theatre, radio and television, and many short stories. But rarely, I suspect, can she have struck such a chord as with this romantic souvenir from austerity-ridden, post-war Britain. If, like me, you formed the younger generation in the 1940s/50s, you are probably already swamped with nostalgic memories of that rite

of passage, that eager anticipation of female adulthood, re-
presented by a visit (preferably on a Saturday afternoon) to the
cosmetic counters of bygone Woolworth's stores! Those other
stalwarts – Californian Poppy and Snowfire Vanishing Cream –
also feature in Lucy's Christmas memories. Not that, as a child,
she's allowed to get her hands on any of them – for in Lucy's family
all Christmas presents are ruthlessly recycled year after year,
until long past their sell-by date. 'Night In Paris' is to have several
reincarnations.

Jane Gardam's 'Swan' (from her 1989 short story collection
Showing the Flag) ends up at Christmas-time, but it is much more a
story about schooldays, or rather, an extra-curricular activity.
Pratt and Jackson are London schoolboys at 'the private school on
the rich side of the river' and one afternoon a week they go south
of the river to help people less privileged than themselves. Jackson's 'project' is painting old Nellie's kitchen. Pratt's is Henry
Wu, a Chinese boy who doesn't speak. He seems to have a rapport
though with animals. In this story Jane Gardam has lost none of
her innate ability, previously exhibited in novels such as
Bilgewater, *God on the Rocks*, and *It's a Long Way from Verona*, to
inhabit the minds and hearts of children.

I suppose it is inevitable that Antonia White's story of
schooldays, 'The Saint', as its title suggests, should be set in a convent school. Born in 1899, Antonia White's fiction was heavily
autobiographical, and she was partly educated at a convent. This
was, of course, to provide the background for *Frost in May* (1928),
the first volume of a quartet of novels, which were to be her
major work. 'The Saint', which appeared in *Strangers*, a volume of
short stories published in 1954, is set in the same world as *Frost in
May* and, indeed, has several characters and events in common,
but it is altogether more lighthearted in tone. Nevertheless, the
claustrophobic, emotional atmosphere is still vividly presented
in this ironic tale which postulates that it isn't always easy to
accurately pinpoint a candidate for canonisation!

Penelope Lively has written nine novels and three volumes of
short stories, and her novel *Moon Tiger*, won the 1987 Booker

Prize. 'Clara's Day' (published in her short story collection *Pack of Cards* in 1986) straddles the world of school and the anguished clumsiness of being a teenager with its opening sentence – 'When Clara Tilling was fifteen and a half she took off all her clothes one morning in school assembly.' The school's reaction – it is obviously a good old-fashioned all girls' school – is restrained ('the Head hesitated for a moment – she was reading out the tennis team list – and then went on again firmly') – and kind, 'Everything all right at home?' she is asked later. Of course everything is not all right at home. What teenager's home is?

To my mind, no representative selection of short stories could be regarded as complete without the Irish exponents of the art and two of them continue this teenage section of the Younger Generation.

Clare Boylan is a professional journalist as well as a fiction writer who has now produced two novels and two collections of short stories. The story here, 'A Model Daughter', comes from her second collection *Concerning Virgins* (published 1989). Barbara, the narrator of the story, has a phantom daughter, but the child is by no means the outcome of emotional trauma. 'My daughter was born not of love, not even of sex, but of necessity.' In fact, the invention of a child for the benefit of an actor husband who had left Ireland for Hollywood, success and a second marriage seventeen years previously, has kept Barbara in a very comfortable life style. For Victor has proved gratifyingly generous in the matter of money for his daughter. But now he wants to meet her and Barbara, racking her brains, can see nothing for it but a model agency! After all, her ex-husband's visit to Dublin will only be a brief one. But teenagers will be teenagers, whether legitimate members of the family or not.

Elizabeth Bowen (1899–1973) of course represents a very different Ireland from Clare Boylan's. She personifies that earlier, Anglo Irish, Protestant, landowning class, now immortalised by the novels of Molly Keane. But Elizabeth Bowen, like many of her class, was educated in England, and as an adult, divided her time between London and the family home in County Cork. Thus her novels (*The Heat of the Day*, *The Death of the Heart*, *The House in Paris*) and her numerous short stories, tend more to have an English setting, as does 'Maria'. Even though the word 'teenager' hadn't been invented then, fifteen-year-old Maria herself is a certain candidate for any anthology on appalling adolescents, and Bowen's laconically immediate opening is a wonderful warning of what is to come. '"We have girls of our own, you see," Mrs Dosely said, smiling warmly'; and from that moment on you just know that no previous experience can have prepared this mother of daughters for the likes of Maria. There is also a clear early warning that only the irascible curate, Mr Hammond, is to be Maria's worthy adversary, when Mrs Dosely tells him, '"We shall be one more in the house. Lady Rimlade's little niece Maria is coming to us while her uncle and aunt are away." "Jolly," said Mr Hammond, sombrely, hating girls.'

Despite Maria's feisty rebelliousness, the 1950s Canadian teenagers remembered in Alice Munro's 'Wigtime' seem years older in experience and budding sexuality. Environmentally, too, their world is a much more inhospitable one. How vividly Munro portrays their journey to school through the hostile elements of a Canadian winter – 'struggling head down against the snow that blew off Lake Huron . . . through a predawn world of white fields, icy swamps . . . fading stars and murderous cold.'

Alice Munro has chosen to write short stories more than any other literary form, and *The Beggarmaid* was shortlisted for the 1980 Booker Prize. *Friend of my Youth* (published in 1990), in which 'Wigtime' appears, is her fifth and, for me, most compelling and witty collection. It has been said of her stories that 'whole lifetimes come into focus as men and women recall . . . [what] made them what they are', and this is certainly true of 'Wigtime'. The story begins with middle-aged Anita coming home to small-town Canada to take care of her dying mother. And there she encounters her old school friend, Margot, whom she hasn't seen for more than thirty years. Margot's childhood and schooldays (such as they were) ended abruptly when she became involved with the school bus driver. Then a married man with a wandering eye, thirty years later he is married to Margot, who has a more effective way of dealing with his infidelities than his vulnerable first wife had. In 'Wigtime', as in many of the stories in the collection, relationships and loyalties are tested, and often found wanting.

As a Liverpudlian, Beryl Bainbridge has set several of her novels (*The Dressmaker, Young Adolf* and *An Awfully Big Adventure*) in her native city, and she has used it, too, as a backdrop for some of her short stories. In 'Somewhere More Central' (from *Mum and Mr Armitage*, published in 1985) Alice, the teenage narrator, is travelling to Liverpool with her mother for her grandmother's funeral. Bainbridge is particularly good on the petty frictions of family life. 'Whenever that advert came on the telly, the one about "Make someone happy this weekend – give them a telephone call", Mother rolled her eyes and said "My God!" When she rang Grandma, Grandma picked up the receiver and said "Hallo, stranger."' And on the train from London to Liverpool, Alice reflects 'Just as I'm a disappointment to Mother, she'd been a disappointment to Grandma.'

'Her Mother' by Anjana Appachana was first published in America in 1989, and appeared here in 1990 in *The Inner Courtyard*, a collection of stories by Indian women, edited by Lakshmi Holmstrom. Anjana Appachana was born in India, but in 1984 she left for the United States and she now lives and writes there. 'Her Mother' reflects this biography in that the narrator is an Indian mother replying to her daughter's first letter from America where she has gone to study. It is ironically witty in its portrayal of Asian despair at what can happen to command of the English language in English-speaking America!

'Everything was fine, the daughter said. The plane journey was fine, her professor was nice, her university was very nice, the house was fine, her classes were OK . . . who would have dreamt that her daughter was doing a PhD in Comparative Literature.' But on a more serious note, as the letter proceeds, the reason for the young woman's departure for the States is gradually and subtly revealed. So, too, is the mother's discontent with her married life, as at the same time she presses upon her absent daughter the advantages of an arranged marriage.

Of course, marriage usually provides the younger generation with a whole new set of older relatives, including that much maligned species, the mother-in-law. The tricky balancing-act that has to be practised between mothers and daughters-in-law has been much written about by novelists and journalists, but Winifred Beechey's fresh and original eye in 'The Kiss' (published in *The Reluctant Samaritan* in 1991) makes it come up newly-minted. Never sentimental, she is nevertheless moving in her recognition of bygone hurts that can never now be put right. Thus the narrator of 'The Kiss', now a middle-aged woman herself, recalls how her mother-in-law Beatrice was 'a mother of sons only and I think now that she would have liked me to call her mother; but then such an idea never entered my head'.

But 'The Kiss' is also about a less recorded or even recognised relationship, between the younger newcomer who has married into a family, and other already existing members of it who are more peripheral, but possibly more sympathetic. In 'The Kiss' it is the reserved Beatrice's much older sister 'Aunt Nessy'. Despite a hard life, Aunt Nessy has never lost an affectionate warmth and spontaneity which is absent in Beatrice, the spoiled baby of the family. Winifred Beechey was born in 1910, but it wasn't until 1984 that her first book – her autobiography *The Rich Mrs Robinson* – was published to excellent reviews. Now *The Reluctant Samaritan* confirms that here is a born writer with a unique voice. Oh Mrs Beechey, what took you so long?!

With new writer Nina Fitzpatrick's 'How Slattery Tricked His Mother into Touching Him' (published in *Fables of the Irish Intelligentsia* in 1991) we are in the world of pure comedy, in the best picaresque tradition. Slattery, a raffish academic at University College, Galway (where Ms Fitzpatrick studies Arabic languages), features in three of the fables; and in this, the third and final one, Slattery, a life-long Communist, disorientated and dismayed by the fall of left-wing governments everywhere, goes home to his mother for consolation. But Mrs Slattery has raised five children, and her greeting is somewhat imprecise '"Seamus, is that you? Have you come all the way from Galway?" "Right place, wrong son. It's Bernard."'

Nina Fitzpatrick's uncanny ability as a woman to breath such convincing life into a comic Irishman is doubly impressive when recently it became clear that not only is she not a male, but she isn't Irish either! This revealed itself when *Fables of the Irish Intelligentsia* was declared invalid as the winner of an Irish literary prize on the grounds that the author was, in fact, Polish – born Nina Witoszek. All the more an achievement, say I, to write such beautifully 'Irish' English (you can hear the 'lilt' in the words).

The final story 'Unearthing Suite' (from *Bluebeard's Egg*, published in 1988) is by one of Canada's most distinguished and regarded novelists and poets, Margaret Atwood. Her first novel, *The Edible Women*, was written in 1964, and since then there have been six more novels and three short story collections. Her short stories tend to be 'softer' and funnier, and her sense of humour, which is often disregarded in reviews of her work, is very much in evidence in the *Bluebeard's Egg* stories. The storyteller in 'Unearthing Suite' is, like Slattery, in the final stage of being any kind of 'younger generation' – the mature/middle-aged child with ageing parents, where any minute now the roles will be reversed.

There is deep affection in 'Unearthing Suite', particularly for the 'otherness' of the mother and father. 'My parents' occasional dismay over me was not like the dismay of other parents. It was less dismay than perplexity, the bewilderment of two birds who have found a human child in their nest and have no idea what to do with it.' The daughter treasures details of their lives before she was born. 'My father first saw her sliding down a banister . . . and resolved then and there to marry her; though it took him a while to track her down, stalking her from tree to tree . . . butterfly net at the ready. This is a metaphor but not unjustified.' Atwood's own father was an entomologist! At the beginning of the story the father explains to his daughter that he and her mother had bought their burial urns that day. The daughter is shocked. 'There is nothing wrong with my parents. They are in perfect health. I on the other hand have a cold.' The reminder of their mortality is an unwelcome one. For when they die, she will become, finally and irrevocably, the 'older' generation herself.

As with the first *Woman's Hour* anthology, I have greatly enjoyed finding this second selection of stories that takes us through a lifetime from the cradle of 'Another Marvellous Thing' to the grave of 'Unearthing Suite'. If words were food, I hope you will find here a literary banquet. *Bon appétit*!

Pat McLoughlin
Serials' Producer, *Woman's Hour*

BABIES

ANOTHER MARVELLOUS
THING

———— ◆ ————

Laurie Colwin

On a cold, rainy morning in February, Billy Delielle stood by the window of her hospital room looking over Central Park. She was a week and a half from the time her baby was due to be born, and she had been put into the hospital because her blood pressure had suddenly gone up and her doctor wanted her constantly monitored and on bed rest.

A solitary jogger in bright red foul-weather gear ran slowly down the glistening path. The trees were black and the branches were bare. There was not another soul out. Billy had been in the hospital for five days. The first morning she had woken to the sound of squawking. Since her room was next door to the nursery, she assumed this was a sound some newborns made. The next day she got out of bed at dawn and saw that the meadow was full of sea gulls who congregated each morning before the sun came up.

The nursery was an enormous room painted soft yellow. When Billy went to take the one short walk a day allowed her, she found herself averting her eyes from the neat rows of babies in their little plastic bins, but once in a while she found herself hungry for the sight of them. Taped to each crib was a blue (I'M A BOY) or pink (I'M A GIRL) card telling mother's name, the time of birth, and birth weight.

At six in the morning the babies were taken to their mothers to be fed. Billy was impressed by the surprising range of noises they made: mewing, squawking, bleating, piping, and squealing. The fact that she was about to have one of these creatures herself filled her with a combination of bafflement, disbelief, and longing.

For the past two months her chief entertainment had been to lie in bed and observe her unborn child moving under her skin. It had knocked a paperback book off her stomach and caused the saucer of her coffee cup to jiggle and dance.

Billy's husband, Grey, was by temperament and inclination a naturalist. Having a baby was right up his street. Books on neonatology and infant development replaced the astronomy and bird books on his night table. He gave up reading mysteries for texts on childbirth. One of these books had informed him that babies can hear in the womb, so each night he sang 'Roll Along Kentucky Moon' directly into Billy's stomach. Another suggested that the educational process could begin before birth. Grey thought he might try to teach the unborn to count.

'Why stop there?' Billy said. 'Teach it fractions.'

Billy had a horror of the sentimental. In secret, for she would rather have died than showed it, the thought of her own baby brought her to tears. Her dreams were full of infants. Babies appeared everywhere. The buses abounded with pregnant women. The whole process seemed to her one half miraculous and the other half preposterous. She looked around her on a crowded street and said to herself: 'Every single one of these people was *born*.'

Her oldest friend, Penny Stern, said to her: 'We all hope that this pregnancy will force you to wear maternity clothes, because they will be so much nicer than what you usually wear.' Billy went shopping for maternity clothes but came home empty-handed.

She said, 'I don't wear puffed sleeves and frilly bibs and ribbons around my neck when I'm not pregnant, so I don't see why I should have to just because I am pregnant.' In the end, she wore Grey's sweaters, and she bought two shapeless skirts with elastic waistbands. Penny forced her to buy one nice black dress, which she wore to teach her weekly class in economic history at the business school.

Grey set about renovating a small spare room that had been used for storage. He scraped and polished the floor, built shelves, and painted the walls pale apple green with the ceiling and mouldings glossy white. They had once called this room the lumber room. Now they referred to it as the nursery. On the top of one of the shelves Grey put his collection of glass-encased bird's nests. He already had in mind a child who would go on nature hikes with him.

As for Billy, she grimly and without expression submitted herself to the number of advances science had come up with in the field of obstetrics.

It was possible to have amniotic fluid withdrawn and analysed to find out the genetic health of the unborn and, if you wanted to know, its sex. It was possible to lie on a table and with the aid of an ultrasonic scanner see your unborn child in the womb. It was also possible to have a photograph of this view. As for Grey, he wished Billy could have a sonogram every week, and he watched avidly while Billy's doctor, a handsome, rather melancholy South African named Jordan Bell, identified a series of blobs and clouds as head, shoulders, and back.

Every month in Jordan Bell's office Billy heard the sound of her own child's heart through ultra sound and what she heard sounded like galloping horses in the distance.

Billy went about her business outwardly unflapped. She continued to teach and she worked on her dissertation. In between, when she was not napping, she made lists of baby things: crib sheets, a stroller, baby T-shirts, diapers, blankets. Two months before the baby was due, she and Penny went out and bought what was needed. She was glad she had not saved this until the last minute, because in her ninth month, after an uneventful pregnancy, she was put in the hospital, where she was allowed to walk down the hall once a day. The sense of isolation she had cherished – just herself, Grey, and their unborn child – was gone. She was in the hands of nurses she had never seen before, and she found herself desperate for their companionship because she was exhausted, uncertain, and lonely in her hospital room.

Billy was admitted wearing the nice black dress Penny had made her buy and taken to a private room that overlooked the park. At the bottom of her bed were two towels and a hospital gown that tied up the back. Getting undressed to go to bed in the afternoon made her feel like a child forced to take a nap. She did not put on the hospital gown. Instead, she put on the plaid flannel nightshirt of Grey's that she had packed in her bag weeks ago in case she went into labour in the middle of the night.

'I hate it here already,' Billy said.

'It's an awfully nice view,' Grey said. 'If it were a little further along in the season I could bring my field glasses and see what's nesting.'

'I'll never get out of here,' Billy said.

'Not only will you get out of here,' said Grey, 'you will be released a totally transformed woman. You heard Jordan – all babies get born one way or another.'

If Grey was frightened, he never showed it. Billy knew that his way of dealing with anxiety was to fix his concentration, and it was now fixed on her and on being cheerful. He had never seen Billy so upset before. He held her hand.

'Don't worry,' he said. 'Jordan said this isn't serious. It's just a complication. The baby will be fine and you'll be fine. Besides, it won't know how to be a baby and we won't know how to be parents.'

Grey had taken off his jacket and he felt a wet place where Billy had laid her cheek. He did not know how to comfort her.

'A mutual learning experience,' Billy said into his arm. 'I thought nature was supposed to take over and do all this for us.'

'It will,' Grey said.

Seven o'clock began visiting hours. Even with the door closed Billy could hear shrieks and coos and laughter. With her door open she could hear champagne corks being popped.

Grey closed the door. 'You didn't eat much dinner,' he said. 'Why don't I go downstairs to the delicatessen and get you something?'

'I'm not hungry,' Billy said. She did not know what was in front of her, or how long she would be in this room, or how and when the baby would be born.

'I'll call Penny and have her bring something,' Grey said.

'I already talked to her,' Billy said. 'She and David are taking you out to dinner.' David was Penny's husband, David Hooks.

'You're trying to get rid of me,' Grey said.

'I'm not,' Billy said. 'You've been here all day, practically. I just want the comfort of knowing that you're being fed and looked after. I think you should go soon.'

'It's too early,' said Grey. 'Fathers don't have to leave when visiting hours are over.'

'You're not a father yet,' Billy said. 'Go.'

After he left she waited by the window to watch him cross the street and wait for the bus. It was dark and cold and it had begun to sleet. When she saw him she felt pierced with desolation. He was wearing his old camel's hair coat and the wind blew through his wavy hair. He stood back on his heels as he had as a boy. He turned around and scanned the building for her window. When he saw her, he waved and smiled. Billy waved back. A taxi, thinking it was being hailed, stopped. Grey got in and was driven off.

Every three hours a nurse appeared to take her temperature, blood pressure, and pulse. After Grey had gone, the night nurse appeared. She was a tall, middle-aged black woman named Mrs Perch. In her hand she carried what looked like a suitcase full of dials and wires.

'Don't be alarmed,' Mrs Perch said. She had a soft West Indian accent. 'It is only a portable fetal heart monitor. You get to say good morning and good evening to your baby.'

She squirted a blob of cold blue jelly on Billy's stomach and pushed a transducer around in it, listening for the beat. At once Billy heard the sound of galloping hooves. Mrs Perch timed the beats against her watch.

'Nice and healthy,' Mrs Perch said.

'Which part of this baby is where?' Billy said.

'Well, his head is back here, and his back is there and here is the rump and his feet are near your ribs. Or hers, of course.'

'I wondered if that was a foot kicking,' Billy said.

'My second boy got his foot under my rib and kicked with all his might,' Mrs Perch said.

Billy sat up in bed. She grabbed Mrs Perch's hand. 'Is this baby going to be all right?' she said.

'Oh my, yes,' Mrs Perch said. 'You're not a very interesting case. Many others much more complicated than you have done very well and you will, too.'

At four in the morning, another nurse appeared, a florid Englishwoman. Billy had spent a restless night, her heart pounding, her throat dry.

'Your pressure's up, dear,' said the nurse, whose tag read 'M. Whitely.' 'Dr Bell has written orders that if your pressure goes up you're to have a shot of hydralazine. It doesn't hurt baby – did he explain that to you?'

'Yes,' said Billy groggily.

'It may give you a little headache.'

'What else?'

'That's all,' Miss Whitely said.

Billy fell asleep and woke with a pounding headache. When she rang the bell, the nurse who had admitted her appeared. Her name was Bonnie Near and she was Billy's day nurse. She gave Billy a pill and then taped a tongue depressor wrapped in gauze over her bed.

'What's that for?' Billy said.

'Don't ask,' said Bonnie Near.

'I want to know.'

Bonnie Near sat down at the end of the bed. She was a few years older than Billy, trim and wiry with short hair and tiny diamond earrings.

'It's hospital policy,' she said. 'The hydralazine gives you a headache, right? You ring to get something to make it go away and because you have high blood pressure everyone assumes that the blood pressure caused it, not the drug. So this thing gets taped above your bed in the one chance in about fifty-five million that you have a convulsion.'

Billy turned her face away and stared out the window.

'Hey, hey,' said Bonnie Near. 'None of this. I noticed yesterday that you're quite a worrier. Are you like this when you're not in the hospital? Listen, I'm a straight shooter and I would tell you if I was worried about you. I'm not. You're just the common garden variety.'

Every morning Grey appeared with two cups of coffee and the morning paper. He sat in a chair and he and Billy read the paper together as they did at home.

'Is the house still standing?' Billy asked after several days. 'Are the banks open? Did you bring the mail? I feel I've been here ten months instead of a week.'

'The mail was very boring,' Grey said. 'Except for this booklet from the Wisconsin Loon Society. You'll be happy to know that you can order a record called "Loon Music". Would you like a copy?'

'If I moved over,' Billy said, 'would you take off your jacket and lie down next to me?'

Grey took off his jacket and shoes, and curled up next to Billy. He pressed his nose into her face and looked as if he could drift off to sleep in a second.

'Childworld called about the crib,' he said into her neck. 'They want to know if we want white paint or natural pine. I said natural.'

'That's what I think I ordered,' Billy said. 'They let the husbands stay over in this place. They call them "dads".'

'I'm not a dad yet, as you pointed out,' Grey said. 'Maybe they'll just let me take naps here.'

There was a knock on the door. Grey sprang to his feet and Jordan Bell appeared.

'Don't look so nervous, Billy,' he said. 'I have good news. I think we want to get this baby born if your pressure isn't going to go down. I think we ought to induce you.'

Billy and Grey were silent.

'The way it works is that we put you on a drip of pitocin, which is a synthetic of the chemical your brain produces when you go nto labour.'

'We know,' Billy said. 'Katherine went over it in childbirth class.' Katherine Walden was Jordan Bell's nurse. 'When do you want to do this?'

'Tomorrow,' Jordan Bell said. 'Katherine will come over and give you your last Lamaze class right here.'

'And if it doesn't work?'

'It usually does,' said Jordan Bell. 'And if it doesn't, we do a second-day induction.'

'And if that doesn't work?'

'It generally does. If it doesn't, we do a cesarean, but you'll be awake and Grey can hold your hand.'

'Oh what fun,' said Billy.

When Jordan Bell left, Billy burst into tears.

'Why isn't anything normal?' she said. 'Why do I have to lie here day after day listening to other people's babies crying? Why is my body betraying me like this?'

Grey kissed her and then took her hands. 'There is no such thing as normal,' he said. 'Everyone we've talked to has some story or other – huge babies that won't budge, thirty-hour labours. A cesarean is a perfectly respectable way of being born.'

'What about me? What about me getting all stuck up with tubes and cut up into little pieces?' Billy said, and she was instantly ashamed. 'I hate being like this. I feel I've lost myself and some whimpering, whining person has taken me over.'

'Think about how in two months we'll have a two-month-old baby to take to the park.'

'Do you really think everything is going to be all right?' Billy said.

'Yes,' said Grey. 'I do. In six months we'll be in Maine.'

Billy lay in bed with her door closed reading her brochure from the Loon Society. She thought about the cottage she and Grey rented every August in Jewell Neck, Maine, on a lagoon. There at night with blackness all around them and not a light to be seen, they heard hoot owls and loons calling their night cries to one

another. Loon mothers carried their chicks on their back, Bill
knew. The last time she had heard those cries she had been jus
three months pregnant. The next time she heard them she woul
have a child.

She thought about the baby shower Penny had given her –
lunch party for ten women. At the end of it, Billy and Grey'
unborn child had received cotton and wool blankets, little sweat
ers, tiny garments with feet, and two splendid teddy bears. Th
teddy bears had sat on the coffee table. Billy remembered th
strange, light feeling in her chest as she looked at them. She ha
picked them both up and laughed with astonishment.

At a red light on the way home in a taxi, surrounded by boxe
and bags of baby presents, she saw something that made her hear
stop: Francis Clemens, who for two years had been Billy's illici
lover.

With the exception of her family, Billy was close only to Gre
and Penny Stern. She had never been the subject of anyone'
romantic passion. She and Grey, after all, had been fated to marry
She had loved him all her life.

Francis had pursued her: no one had ever pursued her before
The usual signs of romance were as unknown to Billy as the work
ings of a cyclotron. Crushes, she had felt, were for children. Sh
did not really believe that adults had them.

Without her knowing it, she was incubating a number of curi
ous romantic diseases. One day when Francis came to visit wear
ing his tweed coat and the ridiculously long paisley scarf h
affected, she realised that she had fallen in love.

The fact of Francis was the most exotic thing that had eve
happened in Billy's fairly stolid, uneventful life. He was as bril
liant as a painted bunting. He was also, in marked contrast t
Billy, beautifully dressed. He did not know one tree fron
another. He felt all birds were either robins or crows. He wa
avowedly urban and his pleasures were urban. He loved opera
cocktail parties, and lunches. They did not agree about economi
theory, either.

Nevertheless, they spent what now seemed to Billy an enor

mous amount of time together. She had not sought anything like this. If her own case had been presented to her she would have dismissed it as messy, unnecessary, and somewhat sordid, but when she fell in love she fell as if backward into a swimming pool. For a while she felt dazed. Then Francis became a fact in her life. But in the end she felt her life was being ruined.

She had not seen Francis for a long time. In that brief glance at the red light she saw his paisley scarf, its long fringes flapping in the breeze. It was amazing that someone who had been so close to her did not know that she was having a baby. As the cab pulled away, she did not look back at him. She stared rigidly frontward, flanked on either side by presents for her unborn child.

The baby kicked. Mothers-to-be should not be lying in hospital beds thinking about illicit love affairs, Billy thought. Of course, if you were like the other mothers on the maternity floor and probably had never had an illicit love affair, you would not be punished by lying in the hospital in the first place. You would go into labour like everyone else, and come rushing into Maternity Admitting with your husband and your suitcase. By this time tomorrow she would have her baby in her arms, just like everyone else, but she drifted off to sleep thinking of Francis nonetheless.

At six in the morning, Bonnie Near woke her.

'You can brush your teeth,' she said. 'But don't drink any water. And your therapist is here to see you, but don't be long.'

The door opened and Penny walked in.

'And how are we today?' she said. 'Any strange dreams or odd thoughts?'

'How did you get in here?' Billy said.

'I said I was your psychiatrist and that you were being induced today and so forth,' Penny said. 'I just came to say good luck. Here's all the change we had in the house. Tell Grey to call constantly. I'll see you all tonight.'

Billy was taken to the labour floor and hooked up to a fetal heart monitor whose transducers were kept on her stomach by a large elastic cummerbund. A stylish-looking nurse wearing hospital greens, a string of pearls, and perfectly applied pink lipstick poked her head through the door.

'Hi!' she said in a bright voice. 'I'm Joanne Kelly. You're my patient today.' She had the kind of voice and smile Billy could not imagine anyone's using in private. 'Now, how are we? Fine? All right. Here's what we're going to do. First of all, we're going to put this IV into your arm. It will only hurt a little and then we're going to hook you up to something called pitocin. Has Dr Bell explained any of this to you?' Joanne Kelly said.

'All,' said Billy.

'Neat,' Joanne Kelly said. 'We *like* an informed patient. Put your arm out, please.'

Billy stuck out her arm. Joanne Kelly wrapped a rubber thong under her elbow.

'Nice veins,' she said. 'You would have made a lovely junkie.

'Now we're going to start the pitocin,' Joanne Kelly said. 'We start off slow to see how you do. Then we escalate.' She looked Billy up and down. 'Okay,' she said. 'We're off and running. Now, I've got a lady huffing and puffing in the next room so I have to go and coach her. I'll be back real soon.'

Billy lay looking at the clock, or watching the pitocin and glucose drip into her arm. She could not get a comfortable position and the noise of the foetal heart monitor was loud and harsh. The machine itself spat out a continual line of data.

Jordan Bell appeared at the foot of her bed.

'An exciting day – yes, Billy?' he said. 'What time is Grey coming?'

'I told him to sleep late,' Billy said. 'All the nurses told me that this can take a long time. How am I supposed to feel when it starts working?'

'If all goes well, you'll start to have contractions and then they'll get stronger and then you'll have your baby.'

'Just like that?' said Billy.

'Pretty much just like that.'

But by five o'clock in the afternoon nothing much had happened.

Grey sat in a chair next to the bed. From time to time he checked the data. He had been checking it all day.

'That contraction went right off the paper,' he said. 'What did it feel like?'

'Intense,' Billy said. 'It just doesn't hurt.'

'You're still in the early stages,' said Jordan Bell when he came to check her. 'I'm willing to stay on if you want to continue, but the baby might not be born till tomorrow.'

'I'm beat,' said Billy.

'Here's what we can do,' Jordan said. 'We can keep going or we start again tomorrow.'

'Tomorrow,' said Billy.

She woke up exhausted with her head pounding. The sky was cloudy and the glare hurt her eyes. She was taken to a different labour room.

In the night her blood pressure had gone up. She had begged not to have a shot – she did not see how she could go into labour feeling so terrible, but the shot was given. It had been a long, sleepless night.

She lay alone with a towel covering one eye, trying to sleep, when a nurse appeared by her side. This one looked very young, had curly hair, and thick, slightly rose-tinted glasses. Her tag read 'Eva Gottlieb'. Underneath she wore a button inscribed EVA: WE DELIVER.

'Hi,' said Eva Gottlieb. 'I'm sorry I woke you, but I'm your nurse for the day and I have to get you started.'

'I'm here for a lobotomy,' Billy said. 'What are you going to do to me?'

'I'm going to run a line in you,' Eva Gottlieb said. 'And then I don't know what. Because your blood pressure is high, I'm supposed to wait until Jordan gets here.' She looked at Billy carefully. 'I know it's scary,' she said. 'But the worst that can happen is that you have to be sectioned and that's not bad.'

Billy's head throbbed.

'That's easy for you to say,' she said. 'I'm the section.'

Eva Gottlieb smiled. 'I'm a terrific nurse,' she said. 'I'll stay with you.'

Tears sprang in Billy's eyes. 'Why will you?'

'Well, first of all, it's my job,' said Eva. 'And second of all, you look like a reasonable person.'

Billy looked at Eva carefully. She felt instant, total trust. Perhaps that was part of being in hospitals and having babies. Everyone you came in contact with came very close, very fast.

Billy's eyes hurt. Eva was hooking her up to the fetal heart monitor. Her touch was strong and sure, and she seemed to know Billy did not want to be talked to. She flicked the machine on, and Billy heard the familiar sound of galloping hooves.

'Is there any way to turn it down?' Billy said.

'Sure,' said Eva. 'But some people find it consoling.'

As the morning wore on, Billy's blood pressure continued to rise. Eva was with her constantly.

'What are they going to do to me?' Billy asked.

'I think they're probably going to give you magnesium sulphate to get your blood pressure down and then they're going to section you. Jordan does a gorgeous job, believe me. I won't let them do anything to you without explaining it first, and if you get out of bed first thing tomorrow and start moving around you'll be fine.'

Twenty minutes later, a doctor Billy had never seen before administered a dose of magnesium sulphate.

'Can't you do this?' Billy asked Eva.

'It's heavy-duty stuff,' Eva said. 'It has to be done by a doctor.'

'Can they wait until my husband gets here?'

'It's too dangerous,' said Eva. 'It has to be done. I'll stay with you.'

The drug made her hot and flushed, and brought her blood pressure straight down. For the next hour, Billy tried to sleep. She had never been so tired. Eva brought her cracked ice to suck on and a cloth for her head. The baby wiggled and writhed, and the fetal heart monitor gauged its every move. Finally, Grey and Jordan Bell were standing at the foot of her bed.

'Okay, Billy,' said Jordan. 'Today's the day. We must get the

baby out. I explained to Grey about the mag sulphate. We both
agree that you must have a cesarean.'

'When?' Billy said.

'In the next hour,' said Jordan. 'I have to check two patients
and then we're off to the races.'

'What do you think,' Billy asked Grey.

'It's right,' Grey said.

'And what about you?' Billy said to Eva.

'It has to be done,' Eva said.

Jordan Bell was smiling a genuine smile and he looked dashing
and happy.

'Why is he so uplifted?' Billy asked Eva after he had dashed
down the hall.

'He loves the OR,' she said. 'He loves deliveries. Think of it this
way: you're going to get your baby at last.'

Billy lay on a gurney, waiting to be rolled down the hall. Grey,
wearing hospital scrubs, stood beside her holding her hand. She
had been prepped and given an epidural anesthetic, and she could
no longer feel her legs.

'Look at me,' she said to Grey. 'I'm a mass of tubes. I'm a
miracle of modern science.' She put his hand over her eyes.

Grey squatted down to put his head near hers. He looked
expectant, exhausted, and worried, but when he saw her scanning
his face he smiled.

'It's going to be swell,' Grey said. 'We'll find out if it's little
William or little Ella.'

Billy's heart was pounding but she thought she ought to say
something to keep her side up. She said, 'I knew we never should
have had sexual intercourse.' Grey gripped her hand tight and
smiled. Eva laughed. 'Don't you guys leave me,' Billy said.

Billy was wheeled down the hall by an orderly. Grey held one
hand, Eva held the other. Then they left her to scrub.

She was taken to a large, pale green room. Paint was peeling on
the ceiling in the corner. An enormous lamp hung over her head.
The anesthetist appeared and tapped her feet.

'Can you feel this?' he said.

'It doesn't feel like feeling,' Billy said. She was trying to keep her breathing steady.

'Excellent,' he said.

Then Jordan appeared at her feet, and Grey stood by her head.

Eva bent down. 'I know you'll hate this, but I have to tape your hands down, and I have to put this oxygen mask over your face. It comes off as soon as the baby's born, and it's good for you and the baby.'

Billy took a deep breath. The room was very hot. A screen was placed over her chest.

'It's so you can't see,' said Eva. 'Here's the mask. I know it'll freak you out, but just breathe nice and easy. Believe me, this is going to be fast.'

Billy's arms were taped, her legs were numb, and a clear plastic mask was placed over her nose and mouth. She was so frightened she wanted to cry out, but it was impossible. Instead she breathed as Katherine Walden had taught her to. Every time a wave of panic rose, she breathed it down. Grey held her hand. His face was blank and his glasses were fogged. His hair was covered by a green cap and his brow was wet. There was nothing she could do for him, except squeeze his hand.

'Now, Billy,' said Jordan Bell, 'you'll feel something cold on your stomach. I'm painting you with Betadine. All right, here we go.'

Billy felt something like dull tugging. She heard the sound of foamy water. Then she felt the baby being slipped from her. She turned to Grey. His glasses had unfogged and his eyes were round as quarters. She heard a high, angry scream.

'Here's your baby,' said Jordan Bell. 'It's a beautiful, healthy boy.'

Eva lifted the mask off Billy's face.

'He's perfectly healthy,' Eva said. 'Listen to those lungs.' She took the baby to be weighed and tested. Then she came back to Billy. 'He's perfect but he's little – just under five pounds. We have to take him upstairs to the preemie nursery. It's policy when they're not five pounds.'

'Give him to me,' Billy said. She tried to free her hands but they were securely taped.

'I'll bring him to you,' Eva said. 'But he can't stay down here. He's too small. It's for the baby's safety, I promise you. Look, here he is.'

The baby was held against her forehead. The moment he came near her he stopped shrieking. He was mottled and wet.

'Please let me have him,' Billy said.

'He'll be fine,' Eva said. They then took him away.

The next morning Billy rang for the nurse and demanded that her IV be disconnected. Twenty minutes later she was out of bed slowly walking.

'I feel as if someone had crushed my pelvic bones,' Billy said.

'Someone did,' said the nurse.

Two hours later she was put into a wheelchair and pushed by a nurse into the elevator and taken to the Infant Intensive Care Unit. At the door the nurse said, 'I'll wheel you in.'

'I can walk,' Billy said. 'But thank you very much.'

Inside, she was instructed to scrub with surgical soap and to put on a sterile gown. Then she walked very slowly and very stiffly down the hall. A Chinese nurse stopped her.

'I'm William Delielle's mother,' she said. 'Where is he?'

The nurse consulted a clipboard and pointed Billy down a hall-way. Another nurse in a side room pointed to an isolette – a large plastic case with porthole windows. There on a white cloth lay her child.

He was fast asleep, his little arm stretched in front of him, an exact replica of Grey's sleeping posture. On his back were two discs the size of nickels hooked up to wires that measured his temperature and his heart and respiration rates on a console above his isolette. He was long and skinny and beautiful.

'He looks like a little chicken,' said Billy. 'May I hold him?'

'Oh, no,' said the nurse. 'Not for a while. He mustn't be stressed.' She gave Billy a long look and said, 'But you can open the windows and touch him.'

Billy opened the porthole window and touched his leg. He shivered slightly. She wanted to disconnect his probes, scoop him up, and hold him next to her. She stood quietly, her hand resting lightly on his calf.

The room was bright, hot, and busy. Nurses came and went, washing their hands, checking charts, making notes, diapering, changing bottles of glucose solution. There were three other children in the room. One was very tiny and had a miniature IV attached to a vein in her head. A pink card was taped on her isolette. Billy looked on the side of William's isolette. There was a blue card and in Grey's tiny printing was written 'William Delielle'.

Later in the morning, when Grey appeared in her room he found Billy sitting next to a glass-encased pump.

'This is the well-known electric breast pump. Made in Switzerland,' Billy said.

'It's like the medieval clock at Salisbury Cathedral,' Grey said, peering into the glass case. 'I just came from seeing William. He's much *longer* than I thought. I called all the grandparents. In fact, I was on the telephone all night after I left you.' He gave her a list of messages. 'They're feeding him in half an hour.'

Billy looked at her watch. She had been instructed to use the pump for three minutes on each breast to begin with. Her milk, however, would not be given to William, who, the doctors said, was too little to nurse. He would be given carefully measured formula, and Billy would eventually have to wean him from the bottle and onto herself. The prospect of this seemed very remote.

As the days went by, Billy's room filled with flowers, but she spent most of her time in the Infant ICU. She could touch William but not hold him. The morning before she was to be discharged, Billy went to William's eight o'clock feeding. She thought how lovely it would be to feed him at home, how they might sit in the rocking chair and watch the birds in the garden below. In William's present home, there was no morning and no night. He had never been in a dark room, or heard bird sounds or traffic noise, or felt a cool draft.

William was asleep on his side wearing a diaper and a little T-shirt. The sight of him seized Billy with emotion.

'You can hold him today,' the nurse said.

'Yes?'

'Yes, and you can feed him today, too.'

Billy bowed her head. She took a steadying breath. 'How can I hold him with all this hardware on him?' she said.

'I'll show you,' said the nurse. She disconnected the console, reached into the isolette, and gently untaped William's probes. Then she showed Billy how to change him, put on his T-shirt, and swaddle him in a cotton blanket. In an instant he was in Billy's arms.

He was still asleep, but he made little screeching noises and wrinkled his nose. He moved against her and nudged his head into her arm. The nurse led her to a rocking chair and for the first time she sat down with her baby.

All around her, lights blazed. The radio was on and a sweet male voice sang, 'I want you to be mine, I want you to be mine, I want to take you home, I want you to be mine.'

William opened his eyes and blinked. Then he yawned and began to cry.

'He's hungry,' the nurse said, putting a small bottle into Billy's hand.

She fed him and burped him, and then she held him in her arms and rocked him to sleep. In the process she fell asleep, too, and was woken by the nurse and Grey, who had come from work.

'You must put him back now,' said the nurse. 'He's been out a long time and we don't want to stress him.'

'It's awful to think that being with his mother creates stress,' Billy said.

'Oh, no!' the nurse said. 'That's not what I mean. I mean, in his isolette it's temperature controlled.'

Once Billy was discharged from the hospital she had to commute to see William. She went to the two morning feedings, came home for a nap, and met Grey for the five o'clock. They raced out for dinner and came back for the eight. Grey would not let Billy stay for the eleven.

Each morning she saw Dr Edmunds, the head of neonatology. He was a tall, slow-talking, sandy-haired man with horn-rimmed glasses.

'I know you will never want to hear this under any other circumstances,' he said to Billy, 'but your baby is very boring.'

'How boring?'

'Very boring. He's doing just what he ought to do.' William had gone to the bottom of his growth curve and was beginning to gain. 'As soon as he's a little fatter he's all yours.'

Billy stood in front of his isolette watching William sleep.

'This is like having an affair with a married man,' Billy said to the nurse who was folding diapers next to her.

The nurse loked at her uncomprehendingly.

'I mean you love the person but can only see him at certain times,' said Billy.

The nurse was young and plump. 'I guess I see what you mean,' she said.

At home William's room was waiting. The crib had been delivered and put together by Grey. While Billy was in the hospital, Grey had finished William's room. The teddy bears sat on the shelves. A mobile of ducks and geese hung over the crib. Grey had bought a second-hand rocking chair and had painted it red. Billy had thought she would be unable to face William's empty room. Instead she found she could scarcely stay out of it. She folded and refolded his clothes, reorganised his drawers, arranged his crib blankets. She decided what should be his homecoming clothes and set them out on the changing table along with a cotton receiving blanket and a wool shawl.

But even though he did not look at all fragile and he was beginning to gain weight, it often felt to Billy that she would never have him. She and Grey had been told ten days to two weeks from day of birth. One day when she felt she could not stand much more Billy was told that she might try nursing him.

Touch him on his cheek. He will turn to you. Guide him towards the breast and the magical connection will be made.

Billy remembered this description from her childbirth books. She had imagined a softly lit room, a sense of peacefulness, some soft, sweet music in the background.

She was put behind a screen in William's room, near an isolette containing an enormous baby who was having breathing difficulties.

She was told to keep on her sterile gown, and was given sterile water to wash her breasts with. At the sight of his mother's naked bosom, William began to howl. The sterile gown dropped onto his face. Billy began to sweat. All around her, the nurses chatted, clattered, and dropped diapers into metal bins and slammed the tops down.

'Come on, William,' Billy said. 'The books say that this is the blissful union of mother and child.'

But William began to scream. The nurse appeared with the formula bottle and William instantly stopped screaming and began to drink happily.

'Don't worry,' the nurse said. 'He'll catch on.'

At night at home she sat by the window. She could not sleep. She had never felt so separated from anything in her life. Grey, to distract himself, was stencilling the wall under the moulding in William's room. He had found an early American design of wheat and cornflowers. He stood on a ladder in his blue jeans carefully applying the stencil in pale blue paint.

One night Billy went to the door of the baby's room to watch him, but Grey was not on the ladder. He was sitting in the rocking chair with his head in his hands. His shoulders were shaking slightly. He had the radio on, and he did not hear her.

He had been so brave and cheerful. He had held her hand while William was born. He had told her it was like watching a magician sawing his wife in half. He had taken photos of William in his isolette and sent them to their parents and all their friends. He had read up on growth curves and had bought Billy a book on breast-feeding. He had also purloined his hospital greens to wear each year on William's birthday. Now *he* had broken down.

She made a noise coming into the room and then bent down and stroked his hair. He smelled of soap and paint thinner. She put her arms around him, and she did not let go for a long time.

Three times a day, Billy tried to nurse William behind a screen and each time she ended up giving him his formula.

Finally, she asked a nurse, 'Is there some room I could sit in alone with this child?'

'We're not set up for it,' the nurse said. 'But I could put you in the utility closet.'

There amidst used isolettes and cardboard boxes of sterile water, on the second try William nursed for the first time. She touched his cheek. He turned to her, just as it said in the book. Then her eyes crossed.

'Oh, my God!' she said.

A nurse walked in.

'Hurts, right?' she said. 'Good for him. That means he's got it. It won't hurt for long.'

At his evening feeding he howled again.

'The course of true love never did run smooth,' said Grey. He and Billy walked slowly past the park on their way home. It was a cold, wet night.

'I am a childless mother,' Billy said.

Two days later William was taken out of his isolette and put into a plastic bin. He had no temperature or heart probes, and Billy could pick him up without having to disconnect anything. At his evening feeding when the unit was quiet, she took him out in the hallway and walked up and down with him.

The next day she was greeted by Dr Edmunds.

'I've just had a chat with your pediatrician,' he said. 'How would you like to take your boring baby home with you?'

'When?' said Billy.

'Right now, if you have his clothes,' Dr Edmunds said. 'Dr Jacobson will be up in a few minutes and can officially release him.'

She ran down the hall and called Grey.

'Go home and get William's things,' she said. 'They're springing him. Come and get us.'

'You mean we can just walk out of there with him?' Grey said. 'I mean, just take him under our arm? He barely knows us.'

'Just get here. And don't forget the blankets.'

A nurse helped Billy dress William. He was wrapped in a green and white receiving blanket and covered in a white wool shawl. On his head was a blue and green knitted cap. It slipped slightly sideways, giving him a raffish look.

They were accompanied in the elevator by a nurse. It was hospital policy that a nurse hold the baby, and hand it over at the door.

It made Billy feel light-headed to be standing out of doors with her child. She felt she had just robbed a bank and got away with it.

In the taxi, Grey gave the driver their address.

'Not door to door,' Billy said. 'Can we get out at the avenue and walk down the street just like everyone else?'

When the taxi stopped, they got out carefully. The sky was full of silver clouds and the air was blustery and cold. William squinted at the light and wrinkled his nose.

Then, with William tight in Billy's arms, the three of them walked down the street just like everyone else.

(Shelley Thompson read this story on *Woman's Hour* in October 1987.)

THERE'S A WAR ON

———— ◆ ————

Cora Sandel

Translated by Elizabeth Rokkan

Night. Pitch darkness. Not a ray of light betrays the fact that people live here, masses of people, millions of them; that they are packed together like bees in a honeycomb, beside each other and on top of each other in cell beside cell, cell above cell; that this is a metropolis.

At long intervals greyness falls on a section of pavement. A street lamp is burning there, turned low, wearing a large black hat. The glow it casts is apportioned so miserly, so thinned down and rubbed out, that it is not much more than a smudge in the darkness, a discolouration.

But the light comes, cleaving the night like a blade, hacking into it in all directions. It is met by other blades. As if combining to impale some object, they pursue each other all over the sky. And a wailing breaks out, brutal, idiotic, an insult against all reason, all calm, all quiet effort. In the murk at the bottom of the chasms of the streets it bellows out on two notes, stressing the second: *doo, doo-oo, doo, doo-oo, doo, doo-oo. . . .*

Black shadows dart from lamp to lamp. Behind them the darkness folds up completely and is universal. The blades of light remain in its boundlessness, meet, accompany one another, part, meet again and suddenly stand still at a tiny point, nothing but a dot, while the wailing continues to bellow at the bottom of the chasm.

When it is again possible to distinguish sounds, the drone of a motor can be heard from out in space.

————

No outward sign betrays it, but now the houses have come to life, an inner, whispering, stealthy life. People are coming out of the doors at all levels. Ghostly figures, people dressed in only the most necessary clothing – a nightdress, a warm coat – with flash-lights directed at one another as if at burglars, are shuffling down the stairs. But some merely open the door a crack and look out at the others. And some do not open up at all.

Old people are helped down, step by step, sleeping children are carried: big, sleeping children, who have become used to being dragged awake, and have made up their minds to sleep in spite of everything.

The wailing has stopped. A stillness as if before a storm has suc-ceeded it. The slightest sound can be heard in it, and the people are as sensitive to them as animals or wild things. They listen, as they listened in caves and catacombs, when night and danger allied themselves together and encircled them. They exchange a few words now and then, attacking the stillness, but under their breath as if to avoid being outwitted by whatever it is out there. They light candles, tiny, flickering flames, grouped in cellars as in chapels, blink sleepily at them and yawn, exchange a few words again, trying to see each other through the gloom: 'Are you there?'

'Yes, are *you* there?'

'A nice how-d'ye-do!'

'There's a war on.'

But some of them choose to retreat into the darkness.

'What's that?'

'Nothing. A door banging. There it goes again.'

Madame Leroux and old Monsieur Dubois. Madame Leroux is always the first to hear things, and Monsieur Dubois the one to counteract it. He is sitting there with a certain responsibility for the whole cellar and for the atmosphere in it. Nervousness must not be allowed to spread.

Mlle Leroux is not present; Mlle Leroux is lying in her bed. She stands from morning till night in one of the big department

stores and refuses to budge now. But Madame Leroux has other
children, she has a son at the war, and can find no peace either
upstairs or down.

'Sit down, madame,' counsels Monsieur Dubois, offering her a
camp-stool. 'One must be a fatalist. It's the only way.'

'Are you a fatalist?' asks Madame Leroux drily, refusing to sit
down. Monsieur Dubois is a childless old man and ought to
abstain from such remarks.

There is a distant explosion.

'There they are!'

'No, that was a gun. It was one of ours.'

Another explosion.

'This time . . .'

'Yes, this time . . .'

'There are several of them, more than one.'

An explosion close by, making the air vibrate.

'My daughter!' cries Madame Leroux. But Madame Bourg puts
her knitting down in her lap and asks after Bernard. He ought to
be here by now.

Madame Bourg always knits: one thick, man's sock after the
other, in the cellar as well. The clicking of her needles is domestic,
reassuring, a pleasant little sound with something enduring about
it. After each explosion it surfaces exactly as before. Like the
practised family knitter she is, Madame Bourg casts off and
decreases almost without looking at what she is doing. With the
yarn hooked over her finger and a knitting-needle stuck in her
mouth, she lifts her work up to the light for a moment, leans
foward slightly, mutters, and it is done. She sits there again, with
an absorbed, patient expression. Now and again it is as if she gathers her wits: she looks about her, pursing her lips maternally at
the children who, lying on their mothers' laps, are sleeping again
after the explosions; she searches in the darkness for those who
are sitting there with no children on their laps, because they are
somewhere quite different; she asks after Bernard.

'We can hear him coming' is the reply from the staircase.

Bernard always comes last. But then he does live at the top of the house, on the sixth floor. He has a long way to come, and he arrives in procession, bringing a large proportion of his belongings with him.

He is really called, quite simply, Bernhardt. But in the country in which he finds himself his name becomes Bernard. The country is at war; the war is being fought in the country, not so very far from the city where Bernard resides. He is involved just as much as the others, moving perpetually down six floors and up six floors, and must be presumed to hear both sirens and bombs. Nevertheless he is outside, apart from it all, understanding nothing, but is, so far as is known, neither blind, nor deaf, nor dumb.

He is three weeks old.

When his basket appears on the cellar stairs, illuminated from below, several pairs of arms stretch out to receive him. 'Let me!' 'No, let me, I can do it more easily.' 'Thank God he's here!'

An exhausted young man, without a tie and with his collar turned up – besides old Monsieur Dubois he is the only man in the whole cellar, and definitely the only *young* man – slings him down. Then an exhausted, distracted mother arrives. She nods her thanks in silence to these helpful people, and simply sits down and stares at Bernard. 'He ought not to be in the air of the cellar so much,' she occasionally mutters dazedly to herself. Or, 'He ought to have sun.'

Two irresponsible young artists from Scandinavia, who hadn't the good sense to get back home in time, and were even more lacking in sense when they went and acquired Bernard in the middle of all this. But now it has happened, and a child is a child. The unfortunate little family have become the centre of attention in the cellar, even though they ought to have stayed where they came from with their painting and child rearing in times like these, when able-bodied young men are lying out in the trenches among rats and lice, in blood and mud, shooting and being shot, and when every drop of milk and every pat of butter, every piece of coal, every gramme of flour and sugar are in short supply.

But never mind about that. It's not Bernard's fault. And in this situation, only a monster would say anything.

When he appeared in the cellar for the first time he was like all infants, and nine days old. Now he is almost smaller than when he arrived, his cry more miserable and more angry, his sleep restless. When he opens his eyes they are more expressive than they should be, with an experienced and reproachful look that has an unnatural effect in a baby's face. His tiny fingers are blue as if Bernard is always freezing, even though he is well wrapped up, with hot-water bottles around him. To say it plainly, Bernard is starving.

As if to emphasise his untimely arrival in this world, the powers that be have cut off the sources of his nourishment. Nothing helps, not even the bean flour that bedouin women use in the desert, and which Madame Bourg has got hold of. His mother sits there, lacking sleep, looking as if she were guilty of dereliction of duty. And whatever Bernard gets instead is not much use, however carefully they weigh it and measure it out. He drinks ravenously, and – a belch – he is empty again. He looks up with reproachful eyes, sucks in empty air, screams. He has not given up, but fights for his existence as best he can.

Mlle Blanchard brings up the rear of the procession, laden like a pack-horse. She lives on the same floor as Bernard and helps to carry things. Nobody has more than two hands. Bernard's father carries the baby basket with his. His mother has to hold on to the banisters with the one, and in the other she has the stand with the bottles, prepared ready. Who would carry the baby clothes and the primus and the powder and the rest of it if not Mlle Blanchard? A visit to the cellar can last for minutes or hours. If the house is hit, it may be days becore they can get out of the ruins; there have been plenty of examples of that. In such a situation one must be able to hold out as long as possible.

Like certain waiters Mlle Blanchard has become adept at carrying the most incredible number of objects, and at putting them down without mishap. Only then does she think of her own concerns and disappears into a dark corner, where she is noticed subsequently only because of a slight rattling, the sound of her rosary as she sits telling the beads.

She is not the kind who is good at bending over Bernard and making expert remarks. Nor does she pretend she can. But she knows how to carry things, and what she knows about, she does.

In fact Mlle Blanchard does more for Bernard than most of the others in the cellar. But as happens frequently, others reap the praise. Madame Bourg reaps the most, even though it is far from her intention to put anyone in the shade. She can give advice, she calls his mother *mon enfant* and Bernard *notre p'tit vieux*, lifting him out of his basket in the way he ought to be lifted, so that his head doesn't loll and his back is properly supported, doing it fearlessly and firmly, quite differently from his mother, who is anxious and fumbling.

Madame Bourg has sons herself. Like all mothers she loves looking back, cherishing the memory of a helplessness so great that it laid total claim on her, and of progress that did not yet threaten to lead away from her. She looks at Bernard and says, 'Pierre at that age . . .', 'Louis at that age. . .'. Perhaps she forgets for a moment that Pierre and Louis are grown boys and gone to the war. Then she must remember it again, for she sighs.

But Mlle Blanchard is in the post office and for years has been a good daughter and supported and finally buried her widowed mother. Mlle Blanchard can wield pens and die-stamps, that's her province; she can be patient with old people and read boring things aloud to them. The longer the war lasts, the fewer are her chances of ever experiencing anything else. Her generation is condemned to spinsterhood and barrenness; it can already be demonstrated statistically. In fact they might just as well withdraw into the shadows at once, so that it is done voluntarily, so to speak, and with dignity. If it were not for Bernard, Mlle Blanchard, too, would perhaps be in her bed, like Mlle Leroux, like many along with her. In resignation, in disgust.

She had wished to go out and nurse the wounded, had wished to become part of a greater unity and feel that she was doing so. But a woman in the post office is needed in the postal service now more than ever. Everyone said so, and she heard it wherever she turned. She remained at the window in the dark, old-fashioned post office in the side-street. Another quiet deed of heroism, like everything else that Mlle Blanchard undertakes in this world.

The employment of a person who might be able to save Bernard is out of the question for the unfortunates in the attic. It does not occur to anyone to suggest such a thing. Besides, the country women are no longer earning their living by meeting the require-ments of the city; they can't, even if they were promised the moon. They are needed behind plough and harrow, spade and fork, everywhere where the men left off. They can't even be found, but have gone home, leaving everyone in the lurch.

All those who can, have left, and rightly. At least it means fewer mouths to feed. In the country there is peace and quiet, fresh air and sunshine, all sorts of possibilities. Bernard ought to leave too. The doctor has said so, everyone says so, Bernard's parents admit it. But to take action, to find documents, travel permits, seats on one of the overcrowded trains – all the things that take time and must be begun as soon as possible, these they do not do. Nobody drops hints about it any more.

Madame Bourg has made inquiries privately at the nearest children's hospital. It was overcrowded. And then there was the matter of the country women. Nobody can force them to stay. The few who were left were far from sufficient. But if Madame Bourg tried another hospital, in another part of the city, then perhaps. . . .

Madame Bourg went home. It is impossible to carry Bernard to distant parts of the city. Even if there are trams, they are subject to the fortunes of war. A hole in the street, a torn-up rail, and they are brought to a standstill.

It has become ridiculous to hide in the cellar. Fewer and fewer people bother. One would have to live there. No sooner are you back in bed than the alarm goes again. It goes in the daytime. Destruction swoops from a clear sky, a sky without a speck in it and in full sunshine, makes craters in the asphalt, explodes and is gone. It's beyond human understanding. People stare upwards, fail to reach any conclusion, then return to their affairs. If one cannot do anything else, one can at least do that, contribute to law and order. The eleven-year-old girl on the third floor is called back from the window and made to play her C major scale over again. That's her contribution.

Then somebody finds a piece of a missile. The mystery is a gun. A phenomenon of a gun, of which the world has never seen the like before in its ability to shoot far.

It is obvious to the most inexperienced that Bernard's stay in this inhospitable life seriously threatens to be short. He still uses his strength, such as it is, to protest; when he is asleep he drinks in his dreams, so he can be heard all over the cellar. But he plucks at the sheet with tiny restless fingers, a gesture that has become a habit, whether it is a helpless attempt to get what nobody can provide him with, or the fumbling of the dying for something to cling to.

His mother sits staring at him, as if she is trying to hold him fast in her gaze. His father? He trudges round half the city looking for milk, stands in queues for hours, and in between comes home again empty-handed. An infant's ration does not go very far on the days when supplies are lacking. He glances at Bernard, looks away again and down at the floor. If he is thinking that maybe it would be better if it were all over, this is perhaps no more than human.

'What if we were to fetch Ernestine?'

It is a night when the stillness that follows the alarm signal seems never-ending. It hovers intolerably between the cellar walls, interrupted only by Bernard's perpetual sucking in his dream and his sudden small cries of misery. Nobody talks, even Mlle Blanchard's rosary is not rattling. Nothing is happening outside. No explosions, no all-clear. The little group of people who still – whether from old habit or for Bernard's sake – go down to the cellar, seem forgotten down there.

But suddenly thin little Madame Mialon, from the first floor above the courtyard, who works as a domestic help and is the most reserved, the least domineering of them all, appears in the middle of the room, with a proposal. And what a proposal! As simple as fitting a sock to the foot and daring as an emergency manoeuvre. 'What if we were to fetch Ernestine? Her youngest is fourteen months, and he's like *this*.' Madame Mialon's gesture implies something decidedly round. She is speaking louder than before, with increasing assurance.

'Ernestine?' Madame Bourg drops her knitting.

'The wife of the caretaker in No. 30, madame. Four children. As healthy as you and me. If I hadn't been afraid of seeming to interfere, I'd have suggested it long ago.'

'He ought, at any rate, to have hydrotherapy first,' says Madame Bourg, feeling her way.

'Doctors' invention, madame. We don't need to make such a fuss. He's hungry. He needs food, not water.'

Silence.

Madame Bourg takes off her spectacles and polishes the lens. This is no easy matter. No, God knows. Much is concealed in it, the one problem within the other. She turns towards Bernard's basket. 'You will have to decide, mes enfants,' she says, strangely tired.

Decide? Two distracted, exhausted faces look up at each other. Then old Monsieur Dubois speaks with the voice of authority. 'If she will come, this Madame Ernestine, it seems to me that there is no choice to be made. It's a matter of alternatives, isn't it?'

'That's my opinion precisely,' says Madame Mialon.

Madame Bourg looks into the half-dark again, where the mother is sitting. And the mother nods, her eyes shining with tears.

'Go and ask her!' says Madame Bourg. 'One can always ask.'

Madame Mialon disappears up the stairs and out into the darkness, quick on her feet as a rat, used to making the least possible noise when she comes and goes. And the stillness is there again, worse than ever, burdened with doubt and uncertainty. When finally there can be heard a rustle of skirts, children's tripping feet, a whining and scolding at the entrance to the cellar, it feels like a deliverance. It really is Ernestine. Fate wills that it is she.

'My husband's at the war, and I have four children,' she announces by way of introduction. 'I'm not leaving them, here they are. If anything should happen, it's best we all go. All at once. In addition I'm a caretaker's wife. I'm risking my job by leaving the house in the middle of the night.'

She stands in the glow of the candle that Madame Bourg is holding up, an ordinary looking person, of average height, average width, not very good tempered and with a sturdy, sleeping child in her arms. Three more are clinging to her skirts, rubbing their eyes sleepily with their fists, and whining.

'There's a war on,' says Madame Bourg, with a sudden smile; an experienced smile of complicity, as one who has immediately sized up Ernestine and knows her.

'There's a war on. We must help one another. Here I am. Where is this lady and her child?'

Madame Bourg shines the light on Bernard, on the whole pathetic little group. And Ernestine's severe caretaker's expression breaks up into a motherly pursing of the lips. 'Heavens above, look at him!'

Then she hands over the sturdy child to other arms, lifts Bernard out of the basket and sits down comfortably with him. She scolds him and slaps his bottom to get him going. And then an explosion shakes the walls.

In the stillness that follows, Ernestine's children's howling is the first sound. 'Be quiet, Pierre! Shut up, Simone! Don't roar like that, Jean! We're all of us here, can't you see?'

Then there follows a sound, a tiny sound of life itself, present in spite of the clamour of death: the regular gurgling of a baby sucking and finding nourishment.

The cellar holds its breath and listens, not to what is happening outside, but inside. Face after face moves into the meagre glow of the candle, stays there a moment, staring with open mouth, then gives way to another. Something is happening that is right and proper, something is beginning to grow as women think it should grow; nothing is being destroyed, something is being protected. Mlle Blanchard says over and over, 'He's drinking, he's drinking!' Old Monsieur Dubois keeps to the fringe so that the women may watch; he is rubbing his hands with pleasure. Once or twice the tiny sound is drowned by an explosion, but it surfaces again.

Someone has found an oil-lamp. It is standing on a crate shining richly and steadily on Bernard and Ernestine who are combined in a figure of total serenity. Ernestine's surly everyday expression is composed and still and beautiful. She, like many another, might be a madonna.

Among the other faces, the mother's. It is as if she, too, is drinking. New life is streaming beneath her skin into her features, into her eyes. And the father's, a mask of harsh defiance, gradually dissolving.

Suddenly Bernard is asleep. He has not taken so very much, but he has decided to sleep on it, to put it to use. Ernestine gets cautiously to her feet and puts him in the basket. It is a decisive moment.

Bernard is asleep. The tiny fingers are quite still, splayed out motionless above the sheet. The magical peace that streams out from a sleeping child is already in the atmosphere, shared to a greater or lesser degree by them all.

'Well, I declare – I think I'm fond of him already,' says Ernestine.

Together with Bernard, his mother has fallen asleep. With her head on her husband's shoulder she sleeps as profoundly and quietly as her child. She is not awakened by the next explosion, nor by the signal announcing the all-clear.

(Rowena Cooper read this story on *Woman's Hour* in May 1992.)

CHILDREN IN THE FAMILY

THE GYPSY'S BABY

◆

Rosamond Lehmann

I

At the bottom of the lane that ran between our garden wall and the old row of brick cottages lived the Wyatt family. Their dwelling stood by itself, with a decayed vegetable patch in front of it, and no grass, and not a flower; and behind it a sinister shed with broken palings, and some old tyres, kettles and tin basins, and a rusty bicycle frame, and a wooden box on wheels: and potato peelings, bones, fish heads, rags and other fragments strewn about. The impression one got as one passed was of mud and yellowing cabbage stalks, and pools of water that never drained away. After a particularly heavy rainfall there was water all round the door and even inside, on the floor of the kitchen. Cursing but undaunted, wearing a battered cloth cap on her head, Mrs Wyatt drove it out again and again, year after year, with a mop. It was an insanitary cottage with no damp course, mean little windows in rotting frames and discoloured patches on the walls.

Mr Wyatt was shepherd to Mr Wilson the farmer, who was, I suppose, a shocking landlord; but this idea only strikes me now. It merely seemed, then, that the wretched cottage with all its litter and pieces of shored-up life suitably enclosed the Wyatt brood, and that one was inseparable from the other. Mrs Wyatt accepted her circumstances in a favourable spirit, and gave birth each year to another baby Wyatt. She was a small crooked-hipped exhausted slattern with a protruding belly and black rotten stumps of teeth. Her beautiful wild eyes were of a fanatical blue, and when she fixed them on you they seemed to pierce beyond the back of your skull. Her face was worn away to bone and stretched skin, and in the middle of each hollow cheek was a stain of rose, like one live petal left on a dead flower.

Maudie, Horace, Norman, Chrissie Wyatt – these names I remember, and can differentiate the owners clearly. Then came three more who reappear to me only as a composite blur, and their names escape me, except that one must have been Alfie, and I still believe the baby's name was Chudleigh. All but one, they took after Mr Wyatt, and had flat broad shallow skulls, sparse mousish hair – foetus hair – coming over their foreheads in a nibbled fringe, pale faces with Mongolian cheekbones and all the features laid on thin, wide and flat. Their eyes were wary, dull, yet with a surface glitter. They were very undersized, and they wore strange clothes. Maudie owned an antique brown sealskin jacket with a fitted waist and flaring skirts to it. Horace had a man's sporting jacket of ginger tweed that flapped around his boots. The younger ones could not be said to be dressed, in the accepted sense. They were done up in bits of cloth, baize or blanket; and once I saw the baby in a pink flannel hot-water bottle cover. There was something sharp, gnawing, rodent about them; a scuttling quietness in their movements. Their voices too were extremely quiet, delicate, light; entirely without the choking coarseness of the local drawl.

Chrissie was the different one. She had a mop of curly brown hair with auburn stripes in it, a dark, brilliant skin, hollow cheeks, and large rolling eyes like her mother's, only dark. Her brow was knobbly, over-developed, disquieting with its suggestion of pre-cocity, of a fatal excess. She frowned perpetually in a fierce worried way, and her prominent mouth would not shut properly. It made a sharp rather vicious looking circle of red round her tiny white teeth. Some charitable person had given her a frock of black and scarlet plaid that fitted tightly to her miniature form and gave her the enhanced reality, or the unreality, of a portrait of a child. I don't think I ever saw her, except once, in any other garment in the whole space of time – how long was it – during which our orbit touched the orbit of the Wyatt family. The frock did get more and more exiguous; but Chrissie did not grow much, or fill out at all. Against the dun background of her sister and brothers she was isolated and set off: as if her mother's degenerating flesh and bone had combined with the nondescript clay of her father to produce the rest; but Chrissie had been conceived from that bright splash of living blood in her mother's cheek.

Whereas the others all looked, curiously enough, clean in a superficial way, she was always excessively dirty, and this increased her look of a travel-stained child from a foreign country: a little refugee, we would think now. If one met her in the field path and said: 'Hallo, Chrissie,' one said it with apprehension: might she not spit, screech like a monkey, blaze out a stream of swear words? She never did, though. She bent rapidly down and started to tear up handfuls of turf. When one passed on, she followed, at a little distance, her eyes rolling fiercely, like a colt's, not focusing.

She was often alone, but the others seemed always in a cluster, moving up and down the lane, or hanging over their broken fence. When we went by we always said 'Hallo,' kindly and they breathed the words back to us in a soft wheezing chorus. They always had colds on their chests. Then, after a brief distance had been established between us, they were apt to direct a piercing whistle after our dog Jannie, a Dandie Dinmont whose long low trotting form riveted them always into a pin of concentrated attention. Patiently bouncing along, as only Dandie Dinmonts do, his shaggy topknot over his eyes, his heavy pantomime head as if barely supported between invisible shafts, he seemed altogether to ignore this magnetising influence. Seemed, I say: we knew he had another life; that *nostalgie de la boue* drove him at dawn and dusk, himself all grey, a shade, to explore the lowest districts and there regale himself with nauseous garbage. We suspected that the Wyatts' back door furnished him a toothsome hunting ground.

Another trait which we could not ignore, but kept firmly on the outskirts of our relationship with him, was his habit of killing

cats. He was death on cats. It was curious, for he was a total failure
with rabbits, and if he blundered on one in the course of one of his
Walt Disney gallops over the fields, he winced if anything and
seemed upset. A great many cats visited our garden up till – not
after – the time when Jannie, shaking off puppyhood, was beginning to know his own nature; and once he killed three in a week.
He left a specimen corpse in the broccoli bed and our gardener
came upon it unexpectedly. It was his own cat, a tortoiseshell. The
sight turned him up, he said; he hadn't been able to fancy his dinner. We grew to be nervous of exploring the shrubbery, just in
case. My father got bored after paying up several high death
claims, and gave orders to the outdoor staff to bury at sight and
say nothing. At the same time, to our despair, he steeled himself
to purchase a muzzle for Jannie. Tearful and crimson, Jess
adjusted it, muttering in his ear that it hurt her more than him.
But Jannie went out into the paved garden, and beat with his
muzzle on the ground like a thrush cracking a snail shell, and
within the hour he had got the better of it and came in again wearing it as it might be some kind of Central European military
helmet, rakishly, over one eye. Attempting to conceal from him
our laughter, we rolled about on the ground and squealed and bit
our fingers. We muzzled him a few more times in a spirit of pure
frivolity, to await the intoxicating result; but when that delight
lost its freshness, the device was altogether discarded; and he
ranged once more in all his wild dignity and freedom.

Now we entered upon a halcyon period. No cat, living or dead,
haunted the garden any longer. Innocently Jannie's smoke-blue
form wove in and out of the berberis and laurel. We told ourselves it was an adolescent phase outgrown.

One evening the back door bell rang. Shortly afterwards a note
was carried through and presented: a grimy note of poorest
quality.

It seems strange in retrospect how many of the dramas of our
lives opened with the loud ping of the back door bell, and were
passed along up to the front through a number of doors and
voices of announcement. 'A person at the back door, 'M, wishes

to speak to you.' 'What kind of a person, Mossop?' 'I reelly couldn't say, 'M. Mrs Almond give me the message.'

Ladies and gentlemen to the front door, persons to the back. The former could scarcely engage one's imagination: they and the nature of their visits were easily calculable. But a person at the back door emerged, portentous in anonymity, from that other world that ever beckoned, threatened, grimaced, teeming with shouts and animal yells and whipping tops and hopscotch, with tradesmen's horses and carts, and the bell of the muffin man and words chalked up on palings, just beyond our garden wall. Now and then someone came through the wall and appeared before us, and occasionally it was by the pressure of some extreme urgency – a fatality, a case for the hospital poste-hast – so that the sight of one or other of my parents walking from the room in answer to such a summons always caused in us a stirring of the bowels.

It was my father who received this note: my mother was out. He scanned it in silence, then said:

'Is someone waiting for an answer, Mossop.'

'Yes, sir. I understand a young lad. I couldn't say who it would be.'

'Tell him I'll come along presently and see his mother.'

Then he handed the note to Jess. It said that Mrs Wyatt presented her compliments and our dog had taken and killed their dear little black cat they'd had for a pet three years. It was a bald statement of fact translated with a world of labour into demented arabesques of scrawl and blot, and signed simply: Mrs Wyatt.

We looked at Jannie sweetly sleeping in his basket by the hearth, and looked away again, seeing a loved face suddenly estranged; angel's face, fiend's face, unaware of crime. 'It's his nature,' muttered Jess; but the pang rooted in the acceptance of such a truth has rarely come home to me more profoundly. This was the first time I knew the inescapable snare of loving a creature with no sense of decency. He was a criminal. We could not change him. We had to love him, go on patching up his betrayals of us, still kiss his tender cruel fur cheeks.

My father sat and smoked a cigarette, and we sat, our books discarded, and waited for him to finish it. He was aware of our feelings and we trusted him. He was never one to blame or to pass a moral sentence. The principle of his life was a humorous benevolence combined with a philosophical scepticism about humanity; and no doubt that perfect generosity of temperament which led him, all his life, to give away his money to anybody who asked him for it, had enabled him frequently to reflect without bitterness: 'It's his nature.' I think the letters in every kind of handwriting, classy, uneducated, youthfully unformed, shaky with age, baring secrets – some trivial, a few tragic – of folly, ill luck, confidence misplaced, with accompanying expressions of everlasting gratitude and pledges of prompt repayment, laid away without comment in a drawer of his desk and found after his death – I think they would fill a volume. The numerous ones beginning: 'Dear Old Man,' were the ones most conducive to cynical reflection. Not that he would have thought so. He never expected to be paid back, and he never was; and in his will he directed that all debts owing to him were cancelled.

We waited in silence, and finally he got up and said: 'Come along, you two, Jess and Rebecca. Down the lane with us.'

Jannie, seeing what looked like the prospect of a walk, stretched himself and skipped forth from his wicker ark and began to prance. 'Don't let him out,' said my father; and in silence we shut the door on his shining, then anxious, then stricken face. Seeing the light fade totally out of him made us feel that the punishment horribly fitted the crime; but far stronger was the sense of wantonly smiting his innocence. The shame, the blame were ours.

We went down the garden, through the bottom gate. It was a hot June evening, and the lane smelt of privet, of dust and nettles. We walked past the end of the row of stumpy prosperous cottages, each with its tended flowery front plot, and came to where the Wyatts' cottage squatted by itself upon its patch of cracked earth and vegetable refuse. There was a decrepit barren old plum tree just beyond their gate, and beneath it were several little Wyatts, perfectly still: waiting for us. Maudie, the eldest, sat with the bald baby on her knee; another, at the staggering stage and with a faint hatching of down on its skull, was stuffed into a wooden grocery box on wheels. Horace, next in age to Maudie, had this vehicle by one handle, and sat there negligently pushing it back and forth. Chrissie was not there. As we came through the gate, it was as though a wire running through them tautened and vibrated. They watched us advance towards them. My father said benevolently:

'Is your mother in?'

'In the 'ouse,' said Maudie, with a jerk of her head.

We were about to pass on when Horace croaked suddenly:

'Your grey dog got our Fluff.'

My father replied regretfully:

'Ah, dear, yes. We've come to say how very sorry we are.'

'We don't like 'im no more.'

'I can understand that,' said my father. 'He's a very bad dog about cats, yet in other ways he's most gentle and loving. It's strange, isn't it?'

Horace nodded.

'We buried poor Fluff,' he said without emotion.

We went on, and their heads swivelled round after us, watching. My father rapped at the door. The lace curtains covering the front room window twitched sharply. After a pause the door was opened by Mr Wyatt, in his shirt sleeves, smoking a pipe.

'Good-evening, sir!' His tone was bluff and hearty, and his sly little eyes twinkled up at my father in a normal way. I don't quite know what I had expected – that he would burst into tears perhaps, or pronounce a curse upon us – but a grateful relief softened the pinched edges of my heart, and affection for Mr Wyatt came over me in a flood.

'Good-evening, Wyatt. My little girls are dreadfully upset about this business,' said my father, in a serious man-to-man way. 'I've brought them along because they wanted to tell your Missis and the youngsters how they felt about it. Was poor Pussy a great pet? Are they much cut up about her?'

And what should Mr Wyatt do but give a shout of laughter.

'Oh that dog, sir! 'E does give me a laugh – always 'as done. Never seen such a dog – 'e's a proper caution. Never think from the build of 'im 'e'd be so nippy would you? Jiggered if I know 'ow 'e copped that blessed cat. Thought she could look after 'erself. 'E's given 'er many a chase up the tree when 'e's been around. Caught 'er napping – that's what is was.' He chuckled and pulled at his pipe. 'There she was, laid out stiff round by the shed. Not a mark on 'er. 'E done the job double quick – neat, too. Our Chrissie saw 'im at it. She was a bit upset. Fact is,' he added confidentially, 'they was all a bit upset. It's only natural. They thought a lot of that there cat.'

A figure now suddenly materialised behind his shoulder, and it was Mrs Wyatt, straightening her dark blue apron, tucking in wisps of hair, sending out emanations of wild welcome. She seemed completely overcome by the sight of us on her doorstep and kept uttering whimpers of delight, her ruined gap-tooth mouth opening and closing at us, her great eyes shedding over us streams of radiant blue light.

'Won't you come in, sir? Arthur, why don't you ask the gentleman in, and the young ladies, bless their hearts. To tell you the honest truth, I wasn't feeling quite the thing, and I slipped upstairs to have a bit of a lay-down.'

Her voice, piercing, resonant, with an occasional wailing note in it, pinioned us where we stood while continuing to urge us within. It occurred to me suddenly that Mrs Wyatt looked very ill. Her lips were a queer colour – violet – and her cheeks beneath the carnation cheek bones were yellow, cadaverously sunken. She looked mad, driven, loving, exhausted. I stared at her until I felt hypnotised; and to this day her face with that something prophetic stamped upon it which I discerned but did not recognise comes before me in all its waste and triumph.

My father excused us from coming in on the score of its getting on for my bed time; and this threw her into a further paroxysm of enthusiasm. She seemed to dote on me for my early bed time: it was a tribute to our superior way of life.

'To be sure! It would be! Bless 'er! Well! It's ever so good of you, sir, I'm sure to trouble to come down. I said to myself: "Now shall I mention it, or shan't I?" Giving you all such a shock and upset – it didn't seem right. But the children did take on so, I didn't hardly know what to do. I thought: "Mrs Ellison will understand I did it for the best." How is she? Oh she does so much! I'm sure every one in the village worships her. Oh that dog of yours! – artful – it isn't the word. I said to my husband I'd never have believed it. Always round at our back door always welcome the bones and that he's buried, and then to take and kill poor Fluff like that. It seems so cold-blooded if you understand. Many's the plate of scraps he's had off her. I used to pass the remark to my husband, what an appetite! – and then gazing up at you so melting out of his big eyes. Ooh, Chrissie did create – didn't you lovey? Where's she got to now? She's been tight round my legs ever since.' She turned and yelled over her shoulder. 'Chrissie! Chris! Come to Mammie, duck! Dad's buried poor old Fluffie. You won't see her no more.'

These (to us) crude and tactless encouragements seemed to fall upon deaf ears. No Chrissie appeared. My father engaged Mr Wyatt in low-voiced conversation. I saw some silver slip from his hand into the knobby brown-grained hand of the shepherd; and the latter thanked him with a brisk nod and a brief word.

All at once Chrissie darted from the obscurity of the cottage towards her mother. I caught a glimpse of her grimy burning face before she buried it passionately in Mrs Wyatt's skirts. Another thing I noticed was that a spasm contracted Mrs Wyatt's lips and forehead, as if the impact made her wince with pain. She put an arm round Chrissie's head and clasped it to her side.

'There's a silly for you!' she cried with rough love. 'Whatever will these young ladies think? She's shy, that's what it is. Ooh, she did create! Never mind, duckie, it's all over now. Mammie'll get you another kitty. Look now, these lovely little ladies have come to see you.'

'To say we're sorry,' muttered Jess heroically.

'Oh dear, and we know they wouldn't have had it happen for the world.'

But Chrissie remained mute, tense, annihilating herself; all of her repudiating us.

My father touched us on the shoulder, and it was all over, and we could go. I had been nervously fingering the wood of the rickety porch, and had my hand raised, picking at the paint blisters. Suddenly I felt it seized and snatched to Mrs Wyatt's lips. I heard her cry wildly:

'Look at her little white hand!'

Tingling from head to foot with blushes, I was unable to join in the mutual expressions of cordiality and farewell. We went away down the cinder path and when we came to the group beneath the tree my father stopped.

'You know, we're dreadfully sad,' he said. 'We love cats as much as you do.'

They stared at us, their eyes pin-pointing from a great distance. But Maudie said politely:

'Oh well, it can't be helped. It don't matter.'

'Dad says 'e'll beg a puppy for us when Jet at the farm 'as pups,' said Horace.

'Good,' said my father. 'Remember puppies like a nice bowl of water – *clean* water – handy for whenever they want to wet their whistle. And I'll tell you a thing they *don't* like. They don't like to be tied up all day. In the end it makes them so cross they feel like biting people. Just as I'd feel. Wouldn't you?'

They looked extremely wary now, their faces blank with suspicion and alarm. Not a word came out of them. My father walked round behind them to the back of the tree and examined in a meditative way a hole freshly dug in the ground.

'That's a fine hole somebody's dug.'

'We done it for Fluff,' said Maudie. ''Orace done it. But our Dad took 'er away and put 'er somewhere else. 'E said Alfie and them would go digging 'er up all day.'

My father stirred the earth with his toe:

'I fancied I saw something shine,' he said. 'What can it possibly ave been? Come and look, one of you.' Cautiously Horace got to his feet and came and stood beside him.

'Just here,' said my father.

Something gleamed in the loose dry soil at the bottom of the hole. Suddenly Horaced crouched and started scrabbling; then he whisked upright again, his face drawn, mottled a dull pink. On his palm lay some earth and a half-crown piece. He was trembling all over.

'Well, I'll be blessed!' said my father. 'What an extraordinary piece of luck that you should have dug just there.'

Maudie picked up the baby and came and stood beside her brother. The one in the box clambered out and joined them. Finally Horace said in a toneless whisper:

''Oo do it belong to?'

'Why, to the lot of you,' said my father. 'Finding's keeping, you know, when it's buried treasure.'

We went out of the gate, and when I looked back I saw Horace scuttling after him. Only Maudie remained under the plum tree, her stomach stuck out to support the weight of the child in her arms, staring after us.

'You did drop it in, didn't you, Daddy?' said Jess, who liked to have everything shipshape, with no excuse for mystification.

'I saw you,' I said; and I had; and was in consequence brooding beneath the cloud of too much light. For it had come home to me in a flash, as the coin left his pocket for the earth, that my reading of *The Treasure Seekers* had been at fault, and that my father and Albert Next Door's Uncle had practised an identical deception. This was an absolutely new idea to me, and caused me a shock of disillusionment.

My father sighed and smiled.

Surreptitiously, for fear of Jess's eye, I squinted sideways at my little white hand.

II

That was the first act in our relationship with the Wyatts, unpropitious, fraught with omens. It was my younger sister Sylvia who subsequently insinuated them, first into the garden, then into the house; and so forever into memory and imagination.

Sylvia had long ago swept away any class barriers which she considered irksome, and for preference selected comrades from among the back lane children. In the self-created role of Lone Scout, wearing a personally designed uniform girt with a stiff leather belt and stuck with knives, ropes, whistles, assuming a gruff husky voice and a sort of backwoodsman's accent, she roamed the lane and mingled in the seasonal hop-scotch and top-whipping. She knew every single one of the children, name, age, details of private life and all. Her experiences must have been interesting – much more so, factually speaking, than my own. I feared the caterwauling noises that floated up in the evenings to the nursery window; I shrank from the drawings and inscriptions upon the pillars of the railway arch. They printed themselves with scorching precision upon the cavern walls behind my eyes, but I passed them furtively, hoping they would – wouldn't – would be rubbed out; as they sometimes were – only to reappear again – by some anonymous purifier working secretly with an indiarubber in the night.

I never thought of the back lane kids as children like myself: they were another species of creature, and, yes, a lower. I imagined their bodily functions must in some nameless way differ from my own. But for Sylvia they were objects of whole-hearted fascination, beings to be emulated and admired. Such posted announcements as: *Rosie Gann goes with Reggie Hiscock*, with accompanying symbols, were transcripts of mysteries into which she had initiated herself without dismay or shame. There never was a little girl less likely to see something nasty in the wood shed. What she did see she accepted with an unwavering speculative eye – an eye that from birth had met the shocks of life impenetrably with one cold answer: 'Just as I expected.' I was fluid, alternately floored and ecstatic; but she was what I believe theosophists call an old soul, and the parents, nurses, governesses, schoolmistresses of the world impressed on her nothing except a tacit determination to resist their precepts. Jess cried out fiercely: 'Unfair! Unjust!'; and I wept, and hastened to be accommodating, because of a wish to be loved by everybody; but Sylvia gave away no clue that might have provided an opportunity for character-moulding. She learned a number of interesting words and rhymes in the back lane; and sometimes she came in from play with a faintly stupefied expression, as if there had been a good deal to take in.

She used to conduct parties into the garden by the bottom gate, and lurk with them among the shrubbery. My parents were democratic in their ideas, but I doubt if they would have encouraged their visitors, had they been aware of their presence. So far as I know, they never were precisely aware of it. The shrubbery was profuse, in the late Victorian style, containing many a secret chamber and named vantage point. The game was to see unseen. Generally all was silence, but now and then owl hoots, unseasonable cuckoo calls issued from the depths of the foliage: ritual cries, maybe, or merely a leg-pull for the gardeners. But gardeners are, I think, particularly unsusceptible to leg-pulls based on natural phenomena; or perhaps it is that custom has dulled their response to the calls of birds: anyway they gave no outward sign of attention or perplexity.

There were also occasional raids on the cherry, plum and apple orchards during the ripe seasons – triumphs of strategy one and all; differently organised indeed from the wretched affair of the ungentlemanly Barstow boys and the peaches, to which I lent myself: but that is another story.

These were the days when each portion of the garden, every shrub-girdled bay of grass and rose bushes, every dark sour-smelling haunt of fern and creeping ivy beneath the laurel-planted walks had its particular myth, its genius or indwelling spirit. Now, when I go back home, I am confused sometimes by double vision. A veil clouds my eyes, and at the same time a veil is stripped off; for a moment time's boomerang splits me clean in two, and presences evanescent and clinging as webs, or the breath of flowers on the wind, drift in the familiar places, exhaling as they pass a last tingling echo of primeval rapture. Almost I remember what, beside myself, hid in the forests of asparagus; what whispered in the bamboos round the pond, and had power over the goldfish and the water-lilies; what complex phantom rose up from the aromatic deeps of lavender when I brushed white butterflies in flocks off the mauve bushes.

Sylvia's myths, intense as mine, were different in their nature, and we never exchanged or shared them. Mine leaned to prettiness and fairies; hers, I feel sure, were bonier, more unromantic, masculine. We ranged ourselves roughly as it were – *Little Folks* against the *B.O.P.* Jess took in *The Children's Encyclopædia*, and she cleaned out the rabbit hutches and nursed the puppies through distemper, and knitted scarves and mittens – proper, wearable ones – for my father and my brother, while daemonically we roamed in the sacred wood with bloomers torn, and black powder off branches in our matted hair.

Sylvia's customary visitors never came near the house, let alone into it: but the Wyatts did come. They worked away noiselessly, like termites, and in the end our foundations collapsed, and they were in the nursery. It was the summer my mother went back to New England to see her people, and took Jess with her. Our infant brother was sent to the seaside with Nurse, our unpopular Belgian governess returned to her native country for a lovely long holiday, and Sylvia and I remained at home to keep our father company, with only Isabel the nursemaid to supervise us.

It was a beautiful time. All over the household a slackening of moral fibre took place. Mrs Almond our cook had friends in most afternoons, and we showed off to them and made them clap their hands over their mouths to gasp and giggle and exclaim that we were cough-drops, cures or cautions. Mossop imported a fascinating curly-haired nephew called Charlie, a professional soldier, who played the concertina and encouraged us to sit on his lap. I stayed up to dinner every night. The Wyatts advanced their operations.

One day Sylvia said in an off-hand way:

'Isabel, the Wyatts are in the garden. They want to come up and see our toys.'

Another time Isabel might have replied that want must be their master, or: 'And so does the sweep's grandmother, I dare say. The very idea! What next?' – but she was in particularly mellow spirits that afternoon and she answered:

'Well, I can't see the harm in that. A cat may look at a king, so I've heard tell;' and she went on pinning together the cut-out front portions of a new blue sateen blouse over her opulent bosom, and humming snatches of 'After the ball was over'.

She was a strapping girl with red cheeks and a full blue marble eye. She sang loudly, in operatic style, with maniac tremolos, as she went about her work. She had a bottom drawer, and a bone in her leg, and saw handsome strangers in the tea-leaves, and bade us leave a little for Miss Manners, and threatened to give us what Paddy gave the drum; and was apt to answer our questions obliquely with a tag or a saw. She was without tenderness. Her mind was not on us. A set-back in her private life on her day out, or a telling-off from Nurse occasionally made her sulky, and then she was apt to give us sharp pushes and be rough with the comb; but she had a fund of easy animal good nature, and we liked her very much, and admired her looks as much as she did herself.

Sylvia went away, and came back with three Wyatts behind her: Maudie, Horace, Chrissie. They stood in a block at the nursery door.

I said would they like to look in the toy cupboard; but they made no answer. 'There's the rocking-horse,' said Sylvia; but their eyes darted up and down, over the walls, along the floor, not focusing. A deep flush came up and began to burn in Sylvia's cheeks. Nothing more happened. Then in came Isabel, swinging her hips, looking particularly pleased with herself – I suppose the blouse was turning out a nice fit – and crying amiably: 'Well, here's a lot of smiling faces, and no mistake!'

We giggled, abashed, and the Wyatts looked at her in a stunned way. Then a minute ventriloquist's voice came out of Maudie, remarking politely:

'Hope it's no trouble.'

'Trouble? I've got trouble enough without troubling about you. All my ironing to do. Mind the wind doesn't change on those doleful dials of yours, that's all, or we'll all have something extra

to mope about. We don't eat children in this nursery, you know.'
She picked Chrissie up in her arms and gave her a little shake; and
Chrissie strained back, her wreath of hair slipping forward and
hiding her face as she bowed it low, low on to her chest, out of
Isabel's sight. 'Curlylocks! Oo, aren't you a thin mite! We'd never
get a square meal off you, would we?'

A tiny doll's titter issued from the other two, and at that
encouraging symptom Sylvia and I broke out in hearty laughs of
relief. A section of Chrissie's eye was visible, frantically rolling.
Suddenly she pitched forward in Isabel's grasp, flung both arms
round Isabel's neck and hung there convulsively, buried and
silent.

'Lor' love a duck!' said Isabel after a second's pause, her voice
taking on a startled gentler note. 'You cling on like a little monkey, don't you? Just like a little monkey on a stick.'

She carried Chrissie over to the musical box, wound it up and
put on a disc. Out tinkled 'After the ball was over' in liquid
midget notes. She gave Chrissie a kiss and set her down, saying:
'Be a good girl now, there's a love. You're all right.' Then she gave
a nod to Maudie and tweaked Horace's ear and went out.

It was all right then: the paralysis was dissolved. Horace
mounted the rocking-horse, dubiously at first, clutching its mane
and letting out a sharp panicky 'Hey!' whenever it moved; gradually with increasing bravado. Maudie walked softly about, looking
at the rugs, the fireguard, the screen we had plastered with cut-
out pictures from magazines and seedsmen's catalogues. She
looked at the doll's house, and the doll's cot, but she never so
much as put out a finger to touch anything. Playing seemed a con-
cept unknown to her. She threw off polite remarks, such as: 'Ain't
it a big room?' and: 'Is that your picture book?' She stood with her
sagging, broken-down working woman's stance, and looked long
at the coloured print of Madame Vigée Lebrun and her daughter
above the mantelpiece. I explained that they were mother and
child, and that the lady in the picture had executed the work herself. She said: 'Is it hand-painted, then?' I said dubiously I thought
it was a copy but that the original was indeed hand-painted. She

said how ever did she manage then, when she'd got both arms round the kid? I was stumped.

After that she said: 'Where d'you keep your clothes and that, then?' and I conducted her to my bedroom, and opened the cupboard. Our wardrobe was far from extensive, but I felt a mounting possessive complacence as I displayed my frocks. She still seemed apathetic, but at the back of her eyes I could now see a fixed point of glittering light. I was overcome by the desire to present her with a pink cotton frock which I disliked. Though I was nine and she rising thirteen I was fully as tall as she. This wish strove with the fear of being scolded should the transaction be discovered, and the resulting conflict held me powerless.

She said: 'Which is your best, then?' and for a climax I took down my dancing-class frock of crimson accordion-pleated silk. She put out her hand to touch it, but did not do so.

'We've got bridesmaids' frocks too, from our cousin's wedding,' I said. 'Apricot satin with pearls embroidered on the belt.'

'Where are they, then?' she said.

'Oh, they're put away,' I said. 'We're not allowed to take them out of their tissue paper.'

Feeling suddenly a peculiar revulsion from clothes, I led her back to the nursery, where Horace was still on the rocking-horse, and Chrissie still crouched by the musical box, with Sylvia putting on 'Robin Adair', 'The Bluebells of Scotland' and 'After the Ball' for her in unbroken succession.

A noticeable thing was their apprehensiveness about any spontaneous moves. We were accustomed to the uninhibited pounces and rushes of our social equals when they came to tea; but the springs of these children were crushed back and could not leap out.

There came a battering and a whimpering at the door, and who should tear in but Jannie, fresh from some round of local visits. We were embarrassed; but they looked at him without ill-will while he gave himself up to the raptures of reunion. Horace even bent to stroke him, remarking:

'You copped our Fluff, you did.'

''E still comes round our back door,' said Maudie. 'Our Mum says she can't like hold anythink against a dumb animal when it's their nature.'

We could think of no suitable reply.

Then Isabel came carolling back, and swung Chrissie up again and set her on her lap, saying cheerfully: 'Well now, let's have a look at you. Found your tongue yet? Eh?'

Chrissie nestled against her shoulder, half-hiding, but relaxed, coy. The others came and stood close beside Isabel, trustful, smiling faintly.

'You're all right, Chris,' said Horace.

'Our Mum say's she's a funny girl,' said Maudie. 'She says she don't know where she come from. She's not like the others, she says.'

'She can't arf bite when she gets 'er temper up,' said Horace.

'Yes, I bites,' whispered Chrissie, beaming.

I think it was the only thing I ever heard her say.

Isabel burst out laughing.

'Oo, you little sinner!' she cried. 'Don't you know what happens to little girls who bite? They get turned into nasty little dogs, they do. Don't you ever do such a shocking thing ever again.' She tilted Chrissie's chin up and looked at her indulgently. It was plain that the beauty of the creature had caught her fancy. 'Twopennyworth of bad ha'pence, that's what you are,' she said; and then, good-naturedly, she swept us all out to the garden and told the Wyatts to mind and run along home at once now.

So we accompanied them to the bottom gate, and bade them goodbye.

The visit had been a success. Yet for the rest of the day I felt depressed. I wished never to have known the Wyatts.

A few days afterwards, Sylvia told me that the Wyatts wished to come to tea.

'Did you ask them?' I said.

'No – they asked themselves.'

'I don't really want them much. Do you?'

'I don't mind. Anyway I've told them they can come.'

'I think Isabel might be cross.'

'I shall ask Dad. If he says yes, she'll have to.'

A stubborn sense of obligation was driving her, I could see. Her feelings about the Wyatts were undoubtedly purer, warmer than mine; but in her too, I think, they were beginning to get muddied. Uneasiness was creeping over both of us. We had got what the Wyatts wanted; sense of guilt deprived us of any concentration of forces such as theirs to oppose to them. Jannie had killed their Fluff. We were at their mercy.

That evening Sylvia said: 'Dad, can I have some children to tea?' – and of course he said: 'Yes, my pet,' and inquired no further. So when next morning at breakfast Sylvia announced: 'Dad says we can have the Wyatts to tea,' some flouncing movements were the only outward signs of revolt that Isabel could permit herself.

'Oh, indeed, by all means, have the whole lot in,' she said sweetly. She rattled the crockery on to the tray, and added what I had been waiting for: '*And* the crossing-sweeper's family, do, by all means.' This relieved her feelings, and she added with only normal tartness: 'I suppose you've got round your father again to allow it.'

She went out with the tray, and no doubt told them downstairs that next time she'd speak her mind. She was having a bit of an off-day, unfortunately; but also I suspect that the previous visit had been condemned in the servants' hall. The Wyatts had a very low local reputation.

That afternoon Maudie, Horace, Chrissie came to tea. Their hands and faces showed signs of scrubbing, and they were dressed for the occasion. Maudie wore a strange box-pleated dress of violet alpaca, made originally for a far larger and fuller frame. It lent a saffron tinge to her sallow complexion. Chrissie, in a discoloured scrap of pallid Jap silk, had almost lost her personality.

I had expected them to fall on their food and stuff it down with both fists, after the manner of the ravenous in fiction, but they seemed uninterested in tea. I wondered – so full of surprises are

people's home lives – if possibly they were accustomed to daily
feasts of cream buns and iced cake, and were utterly disgusted by
our simple fare. They chewed without appetite at a slice of bread
and butter each, and refused ginger-bread, and clearly gave Isabel
the pip by their unnatural abstraction from the board. I could
hear the caustic comments she was not expressing. Nothing is so
likely to produce hatred and contempt in a hostess as distaste
manifested at table by her visitors; and when the latter are a trio
of despicable, scrubby, under-nourished little brats, the feeling
must be deeply intensified. I suppose one factor was that they
were so unaccustomed to the ordinary diet of childhood or indeed
to regular meals of any sort that they had become more or less
indifferent to food. I have often noticed how much less greedy
children of the proletariat are than others. One would imagine
that they would be more absorbed in the problem of stoking up
than the pampered young of the middle and upper classes; but it is
not so. They are spare and delicate of appetite, extremely cautious
of experimenting, and seem not to wish to stuff themselves even
when there is a real opportunity for a blow-out. But when I look
back, I see that as regards this particular tea-party it was excess of
emotion that deprived the Wyatts of all appetite. At last they had
compassed their objective: they had come to tea.

Everybody was quite silent. This time Isabel did not help. It
was a relief when the meal was over. Chrissie scuttled to the musical box. Horace to the rocking-horse. Maudie lingered about,
looking apathetically at various objects. As soon as Isabel had
gone out with the tray, she said to me in her dull voice:

'Where does your mother keep her dresses and that, then?'

My heart sank.

'Oh, some in her room, some in the cupboard in the passage.'

'Let's have a look at them, then.'

Feeling dishonoured and sensing doom, I led the way to my
mother's bedroom. I came to the door which since her departure I
had not had the courage to open; and desolation swamped me as I
turned the handle. There was the shrine, empty, its fresh chintzes
as if frozen beneath a film of thin green ice, the bed shrouded, the

gleaming furniture, the cut-glass bottles, the photographs, the pastel drawing of three little girls in white frocks and blue sashes – ourselves – speaking at me with cold, mourning minatory voices. All her possessions had become taboo. This was desecration. I loathed Maudie.

'Ain't she got any velvets, then?' said the relentless voice.

'She's taken all her best frocks to America,' I said. 'I think everything's locked, anyway. We'd better go back to the nursery.'

'Go on. Try.'

Fearing she was about to lay hands upon the cupboard, I sprang towards it, and at my touch the carved olive wood door yawned open with a soft complaint, and revealed the long attenuated draperies of various garments hanging down.

'That's her black velvet tea gown,' I said touching it hurriedly.

'What's that?' said Maudie, pointing.

'That's an evening dress. It's got silver water lilies on.'

'Let's see it, then.'

I took down the green and silver brocade on its hanger, and laid it out on the couch.

'Ain't that 'er best, then?'

'It's one of her best, but she didn't take it because sea journeys tarnish silvery things.'

For a few moments, pride of showmanship overcame my nausea. If I had to go through with it, at least I could tell myself I had done Maudie proud. The dress flowed along the couch, a glittering delight. It was my particular favourite, appearing in my imagination as a sort of transformation scene – a magic pool, a fairy ring in an enchanted wood. I glanced at Maudie, and saw in her eye the same gloating point heightened now to an inexpressible degree. It was the look of someone in a trance-like state of obsession.

It was at this moment that Isabel swept in upon us. The rest is lost in horror and humiliation. We were driven back to the nursery, and the Wyatts were told it was high time to get along home. Off they bundled, noiseless, wary, unresisting. Through a mist, I saw Chrissie in the doorway break from formation, dart back to the musical box, make as if to pick it up, snatch her hands off it, dart back, dumb, to Maudie's side again. Afterwards I was enveloped in a whirlwind of scolding. Explanation was fruitless; I did not attempt it.

That night in bed I wept myself to a pulp and knew that my mother would die in America and that it would be entirely my fault; and nobody came magically to comfort me.

Isabel was particularly nice to us after that episode. I suppose she felt some responsibility with us for the catastrophe; I heard her say to the kitchen maid that those dratted Wyatt kids were on her mind. 'And another any day now,' said Alice; and then they whispered together. She gave us little treats, and encouraged us to have a picnic party of friends of our own class, and helped to make it go with a bang. Then, perhaps to demonstrate the difference between riff-raff like the Wyatts and well brought up inferiors, she asked little Ivy Tulloch to tea with us.

Ivy was the only child of the head gardener at Lady Bigham-Onslow's, impressive neighbour, and Mrs Tulloch and Isabel were dearest friends. Isabel had tried before to offer us little Ivy, but we had always vigorously rejected her. This time we felt our position shaky, and dared not protest.

She was a fat bland child with bulbous cheeks and forehead, and we despised her prim smug booted legs and her pigtails bound with glossy bows. She had far more and smarter frocks than we, and insertion and lace frills to the legs of all her knickers; whereas we had only one ornamental pair apiece, for parties. She was kept carefully from low companions, never played in the lane, and was made ever such a fuss of by Her Ladyship.

The arrangement made without consulting us was that she should trot along about four o'clock for a nice game with us, and that her Mummy should pop in after tea to have a chat with Isabel before taking her home.

Four o'clock came and went: no Ivy. We began to feel hopeful: she had forgotten the day, perhaps, or been struck down by measles. At five we ate the doughnuts bought to tempt her dainty appetite. By five-thirty we had totally erased her distasteful image from our minds, and were agreeably immersed in our own pastimes. Then we heard the back door bell ring sharply: and Isabel, exclaiming: 'There!' went rustling down at top speed. Shortly afterwards, two pairs of footsteps returned, two voices sounded in the passage, engaged in emphatic thrust and counterthrust. We recognised the refined and breathy tones of Mrs Tulloch, and the punctuating gasps and exclamations of Isabel. They went into the night nursery, hissed together for a little longer, then flung open the dividing door and descended upon us.

A flaming spot stood in either cheek of Mrs Tulloch, and there was a look about her, we saw it at a glance, of the mother fowl defending its young. She kept saying: 'Don't give it another thought, Isabel, I beg. I wouldn't want to cause any trouble, not when it's children'; and Isabel kept repeating that she never would have credited it, never, the wickedness.

Chaotically, the facts emerged. Stunned, we pieced them together. They were these. Little Ivy, dressed in her best and feeling a wee bit shy, bless her, but innocently trusting to be met as arranged by Isabel at the back door, had come tripping across the fields at the appointed time. But at the turn of the lane, who should be lurking in wait, pressed up against a small wooden side door in our garden wall – who but Chrissie? And then what happened? Chrissie Wyatt had had the downright demon wickedness to declare to Ivy she wasn't wanted inside, that she, Chrissie, had been specially posted there by us to tell her so; that it was horrible, awful in there anyway, a kind of torture chamber: nobody was allowed to talk, *not even to smile* at the tea-table; and Ivy had best run along home quick before anybody appeared to beckon her within. So what was left for Ivy but to hurry back home to her Mummy, frightened out of her little wits, sobbing her little heart out?

'Wait till I catch her!' muttered Isabel. 'I'll give her not even smile at tea. When I think! ... Cuddling up to me so loving and .. The spitefulness! It only shows ... And I hope it'll be a lesson. If I hadn't got your word for it, Doll, I'd never have credited it, never. Who'd ever fancy a 'uman child could have the artfulness, the wicked artfulness – a scrap of a thing like her. The downright impudence! Makes you think she can't be right in her head . . .'

'The devil's in her, if you ask me,' said Mrs Tulloch; adding sweetly: 'You said they came to tea last week, did you, dear?'

'It wasn't my doing,' said Isabel. 'They got round their father, as per usual.'

'Ah well! We all know a certain gentleman's kind heart. But as I always say, it's all very well. Right's right, when all's said and done.'

'Ah, and it's easy to be soft when it's others have the trouble. That's where it is.'

'And some will always take advantage, that's one thing certain.'

Together they went on intoning judgment and sentence on Chrissie.

'Makes you wonder where she'll finish up.'

'Mark my words, if she goes on like this, she'll come to a bad end.'

'It's the bringing-up – you can't wonder really.'

'Bringing-up it may be, but I always say when a nature's bad, bad it is. You can't alter it. Be your station high or low. Many's the time I've passed the remark to Tulloch.'

Meanwhile we were dumb, aghast. Had we been told that Chrissie had laid a charge of dynamite at our gate and blown up Ivy, the shock could not have been greater. We had to agree, it only showed, we must let it be a lesson. Yet we could not regret the catastrophe to Ivy, or feel drawn towards the injured parent, in whose strokes at the Wyatts we apprehended a back-hander at ourselves; and whom in any case we were debarred from liking owing to her squint and her manner – genteel, patronising, obsequious.

'Now take my advice, dear, and put your foot down another time. If you'll excuse me mentioning it, right's right, and it's best to start as you mean to go on. I dare say it's not my place, but they hadn't ever ought to have set foot, dear, and you know it – though far be it from me to blame you. Still – they're not exactly a clean lot, are they? You wouldn't want yours to pick up anything, would you? – not with their mother away.'

With that she rose and adjusted her hat and said she mustn't stop. She'd only popped along because she knew we'd be worried.

'I left the poor mite sitting on her Daddy's knee, but she'll be fretting for me if I don't get back. Oh, Tulloch, he was upset! You know what men are – he thinks the world of her, it's only natural. I don't know what he didn't want to do. But I said, now we don't want to make trouble, not when it's children. And don't go worrying her Ladyship with it, I said. Her Ladyship takes ever such an interest in Ivy, you know, always has done since she was a mite in a pram. I said, you'll only upset her – there's no need to go worrying her.'

'Well, I'm sure I hope,' said Isabel, with a stony glance at us, 'you'll find it in you to let her come another day instead. I'm sure the girls are as upset as me to think it should have occurred.'

'Thanks, dear,' said Mrs Tulloch, with a sort of repudiating graciousness. 'Perhaps later on when she's over the shock. She's such a sensitive wee soul – you never know what a shock like that will do to a sensitive child. Bless her, she'd got herself quite worked up. "Oo, Mummy," she said to me when I was changing her, "will they have rosebuds on their frocks like me?" The things children think of! "Shall I take my new dolly?" she said. "Will they have some big dollies there – bigger than mine?"' She uttered a tender deprecating laugh, and cast a glance round our doll-less nursery. 'Well, ta ta, dear. Now don't brood about it, I do beg.'

'I've a good mind,' said Isabel, 'to go down this very minute and speak my mind to her mother.'

'Now, dear, take my advice and don't do no such thing. You never know what sort of answer you'll get from that sort of person. She might turn reely rude, and then you'd regret you ever gave her the opening.'

'You may be right,' said Isabel. 'Still –'

Still – later on that evening, after we were in bed, Isabel stood by our bedroom window, fingering the curtain, looking out over the garden, arrested in an unfamiliar pose, a quietness that suggested brooding, almost dejection. From this window, the chimney of the Wyatts' cottage was just visible between the poplars. Flat on our pillows, we watched her. Suddenly we heard her say quietly: 'It was jealousy.' She was speaking to herself. Then: 'Poor little beggar.' She heaved a deep sigh, shook her head. 'Ah, well, what you can't cure, you'd best let alone.'

She bade us good-night with customary briskness, and went away.

Next morning, I wanted to go to the creek to hunt for some particular water plant for my collection of pressed wild flowers. Short of making a long and dreary detour through the village, it meant passing the Wyatts' cottage; and the idea of running into a group of them was painfully embarrassing. But Sylvia lent me moral courage, and, declaring that since we obviously could not avoid the lane for the rest of our lives it was best to bare our bosoms at once for the encounter, offered to accompany me. We went together down the lane, and the way was clear. The cottage looked deserted. But when we came back about lunch time they were all there, every one of them, in a huddle by their gate. The next to youngest sat in his soap box, the baby lolled its head on Maudie's shoulder. There was no movement among them except the slight turn of their heads as they watched us approach.

'Hallo,' we said sheepishly, not looking at any particular one of them.

''Allow.'

As we passed, Horace croaked suddenly:

'Our mum's gorn to the 'ospital. She's bad. The amb'lance come for her.'

'Last night,' said Norman, 'our dad 'ad to go for the doctor. Then the amb'lance come.'

''Er 'ead was bad,' said Alfie.

One of the younger ones piped:

'Make it better at the 'ospital. Then she come back.'

'Our dad's gone on 'is bike to see 'er,' said Horace.

We said we hoped she would be better soon. We could feel the after-quivers of catastrophe reverberating through the group, but we could not think of anything else to say.

Maudie had not spoken a word. Awkward, wishing to make a friendly gesture, I approached her. I had a weakness for holding babies, and though I could not feel drawn to this one, still it was a baby; and I asked her timidly if she thought it would come to me.

''E's all right,' she said indifferently, scarcely glancing at me. Impossible to believe that this was the same Maudie whose stoat-like concentration had so weighed upon me. Then I heard her mutter, in the voice of a sleep-walker:

'We got enough babies, anyway.'

Then, as if accosting a stranger to ask the way, she looked at me with a faint contraction between the eyes and said ungraciously:

'Where is the 'ospital, then?'

I did not know.

'It's a good way off,' she said. 'That I do know.'

She shifted the baby a bit and relapsed into indifference. Chrissie was hiding behind her, and involuntarily I caught a glimpse of her face. It was pinched, sallow, drab, and she was almost indistinguishable from the others.

We hurried home to tell Isabel, and found that news of the calamity had already reached her. She shut us up when we attempted to question her, but asked us rather sharply if they'd said whether they'd had their dinners. We had not thought of this. For us, meals were things that appeared automatically on the table at punctual intervals, were eaten, removed again. She appeared absent all through lunch, bit her finger, and after she had cleared away, came to us and said:

'Now be good girls and sit down with your books a bit, like your mother wished you to do. I'm just going to pop down and see if those young Wyatts are all right.'

Feeling a warm rush of affection for Isabel, we obeyed her. She came back not long after, still laconic, and merely said they were all right, various neighbours had taken them in and given them their dinners. They were playing now in the lane, along with some others, and seemed quite bright.

The kitchen maid ran upstairs with a belated post-prandial cup of tea for her, and they retired together to the nursery pantry while she drank it. Terrific whispers came forth, and my ears, ever agog, caught such words as 'raving' and 'water on the brain' as I lingered past them on my way to the bathroom.

I told my father that evening when he got back from London, where he went four days a week to edit a literary journal; and immediately he took his hat and walking stick and went down the garden to see Mr Wyatt. He was away some time, and when he came back, his face looked sorry. He told us that poor Mr Wyatt was very worried. Mrs Wyatt was dreadfully ill. After all his long bicycle ride, they had not allowed him to see her: she was too ill. She had had a baby, and the baby had died. I knew, and did not know, and could not ask about the unmentionable connection between this and her mortal sickness.

Then he rang the bell and told Mossop to telephone to the hospital first thing in the morning, and inquire for Mrs Wyatt, and get the message sent down to Mr Wyatt. Then he went over to the garage and told Gresham, our chauffeur, to hold himself ready to drive Mr Wyatt to the hospital at any moment of the day or night.

We felt comforted and elated. Our father had the situation in hand, and everything would probably be all right.

It was the next night after supper. Sylvia had gone to bed, and I had been allowed an extra half-hour for *David Copperfield*. My father and I sat reading in the library. It must have been nearly nine o'clock. There had been a heavy thunderstorm earlier in the evening, and the sky, instead of clearing in the west with sunset, had remained dun, murky, overcast; and we had drawn the curtains to shut out the lugubrious dusk. All of a sudden came a sound of running on the gravel path outside. Then a frantic drumming on the French windows. My father went white as paper, as he always did at any sudden shock. Again. Again. Paralysed with terror, I watched him walk across the room, draw back the curtains, press down the handle. The doors fell back and there on the step stood Mr Wyatt, hatless, haggard, wild.

'Wyatt, my dear chap, come in, come in,' said my father, all haste and gentleness, taking his arm and drawing him across the threshold. They stood together in the bay of the window, silent, their heads bowed down; one so tall, dignified, white-haired, the other so small, brown and gnarled, his poor coat hanging off him, his hair plastered in dark dishevelled strips over his bald head. He drew great labouring breaths as if he had been running for miles, and I saw that his clothes were soaked with rain and sweat. His throat and lips kept moving and contracting, but no sound came. My father stole an arm around his shoulders. At that he cried out suddenly in a terrible threatening voice, like an Old Testament prophet:

'She's gone, sir!'

My father nodded. I heard him murmur: 'Rebecca, run along,' but I was too petrified to make a quick move, and next moment the storm was loosed. Mr Wyatt began to walk up and down, up and down. The appalling dry sobs torn out of his chest seemed to fling him about the room. He passed my chair with glaring eyes fastened upon me, and took no notice of me. An overpowering smell emanated from him – his clothes, his body, his agony – and his terrible voice went on racking him, bursting and crying out.

'She's gone, sir! They never let me see 'er – not once since they took 'er away. Not till the end. Better not, they said, she won't know you, Mr Wyatt – she was raving, that was it. They sent word down at dinner-time – come at once. Thanks to your kindness, sir, I got there quick. 'E was good, your shuvver – 'e give me a packet of fags and 'e never stopped for nothink. She's going, they said . . . It's all for the best, Mr Wyatt . . . It was 'er brain went – brain fever or that – some word or other – I never did understand sickness. Why should a thing like that fly all over 'er like, in a couple o' days? She was always strong and 'ealthy, wasn't she? She never complained – only to say she was fagged like these last few months – and a bit of a backache. I thought that 'ud right itself when 'er time come. I thought – I never thought . . . She never . . . She 'ad the best of attention, didn't she, sir? Do you think they give 'er proper attention there?'

'My poor Wyatt, I feel convinced they did,' said my father.

'I never saw no doctor. They don't always trouble so much about poor people and that's a fact, sir. She's going, Mr Wyatt, the nurse said . . . She was a pleasant spoken woman. She won't know you, she said. They'd got 'er in a room separate . . . She died private anyway – not in a ward along of . . . She didn't fancy the thoughts of that . . . She never wanted to go to the 'ospital. "Don't let them take me, Jim," she says that night – just before she come on so queer, "I'll never come out alive." "Don't talk so foolish, girl," I says. 'You'll be back along of us all next week." What could I do, sir? I 'ad to let 'er go, didn't I? I 'ad to abide by what the doctor said?'

'Of course, of course. It was the only thing to do, Wyatt. It was a hundred to one chance, you know. We knew that.'

'A 'undred to one chance – Ah! . . . She was peaceful when they took me in. She died peaceful anyway. She 'ad 'er 'ands laid out on the sheet – 'er eyes shut . . . "Now, my girl," I says . . . Oh, but 'adn't she fallen away in the short time! It would 'ave 'urt you to see 'er. It 'urt me crool. "Now my girl," I says. "We want you back 'ome, don't we? The little 'uns is fretting for you." I thought that might rouse 'er. . . . She never stirred nor took no notice. . . . I sits there beside 'er, on and on. Then I leans over to 'ave another look at 'er. All on a sudden 'er eyes flies open as wide as . . . She stares right up at me . . . She knew me at the last, that I do know. That nurse comes in again then . . . "She's gone," she says. "Poor dear," . . . and covers 'er face over . . . Sir, do you know what they says to me? She didn't never ought to 'ave 'ad another, they says. It was 'er time of life. She was too wore out, they says. She'd 'ad too many. I . . .' He struck his forehead with his clenched fist. 'God knows we 'ad enough mouths to feed.' His voice broke, trailed off; hopelessly he shook his head. Then he cried out: 'I loved my wife, sir! They can say what they like – nobody can say different. We was happy . . . A happy family . . . She thought the world of them – the 'ole blessed lot. "I wouldn't be without one o' them," she'd say. . . .'

He fell silent, but went on walking up and down. My father took the opportunity to come over to me and whisper that I was to go to bed – he would come presently and see me. He gave me a kiss. Doubtful whether or not it would be correct to say goodnight to Mr Wyatt, I hazarded it finally in a tiny voice scarcely expecting any response. But he answered with dignity:

'Goodnight, missy, God bless you. I must ask your pardon, sir for coming like this upsetting you and little missy here. I 'ad ought to 'ave thought. I thank you for all your kindness. You've been a friend, sir. Yes, a friend. I must get along 'ome to the young 'uns. Got to think of them now, haven't I? Got to break it to them. Maudie, she's a good girl, but . . .' He shook his head with the same hopeless perplexity, and adding: 'Goodnight, sir, God bless you,' made for the window.

'Wyatt, my poor fellow, don't dream of going like that,' said my father tenderly. 'Sit down and rest yourself and take a drop of brandy with me. You're thoroughly exhausted. Here.'

He pulled forward an armchair and Mr Wyatt sank immediately into it without another word, his elbows on his knees and his head in his hands. The decanters were on the table and my father was pouring out brandy in liberal measure as I slipped out of the room.

I told Isabel what had happened, and she was kind to me and brought me hot milk to stop my shivering after she had helped me to bed. Great tears dripped down her face, and she blew her nose loudly and muttered if only there was something she could do.

A little later I heard voices in the garden and crept to my window to look out. The moon was up now, softly breaking the clouds, and I saw Mr Wyatt and my father walking together across the misty lawn towards the lower gate. Their voices rose and fell. Mr Wyatt was quiet now. The prophetic howl had gone out of his throat, and his guttural voice, his voice that seemed almost choked with soil, twined with thick roots, with tubers, sounded much as usual; and my father's voice, which was both light and rich, answered him musically.

Still later on, he came up and sat on my bed and told me how very sorry he was I had had to witness so painful a scene. He explained and comforted as best he could, and made me feel better. I could bear to accept the fact that that was how human beings behaved in the first anguish and indignation of bereavement. What I could not bear, then, was to see him wipe away the tears that kept rolling down his face.

I lay awake and imagined all the children huddled crying and wailing in the cottage. I saw Maudie's face; I tried to imagine Chrissie's; and I saw Mrs Wyatt stretched dead, her hands folded, in the hospital bed, taking absolutely no notice of them all. I thought the two stains of colour must still lie in her snow cheeks, like roses in December.

After that, the sinister pattern broke. We went away to join our infant brother and nurse at the seaside; and plunged in the happy trance of waves, rocks, sand, we let slip the Wyatts from our minds. My father joined us for a week, brought us all home, and then went to Liverpool to meet my mother and Jess.

We painted WELCOME HOME in white letters on a strip of scarlet bunting, and were busy attaching it to the gateposts of the drive, when we saw Horace, Norman, Alfie and the soap-box one standing under the wall, watching us.

'Hallo,' we said.

''Allow.'

We looked at them furtively and they seemed much as usual except that the three younger ones had new suits on. They watched us with their usual mixed look, incurious yet attentive, as we sat each astride a brick post and lashed rope round the stone ball on the top to hold our banner in position. I felt suddenly that we were doing something silly; and directly I had said: 'Our mother's coming back from America this evening,' I blushed deeply, realising the tactlessness of mentioning the return of a mother.

'It's nice,' stated Norman, in a flat way.

We called directions to each other, and they went on watching, and by and by we got down and surveyed our work. It was a bit crooked but it flared out with loud brilliance upon the shining blue September air. In another hour our parents and Jess would drive in under it. We could not help wondering if Jess would wholeheartedly approve of such a blatant display of feeling.

Horace said:

'They're going away tomorrow – the three of 'em.'

'Where are they going?'

'To the Institution.'

Silence. We did not know what he meant.

'Our dad said for us all to stay together and we'd manage, but that lady said it was all too much for Maudie, she hadn't ought to do it. She come and see 'er. She said Maudie couldn't give 'em what they needed, so she spoke to our dad.'

'Our dad cried,' said Alfie.

'So she said they'd be better off in the Institution. She wanted for the baby to go too, but Maudie wouldn't let 'im go.'

'Maudie cried,' said Alfie.

'The lady said it was ever so nice there. They was ever so kind to children. They 'ave a Christmas tree and all. So our dad said to 'em to be good boys and learn their lessons and 'e'd 'ave 'em out soon. 'E's going to get a better job and then we'll 'ave a reel 'ousekeeper and it won't come so 'ard on Maudie. 'E bought 'em new suits.'

'And we got sixpence each to buy sweets,' said Norman.

'And a horange,' said Alfie.

'What about Chrissie?' I said.

'Chrissie's going to stop at 'ome. She went and 'id 'erself when the lady come. One of our aunties wrote a letter. She said she'd take Chrissie and bring 'er up just like 'er own. But Chrissie created so our dad said for 'er to stop at 'ome.'

'So there'll only be the four of us at 'ome now,' said Norman.

'Maudie and 'Orace and Chrissie and baby,' said Alfie.

Their voices were important, not pathetic. The family had obviously been the object lately of many a local charitable scheme, both private and official: and this had set them all up in their own estimation. I felt vaguely that a number of well-disposed people were interested, many benefits were being conferred, and everything was turning out as well as could be expected.

It was time to go and tie a festal bow on to Jannie's collar, so we said good-bye, and went away.

But when I asked Isabel what the Institution was and she replied the workhouse, I knew enough about society to know that disgrace had come upon the Wyatts; and though I was sorry and disturbed, I felt once again what a very low family they were, and how they and their house and their misfortunes emanated a kind of miasma which the neighbourhood could neither purify nor disregard: as if a nest of vermin had got lodged under the boards, rampant, strong-smelling, not to be obliterated.

Now and then I saw Chrissie passing to and from school or playing in the lane among a group of contemporaries. She looked as usual, in her plaid frock. She never smiled, or took any notice of me. Mr Wyatt continued to be seen about the sheep folds, smoking his pipe. My mother went to see him, and they went again and took Maudie some clothes. Maudie told her she was managing nicely. Dad helped her in the evenings when he got home from work. Sometimes he undressed the baby all himself and gave him a wash and put him to bed: he'd never taken so much notice of any of them as he did of this baby. Yes, the baby had a cold on his chest, but she'd rubbed him, and he was ever so bright and eating well.

There was a neighbour, Mrs Smith the washerwoman, who was kind. Once I ran down with a message from Nurse to ask her to wash the nursery sofa cover in a hurry and Maudie was there, sitting slumped in a kitchen chair, drinking a cup of tea, silent, grimy, greasy, her hair screwed and scraped up into a bun with huge hairpins. She had put it up, I suppose, to mark the fact that she was now a woman: one of a thousand thousand anonymous ones who bear their sex, not as the unconscious, fluid, fructifying centre, as women who are loved bear it and are upborne by it; but as it were extraneously, like a deformity, a hump on their backs, weighing them down, down, towards the sterile stones of the earth.

In October, the gipsies came back. They came twice a year, in spring and autumn, streaming through the village in ragged

procession, with two yellow and red caravans; men in cloth caps
with handkerchiefs knotted round their throats, women in black
with cross-over shawls and voluminous skirts, some scarecrow
children, and several thin-ribbed dogs of the whippet race running on leads tied, much to Jess's disquiet, under the shafts of the
caravans.

They were a raffish, mongrel lot, with bitter, cunning, wizened
faces and no glint of the flash and dash that one is conditioned to
expect. But there was one noble beauty, a middle-aged woman,
short, ample of figure, with gold earrings and a plumed black hat,
who came regularly to the back door with a basket of clothes pegs
to sell. The eyes in her darkly rich, broad face glowed with a veiled
and mystic fire, and her voice came out of her throat with an
indescribable croon on one low note. Isabel always went flying
down to buy some pegs – it brought bad luck to turn the gipsies
from the door – and once I went with her to watch the transaction. Superstition made Isabel excessively polite, not to say
conciliatory, quite unlike her usual style of bridling badinage and
repartee with the tradespeople.

I smiled at the woman, and at once her face seemed both to
melt and to sharpen, and she caught my hand in hers and began to
mutter. I felt the hardness and dryness of her strong hand. My
eyes sought hers and were immediately lost in the fathomless gaze
she bent upon me. I could not look away, and my panicking senses
began to swoon beneath the torrent of unintelligible words
poured over me. Something in my face, she said – my fate, my
future, a long, long journey . . . something I could not bear to
hear. Then suddenly it stopped; and she asked in quite a different
whining voice if there were any old clothes today – any shoes – a
pair or two of the little lady's cast-off shoes now for the children
– a coat, now – an old jacket for her man. I heard her drilling away
at the resisting Isabel as I made off upstairs, my heart still
thumping loud with terror. After that I was convinced that
the gipsies designed to steal me, and ventured to tell Isabel so; and
though Isabel told me not to be so soft, all old gipsy women went
on like that, I would never, after this incident, go through the

gravel pit field where they always camped so long as the caravans were there.

The gravel pit itself was a romantic spot, overgrown with grasses, clover, brambles, wild rose bushes and bryony. In spring it harboured the most exciting birds' nests – once I found a gold-finch's – but in autumn it was particularly enchanting, when one could rove from one slope to another picking blackberries, hips, and branches of the dogwood that flushed the air so rosily on grey days and blue. Also there were fossilised sea-urchins, petrified fragments of shells lurking among the stones and sand of the old quarry-workings. I spent hours of my childhood there, wandering in a voluptuous, collector's daydream, or lying hidden in one of the many secretive hollows.

It was October. From the nursery window I looked out over the familiar view of shrubbery, lawn and apple orchard, and saw between the thinning boughs of the poplars that bordered it a glimpse, a mile or so away, up the hill, of two red and yellow cara-vans nestling in a corner of the gravel pit field. The beech woods rose up directly behind them, clasping them as in the curve of a tender shoulder. I saw blue smoke rising, figures sitting on the steps, children tumbling in the grass. I could also see a group of local children hanging over a gate, watching them, a little distance away: the scarlet frock of Chrissie was among the group. I remem-ber thinking then what a fascination the bright roving caravans must have for her; how congruous a part she would seem of the life of fairs and gipsies. I felt faintly anxious and depressed, won-dering if the woman had yet been to the back door, hoping that next day the corner of the field would be empty of its load of alien humanity. All the reasons I had for melancholy came down to weigh upon me: Jess, who had not been very well, absent for the winter, gone to share bracing air, riding and education with some cousins near Brighton; our unpopular governess back from Belgium in a day or so, and myself left to bear the brunt of her without Jess. Then I remembered Mrs Wyatt whom I sought to forget, and how she also had seized my hand; and felt I was singled out in a disquieting if gratifying way by this coincidence:

wild forces both, and I, so passive, their inexplicable point of explosion.

What happened next is hard to put down in any exact way, because so much was concealed from us, we had so much to conceal, that sometimes I think I dreamed it all. Suddenly one day out broke the melodrama; but at once we were hurried away from it, and its development reached us only as it were in snatches, in disjointed echoes from the wings or by the furtive peeps we contrived through the lowered curtain. Horror toppled above the village for a short while, then sank back and vanished; and everybody drew a great breath and burst out in chattering, exclaiming, head-shaking; and all the children who had been snapped indoors after school by wrought-up parents were let out to play again; and everything was as before, except for the usual scatter of flotsam left by the retreating tide; and except for one small figure carried away on it, vivid but dwindling.

The gipsies went away. Two or three days later, a peculiar vibration began in the village. It was confined at first to the children. In the afternoon, we were messing about in the laurels by the garden gate, when two of Sylvia's associates, sisters called Cissie and May Perkins, came past and beckoned portentously to us. They said:

'Can you keep a secret?'

We said yes. They said:

'There's a little dead biby in the gravel pit. We ain't allowed to tell 'ow we know, but we do know. Cross your hearts and swear by the Bible you won't tell no one.'

We did so. They said:

'We know because Chrissie told us. She found it. It's under some bramble-bushes. It's got no clothes on. It's a biby boy. She says the gipsies left it there.'

'Do you mean they killed it?' we said.

'Dunno.'

We were silent, beholding the monstrous image of a dead naked baby boy under the bramble bushes. We said:

'Oughtn't somebody to be told?'

'She says on our solemn oath we're not to. We're not to tell our mums nor no one. She says after three days the gipsies may come back and take it away. She's going up tomorrow to see.'

'Why does she think they'll come back for it?'

'Dunno. She says that's what they do. She says if the gipsies knew she'd found it they'd do something downright awful to her.'

'What would they do?'

'Murder 'er and bury 'er.' They added: 'Be down by the gate tomorrer afternoon when we come out of school. We'll tell you if it's still there.'

Next day at the appointed hour they said:

'She's been up to look, and it's still there.'

We were to wait another day, and cross our hearts we'd tell no one.

But that evening some overwrought child broke down and unloaded the news to its parents. All the village began to hum. We were made aware of this by the gathering and whispering of Nurse, Isabel and the others in the servants' hall; and by the fact that our mother called us to her and said with some severity:

'Now girls, I want you to promise – especially you, Sylvia – not to talk to any children in the lane just at present. If they see you in the garden and call out to you just wave politely and go away. There may be a case of measles in the village and I don't want you to run any risk of contact. I don't say it *is* measles, we must wait a few days to make sure. But you needn't give any reason. Do you understand? Promise now.'

We promised.

That night while Isabel was brushing my hair, she remarked to Nurse:

'Not mentioning any names, someone told me they're under suspicion, that lot, for the same line of thing before; only they never could fasten it on them like. Nice, isn't it?'

Nurse shook her head and uttered a series of sharp tongue clickings. She said:

'Ah, there's more in it than meets the eye.'

'Mark my words,' said Isabel. 'It's that man. You know the one

– the older one with the nasty expression of face. I always did think he looked the part.'

'If you ask *me*,' said Nurse, 'they're all in it. The shock for that little mite – I can't get her off my mind.' After a pause she said: 'Have they got back, did you hear by any chance?'

'Mm,' said Isabel.

Nurse queried with her eyebrows.

'No,' said Isabel. 'It's inky black out. Him and old Gutteridge had lanterns, but I don't think they fancied the job in the dark, if you ask *me*.' She giggled. 'I don't blame them neether.'

Nurse told her rather sharply to get on with our hairs, do, and not chatter so.

We understood that an expedition of householders had visited the pit with lanterns, and returned empty-handed.

Next day as I came back at noon from my hour of German with Miss La Touche (cultured spinster and traveller), I saw a sight that froze my blood. It was the local constable emerging from the school-yard, grasping Chrissie by the hand. Her face was down on her chest, her hair over it. With every step she struggled to fling herself back. The constable seemed to be attempting genial encouragement, but he was not built or endowed for soothing. He was the very type of rustic policeman – burly, beefy, flaxen, slow of wits and speech. He was plainly embarrassed by his task and wore a sheepish grin. There was not another child in sight: all kept in. Together, slowly but surely, they turned up the hill towards the gravel pit.

Later on, in the afternoon, another kind of hum began to develop. The silence that had hung over the lane gave place to the customary commotion. The sounds that came out of the servants' hall seemed to contain gasps of staggered somewhat ghoulish incredulity. There seemed also a note of disappointment or disgust – as if there had been a let-down after a promised sensation. I heard Nurse say to Isabel that's what came of letting your nasty imagination run away with you.

'Whose nasty imagination?' said Isabel, going red down her neck.

'Yours,' said Nurse simply. 'And a lot of other silly gossips I could mention. I never did believe it from the start.'

'Oh, didn't you indeed! I'm surprised,' said Isabel, with impertinent emphasis.

Nurse actually let this pass, and hurried on to say in a different, confidential tone: 'But talk of nasty imaginations! . . .' and they went murmuring and hissing down the passage together.

Shortly after, Nurse said in a crisp yet off-hand way: 'Look here, you two – especially you, Sylvia – if you happen to speak to any of those children that hang around by the gate and they go telling you any nasty nonsense they've picked up, don't you take any notice. They may have got hold of some silly story or other that's been going about. I'm sure I don't know what they *don't* pick up, those children – nobody cares, more's the pity, and if I had my way—' She broke off, then added: 'Well now, you've heard what I say. If they repeat it, you just tell them there's nothing in it and never was and say I said so.'

'All right,' we said.

My mother went out about tea-time. As soon as the car had driven away with her, we made our way to the bottom of the garden, where Cissie and May were awaiting us. They said:

'The biby wasn't there.'

'Had the gipsies taken it away?'

'No. There wasn't no biby. She mide it all up.'

'! ! !'

'The p'liceman come to school this morning. 'E said for Chrissie to come along with 'im to show 'im the plice. Teacher was ever so upset. Chrissie didn't want to go. She fought 'im. She bit 'is 'and. But 'e took 'er along. When they got up to the pit, she took 'im to a plice and she says there, that's where it was. Well, it's not there no more, 'e says. It's gorn, she says. So 'e said for 'er to come along at once to the p'lice station. So she begun to take on and said she didn't want to go. Then she said there 'adn't ever been no biby. She'd mide it all up. So 'e brought 'er back and 'e told teacher she was a bad wicked little liar, wasting 'is time. So teacher mide 'er stand up in front of the 'ole class and tell us she'd mide it up. Teacher asked 'er what she wanted to tell such 'orrible wicked lies for. She never said nothink. She was shivering and shaking all over. So teacher took 'er into 'er own room and put 'er to sit down in a big chair with a rug round 'er, and she said she'd speak to 'er later. She's still there. Teacher's going to keep 'er there till 'er dad comes from work, and they take 'er back 'ome. Our mum says she's a bad bad girl and we're not to 'ave anythink to do with 'er. She says she 'ad ought to be sent to a reformary.'

We never saw Chrissie again. The problems of her disgrace, her punishment, her future – all were kept from us; and even the know-alls of the lane were more or less in the dark about her destination when she vanished from the village.

We knew that our mother, ever combining prompt with humanitarian action, had taken charge of Chrissie's case. We did venture to ask Isabel whether it was true that Chrissie had been sent to a reformatory, but she said sharply, stuff and nonsense: Chrissie had gone right away to live with some kind people who loved her, and who would give her a mother's care and perhaps adopt her if she mended her ways and tried to be a good girl. She added: 'And if she grows up a decent ordinary being after all instead of a wild wicked demon, she'll have your mother's trouble and your father's generousness to thank for it.' So we knew that something impressive had been accomplished, and that our parents were paying for it.

This was before the days of child guidance clinics.

I remember only one or two more things about the Wyatts. Later on in October I plucked up courage to go past their cottage by myself: an act I had been unable to face since the death of Mrs Wyatt. The lane was strewn with the drenched, honey drifts of poplar and chestnut leaves, and their sweet and pungent smell of death made my heart turn over. High over the fences of the little gardens, sunflowers flopped their harsh tawny faces. I came to the Wyatts' cottage, and Maudie was there, standing by the gate. One of her hands was bandaged and in a dirty sling; with the other she supported the baby who sat astride her crooked hip.

'Hallo,' I said timidly.

''Allow,' she said, unsmiling.

'What a lot he's grown,' I said.

She looked down at him and said in her indifferent way: 'Yes. 'E's getting on all right. 'E goes all over the place now.'

'Isn't he heavy for you to carry?'

'I don't mind. 'E likes a ride.' Suddenly she put her cheek down against his and cried: 'Don't you, ducks?'

He peeped out at me with a coy grin; then hid his face in her shoulder. A faint smile went over her face, maternal, indulgently mocking. He was bald, rickety, exactly like his brothers, but the hiding gesture reminded me of Chrissie; and what with that, and Mrs Wyatt vanished for ever, and the desolate look of the cottage with Maudie standing alone there with the baby, and only two more to come home out of all the nine, I felt most terribly miserable and feared to disgrace myself by tears. I said:

'What have you done to your hand?'

'Got a poisoned thumb.'

'Does it hurt?'

'It throbs painful at nights. I 'ad it lanced but it goes on. The nurse comes to see to it. She says it got bad because it wasn't done up sooner. Still, I got to use it a bit – you can't do all your work with one 'and.'

I said I hoped it would soon be better, and then there was nothing more to say, and I said goodbye and went on. When I reached the corner I glanced over my shoulder, but she was not looking after me. Maudie had given up wanting anything I had got.

That winter they all went away. Mr Wyatt got another job, over the other side of the country. I don't know if it was a better job. He came to say goodbye to my parents. I was not present during this interview, but later on, looking over the stairs, saw my father showing him out of the front door.

'Goodbye, Wyatt, my dear chap,' said my father warmly. 'The best of luck to you and yours.'

Mr Wyatt went on wringing his hand, speechless, for a long time, then said brokenly: 'God bless you, sir,' and went away.

They left the cottage in such a state that it had to be fumigated and washed down with lysol from ground floor to attic. It stayed empty for a bit; then the landlord did a few repairs and put a coat of paint on, and another family came to live there. They planted vegetables and sowed a little plot of front lawn and cut out some little flower beds and made a little tile-bordered path to run exactly through the middle; and after a while it looked quite like the other cottages.

(Emily Richard read this story on *Woman's Hour* in November 1988.)

SOME DAY MY
PRINCE WILL COME

_____ ◆ _____

Deborah Moggach

I was woken up by Tilly prising open my mouth. They'd had the school dentist yesterday, that was why. She was smug because they had found nothing wrong with her.

'Wider,' she said. Small ruthless fingers pushed back my lips, baring my gums. I was lying in bed and she was sitting on top of me. 'There's these bits here . . . yellowy bits . . . round the edges of your teeth.' Her calm eyes gazed into my mouth. 'It's called plaque, ' she said. 'You should brush your teeth gooder.'

Beside me, Martin grunted. 'Seen the time?'

Tilly was now yanking down my lower jaw. 'Oooh, look at all your silver stuff.'

'Half past six,' said Martin, and went back to sleep.

'You've got lots of holes, didn't you,' she said.

Most of them, I thought, when I was pregnant with you. I lay, mute as a cow, under her gaze. She was only five and already she made me feel inferior. She would say things like: 'You shouldn't smoke.' I hadn't the heart to reply: I didn't till recently.

Tilly settled down to deeper inspection. I was going to say: go and look at Daddy's teeth. Then I thought: better not, he had a hard day yesterday, at the office. A long day ahead, too. It's Saturday, Working on the House Day. Every Saturday and every Sunday . . . weekends of the whirring Black & Decker, and fogs of dust, and muffled curses from the closed door behind which he toiled . . . of tripping over the plumbing pipes, and searching for one small sandal in the rubble, and keeping out of Daddy's way . . . So much of the time I spent protecting Martin from his children.

Tilly got bored and padded off in her nightie, sucking her thumb. From the back she suddenly looked terribly young. Outside I heard a thud: she had knocked down a roll of wallpaper.

'Hey!' Martin's head reared up. Where his tools were concerned his reaction was so sharp. I swear he could hear a chisel shifting in its box three rooms away. Funny how he could sleep through all the children's noises – the cries to be potted, the thud as *they* rolled over and fell out of bed.

However, this seemed a churlish waking thought, with a weekend ahead. I ticked myself off, running through the litany to make myself a more loving wife: Remember, Martin's slaving away just for us. Wasn't it me who wanted this house, such a lovely one right near the common, and we could never have afforded a done-up one in a street like this. And I bet he would rather spend the weekends playing football and watching the telly and drinking cans of lager . . . He would probably even prefer to spend them striding over the common with Tilly on his shoulders, like fathers did in Building Society advertisements. He had never done that. He said: there's so much to do.

Did your character change when you had children? Mine did. Trouble is, it's crept up on me so gradually and by now I simply can't remember what I was like before . . . What *we* were like. What did Martin and I do, those three years of long, child-free weekends in our flat? What does one do? Did we actually sit and talk, and read books unmolested, and wander off to the cinema on impulse, go anywhere on impulse, go to pubs . . . And dawdle in shops unembarrassed by clumsy infants and cold, shopgirl stares, and make love in the afternoons? That bit I do remember . . . I remember that.

Anyway, that Saturday I got up, and fed the children, and peeled off their Plasticine from Martin's hammer before he saw it . . . Really, compared to the rest of the week, weekends were such a strain . . . And pulled a nail out of Tilly's plimsoll. She made such a fuss that I tried to shut her up by telling her the story about

Androcles and the Lion, but I couldn't remember what had happened. Didn't Kirk Douglas play Androcles? By this time Tilly was wearing her schoolmistressy look. And Adam had just fallen down and was shrieking so loudly that Martin could hear him over the electric sander.

After lunch Martin went out. He had all these errands to do on Saturdays, like getting his hair cut and the car repaired, and things mended that I had forgotten to do during the week or that I had been too busy to fetch – he can't understand that I'm busy, when there's nothing to show for it. No floors re-laid, nothing like that. And he has to go to all those proper little shops with old men in overalls who take hours; he refuses to go to the big help-yourself places because he says they're soulless.

It's taking ages, our house. It's like one of those fairy stories where Mrs Hen won't give an egg until she's been given some straw, and Mr Horse won't give any straw until he's been given some sugar. You can't plumb in the bath until the skirting's fixed, and you can't fix the skirting until the dry rot's been done . . . I told this to Martin and he gazed at me and then he said: 'That reminds me. Forgot the Nitromors.'

It was two thirty and raining outside. Do you ever have those moments of dulled panic: what on earth can one possibly do with the children until bedtime? The afternoon stretched ahead; Adam was staggering around, scattering wood shavings. Then I looked in the local paper and saw that *Snow White* was on.

So I wrote a note to Martin and heaved out the double buggy and spent 23½ minutes searching for their gumboots and gloves . . . I actually went to college once, would you believe, and I can still add up . . . 12½ minutes to find my bag, and the teddy that Adam has to suck.

I pushed the children along the street – at least, Adam sat in the buggy (he's just three) and Tilly walked beside me because she only sits in the buggy when she's sure not to meet any of her friends.

'Does Snow White wear a beautiful pink dress?' she asked. 'With frillies?' She's obsessed with pink.

'Can't remember,' I said. 'I was your age when I saw it. I loved it more than any film I've ever seen.'

'Snow White gets deaded,' said Adam.

'She doesn't!' I cried. 'She's only asleep.'

'Deaded in a box. Seen the picture.'

'She isn't! She's just sleeping. And do you know how she wakes?'

'Got worms in her.'

'Shut up. She wakes when the Prince comes along,' I said.

'Why?'

'He kisses her.'

When did Martin last kiss me? Properly. Or when, indeed, did I last kiss him?

The Prince just touches her forehead, or is it her lips? Just a peck, really. Just like when Martin comes home from the office.

No, not like that at all.

'Mummy! I said what happens after that?' Tilly's addressing-the-retarded voice. 'Does she get a baby? Does she get married?'

'Oh yes, they marry all right. He takes her off to his castle in the sunset, on the back of his big white horse.'

We arrived at the cinema; a peeling brick cliff, its neon lights glaring over the grey street. How could such buildings house such impossible dreams?

Inside I saw him. I saw him straight away; the place was half-empty. But I would have spotted him, I bet, in a crowd of a thousand. He was flung back in his seat, in that abandoned way he had, with his hair sticking up like it always had. He had never taken care of himself. The lights were still up; if I'd dared I'd have looked longer.

I had sat next to him in fifty cinema seats . . . Him beside me, flung back in that restless, tense way, never settled . . . his arm lying along the back of the seat. But now his arms were flung each side of his children.

'Let's go here!' Tilly demanded.

I pulled her away.

'Mummy! We can see over the edge!'

'Come on. This way.'

'Don't be silly! There's all these seats.'

'Silly bum-bum,' said Adam.

I dragged the buggy further away.

'Wanna sit here,' cried Adam.

'Ssh!'

I sat them down at last, pulling off their anoraks and trying to shove the buggy under the seat. The cinema darkened.

'Gimme the popcorn!' said Adam.

I rummaged in my carrier-bag. While I did it, I stole another look. A red point glowed . . . She hadn't stopped him smoking, then.

'You said half!' Tilly hissed.

'Have a handful each.'

'S'not fair! He's –'

'Ssh! It's starting.'

Snow White was washing the steps, scrubbing and singing, the birds cheeping. I thought: forgot the Daz, and now I've missed the shops.

'When's the Prince coming?' hissed Tilly, her mouth full of popcorn.

'Hang on,' I replied. 'Don't be impatient.'

'Will he come on his horse?'

'Of course.'

He'd had a motorbike, an old Triumph. I'd sat behind him, gripping him with my arms, my face pressed against the leather. Ah, the ache, that his skin was hidden . . . The physical pain, that I couldn't get my hands on him. I wanted him all the time. Where did we go? Transport cafés at four in the morning. The glare of the light, the suddenness of all those strangers, after we had been alone for so long . . . He'd take off his gloves and hold my hand; I stroked his hard fingernails, one by one, and then the wider nail of his thumb.

Afterwards, driving oh too fast – he had a death wish all right – driving just for the heck of it . . . Then back to my digs, lying naked on the twisted sheets, the sun glowing through the curtains and the children down in the street whooping on their way to school – they seemed a hundred miles away . . . And me missing my lectures.

I wish you had met him. You'd probably think he was wildly unsuitable, far too neurotic. My parents did. They were terrified that I would marry him. And I didn't, did I?

I wonder if you'd have thought him beautiful. I wondered if he still was. It was too dark to see. All I'd heard was that he had married a social worker and had two children. She was called Joyce. I'd pictured somebody with a political conscience and thick ankles, who would care for him and see that he ate. Well, that's how I liked to picture her. Today she must be staying home, making flans for the freezer. Did he write her poetry, like he had written for me? Did anybody, once they got married? Joyce . . . With a name like that, she must be overweight.

'*Mirror mirror on the wall, who's the fairest one of all?*'

The Dark Queen was up on the screen, with her bitter, beautiful face. The light flared on her.

A hand gripped mine. 'She's horrid!' said Tilly.

'She's jealous,' I whispered.

'I hate her.'

'Ssh.'

Where did he live? It must be around here. On the other hand, on a wet Saturday afternoon he might have crossed London to see *Snow White*.

I would follow him home. I'd find out where he lived and press my nose against the window and gaze into his life, his lamplit family life all unknown to me, where I was not needed . . .

'Ugh!' The hand squeezed. 'She's turning into a witch!'

'Look at her horrid nose!'

'Isn't she ugly.'

'I don't like her!'

Tilly said in her posh voice: 'It's because she's got ugly thoughts.'

She took away her hand and sat there primly. She was wearing her kilt that she'd chosen herself, and her awful orange plastic necklace, and her I'VE SEEN WINDSOR SAFARI PARK badge.

Snow White was in the forest now; it was blacker than Windsor Park and the trees were swaying and moaning, warning her of danger. I thought that Tilly would be frightened here but she didn't show it. I had a sudden desire to grip my growing, wayward girl, so cool and so young. I wanted to grip her and protect her from what lay ahead. But she disliked shows of emotion.

Snow White had arrived at the dwarfs' cottage and, little housewife that she was, she was clearing up, dusting, polishing, a song on her lips (well, she had about twenty squirrels and rabbits to help). I looked round. He was getting up.

I felt panic. But he was only carrying out one of his children, down the aisle. They must be going to the lavatory. He passed quite close, gripping the child. He was wearing a pale pullover and he held the child so tenderly. Ten years later and he looked just the same, no fatter. I thought how easily that child could have been ours. It could have been us sitting there, and no Tilly. No Adam. Or a different Tilly . . .

'Mummy, you're hurting!'

I had been squeezing her hand, so I took mine away. But then she groped for it – both of them did – because the witch was knocking on the door of the cottage.

I feared for his remaining child, left alone. But I stopped myself. It wasn't my child to worry about. Besides, there he was, his hair haloed by the screen, bowed so he wouldn't block the view of this terrifying, powerful film.

Snow White let in the witch. As she took the apple, the audience sat absolutely still. All those children – not a sweet-paper rustled. Nothing.

When she bit the apple, Tilly hid her face. My cool, superior Tilly. I pressed my hand against her eyes.

'It's all right,' I whispered.

'I want to go.'

'It's all right,' I said desperately. 'I told you – the Prince will come.'

He came, of course, as you knew he would. He rode upon his muscular white horse. Tilly took away her hand; she sat there, calm as ever. She knew it would turn out all right.

The Prince knelt down to kiss Snow White. And then she was in his arms and he was lifting her on to the back of his horse. Not a motorbike – a stallion with a thick curved neck, and the sun cast long shadows between the trees as they rode off, and ahead lay the castle, radiant.

Businesslike, Tilly was rummaging in the bottom of the popcorn bag. I sat limp; I felt her busy concentration. She knew the Prince would come, she believed it. Every girl must believe it, because wouldn't life be insupportable if they didn't?

'Come on.' She was standing up.

Every girl . . . Every boy too. All those young, believing children.

'Where's your hanky?' I muttered.

She had this hideous little diamanté handbag that Aunt Nelly had given her; she carried it everywhere. I took the hanky and blew my nose. The lights came on.

'Don't be soppy,' she said. 'It's only a story.'

I saw him ahead of us in the foyer. He had sunk down in front of his child and was zipping up its anorak. He was speaking but I couldn't hear the words.

Outside it was dark, and still raining: a soft November drizzle. I saw him quite clearly standing at the bus stop on the other side of the road. His children looked younger than mine.

I wanted to follow him. I couldn't face meeting him but I wanted to see where he lived. I wanted to set him into a house and give him a locality. I would be able to dream about him better then. All these years he had just been the same set of memories, stale and repeated; his present life was a vacuum. I hungered even for the name of his street.

'I'm wet!'

'Wanna Slush Puppy!'

'I want to go home.'

I wonder if you would have followed him.

I didn't. It was cold out there, and dark, and fumey as people revved up their cars. The warmth of the cinema, the dreams, they had vanished like that castle into the raw air of this South London road. Really, what was the good? Besides, the person I was seeking belonged to somebody who no longer existed.

They both sat in the buggy, they were so sleepy. I gazed down at their two anorak hoods, lolling, brown in the sodium light. Some day, I thought, will your Prince come? If you get lost in the dark wood, as you will, and I can't always be there to protect you . . . If you get lost, will somebody find you? Will you be happy?

Twenty minutes later I was walking up our street. The cardboard eye of our bedroom looked at me blankly. It said: *shouldn't have gone, should you?*

Our car was outside and the house lights were on. Martin must be home. The rain had stopped but I wiped my face on my sleeve. Besides, he would just think my face was wet from the rain. If, that is, he ever noticed anything about me.

I went into the house, with its naked lightbulb hanging down. The light shone on a lot of planks, propped against the wall; they made a forest of the hallway. He had been to the timber merchant.

Adam stirred and started to whine. Tilly climbed out of the pushchair and they went into the living-room. A burst of canned laughter; they had switched on the TV.

Martin didn't come out of the kitchen. No buzzing drill. I hesitated. Could he feel my thoughts? In the sitting-room the advertisements came on; I heard the jingle for the Midland Bank. The children call it the Middling Bank.

Then I thought: he's made me a surprise.

I stood still, the realisation filling me, through my limbs, like warm liquid.

You know how, just when the children are driving you insane, when you can't stand another minute . . . You know how, suddenly, they do something terribly touching? Like drawing you a card with I LOVE MUM on it or trying, disastrously, to do the

WOMAN'S HOUR BOOK OF SHORT STORIES

washing up?

Martin had made the supper. Hopelessly, because he couldn't cook. But he had cleared the table, and bought a bottle of wine and lots of pricey things from the deli. He had realised how I'd been feeling lately.

I opened the door. But this wasn't a story. Life is not that neat, is,it? No fairy tale.

There sat Martin, with a can of beer in front of him and the lunch plates still piled in the sink. Packets were heaped on the table: not exotic cheeses but three-point plugs and boxes of nails.

'Hello.' He looked up. 'Didn't hear you come in.'

'Exhausted?'

He nodded. Fiction is shapely. A story billows out like a sheet, then comes the final knot. *The End*. Reared up against the suffused, pink sky there stands a castle, lit from within. The end.

A silence as he poured the lager into his glass. The froth filled up; we both watched it. He said: 'The end is in sight. I think I can finally say I've finished this bloody kitchen.'

(Caroline John read this story on *Woman's Hour* in March 1988.)

A VIEW OF EXMOOR

◆

Sylvia Townsend Warner

From Bath, where Mr Finch was taking the waters, the Finches travelled by car into Devonshire to attend the wedding of Mrs Finch's niece, Arminella Blount. They made a very creditable family contribution – Mrs Finch in green moiré, Cordelia and Clara in their bridesmaids' dresses copied from the Gainsborough portrait of an earlier Arminella Blount in the Character of Flora, Mr Finch in, as his wife said, his black-and-grey. Arden Finch in an Eton suit would have looked like any other twelve-year-old boy in an Eton suit if measles had not left him preternaturally thin, pale, and owl-eyed.

All these fine feathers, plus two top hats, an Indian shawl to wrap around Arden in case it turned cold, and a picnic basket in case anyone felt hungry, made the car seem unusually full during the drive to Devonshire. On the return journey it was even fuller, because the Finches were bringing back Arminella's piping bull-finch and the music box that was needed to continue its education, as well as the bridesmaids' bouquets. It was borne in on Mr Finch that other travellers along the main road were noticing his car and its contents more than they needed to, and this impression was confirmed when the passengers in two successive charabancs cheered and waved. Mr Finch, the soul of consideration, turned into a side road to spare his wife and daughters the embarrassment of these public acclamations.

'"Pember and South Pigworthy",' Mrs Finch read aloud from a

signpost. 'The doctor who took out my tonsils was called Pember It's so nice to find a name one knows.'

Mr Finch replied that he was taking an alternative way home After a while, he stopped and looked for his road map, bu couldn't find it. He drove on.

'Father,' said Cordelia a little later, 'we've been through thi village before. Don't you think we had better ask?'

'Is *that* all it is?' said Mrs Finch. 'What a relief. I thought I wa having one of those mysterious delusions when one half of m brain mislays the other half.'

Mr Finch continued to drive on. Arden, who had discovered that the bars of the bird cage gave out notes of varying pitch wher he plucked them, was carrying out a systematic test with a view to being able to play 'Rule Britannia'. Cordelia and Clara and thei mother discussed the wedding.

Suddenly, Mrs Finch exclaimed, 'Oh, Henry! Stop, stop There's such a beautiful view of Exmoor!'

Ten-foot hedges rose on either side of the lane they were in the lane went steeply uphill, and Mr Finch had hoped that he hac put any views of Exmoor safely behind him. But with unusua mildness he stopped and backed the car till it was level with a gate Beyond the gate was a falling meadow, a pillowy middle distance of woodland, and beyond that, pure and cold and unimpassioned the silhouette of the moor.

'Why not,' Mr Finch said, taking the good the gods provided 'Why not stop and picnic?' It occurred to him that once the ca was emptied, the road map might come to light.

The Finches sat down in the meadow and ate cucumbe sandwiches. Arden wore the Indian shawl; the bullfinch in its cage was brought out of the car to have a little fresh air. Gazing at the view, Mrs Finch said that looking at Exmoor always reminded he of her Aunt Harriet's inexplicable boots.

'What boots, Mother?' Cordelia asked.

'She saw them on Exmoor,' Mrs Finch said. 'She and Uncle Lionel both saw them; they were children at the time. They were picking whortleberries – such a disappointing fruit! All these folk-art fruits are much overrated. And nobody's ever been able to account for them.'

'But why should they have to be accounted for?' Clara asked. 'Were they sticking out of a bog?'

'They were in a cab.'

'Your Aunt Harriet –' Mr Finch began. For some reason, it angered him to hear of boots being in a cab while he was still in doubt as to whether the map was in the car.

'Of course,' Mrs Finch went on, 'in those days cabs were everywhere. But not on Exmoor, where there were no roads. It was a perfectly ordinary cab, one of the kind that open in hot weather. The driver was on the box, and the horse was waving its tail to keep the flies off. They looked as if they had been there quite a long time.'

'Days and days?' Arden asked.

'I'm afraid not, dear. Decomposition had not set in. But as if they had been there long enough to get resigned to it. An hour or so.'

'But how could Aunt Harriet tell how long –'

'In those days, children were very different – nice and inhibited,' Mrs Finch said. 'So Aunt Harriet and Uncle Lionel observed the cab from a distance and walked on. Presently, they saw two figures – a man and a woman. The man was very pale and sulky, and the woman was rating him and crying her eyes out, but the most remarkable thing of all, even more remarkable than the cab, was that the woman wasn't wearing a hat. In those days, no self-respecting woman would stir out without a hat. And on the ground was a pair of boots. While Harriet and Lionel were trying to get a little nearer without seeming inquisitive, the woman snatched up the boots and ran back to the cab. She ran right past the children; she was crying so bitterly she didn't even notice them. She jumped into the cab, threw the boots onto the opposite seat, the driver whipped up his horse, and the cab went bumping and jolting away over the moor. As for the man, he walked off looking like murder. So what do you make of that?'

'Well, I suppose they'd been wading, and then they quarrelled and she drove away with his boots as a revenge,' said Clara.

'He was wearing boots,' said Mrs Finch.

'Perhaps they were eloping,' Clara said, 'and the boots were part of their luggage that he'd forgotten to pack, like Father, and she changed her mind in time.'

'Speed is essential to an elopement, and so is secrecy. To drive over Exmoor in an open cab would be inconsistent with either,' said Mr Finch.

'Perhaps the cab lost its way in a moor mist,' contributed Arden. 'Listen! I can do almost all the first line of "Rule Britannia" now.'

'But Clara, why need it be an elopement?' Cordelia asked. 'Perhaps she was just a devoted wife who found a note from her husband saying he had lost his memory or committed a crime or something and was going out of her life, and she seized up a spare pair of boots, leaped hatless into a cab, and tracked him across Exmoor, to make sure he had a dry pair to change into. And when Harriet and Lionel saw them, he had just turned on her with a brutal oath.'

'If she had been such a devoted wife, she wouldn't have taken the boots away again,' Clara said.

'Yes, she would. It was the breaking point,' Cordelia said. 'Actually, though, I don't believe she was married to him at all. I think it was an assignation and she'd taken her husband's boots with her as a blind.'

'Then why did she take them out of the cab?' inquired Clara. 'And why didn't she wear a hat, like Mother said? No, Cordelia! I think your theory is artistically all right. It looks the boots straight in the face. But I've got a better one. I think they spent a guilty night together and, being a forgetful man, he put his boots out to be cleaned and in the morning she was hopelessly compromised, so she snatched up the boots and drove after him to give him a piece of her mind.'

'Yes, but he was wearing boots already,' Cordelia said.

'He would have had several pairs. At that date, a libertine would have had hundreds of boots, wouldn't he, Mother?'

'He might not have taken them with him wherever he went, dear,' said Mrs Finch.

Mr Finch said, 'You have both rushed off on an assumption. Because the lady drove away in the cab, you both assume that she arrived in it. Women always jump to conclusions. Why shouldn't the cab have brought the man? If she was hatless, she might have been an escaped lunatic and the man a keeper from the asylum, who came in search of her.'

'Why did he bring a pair of boots?' Cordelia asked.

'Ladies' boots,' said Mr Finch firmly.

'He can't have been much of a lunatic-keeper if he let her get away with his cab,' Clara said.

'I did not say he was a lunatic-keeper, Clara,' said Mr Finch. 'I was merely trying to point out to you and your sister that in cases like this one must examine the evidence from all sides.'

'Perhaps the cabdriver was a lunatic,' said Arden. 'Perhaps that's why he drove them onto Exmoor. Perhaps they were *his* boots, and the man and the woman were arguing as to which of them was to pay his fare. Perhaps –'

Interrupted by his father and both his sisters, all speaking at once, Arden returned to his rendering of 'Rule Britannia'. Mrs Finch removed some crumbs and a few caterpillars from her green moiré lap and looked at the view of Exmoor. Suddenly, a glissando passage on the bird cage was broken by a light twang, a flutter of wings, a cry from Arden. The cage door had flipped open and the bullfinch had flown out. Everybody said 'Oh!' and grabbed at it. The bullfinch flew to the gate, balanced there, flirted its tail, and flew on into the lane.

It flew in a surprised, incompetent way, making short flights, hurling itself from side to side of the lane. But though Cordelia and Clara leaped after it, trying to catch it in their broad-brimmed hats, and though Arden only just missed it by overbalancing on a bough, thereby falling out of the tree and making his nose bleed, and though Mr Finch walked after it, holding up the bird cage and crying 'Sweet, Sweet, Sweet' in a falsetto voice that trembled with feeling, the bullfinch remained at liberty and, with a little practice, flew better and better.

'Stop, all of you!' said Mrs Finch, who had been attending to Arden, wiping her bloodstained hands on the grass. 'You'll frighten it. Henry, do leave off saying "Sweet" – you'll only strain yourself. What we need is the music box. If it hears the music box it will be reminded of its home and remember it's a tame bull finch. Arden, dear, please keep your shawl on and look for some groundsel, if you aren't too weak from loss of blood.'

The music box weighed about fifty pounds. It was contained in an ebony case that looked like a baby's coffin, and at every movement it emitted reproachful chords. On one side it had a handle; on the other side, the handle had fallen off, and by the time the Finches had got the box out of the car, they were flushed and breathless. His groans mingling with the reproachful chords Mr Finch staggered up the lane in pursuit of the bullfinch with the music box in his arms. Mrs Finch walked beside him, tenderly entreating him to be careful, for if anything happened to it, it would break Arminella's heart. Blithesome and cumberless, like the bird of the wilderness, the bullfinch flitted on ahead.

'I am not carrying this thing a step further,' said Mr Finch, setting down the music box at the side of the lane. 'Since you insist, Elinor, I will sit here and play it. The rest of you can walk on and turn the bird somehow and drive it back till the music reminds it of home.'

Clara said, 'I expect we shall go for miles.'

Seeing his family vanish around a bend in the lane, Mr Finch found himself nursing a hope that Clara's expectation might be granted. He was devoted to music boxes. He sat down beside it and read the list of its repertory, which was written in a copperplate hand inside the lid: 'Là ci darem la Mano'; 'The Harp that once through Tara's Halls'; The Prayer from *Moïse*; the 'Copenhagen Waltz'. A very pleasant choice for an interval of repose, well-earned repose, in this leafy seclusion. He ran his finger over the prickled cylinder, he blew away a little dust, he wound the box up. Unfortunately, there were a great many midges, the inherent pest of leafy seclusions. He paused to light cigar. Then he set off the music box. It chirruped through three and a half tunes and stopped, as music boxes do. Behind him, a voice said somewhat diffidently, 'I say. Can I be any help?'

Glancing from the corner of his eye, Mr Finch saw a young man whose bare ruined legs and rucksack suggested that he was on a walking tour.

'No, thank you,' Mr Finch said. Dismissingly, he rewound the music box and set it going again.

Round the bend of the lane came two replicas, in rather bad condition, of Gainsborough's well-known portrait of Arminella Blount in the Character of Flora, a cadaverous small boy draped in a blood-stained Indian shawl, and a middle-aged lady dressed in the height of fashion who carried a bird cage. Once again, Mr Finch was forced to admit the fact that the instant his family escaped from his supervision they somehow managed to make themselves conspicuous. Tripping nervously to the strains of the 'Copenhagen Waltz', the young man on a walking tour skirted round them and hurried on.

'We've got it!' cried Mrs Finch, brandishing the bird cage.

'Why the deuce couldn't you *explain* to that young man?' asked Mr Finch. 'Elinor, why couldn't you explain?'

'But why should I?' Mrs Finch asked. 'He looked so hot and careworn, and I expect he only gets a fortnight's holiday all the year through. Why should I spoil it for him. Why shouldn't he have something to look back on in his old age?'

(Edward Petherbridge read this story on *Woman's Hour* in October 1989.)

CHRISTMAS
MEMORIES

VIOLETS
AND STRAWBERRIES
IN THE SNOW

———— ◆ ————

Shena Mackay

As he lay reflecting on the procession of sad souls who had occupied this bed before him, the door burst open with an accusing crack.

'You know smoking is forbidden in the dormitories!'

'I'm terribly sorry, nurse. I must have misread the notice. I thought it said, "Patients are requested to smoke at all times, and whenever possible to set fire to the bedclothes."'

In the leaking conservatory which adjoined the lounge, puddles marooned the pots of dead Busy Lizzies and the brown fronds of withered Tradescantias, and threatened with flood the big empty doll's house that stood incongruously, and desolate, with dead leaves blown against its open door; a too-easy metaphor for lost childhoods and broken homes and lives. At seven o'clock in the morning in the lounge itself, the new day's cigarette smoke refreshed the smell of last night's butts, whose burnt-out heads clustered in the tall aluminium ashtrays. A cup, uncontrollable by a shaking hand, clattered in a saucer. The Christmas-tree lights were winking red and green and yellow and blue, and on the television, creatures from another sphere were sampling mince pies and sipping sherry in an animated consumer guide to the delights of the worst day of the year. There was port and wine and whisky too, and Douglas Macdougal sat among the casualties of alcohol and watched what once would have been his breakfast vanish down the throats of those to whom nature, or something, had granted a mandate or dispensation, those who were paid in money and fame as well as in the satisfaction, which had brought a virtuous glow to their cheeks, that they were imbibing in the national interest. There were no saucer-like erosions under their eyes, no pouchy sacs of unshed tears; and in subways and doorways, on station forecourts and in phoneboxes, in suburban kitchens a thousand bottles clinked in counterpoint. Cheers.

'You were as high as a kite last night when they brought you in.' The man seated on his left pushed a pack of cigarettes towards Douglas.

'Well I've been brought down now. Somebody cut my string. Or the wind dropped.'

A coloured kite crashed to earth; a grotesquely broken bird among the ashtrays and dirty cups, trailing clouds of ignominy.

Although a poster in the hall showed a little girl, her face all bleared with tears and snot, the victim of a parent's drunkenness, it became apparent that not everybody was here for the same reason. A woman with wild, dilated bright eyes glided back and forward across the room, as if on castors, with a strange stateliness, passing and repassing the television screen, and from time to time stopping to ask someone for a cigarette, from which she took one elegant puff before stubbing it out in the ashtray and continuing her somnambulistic progress. No one refused her a cigarette; Douglas had noticed already a kindness towards one another among the patients, and no one objected when she blocked the television screen where peaches bloomed in brandy and white grapes were frosted to alabaster. No one was watching it. The inmates sat, bloated and desiccated, rotten fruit dumped on vinyl chairs, viewing private videos; reruns of the ruins they had made of their lives, soap operas of pain and shame, of the acts which had brought them to be sitting between these walls bedecked with institutional gaiety, or fastforwarding to scenes of Christmases at home without them; waiting for breakfast time, waiting for the shuffling queue for medication.

To his right a woman was crying, comforted by a young male member of staff.

'Just because a person hears voices in her head, it doesn't give anyone the right to stop them being with their kids on Christmas Day.'

'But I'm sure they'll come up to see you, Mary.'

'But I won't be there when they open their presents . . .'

'But they'll come to see you, I'm sure . . .'

Her voice rose to a wail, 'But they don't like coming here!'

The tissue was a dripping ball in her hand. He patted her fist.

'They'll be coming to see you, Mary – it's Christmas.'

Douglas felt like screaming, 'She knows it's fucking Christmas, that's the point, you creep!' but who was he to say anything?

'You don't understand,' she said, and male, childless, half her age, an adolescent spot still nestling in the fair down on his chin, how could he have understood?

Douglas was shaking. He didn't want any breakfast. Although the routine had been explained by two people he hadn't been able to take it in. He was afraid to go into the kitchen where the smell of dishcloths mingled with the steam from huge aluminium kettles simmering on an old gas cooker. He hovered in the doorway for a minute, taking in the plastic tub of cutlery on the draining board, the smeary plastic box of margarine, the cups and plates, inevitably pale green, that belonged to nobody. *Timor mortis conturbat me*. He had been saying that in the ambulance, but mercifully could remember little else. A faint sickly smell clung to his shirt. He had refused to let them undress him, clinging to a spurious shred of vomity dignity that was all he felt he had left, aware of his bloated stomach, and had slept in his clothes. Up and down staircases, down windowless corridors whose perspectives tapered to madness, past toothless old men who mimed at him, asking for cigarettes, repassing the women with heavy-duty vacuum cleaners, past the closed but festive occupational therapy unit with a plate of cold and clayey mincepies on its windowsill, past the locked library, he ranged on his aching legs, until at last he found a bathroom. As he washed himself, and the front of his shirt and his stubbly face, avoiding the mirror, the words of a song doubled him up with pain, 'Oh Mandy, will you kiss me and stop me from shaking . . .' He used to sing 'Oh Mandy, will you kiss me and stop me from shaving . . .' when his daughter ran into the bathroom and he picked her up and swung her round and dabbed a blob of foam on her nose. If he had a razor now he would have drawn it across his aching throat, across the intolerable ache of remembered happiness.

Downstairs again he was given some coloured capsules in a transparent cup, and then it seemed that his time was his own. It was apparent that, a long time ago, a severely disturbed patient had started to paint the walls with shit and the management had been so pleased with the result that they had asked him to finish the job, and then had been reluctant to break up the expanse of ocherous gloss with the distraction of a lopsided still life painted in occupational therapy and framed in dusty plywood or even one of the sunny postcards which are pinned to most hospital walls, exhorting the reader to smile. The television, with the sound turned down, was showing open-heart surgery; the naked dark red organ fluttered, pulsated and throbbed in its harness of membranes. Douglas turned to the man sitting next to him.

'What do we do now?'

'We could hang ourselves in the tinsel.'

Like several residents, he was wearing a grey tracksuit, the colour of the rain, the colour of despair. He held out his hand.

'I'm Peter.'

'Douglas.'

'I was going to walk down to the garage to get some cigarettes, if you feel like a walk.'

Douglas shook his head. His pockets were empty. If he had had any money at the start of this débâcle, he had none now.

'Do you want anything from the shop, then?'

'Just get me a couple of bottles of vodka, a carton of tomato juice, and a hundred Marlboro.'

'No Worcester?'

'Hold the Worcester. A couple of lemons, maybe, and some

black pepper.'

'You're on, mate.'

Peter was taking orders for chocolate and cigarettes from the others, then he set out into the sheet of rain. Douglas was summoned to see the doctor, a severe lady in a sari: afterwards he remembered nothing of the interview.

Back in the lounge a ghostly boy watched him with terrified eyes, and gibbered in fear when Douglas attempted a smile; whatever the reason for his being here was, it had been something that life had done to him, and not he to himself; some gross despoliation of innocence had brought him to this state. Douglas watched a nurse crouch beside him for half an hour or more, coaxing him to take one sip of milk from a straw held against his clamped bloodless lips; the milk ran down his white chin and she wiped it with a tissue. This sight of one human being caring for another moved him in part of his mind, but he felt so estranged from them, as if he had been watching on television a herd of elephants circling a sick companion. He might have wept then; he might have wept when Peter returned battered by the rain and dropped a packet of cigarettes in his lap; he might have wept when he held Mary's hand while she cried for her imprisonment and for her children, thinking also of his own, but he couldn't cry.

'Perhaps all my tears were alcohol,' he thought. He picked up a magazine. *Don't let Christmas Drive you Crackers*, he read. *Countdown to Christmas*. He thought about his own countdown to Christmas, which had started in good time some two weeks ago, in the early and savage freeze which had now been washed away by the grey rain.

'Slip slidin' away, slip slidin' away . . .' the Paul Simon song was running through his head as he skidded and slid down the icy drives of the big houses where he delivered free newspapers. His route was Nob Hill and the houses were large and set back from the road. 'This is no job for a man' he thought, but it was the only job that this man could find. He had seen women out leafleting, using shopping trolleys to carry their loads, and he had considered getting one himself as the strap of his heavy PVC bag bit into his shoulder, but that would have been the final admission of failure, and the suspicion that nobody wanted the newspapers anyway crystallised his embarrassment to despair.

What struck him most about the houses was the feeling that no life took place behind those windows; standing in front of some of them, he could see right through; it was like looking at an empty film set where no dramas were played out. Beyond the double-glazed and mullioned windows his eye was drawn over the deep immaculate lawn of carpet, the polished frozen lake of dining table with its wintry branched silver foliage of candelabra, past the clumps of Dralon velvet furniture and the chilly porcelain flowers and birds, through the locked french windows to the plumes of pampas grass, the stark prickly sticks of pruned roses in beds of earth like discarded Christmas cake with broken lumps of icing, the bird table thatched and floored with snow and the brown rushes keening round the invisible pond. Latterly ghostly hands had installed, by night, Christmas trees festooned with electric stars that sparkled as coldly and remotely as the Northern Lights. Douglas conceived the idea that the inhabitants of these houses were as cold and metallic as the heavy cutlery on their tables, as hollow as the waiting glasses.

It was late one morning, on a day that would never pass beyond a twilight of reflected snowlight, that he got his first glimpse of life beyond the glass; there had been tyre marks and sledge marks in the silent drives before, but never a sight of one of the inhabitants in this loop of time. Her hair was metallic, falling like foil, heavy on the thin shoulders of her cashmere sweater; he knew that it was cashmere, just as he knew that the ornate knives and forks that she set on the white tablecloth were pewter. Pewter flatware. He had found the designation for these scrolled and fluted implements in an American magazine filched from one of the cornucopias, or dustbins, concealed at the tradesmen's entrance to one of these houses. He stood and watched her as she folded napkins and cajoled hothouse flowers into an acceptable centrepiece. What was her life, he wondered, that so early in the day she had the time, or perhaps the desperation, to set the table so far in advance of dinner. She looked up, startled like a bird, or like one whose path has been powdered with snow from the feathery skirt of a bird, and Douglas retreated. He retrieved a real newspaper, not one of the local handouts which he delivered, from next door's bin and stood in the wide empty road, glancing at the headlines, with a torn paper garland, consigned to the wind, leaking its dyes into the snow at his feet.

Glasgow – World's Cancer Capital, he read. Nicotine and alcohol had given to his native city this distinction.

'Christ. Thank God I left Glasgow when I did.'

He poured the last drop down his throat and threw the little bottle into the snow, taking a deep drag on the untipped cigarette, which was the only sort which gave him any satisfaction now. He coughed, a heavy painful cough, like squashed mistletoe berries in his lungs, and returned to the room he had rented since he had left his wife, and children. The next time that he saw the woman she was unloading some small boys in peaked prep school caps from a Volvo Estate. She was wearing a hard tweed hat with a narrow brim, a quilted waistcoat and tight riding breeches, like a second skin, so that at a distance it looked as if she wasn't wearing any trousers above her glossy boots. Douglas was tormented by her. He looked for her everywhere, seeing her metallic hair reflected in shop windows, in the unlikely mirrors of pubs which she would never patronise. He stood in the front garden staring at her sideboard which had grown rich with crystallised fruits, dates and figs, a pyramid of nuts and satsumas, some still wrapped in blue and silver paper, Karlsbad plums in a painted box, a bowl of Christmas roses; his feet were crunched painfully in his freezing, wet shoes, his shoulders clenched against the wind; he wanted to crack open the sugary shell of one of those crystallised fruits and taste the syrupy dewdrop at its heart. Once he met her, turning from locking the garage, and handed her the paper. He couldn't speak; his heart was sending electric jolts of pain through his chest and down his arms. He stretched his stubbly muzzle, stippled with black, into what should have been a smile, but which became a leer. She snatched the paper and hurried to the house. If a man hates his room, his possessions, his clothes, his face, his body, whom can he expect not to turn from him in hatred and fear? There was nothing to be done, except to wrap himself in an overcoat of alcohol.

Whisky warmed the snow, melted the crystals of ice in his heart; he skidded, slip slidin' away, home to the dance of the sugar-plum fairy tingling on a glassy glockenspiel of icicles, to find the woman who organised the delivery round of the free newspapers on his doorstep. She was demanding his bag. He perceived that she was wearing acid yellow moonboots of wet acrylic fur. She blocked the door like a Yeti.

'There have been complaints,' she was saying. 'We do have a system of spot-checks, you know, and it transpires that half the houses on your round simply haven't been getting their copies. We rely on advertising, and it simply isn't good enough if the papers aren't getting through to potential customers, not to mention the betrayal of trust on your part. There has also been a more serious allegation, of harassment, but I don't want to go into that now. I had my doubts about taking you on in the first place. I blame myself, I shouldn't have fallen for your sob story . . . so if you'll just give me that bag, please . . . and calling me an abominable snowman is hardly going to make me change my mind . . .'

She hoisted the bag, heavy with undelivered papers, effortlessly on to her shoulders and stomped on furry feet out of his life.

So Pewter Flatware had betrayed him. He turned back from the door and went out to re-proof his overcoat of alcohol, to muffle himself against that knowledge, and the interview with the Yeti on the doorstep, and its implications.

A year ago, when he had had a short stay in hospital for some minor surgery, his voice had been the most vehement in the ward expressing a desire to get out of the place. He remembered standing in his dressing gown at the window of the day room, staring across the asphalt specked with frost, at the smoke from the incinerators and the row of dustbins, and saying, 'What a dump.'

The truth was that he had loved it. When he had been told that he could go home, they had to pull the curtains round his bed, but the flowery drapes had not been able to conceal the shameful secret that he sobbed into his pillow. The best part had been at night, after the last hot drinks and medication had been dispensed from the trolley, and the nurse came to adjust the metal headboard and arrange the pillows and make him comfortable for the night. Tucked up by this routine professional tenderness into a memory of hitherto forgotten peace and acceptance, he felt himself grow childishly drowsy, and turned his face into the white pillow and slept. He restrained the impulse to put his thumb in his mouth.

Now he was lying in a bank of snow under the copper beech hedge of the woman with tinfoil hair, a lost dissolute baby, guzzling a bottle. The kind white pillow was soft and pure and accepting; he turned his face into it, into the nurse's white bosom, and slept, deaf to the siren that brought the Silver and Pewter people to their leaded windows at last, and blind to the blue lights spinning over the snow. He was now on the other side of sleep, on a clifftop, wrestling with a huge red demon which towered out of the sea, unconquerable and entirely evil. He woke in the ambulance, gibbering of the fear of death, and was taken to the interrogation room of the mental hospital, in whose lounge he sat now, reading a magazine article on how to prevent Christmas from driving you crackers.

At some stage in the interminable morning, one of the nurses brought into the lounge her own set of Trivial Pursuit, and divided the hungover, the tearful, the deranged, the silent and the illiterate into two teams, but the game never really got off the ground. The red demon of his dream came into Douglas's mind, and at once he realised that it had been the Demon Drink; a diabolical manifestation, a crude and hideous personification of the liquid to which he had lost every battle. But the demon assumed other disguises by day; liquefying into seductive and opalescent and tawny amber temptresses who whispered of happiness, that it would be all right this time, they promised; they would make everything all right and each time that he succumbed he couldn't have enough of them, and their promises were broken like glass, and at night as Douglas lay neither asleep nor awake, the demon took his true shape and led him to glimpses of Hell, or at least to the most grotesque excesses of the human mind. He had not dared to go to sleep in his dormitory bed; all night thin ribbons of excelsior had glittered round the doorframe and the barred windows; it sparkled pink and phosphorescent and crackled in nosegays on the snores of the sleeping men, and danced in haloes of false fire above their restless heads.

'I hate going to bed,' he heard Peter say to a man called Bob, 'it's like stepping into an open grave.' And then, 'I'm so terrified of drinking myself to death that I have to drink to stop myself from thinking about it. Bob was a big gentle man with broken teeth, and his bare forearms were garlanded with tattooed hearts and flowers. Peter asked him what had happened to his teeth, and about a scar on his hand.

'They sent me up to D ward and the nurses broke my teeth. They broke two of my ribs as well.'

He said it quite without rancour: this is what happens when you are sent up to D ward. Unable to bear the implications of Bob's statement, Douglas concentrated on a somewhat haphazard game of Give Us a Clue that was in progress across the room. Charades had been proposed, and abandoned in favour of this idiosyncratic version of the television game, and Douglas was invited to join in. As he rose from his chair, he saw that Peter was crying, and he saw Bob reach out his scarred and flowery hand and place it on Peter's knee and say gently through his broken teeth, 'I wish I could help you with your trouble, Peter.'

In his shamed and demoralised state Douglas felt that he had come as near as he ever would to a saint, or even to Jesus Christ. The sight of the big broken man giving a benediction on the other's self-inflicted wounds moved him so that he sat silent and clueless in the game, unable to weep for anyone else, or for his own worthlessness. Then an old man stood up, his trousers hoisted high over his stomach to his sagging breasts. He extended his arm, closed thumb and forefinger together, and undulated his arm.

'What's that then?' he demanded.

'Snake,' said Douglas.

'Yep. Your go.'

Douglas sat; the embodiment of the cliché: he didn't know whether to laugh or to cry.

> 'For When the One Great Scorer comes
>   To write against your name,
>   He marks – not that you won or lost –
>   But how you played the game.'

The debauched Scottish pedant swayed to his feet, grinning uncertainly through stained teeth, and played the game.

In the afternoon his daughters came to visit. He would have done anything to prevent them, if he had known of their intention. He wanted to hide, but they came in, smelling of fresh air and rain, with unseasonal daffodils and chocolates, like children, he thought, in a fairytale, sent by their cruel stepmother up the mountainside to find violets and strawberries in the snow. He took them to the games room which was empty. Here, too, the ashtrays overflowed; those deprived of drink had dedicated themselves to smoking themselves to death instead. The girls had been to his room, and had brought him clean clothes in a carrier bag, and cigarettes. He was so proud of them, and they, who had so much cause to be ashamed of him, made him feel nothing but loved and missed. They laughed and joked, and played a desultory game of table tennis on the dusty table with peeling bats, and mucked about on the exercise bicycle and rowing machine which no one used, and picked out tunes on the scratched and stained and tinselled piano. There was an open book of carols on its music stand: that will be the worst, he thought, when we gather round on Christmas Day to emit whatever sounds come from breaking hearts. Two of the girls lit cigarettes, which made him feel better about the ash-strewn floor, and Mandy, who did not smoke, let no flicker of disapproval cross her face; all in all they acted as if visiting their father in a loony bin was the most normal and pleasurable activity that three young girls could indulge in on a Saturday afternoon. It was only when the youngest said that she was starving, and he said that there were satsumas, which another patient had given him, in his locker, and she made a face and replied 'Satsumas are horrible this year' that they all looked at each other in acknowledgement that her words summed up the whole rotten mess that he had made of Christmas. The fathers have eaten sour grapes, and the children's teeth are set on edge. Douglas broke the silence that afflicted them by saying, 'Good title for a story, eh?' A reminder that in another life he had been a writer. Someone was waiting for the girls in a car, and as he led them to the front door, he hurried them past a little side room where Bob was hunched in a chair, his great head in his hands, his body rocking in grief. Douglas heard the laughter of staff, a world away, behind the door that separates the drunks from the sober. In his carrier bag he found a razor, electric. Now I can shave myself to death, he thought, as opposed to cutting my throat. There were also some envelopes and stamps, a writing pad and pen. There were no letters that he wished to write, but he took the paper and pen, and wrote 'Satsumas Are Horrible This Year', as if by writing it down he could neutralise the pain; turn the disgrace to art. It would not be very good, he knew, but at least it would come from that pulpy, sodden satsuma that was all that remained of his heart.

Later he went into the kitchen to make a cup of tea for himself and for several of the others: like ten-pence pieces for the phone, and cigarettes, coffee was at a premium here. He was hungry, not having eaten for days, and thought of making a piece of toast, but he did not know if he was allowed to take any bread, and the grill pan bore the greasy impressions of someone else's sausages. He realised then what all prisoners, evil or innocent, learn; that what seems such a little thing, and which he had forfeited, the act of making yourself a piece of toast under your own lopsided grill, is in fact one of life's greatest privileges. He stood in the alien kitchen that smelled of industrial detergent and fat and old washing-up cloths, seeing in memory his children smiling and waving at the door, their resolute backs as they walked to the car concealing their wounds under their coats, forgiving and brave, and carrying his own weak and dissolute genes in their young and beautiful bodies. Violets and strawberries in the snow.

(Trevor Nichols read this story on *Woman's Hour* in December 1987.)

TO UNCLE, WITH LOVE

———— ◆ ————

Rumer Godden

In our family Christmas was a thoroughly kept festival and brought an adamantine necessity of present-giving that was hard on us four small girls at the tail of the family clan. Parcels came from our Worcestershire relations, from relations in Taunton and London, and most sent individual presents, necessitating a return. Aunt Gertrude, for instance, would send, besides three bottles of sherry for our parents, four pretty packets for us. Long before the days of gay packing papers Aunt Gertrude painted roses on her white papers and tied the packets with green and pink ribbons that were slightly scented as if Aunt Gertrude herself were in them. They were so pretty that we longed to send something worthy to her; we worked hard but our prospects were meagre. 'It's the thought that counts,' our nearest Aunt, Aunt Hilda, would say, but to be any use at Christmas the smallest thought had to be embodied – and our pocket-money was only ninepence a week each.

For weeks before Christmas we toiled at bookmarkers, penwipers, raffia table-napkin rings, calendars. The Uncles were particularly difficult. Our little sisters had a monopoly, protected by our mother Mam, of the two things we could make easily and cheaply: one was spills, the other an improbable looking thing called a shaving ball made of rosettes twisted out of paper; the Uncle was supposed to pull a rosette off each morning and wipe his razor on it to save cutting the towels. 'You two big ones must think of your own ideas,' said Mam.

'Yes, Mam,' we said and sighed.

Of all the Uncles, our Uncle Edward was the most difficult. Perhaps even then we realised dimly that he had something that was missing from the other Uncles and Aunts – except perhaps Aunt Gertrude – something not to be ignored, that lingered. I know now that it was quality.

He was our eldest maternal uncle and as English as his name, Edward; his essence was a mildness that held an unruffled strength and his life had flowed, because he had so made it flow, with the steady untroubled peace of one of our English rivers.

Each weekday morning he left the house by taxi – the same taxi – for the office (he kept his old-fashioned snub-nosed two-seater Morris Cowley for weekends and holidays). He was a partner in a firm of solicitors in our seaside town and I can remember his office, full of black tin deed boxes, his desk piled with documents, but its very air deliberate and serene. Every day he lunched at the same table in the restaurant at Boots, the chemist. His friends and colleagues lunched at the Royal Sussex Hotel but there the wine waiter came round and asked, embarrassingly, for orders and my Uncle Edward did not drink. At five o'clock he left the office and took the bus to the corner of his road where he walked up the chalky lane to his house. He was a bachelor and lived with his maiden sister, my Aunt Hilda, on the edge of the rolling green Sussex hills. The house was small but the garden was large and he spent every available moment working in it. As soon as he came in, he changed into a disgraceful tattered Burberry and an old green hat and gardened. At seven o'clock Aunt Hilda called him and they had supper; after supper he sat by the dining-room fire and read *The Times* or *Punch* while my Aunt retired to the drawing-room. At nine o'clock he went in to her and they talked a little and had tea. At ten he wound the clocks, shut the house and went to bed.

Little else happened. Occasionally he watched cricket – the town had a famous cricket ground – and once a year he stayed a few days with his brother in Worcestershire. Every spring he was moved to get out the Morris Cowley and spend whole days in the country; he went to see the poetry of bluebells and wild cherries in the woods and drove by farmhouses with their red-brown Sussex tiled roofs standing in what we, Worcestershire bred, called a blow of apple blossoms. Every autumn he saw the bracken turn in Ashdown Forest and he still kept the canoe he had had at Oxford; now it was paddled on the Little Ouse, a tiny placid river that wound through meadows of buttercups and under tangles of wild roses where the swans floated in the shade.

Uncle Edward's things were curiously elegant for a country solicitor. The canoe, Dream Days, was fitted with velvet cushions in yellow and had monogrammed paddles; Uncle Edward's books had special bindings, his slippers, his handkerchiefs, his pipe, his tobacco, were unusually good. How could we give him a lead pencil, a packet of drawing-pins, a cake of cheap soap, which was all our money would run to? Every year we asked ourselves that question, but the Christmas I was twelve years old, the position was particularly acute; I found myself with only three-pence to spend on Uncle Edward.

'Give him a card,' said Ruth who was happily furnished with a comb-case she had made, but cards were considered paltry and all presents were distributed with horrible publicity from the tree in Aunt Hilda's drawing-room.

Aunt Hilda, in real life, did what the maiden aunt of a family is supposed to do in novels; she kept count of all the family threads and wove them tightly together. There were many threads and all of them, or as many as possible, were gathered into one knot for Christmas.

'Nothing for Uncle Edward!' Aunt Hilda would say, and at four o'clock on that Christmas Eve I had nothing.

We, Ruth and I, were standing outside Fidler's bookshop in the South Parade and I was turning over a tray of second-hand books marked 'All at 3d'. It was the 3d that had attracted me, not the books; they were shabby and dirty and at no moment had I thought of giving Uncle Edward a book. Books were of grown-ups' bestowing. We had been shopping all afternoon and were tired and hungry.

'I'm going home to tea,' said Ruth.

'I can't till I've found him a present,' I said.

I watched Ruth, in her brown school coat and brown soup-plate hat, go up the street. She grew smaller and smaller until she went quite out of sight. My feet were cold, I was miserable with worry; listlessly I turned over the books, and then I saw it.

It was under the tray, under a sheet of newspaper as well; I wonder now if it had been put there for someone to come and fetch quietly away. Lifting the newspaper I caught sight of its cover, which was of clean white vellum stamped with gold. It was a book that looked not unlike some of Uncle Edward's own books and I could not imagine how it came to be in the 3d tray, but cautiously I drew it out, opened it and took a quick look inside. It was poems with a few pictures, and it was obviously quite new; most of the pages were uncut. I felt the end papers which were of satiny white paper stamped with a curious little object in gold that conveyed nothing to me at all, nor did the title that I made out with difficulty. *Sonnets on the Kama Sutra*. I could not stop to read or look very carefully and in any case I was stunned by the beauty of the binding and paper. I could hardly believe my luck.

The custom at Fidler's, for a buyer from the cheap trays, was to take the book of his choice and leave the money in a saucer set on the tray; at that price one could not expect the attention of a bookseller. I had an uneasy feeling that I should have gone in and asked Mr Fidler about this book but, 'It was in the threepenny tray,' I said stoutly to Ruth afterwards and I dropped my three-pence in the saucer, put the book under my coat and ran all the way home.

I showed the book to Ruth but there was no time to do more than glance at it, because Mam was waiting for us to take our presents up to Aunt Hilda's and hang them on the tree for the Christmas afternoon party.

'Do it up,' urged Ruth.

'There's a picture of a naked woman and man in the front,' I said. I had just seen it and it made me hesitate.

'They are probably gods,' said Ruth. Gods, we knew, were allowed to be naked as long as their hands were properly disposed.

Then I saw there was a sub-title and read it aloud: 'Kama Sutra. The Eight Attitudes and Sixty-four Ingredients of Love.' It sounded strange; I had not known that love had attitudes or ingredients. '*Will* it do for Uncle Edward?' I asked, hesitating still more.

'Well, Mam says he is the most loving man we know,' said Ruth, 'and it looks quite new. Hurry. Do it up.'

Uncle Edward opened my parcel almost at the last. I was covertly watching. He undid the string, opened the paper and looked. After a moment I began to think he was stunned himself, he was so still. I took this as a tribute; it was a surprisingly handsome book to come from an obscure niece. He opened the front cover, still keeping the book in its paper, not once did he lift it proudly out to public view as I had hoped; I had written a card, 'To Uncle, with love', with my name underneath and he shot a look in my direction. Then I saw that he had coloured deeply – with pleasure? I wondered – and all at once I was as uncertain as I had been when I saw the naked gods. The next minute he had wrapped it swiftly up again and thrust it under all his other presents and, his fingers trembling a little, began to undo José's packet of spills.

He had been quick but not quick enough for Aunt Alice. 'Why, what have you got there?' she asked.

'Nothing,' said Uncle with strange briefness.

Nothing! My precious book! I opened my mouth but I got a look from my Uncle that I had never had before, a look that quelled me.

'But I saw . . .' said Aunt Hilda.

'It's a book of poems,' said Uncle. 'They are only for me.'

'You funny girl,' said Aunt Hilda, who had caught sight of my card and immediately thought I had written them. 'Poems! Uncle doesn't go in for that sort of thing at all.'

There was a sudden sound from Uncle Edward. 'What's the matter, Edward?' asked Aunt Hilda. I raised my head and looked at him. He was quietly opening his presents but it had sounded like – a chuckle?

Three days after the funeral Aunt Hilda began to cry; she had been quietly through it all, the death, the cremation that was done by Uncle's wish, the return to the empty house, the reading of the will and the task we were busy with at present, the sorting of his things. I had come to help Aunt Hilda and Mam with that. Now we were at tea and I had said something a little inarticulate about Uncle Edward and teas in other times, about his gentleness and goodness. Aunt Hilda had burst into tears, tears that were inexplicable from her because they were bitter.

'I should rather have cut off my hand than have to know this,' she sobbed, and when we asked what 'this' was, she could only sob, 'Edward! Edward of all people, to do *that*!'

'Do *what*, Aunt Hilda?'

'I never meant to tell anyone but I can't keep it to myself,' she sobbed. 'Edward, whom I could have sworn ... I know some men are nasty but not Edward!'

'Nasty?' Mam and I said together; 'Uncle *Edward* nasty?'

'Like dirty postcards!' and Aunt Hilda wept again.

'Aunt Hilda,' I said firmly, 'do please tell us what you are talking about.'

She sat up and dabbed her eyes and then said in a quick, stifled voice, 'Edward kept pornographic books in his drawer – a pornographic book.'

'Edward?' 'Uncle Edward?' We were both stupefied. Then, 'Are you *sure*?' I asked but Aunt Hilda stood up, tears spattering on her blouse, and went across the room to his desk; it was a knee-hole desk and on the right-hand side was a deep drawer; it was locked; she took a key, unlocked the drawer and opened it.

When I looked in I had tears in my own eyes. I had not known that Uncle had really cared for us, but in the drawer were all the presents we children had given him, carefully dated and labelled; home-drawn cards and clumsy spills, a pair of knitted scarlet cuffs sewn crooked, blotters and calendars, pen-wipers, table-napkin rings, unused shaving balls! 'I always knew those things were no use,' I said unsteadily, touching the dusty rosettes with my finger.

'He thought a lot of you children,' said Mam.

'That's what makes it so much worse,' said Aunt Hilda, and her tears ran over again. 'Look,' she said, and as if it were red hot, from underneath everything else, as he had once hidden it under his parcels, she pulled out a book. I recognised it instantly: *Kama Sutra. The Eight Attitudes and Sixty-four Ingredients of Love.*

'But I gave him that,' I said.

'*You!*' She and Mam stared at me appalled.

'Yes. Look.' The book was as new as when I had bought it, its pages were still uncut and my card was where I had put it. To Uncle, with love'. 'Don't you remember . . . ?' I said.

'But – you nasty child!' Aunt Hilda's voice began to rise.

'I was only twelve,' I pleaded but, looking at the book, I wondered that even then I had not guessed what it was; I looked at the end papers with their frank phallic design, the front picture – gods indeed! – at the first lines of a poem; I was a mature, grown woman but I grew hot as I looked and I stood before Aunt Hilda as ashamed as I should have been if Uncle had uncovered it that day. 'I didn't know what it was,' I said, 'I was only twelve.'

'Twelve or not!' snapped Aunt Hilda.

'It was Christmas. . . .'

I stopped. Aunt Hilda paused. We seemed to hear something, something I thought I had heard on that Christmas day long ago; Uncle Edward's chuckle.

We looked at one another and began to laugh.

(Stephanie Cole read this story on *Woman's Hour* in May 1992.)

NIGHT IN PARIS

———— ◆ ————

Patrice Chaplin

For Christmas 1950 when Lucy was eleven, Aunt Ethel sent he
a bottle of perfume. It was called 'Night in Paris' and wa
packaged in a blue box with an Eiffel Tower and a half moon on
the front. It was Lucy's first glamorous present and she was so
thrilled she wanted to keep it forever. That was her first mistake
Her second was standing it on the dressing-table next to the
glossy postcard photographs of her film star favourites, Lauren
Bacall and Robert Taylor. Since she was six she'd wanted to be
film star. The 'Night in Paris' perfume seemed to help that along
Enclosed in the wrapping paper was a note from Aunt Ethel. 'To
My Darling Dearest Little God Daughter. Auntie's so proud
you've won a place at Grammar School.'

In those days Lucy had a shilling a week pocket money invari
ably spent in Woolworth's at the make-up counter. She could bu
a small bottle of Eau de Cologne for tenpence or a mirror and
powder puff in a plastic case for fourpence. Colourless nail var
nish was a shilling, face-powder ninepence. The 'Night in Paris'
perfume adorned Woolworth's counter in many sizes. The delux
bottle cost two and nine. After the glamour shopping she went to
Saturday afternoon pictures at the Odeon. She'd earned the on
and three ticket money washing up in the High Street café.

That Christmas, 1950, her mother received a stiff mauve folde
with a satin bow on the front. The writing paper and envelope
inside smelt of lavender. Lucy had seen the present in Wool
worth's at three and six. Her mother opened the folder. 'Good

Ethel hasn't written in it. I can give it to your Auntie Vi. I don't need posh stuff like this.' And she put it away in the dressing-table.

Auntie Vi arrived Boxing Day and brought not only a present but her daughter, young Violet, also bearing a gift. Lucy's mother rushed into the bedroom and got out the writing paper. She turned the mauve folder over to scribble a greeting on the back. The price, five shillings, was inked boldly in the corner.

'But that isn't right,' said Lucy. 'It's only three and six. I've seen it in Woolworth's.'

'They don't ink in the prices either. That's your Aunt Ethel. Swank as usual. We'll have to give young Violet something.' Her mother looked around wildly. 'Give her the scent. Come on. You can always get some more.'

Lucy was appalled. 'But it's too good even to use.'

'All the better. Not been touched. They can see that. Come on. Hurry up. They've come all the way from Gosport.' Lucy's mother always got her way in those days.

Reluctantly Lucy wrote on the back of the box: 'To my Cousin Violet with love, Christmas 50.' In exchange she received a doll's hood.

In 1952 Lucy again received a bottle of 'Night in Paris' perfume for Christmas. This time it came from the Reverend Maude and his wife who lived in Weymouth. Lucy wouldn't have thought twice about it if she hadn't seen, faintly scratched on the box, 'Cousin Violet . . . 50.'

Her mother said for all the Reverend Maude's snobbery he was a cheapskate. 'But how did they get my present that I passed on to Cousin Violet?'

'Your cousin was made to send it on to the Reverend's wife, that's why. Your Aunty Vi wouldn't let her daughter use that muck. You know the sort who use that.'

That year Lucy had started wearing 'Californian Poppy' per-fume, Woolworth's one and six a bottle, so she decided to put the present in her drawer until the other was finished. When she came to use it, however, it had gone. Her mother had sent it to Aunt

Ethel for her birthday. 'But she sent it to me originally!' Lucy was outraged.

'She won't know. She ought to be glad to get anything. Mutton dressed as lamb.'

The photographs of Lauren Bacall and Robert Taylor had gone too. So had most of Lucy's film star collection which she kept in a shoebox in the wardrobe. She hadn't noticed because she was so passionately in love with Mario Lanza after seeing him in *Because You're Mine* and *The Great Caruso* that only pictures of him adorned her room.

Her mother admitted she'd given them to Cousin Violet. 'You don't want those old photographs. She's only a kid. Gives her something to look at.'

Lucy realised her mother, along with Aunt Ethel, had no respect for possessions. The film stars had taken years to collect. She'd written to the stars care of the studios and usually got a signed glossy photograph in reply. Vera Ellen, Cornel Wilde, Lana Turner, Ava Gardner, Humphrey Bogart, Phyllis Calvert – they'd given dreams and brightened up her dreary schooldays in the suburbs. She tried to explain that to her mother.

'Give all that up. You're not a child. You're nearly fourteen.'

'But I want to be one of them.'

'Make believe. You've got to get on with the real world.' Her mother wanted Lucy to become a private secretary. That's where the status was. Film stars played no part in that job.

The next Christmas Lucy received a stiff mauve folder of writing paper from Aunt Ethel. Written inside in blue ink was, 'To my Darling Little God Daughter with heaps of love and affection for Christmas 1953. P.S. Only a little gift darling but you can write more letters to your Auntie.' A gummed label on the top right hand corner marked the price. Twelve and sixpence. Lucy tore it off and underneath was inked five shillings, the price Aunt Ethel had originally marked it up to when she'd sent it, all festive and indisputably new, to Lucy's mother in 1950. Lucy sniffed the folder. The lavender smell had gone. The mauve silk bow was flattened and frayed and Aunt Ethel had disguised its age by sewing on a cloth rose.

'What a cheek!'

'Doesn't matter.' Lucy's mother grabbed the folder. 'We'll try and scratch the price out and send it to the Reverend Maude and his wife.'

'But Ethel's written in it!'

'They'll never know. They're half blind. I'll stick a label over the message. Ethel's a nuisance, writing all over the presents like that.'

Lucy got an expensive gift from the Reverend Maude and his wife. A bottle of Coty 'Chypre' fragrance in an untampered box. Lucy hadn't seen it in Woolworth's – it was out of that price range.

'I wonder who gave her that,' said Lucy's mother. 'She can't stand scent, old Maude's wife. That's why you've got it.'

By Easter the Mario Lanza pictures were down and the bed-room wall was bare. Lucy had a crush on her gym mistress and was longing to give her a token of the passion. The Chypre fragrance was undeniably right. A memorable gift of love. Lucy began the accompanying note and her mother picked up the bottle.

'Where's this going?'

'To my teacher. It's her birthday.'

'Rubbish. These are Christmas presents. You don't touch these.'

'But it's valuable.'

'All the better. Do for Aunt Ethel. She's come up in the world. She's going to manage a hotel in the Isle of Wight.'

'But it's mine.'

Her mother kept her hands on the Chypre. 'But they're sent out at Christmas. You don't use them.'

Lucy longed for revenge. What better than an incorruptible present, the transitory kind. Next Christmas she'd send out a batch of live things that died. Plants. Unheard of in the Christmas chain. She even considered perishable things like homemade cakes covered in hundreds and thousands or blancmange packed in ice.

Lucy loved Christmas. She loved cards and carols, crackers, coal fires, party games. From the end of November each year she went carol singing with her friends and they saved the money to buy presents. Lucy enjoyed wrapping them, decorating the packages with holly and tinsel. The professional presents upset her.

In the late forties a special present had gone into circulation but it didn't reach Lucy until the mid-fifties. A small tin of Snowfire vanishing cream, Woolworth's one and three. It was considered a suitable professional gift because the tin couldn't be marked and by lifting the lid it was obvious it hadn't been used. It was passed on to Aunt Ethel for Christmas '55 and she recognised its pedigree. In the same wrapping it was despatched to little Beryl in Folkestone. Aged ten, the girl was delighted. Her mother took it away. 'Whatever is Ethel thinking about? You don't want to put much on your face at your age.' She rewrapped it immediately and sent it to Lucy. 'A late present for my pretty niece.' If she put that old cream on her face, Lucy reflected, the adjective might cease to apply. It lay in the darkness of her dressing-table for years. Before they moved in 1959 her mother removed it from the box of jumble. 'Wait a minute. This stuff's never been used. It might come in for someone.' Aunt Ethel got it with a tin of tea the following Christmas.

Lucy had rejected the secretarial path. After school she'd worked in the local rep as ASM and made her way up to juvenile lead. She was glamorous and earned extra money fashion modelling in London. She no longer shopped at Woolworth's. In 1960, after she'd failed to get a small part in a West End pantomime, she was obliged to visit Aunt Ethel. The Reverend Maude and his wife were also staying. It was a subdued Christmas but she did get one laugh. When Aunt Ethel opened her presents Vi and young Violet had sent a folder of writing paper and a slightly battered box of 'Night in Paris' perfume. Fourteen and six was inked outrageously on the side. Aunt Ethel grimaced but her voice was bright. 'How nice. They don't always have such taste about present giving.'

Both the satin bow and cloth rose had gone from the folder and the gluey scar was covered by a handmade paper doll that leaned forward when the folder was opened.

'How original,' said Lucy mischievously.

Aunt Ethel's mouth tightened. 'Yes. Young Violet was always good at craft.' The Reverend Maude's wife received the Snowfire vanishing cream. It was the first time she'd got that. The Coty 'Chypre' fragrance had gone into hiding.

Lucy gave them a completely innocent present. It could not be corrupted. She laid the plucked goose onto the table. They pretended to be grateful but they were very disappointed. Didn't Lucy know the meaning of Christmas?

All three long-term festive missiles ended up in Aunt Ethel's care. She let them freshen up in her dressing-table pungent with the smell of old Christmas soaps and thirties lavender bags for two years. Then she took the 'Night in Paris' scent and removed it from its box. She wrapped it in an Irish linen handkerchief (Christmas '37) and sent it to young Beryl in Folkestone. She removed the handmade doll from the stationery folder, stuck a Christmas label over the glue mark and wrote right across the front of the folder in indelible red pen, 'Happy Christmas'. In a moment of spite she added '1967'. She gave it to the Reverend Maude. He was ninety-four and had a short memory. So did she it seemed in '68 because she gave the Snowfire cream to Lucy for her birthday. She arrived unannounced in the dressing-room of the West End theatre while Lucy was on stage and left a note. 'Just dropped in on a flying visit with little gifts for my clever God-daughter.' Lucy kept the tin in the dressing-room and the other actresses were intrigued by its age, its nostalgia.

The second 'little present' was the film star collection which Lucy had so loved as a child. 'I thought you might like these. I got them for you especially. They're very valuable darling.'

More than Aunt Ethel could know. How she'd got them from Cousin Violet and what circuitous route they'd travelled, Lucy could not guess.

There was an outbreak of the professional presents in 1971 but by then Lucy was in Hollywood. 'Night in Paris' was still going strong. It travelled around as part of a Boots toilet selection. The writing paper had had to come off the circuit in '68. Lucy's mother had received it from the Reverend Maude and the seven of sixty-seven had been changed to a spidery eight. Lucy's mother was licked. She kept it in the dressing-table until she could think of something to do with it.

Aunt Ethel wrote to Hollywood where Lucy was playing small parts. 'We so missed you at Christmas but if you do get back to England there's a welcome home present waiting at your mother's. It may come in useful for your busy career. We're so proud of you.'

When Lucy finally returned in 1976 after her mother's death, she found the little gift in the sideboard. She lifted off the soft blue crepe paper and on a nest of green nineteen-fifties taffeta lay the bottle of 'Night in Paris'. She hadn't seen it for years. Its smell took her back to her school days, Mario Lanza, the crush on the gym teacher, carol singing. It also reminded her of the Christmases of the war. Waking up early in the cold with the blackout still up and under the dim torch light unwrapping a small packet of perfumed crayons, six colours and a drawing book, some nuts wrapped in silver paper, a packet of Cadbury's chocolate with purple wrapping, a monkey up a stick, an apple, an orange. One year there was the magic of a kaleidoscope. She remembered these as being the happy Christmases.

She took the folder of writing paper from her mother's table, smelling of mothballs. She tore off the two strips of satin ribbon and took out a yellowing envelope and sheet of paper. She wrote,

'Thank you Auntie Ethel for all the Christmases.'

(Brenda Blethyn read this story on *Woman's Hour* in December 1990.)

SCHOOLDAYS

SWAN

—— ♦ ——

Jane Gardam

Two boys walked over the bridge.

They were big boys from the private school on the rich side of the river. One afternoon each week they had to spend helping people. They helped old people with no one to love them and younger children who were finding school difficult. It was a rule.

'I find school difficult myself,' said Jackson. 'Exams for a start.'

'I have plenty of people at home who think no one loves them,' said Pratt. 'Two grandparents, two parents, one sister.'

'And all called Pratt, poor things,' said Jackson, and he and Pratt began to fight in a friendly way, bumping up against each other until Jackson fell against a lady with a shopping-trolley on a stick and all her cornflakes fell out and a packet of flour, which burst.

'I'm going straight to your school,' she said. 'I know that uniform. It's supposed to be a good school. I'm going to lay a complaint,' and she wagged her arms up and down at the elbows like a hen. Pratt, who often found words coming out of his mouth without warning, said, 'Lay an egg. Cluck.'

'That's done it. That's finished it,' said the woman. 'I'm going right round now. *And* I'll say you were slopping down the York Road Battersea at two o'clock in the afternoon, three miles from where you ought to be.'

'We are doing our Social Work,' said Pratt. 'Helping people.'

'Helping people!' said the woman, pointing at the pavement.

'We're being interviewed to take care of unfortunate children,' said Jackson.

'They're unfortunate all right if all they can get is you.' And she steamed off, leaving the flour spread about like snow, and passers-by walked over it giving dark looks and taking ghostly footprints away into the distance. Pratt eased as much of it as he could into the gutter with his feet.

'She's right,' he said. 'I don't know much about unfortunate children. Or any children.'

'They may not let us when they see us,' said Jackson. 'Come on. We'd better turn up. They can look at us and form an opinion.'

'Whatever's that mess on your shoes?' asked the Head Teacher at the school on the rough side of the river, coming towards them across the hall. 'Dear me. It *is* a nasty day. How do you do? Your children are ready for you, I think. Maybe today you might like just to talk to them indoors and start taking them out next week?'

'Yes, please,' said Jackson.

'Taking them *out*?' said Pratt.

'Yes. The idea is that – with the parents' consent – you take them out and widen their lives. Most of them on this side of the river never go anywhere. It's a depressed area. Their lives are simply school (or truanting), television, bed and school, though we have children from every country in the world.'

'It's about the same for us,' said Pratt. 'Just cross out television and insert homework.'

'Oh, come now,' said the Head Teacher, 'you do lots of things. Over the river, there's the Zoo and all the museums and the Tower of London and all the lovely shops. All the good things happen over the bridge. Most of our children here have scarcely seen a blade of grass. Now – you are two very reliable boys, I gather?' (She looked a bit doubtful.) 'Just wipe your feet and follow me.'

She opened a door of a classroom, but there was silence inside and only one small Chinese boy looking closely into the side of a fish-tank.

'Oh dear. Whatever . . . ? Oh, of course. They're all in the gym. This is Henry. Henry Wu. He doesn't do any team games. Or – anything, really. He is one of the children you are to try to help. Now which of you would like Henry? He's nearly seven.'

'I would,' said Pratt, wondering again why words kept emerging from his mouth.

'Good. I'll leave you here then. Your friend and I will go and find the other child. Come here, Henry, and meet – what's your name?'

'Pratt.'

'Pratt. HERE'S PRATT, HENRY. He's not deaf, Pratt. Or dumb. He's been tested. It is just that he won't speak or listen. He shuts himelf away. PRATT, HENRY,' she said, and vanished with an ushering arm behind Jackson, closing the door.

Henry Wu watched the fish.

'Hello,' said Pratt after a while. 'Fish.'

He thought, that is a very silly remark. He made it again, 'Fish.'

The head of Henry Wu did not move. It was a small round head with thick hair, black and shiny as the feathers on the diving ducks in the park across the river.

Or it might have been the head of a doll. A very fragile Chinese-china doll. Pratt walked round it to try and get a look at the face, the front of which was creamy-coloured with a nose so small it hardly made a bump, and leaf-shaped eyes with no eyelashes. No, not leaf-shaped, pod-shaped, thought Pratt, and in each pod the blackest and most glossy berry which looked at the fish. The fish opened their mouths at the face in an anxious manner and waved their floaty tails about.

'What they telling you?' asked Pratt. 'Friends of yours, are they?'

Henry Wu said nothing.

'D'you want to go and see the diving ducks in our park?'

Henry Wu said nothing.

'Think about it,' said Pratt. 'Next week. It's a good offer.'

Henry Wu said nothing.

'Take it or leave it.'

Pratt wondered for a moment if the Chinese boy was real. Maybe he was a sort of waxwork. If you gave him a push maybe he'd just tip over and fall on the floor. 'Come on, Henry Wu,' he said. 'Let's hear what you think,' and he gave the boy's shoulder a little shove.

And he found himself lying on the floor with no memory of being put there. He was not hurt at all – just lying. And the Chinese boy was still sitting on his high stool looking at the fish.

Pandemonium was approaching along the passage and children of all kinds began to hurtle in. They all stopped in a huddle when they saw large Pratt spread out over the floor, and a teacher rushed forward. The Head Teacher and Jackson were there, too, at the back, and Jackson was looking surprised.

'Oh dear,' said the teacher, 'his mother taught him to fight in case he was bullied. She's a Black Belt in judo. She told us he was very good at it. Oh Henry – not again. This big boy wants to be kind to you.'

'All I said,' said Pratt, picking himself up, 'was that I'd take him to the diving ducks in the park. What's more, I shall,' he added, glaring at Henry Wu.

'Why bother?' said Jackson. They were on their way home. 'He looks a wimp. He looks a rat. I don't call him unfortunate. I call him unpleasant.'

'What was yours like?'

'Mine wasn't. She'd left. She was a fairground child. They're always moving on. The school seems a bit short of peculiar ones at the moment. I'll share Henry Wu the Great Kung Fu with you if you like. You're going to need a bit of protection by the look of it.'

But in the end Jackson didn't, for he was given an old lady's kitchen to paint and was soon spending his Wednesdays and all his free time in it, eating her cooking. Pratt set out the following week to the school alone and found Henry Wu waiting for him, muffled to just below the eyebrows in a fat grasshopper cocoon of bright red nylon padding.

'Come on,' said Pratt, and without looking to see if Henry followed, set out along the grim York Road to a bus stop. Henry climbed on the bus behind him and sat some distance away, glaring into space.

'One and a half to the park,' said Pratt, taking out a French grammar. They made an odd pair. Pratt put on dark glasses in case he met friends.

It was January. The park was cold and dead. The grass was thin and muddy and full of puddly places and nobody in the world could feel the better for seeing a blade of·it. Plants were sticks. There were no birds yet about the trees, and the water in the lake and round the little island was heavy and dark and still, like forgotten soup.

The kiosk café was shut up. The metal tables and chairs of summer were stacked inside and the Coke machine was empty. Pigeons walked near the kiosk, round and round on the cracked tarmac. They were as dirty and colourless as everything else but Henry looked at them closely as they clustered round his feet. One bounced off the ground and landed on his head.

Henry did not laugh or cry out or jump, but stood.

'Hey, knock that off. It's filthy,' shouted Pratt. 'They're full of disease, London pigeons. Look at their knuckles – all bleeding and rotten.'

A large black-and-white magpie came strutting by and regarded Henry Wu with the pigeon on his head. The pigeon flew away. Henry Wu began to follow the magpie along the path.

'It's bad luck, one magpie,' said Pratt, 'One for sorrow, two for joy,' and at once a second magpie appeared, walking behind. The Chinese boy walked in procession between the two magpies under the bare trees.

'Come on. It's time to go,' said Pratt, feeling jealous. The magpies flew away, and they went to catch the bus.

Every Wednesday of that cold winter term, Pratt took Henry Wu nto the park, walking up and down with his French book or his Science book open before him while Henry watched the birds and said nothing.

'Has he *never* said anything?' he asked the Head Teacher. 'I suppose he talks Chinese at home?'

'No. He doesn't say a thing. There's someone keeping an eye on him of course. A Social Worker. But the parents don't seem to be unduly worried. His home is very Chinese, I believe. The doctors say that one day he should begin to speak, but maybe not for years. We have to be patient.'

'Has he had some bad experiences? Is he a Boat Person?'

'No. He is just private. He is a village boy from China. Do you want to meet his family? You ought to. They ought to meet you, too. It will be interesting for you. Meeting Chinese.'

'There are Chinese at our school.'

'Millionaires' sons from Hong Kong, I expect, with English as their first language. This will be more exciting. These people have chosen to come and live in England. They are immigrants.'

'I'm going to meet some immigrants,' said Pratt to Jackson. 'D'you want to come?'

'No,' said Jackson to Pratt, 'I'm cleaning under Nellie's bed where she can't reach. And I'm teaching her to use a calculator.'

'Isn't she a bit old for a calculator?'

'She likes it. Isn't it *e*migrants?'

'No, immigrants. Immigrants come *in* to a country.'

'Why isn't it innigrants then?'

'I don't know. Latin, I expect, if you look it up. Emigrants are people who go out of a country.'

'Well, haven't these Chinese come out of a country? As well as come in to a country? They're emigrants and immigrants. They don't know whether they're coming or going. Perhaps that's what's the matter with Henry Wu.'

'Henry's not an innigrant. He's a *ninny*grant. Or just plain *nigrant*. I'm sick of him if you want to know. It's a waste of time, my Social Work. At least you get some good food out of yours. You've started her cooking again. And you're teaching her about machines.'

'Your Chinese will know about machines. I shouldn't touch the food, though, if you go to them. It won't be like a Take-Away.'

'D'you want to come?'

'No thanks. See you.'

'Candlelight Mansions,' said the Social Worker. 'Here we are. Twelfth floor and the lifts won't be working. I hope you're fit.'

They climbed the concrete stairs. Rubbish lay about. People had scrawled ugly things on the walls. On every floor the lift had a board saying out of order hung across it with chains. Most of the chains were broken, too, so that the boards hung crooked. All was silent.

Then, as they walked more slowly up the final flights of stairs, the silence ceased. Sounds began to be threaded into it; thin, busy sounds that became more persistent as they turned at the twelfth landing and met a fluttery excited chorus. Across the narrow space were huge heaps. Bundles and crates and boxes were stacked high under tarpaulins with only the narrowest of alleys to lead up to the splintery front door of Henry Wu's flat. A second door of diamonds of metal was fastened across this. Nailed to the wall, on top of all the bundles, were two big makeshift birdcages like sideways chickenhouses and inside them dozens of birds – red and blue and green and yellow – making as much noise as a school playground.

'Oh dear,' said the Social Worker, 'here we go again. The Council got them all moved once but the Wus just put them back; they pretend they don't understand. Good afternoon, Mrs Wu.'

A beautiful, flat Chinese woman had come to the door and stood behind the metal diamonds. She did not look in the least like a Black Belt in judo. She was very thin and small and wore bedroom slippers, a satin dress and three cardigans. She bowed.

'I've just called for a chat and to bring you Henry's kind friend who is trying to help him.'

Mrs Wu took out a key and then clattered back the metal gate and smiled and bowed a great deal and you couldn't tell what she was thinking. From the flat behind her there arose the most terrible noise of wailing, screeching and whirring, and Pratt thought that Jackson had been right about machines. A smell wafted out, too. A sweetish, dryish, spicy smell which sent a long thrill down Pratt's spine. It smelled of far, far away.

'You have a great many belongings out here,' said the Social Worker, climbing over a great many more as they made their way down the passage into the living-room. In the living-room were more again, and an enormous Chinese family wearing many layers of clothes and sitting sewing among electric fires. Two electric sewing-machines whizzed and a tape of Chinese music plinked and wailed, full-tilt. Another, different tape wailed back through the open kitchen door where an old lady was gazing into steaming pans on a stove. There were several birdcages hanging from hooks, a fish-tank by the window and a rat-like object looking out from a bundle of hay in a cage. It had one eye half-shut as if it had a headache. Henry Wu was regarding this rat.

The rest of the family all fell silent, rose to their feet and bowed. 'Hello, Henry,' said Pratt, but Henry did not look round, even when his mother turned her sweet face on him and sang out a tremendous Chinese torrent.

Tea came in glasses. Pratt sat and drank his as the Social Worker talked to Mrs Wu and the other ladies, and a small fat Chinese gentleman, making little silk buttons without even having to watch his hands, watched Pratt. After a time he shouted something and a girl came carrying a plate. On the plate were small grey eggs with a skin on them. She held them out to Pratt.

'Hwile,' said the Chinese gentleman, his needle stitching like Magic. 'Kwile.'

'Oh yes,' said Pratt. (Whale?)

'Eat. Eat.'

'I'm not very . . .'

But the Social Worker glared. 'Quail,' she said.

'Eggs don't agree . . .' said Pratt. (Aren't quails snakes?) He imagined a tiny young snake curled inside each egg. I'd rather die, he thought, and saw that for the first time Henry Wu was looking at him from his corner. So was the rat.

So were the fish, the birds, Mrs Wu, the fat gentleman and all the assorted aunts. He ate the egg which went down glup, like an oval leather pill. Everyone smiled and nodded and the plate was offered again.

He ate another egg and thought, two snakes. They'll breed. I will die. He took a great swig of tea and smiled faintly. Everyone in the room then, except the rat, the fish and Henry, began to laugh and twitter and talk. The old woman slipper-sloppered in from the kitchen bringing more things to eat in dolls' bowls. They were filled with little chippy things and spicy, hot, juicy bits. She pushed them at Pratt. 'Go on,' said the Social Worker. 'Live dangerously.'

Pratt ate. Slowly at first. It was delicious. 'It's not a bit like the Take-Away,' he said, eating faster. This made the Chinese laugh. 'Take-Away, Take-Away,' they said. 'Sweet-and-Sour,' said Mrs Wu. 'Not like Sweet-and-Sour,' and everyone made tut-tutting noises which meant, 'I should just hope not.' Mrs Wu then gave Pratt a good-luck charm made of brass and nodded at him as if she admired him.

'She's thanking you for taking Henry out,' said the Social Worker as they went down all the stairs again.

'She probably thinks I'm a lunatic,' said Pratt, 'taking Henry out. Much good it's done.'

'You don't know yet.'

'Well, he's not exactly talking, is he? Or doing anything. He's probably loopy. She probably thinks I'm loopy, too.'

'She wouldn't let you look after him if she thought you were loopy.'

'Maybe she wants rid of him. She's hoping I'll kidnap him. I'm not looking after him any more if he can't get up and say hello. Or even smile. After all those terrible afternoons. Well, I've got exams next term. I've got no time. I'll have to think of myself all day and every day from now on, thank goodness.'

And the next term it was so. Pratt gave never a thought to Henry Wu except sometimes when the birds began to be seen about the school gardens again and to swoop under the eaves of the chapel. Swallows, he thought, immigrants. And he remembered him when his parents took him out to a Chinese restaurant on his birthday.

'Oh no – not those,' he said.

'They are the greatest Chinese treat you can have,' said his father. 'Quails' eggs.'

'Aren't they serpents?'

'Serpents? Don't you learn *any* general knowledge at that school? They're birds' eggs. Have some Sweet-and-Sour.'

'The Chinese don't have Sweet-and-Sour. It was made up for the tourists.'

'Really? Where did you hear that?'

'My Social Work.'

The exams came and went as exams do and Pratt felt light-headed and light-hearted. He came out of the last one with Jackson and said, 'Whee – let's go and look at the river.'

'I feel great. Do you?' he said.

Jackson said he felt terrible. He'd failed everything. He'd spent too much time spring-cleaning old Nellie. He knew he had.

'I expect I've failed, too,' said Pratt, but he felt he hadn't. The exams had been easy. He felt very comfortable and pleased with himself and watched the oily river sidle by, this way and that way, slopping up against the arches of the bridge, splashy from the barges. 'What shall we do?' he asked Jackson. 'Shall we go on the river?'

'I'd better go over and see if old Nellie's in,' said Jackson. 'I promised. Sorry. You go.'

Pratt stood for a while and the old lady with the shopping-trolley went by. 'Lolling about,' she said.

'I'm sorry about your flour,' said Pratt. Filled with happiness because the exams were over he felt he ought to be nice to the woman.

But she hurried on. Pratt watched her crossing the bridge and found his feet following. He made for Candlelight Mansions.

'Does Henry want to come to the park?' he asked a little girl who peered through the diamonds. Her face was like a white violet and her fringe was flimsy as a paintbrush. There was a kerfuffle behind her and Mrs Wu came forward to usher him inside.

If I go in it'll be quails' eggs and hours of bowing, thought Pratt. 'I'll wait here,' he said firmly. Mrs Wu disappeared and after a time Henry was produced, again muffled to the nose in the scarlet padding.

'It's pretty warm out,' said Pratt, but Mrs Wu only nodded and smiled.

In the park Pratt felt lost without a book and Henry marched wordlessly, as far ahead as possible. The ice-cream kiosk was open now and people were sitting on the metal chairs. Pigeons clustered round them in flustery clouds.

'Horrible,' said Pratt, catching up with Henry. 'Rats with wings. I'll get you a Coke but we'll drink it over there by the grass – hey! Where are you going?'

Henry, not stopping for the pigeons, was away to the slope of green grass that led down to the water. On the grass and all over the water was a multitude of birds and all the ducks of the park, diving ducks and pelicans and geese and dabchicks and water-hens and mallards. Old ducks remembering and new little ducks being shown the summer for the first time. Some of the new ducks were so new they were still covered with fluff – white fluff, fawn fluff, yellow fluff and even black fluff, like decorations on a hat. The proud parent ducks had large Vs of water rippling out behind them and small Vs rippled behind all the following babies. Henry Wu stood still.

Then round the island on the lake there came a huge, drifting meringue.

It was followed by another, but this one had a long neck sweeping up from it with a proud head on the end and a brilliant orange beak and two black nostrils, the shape of Henry Wu's eyes.

The first meringue swelled and fluffed itself and a tall neck and wonderful head emerged from that one, too.

Suddenly Henry pointed a short padded arm at these amazing

things and, keeping it stiff, turned his face up to Pratt and looked at him very intently.

'Swan,' said Pratt. 'They're swans. They're all right, aren't they? Hey – but don't do that. They're not so all right that you ought to go near them.'

'Get that boy back,' shouted a man. 'They'll knock him down. They're fierce, them two.'

'Nasty things, swans,' said someone else.

But Henry was off, over the little green hooped fence, running at the swans as they stepped out of the water on their black macintosh feet and started up the slope towards him. They lowered their necks and started to hiss. They opened their great wings.

'Oh, help,' said Pratt.

'It's all right,' said the man. 'I'm the Warden. I'll get him. Skin him alive, too, if they don't do it first,' and he ran down the slope.

But the swans did not skin Henry Wu alive. As he ran right up to them they stopped. They turned their heads away as if they were thinking. They shifted from one big black leathery foot to another and stopped hissing. Then they opened their wings wider still and dropped them gently and carefully back in place. They had a purple band round each left leg. One said 888. White swans, purple band, orange beaks, red Henry Wu, all on the green grass with the water and the willows about them, all sparkling and swaying.

'Bless him – isn't that nice now?' said the crowd, as the Warden of the swans gathered up Henry and brought him back under his arm.

'You'll get eaten one day,' said the Warden, 'you'll go getting yourself harmed,' but he seemed less angry than he might.

On the way home Henry did not look at Pratt but sat with him on the long seat just inside the bus. It was a seat for three people and Henry sat as far away as possible. But it was the same seat.

Then Pratt went on his summer holidays and when he came back the exam results were out and they were not marvellous. He stuffed miserably about in the house. When Jackson called –

Jackson had done rather well – he said that he was busy, which he wasn't.

But he made himself busy the next term, stodging glumly along, and took the exams all over again.

'Aren't you going to see your Chinese Demon any more?' asked Jackson afterwards. 'Come and meet old Nellie.'

'No thanks.'

'She says to bring you.'

'No thanks.'

But when the results came out this time, they were very good. He had more than passed.

Pratt said, 'How's Nellie?'

'Oh, fine. Much better tempered.'

'Was she bad tempered? You never said.'

'How's Henry Wu? Did you ever get him talking?'

'No. He was loopy.'

But it was a fine frosty day and the sun for the moment was shining and Pratt went to the park and over the grass to the lakeside where one of the swans came sliding around the island and padded about on the slope, marking time and looking at him.

It dazzled. The band round its leg said 887. 'Where's your husband?' said Pratt. 'Or wife or whatever? Are you hungry or something?'

The sun went in and the bare trees rattled. The swan looked a bit lonely and he thought he might go and get it some bread. Instead he took a bus back over the bridge and went to Candle-light Mansions.

They've probably forgotten me, he thought as he rang the bell. The bundles and the birdcages had gone from the landing. He rattled the steel mesh. They've probably moved, he thought. They'll have gone back to China.

But he was welcomed like a son.

'Can I take Henry out?'

Bowings, grinnings, buttonings-up of Henry who had not grown one millimetre.

'Where's the rat?' Pratt asked.

'Nwee-sance,' said Mrs Wu.

'Neeoo-sance,' said the fat gentleman. 'Nee-oosance. Council told them go.'

But the flat was now a jungle of floating paper kites and plants with scarlet dragons flying about in them, mixed with Father Christmases, Baby Jesuses and strings of Christmas tinsel. In the kitchen the old lady stirred the pots to a radio playing *O Come, All Ye Faithful*. Henry, seeing everyone talking together, sat down under a sewing-machine.

'Has he said anything yet?' asked Pratt, eating juicy bits with chopsticks. Everyone watched the juicy bits falling off the chopsticks and laughed. Now and then, when anything reached his mouth successfully, they congratulated him. They ignored the question, which meant that Henry had not.

It was cold in the street and very cold as they stood at the bus stop. Pratt had forgotten that the days were now so short, and already it was beginning to get dark. Far too late to go to the park, he thought. The bus was cold, too, and dirty, and all the people looked as if they'd like to be warm at home in bed. 'Come on – we'll go upstairs and sit in the front,' said Pratt and they looked down on the dreary York Road with all its little half-alive shops and, now and then, a string of coloured Christmas lights across it with most of the bulbs broken or missing. Some shops had spray-snowflakes squirted on the windows. It looked like cleaning-fluid someone had forgotten to wash off. Real snowflakes were beginning to fall and looked even dingier than the shop-window ones.

I should have taken him over the river to see some real Christmas lights in Regent Street, thought Pratt. There's nothing over here.

But there came a bang.

A sort of rushing, blustering, flapping before the eyes.

The glass in the window in front of them rattled like an earthquake and something fell down in front of the bus.

There were screeching brakes and shouting people and Pratt and Henry were flung forward on to the floor.

As they picked themselves up they saw people running into the road below. 'Something fell out of the sky,' said Pratt to Henry Wu. 'Something big. Like a person. Come on – we've got to get out.'

But it was not a person. It was a swan that sat heavy and large and streaked with a dark mark across its trailing wings in the very middle of the road.

'Swan, swan – it's a swan!' Everybody was shouting. 'It's killed itself. It's dead. Frozen dead with fright.'

'It hit a wire,' said someone else – it was the woman with the shopping trolley – 'I saw it. An overhead wire from the lights. They oughtn't to be allowed. They're not worth it. They could have electrocuted that bus.'

'It's killed it, anyway,' said Jackson, who seemed to be with her. 'It's stone dead.'

But the swan was not dead. Suddenly it decided it was not. It heaved up its head and wings and lolloped itself to the side of the road and flopped down again, looking round slowly, with stunned wonder, opening and shutting its orange beak, though with never a sound.

'It was migrating,' said the man from a chipshop.

'Swans don't migrate, they stay put,' said a man from a laundry.

'Anyone'd migrate this weather,' said a man selling whelks and eels. 'Look, it's got a number on it. It's from the park. Look, it's put itself all tidy on the yellow line.'

'Out of the way,' said a policeman. 'Now then. Stand aside. We'll want a basket.' A laundry basket was brought and someone lent the policeman a strong pair of gloves.

'Clear a space,' he said and approached the swan, which proved it was not dead by landing the policeman a thwacking blow with its wing.

'Have to be shot,' said a dismal man from a bike-shop. 'Well, it's no chicken.'

'Course it's no chicken,' said the woman with the trolley. 'If it was a chicken it'd be coming home with me and a bag of chips.'

And then a girl with purple hair began to shriek and scream

because she didn't believe in eating animals, which included birds.

'Anyway, all swans belong to the Queen,' said the trolley-lady. 'I heard it on Gardeners' Question Time.'

'I'm going crazy,' said the policeman, who had withdrawn to a little distance to talk into his radio-set. 'If they all belong to the Queen I hope she'll come and collect this one. I'm not sure I can. Move along now. We have to keep the traffic moving. We can't hold up London for a swan.'

One or two cars sidled by, but otherwise nobody moved. It was a strange thing. In the middle of the dead dark day and the dead dark street sat the open laundry basket and the shining, mute bird with its angel feathers. The road fell quiet.

Then Henry Wu stepped forward, small inside his padding, and put short arms round the bulk of the swan's back and lifted it lightly into the basket where it fluffed up its feathers like rising bread and gazed round proudly at the people.

'Heaven on high!' said everyone. 'The weight!'

'His mother's a Black Belt,' said Pratt proudly.

'That Chinese'll have to be washed,' said the trolley-lady. 'They'd better both come home with us, Jackson, and I'll give them their tea.'

But Pratt and Henry did not go home with old Nellie on that occasion because the policeman asked them to go back to the station with him and the swan. If Henry would be so kind as to assist him, he said. And Henry stroked the swan's docile head twice and then folded it down with its neck behind it – and a big strong neck it was, though very arrangeable – and quickly put down the lid.

The Park Warden came to the police station and he and Henry and Pratt and the swan then went on to the park, where the swan took to the water like a whirlwind and faded into the dark.

'Off you go, 888,' said the Warden. 'There's your missus to meet you. You wouldn't have seen her again if you'd not dropped among friends.

'They can't take off, you see,' he said to the two boys, 'except on water. They're like the old sea-planes.'

Pratt watched the two white shapes fade with the day. 'They're strange altogether, swans,' said the Warden. 'Quite silent!'

'Is it true they sing when they're dying?' asked Pratt. 'I read it. In poetry.'

'Well, that one's not dying then,' said the Warden. 'Gone without a sound. It's funny – most living creatures make some sort of noise to show they're happy. Goodbye, Henry. There'll be a job for you with creatures one day. I dare say when you grow up you'll get my job. You have the touch.'

On the bus back over the bridge to Candlelight Mansions Henry sat down next to Pratt on a double seat and, staring in front of him, said in a high, clear, Chinese-English voice, 'Hwan.

'Hwan,' he said. 'Hwan, hwan, hwan, swan. Swan, swan, SWAN,' until Pratt had to say, 'Shut up, Henry, or they'll think you're loopy.'

(Trevor Nichols read this story on *Woman's Hour* in October 1990.)

THE SAINT

—— ◆ ——

Antonia White

Children, as you know, are supposed to have a special power of discerning saints. A great many years ago, when I was a child at a convent school, a number of us were certain that we had divined one in our very midst.

The name of the saint was Mother Lucilla Ryan. She was about thirty years old, very beautiful in a way that was both spiritual and witty, and she was dying of consumption.

We came back from our long summer holidays to find that the consumption, which for months had moved stealthily, almost invisibly, had begun to gallop. It was too late to send her abroad to the Order's sanatorium at Montreux. She was to die here, in the community infirmary, among her own friends.

Mother Lucilla had been in direct charge of the Junior School, so that we felt her to be peculiarly *our* saint. The tiny notes she scribbled us now and then, exquisitely written notes pencilled on scraps of squared paper torn from an exercise book, we slipped reverently into our missals, convinced that one day they would be sought-after relics. Charlotte, I remember, even went so far as to print on hers 'Actual writing of the Blessed Lucilla Ryan'. We were amazed at her boldness, but we secretly felt that it would be justified.

I think we were just a little disappointed that Mother Lucilla was dying in her bed and not at the stake. Canonisation, we knew, was a long and tedious process, and we wanted quick results.

Martyrdom, as everyone knows, is the royal road to sainthood, and we would have trusted Mother Lucilla under any torture. Her bravery, indeed, was almost legendary. Some of the Senior School could remember how she had caught her finger in the see-saw one day during recreation. Without so much as a grimace, she had folded her wounded hand in her sleeve and stood for the rest of the hour, directing games as usual, with that odd, delicate smile of hers. Not until she had marshalled the children back indoors did anyone know that the top half of one finger had been torn right away.

It can never be an easy task to succeed a saint, especially in the critical eyes of twenty small girls, but few people could have failed more conspicuously than poor Mother MacDowell. There was nothing to appeal to the most charitable imagination about our new mistress. To begin with, she was very plain; small and stocky, with a red, hard-bitten face and thick, refracting glasses. Through these amazing glasses, her small, dull eyes appeared enormous, like the eyes of an insect. Somehow or other we knew that her father had gone blind and that her parents had made her spend an hour every day alone in the dark, so that if she, too, were to go blind she would be less helpless. Had we heard such a story about Mother Lucilla, it would be one more legend of her saintly patience. But it was part of the general unfortunateness of Mother MacDowell that everything that happened to her should seem dull, common, and even rather ridiculous. The very tasks she was given by the community seemed to be chosen to display her at her worst. Besides looking after us, she was mistress of needlework for the whole school, though, even with her glasses, she could hardly see to thread a needle. Her red hands, speckled with pricks, looked clumsier than ever, moving stiffly and painfully over the gauzy linen we were embroidering for altar cloths. Everything about her was unromantic. Her habit was the shabbiest in the convent. Her rosary was broken in three places and mended with wire. She suffered from titanic colds that made her look plainer than ever. And, to crown all, her Christian name was Keziah.

We were prepared to receive her with a cold dislike, but there was something about Mother MacDowell's attitude to our adored Mother Lucilla that ripened the dislike into hostility. I don't mean that she ever said anything uncharitable about Mother Lucilla or that she did not encourage us to pray for her. But the sight of any extravagant devotion, and, above all, any mention of the word 'saint', roused her to unwonted anger.

The four o'clock recreation, when we did not play games, but sat about with our mistress, munching thick slices of bread and jam, was always a time for discussion. I am afraid it was also a favourite time for baiting Mother MacDowell. One afternoon, as we sat round her under the plane-tree on the dusty, stony, Junior School playground, Charlotte said, raising innocent eyes:

'Mother MacDowell, do you think Mother Lucilla is a saint?'

'It is not for us to say who are saints and who are not. That is for God to declare, through the mouth of the Church,' said Mother MacDowell piously.

'But don't you think Mother Lucilla's awfully holy?' persisted Charlotte, who had been a great favourite of Mother Lucilla's, if saints can be said to have favourites.

'Only God can know that. We all need infinite mercy. No doubt we shall all have a great many surprises at the Last Day.'

We looked at each other. The five-minute bell rang.

'Come along, Charlotte, eat your bread and jam. You haven't even begun it,' said Mother MacDowell sharply.

'I don't want it,' said Charlotte self-consciously.

'Don't be absurd, child. Be thankful to the dear Lord who sent it you, and eat up your good food.'

'But – Mother—' Charlotte wriggled.

'Well, child?'

'I wanted to do a penance for Mother Lucilla. You said we all needed prayers. So I thought I'd give up my *goûter* for her.'

We gave Charlotte admiring glances. None of us had thought of doing that.

'God does not want penances of that sort,' said Mother MacDowell very decidedly. 'He would far rather that, instead of showing off like that, you made an act of humility and ate your *goûter* like the others. That would be a real penance.'

Charlotte turned crimson and began to eat her bread in small, martyred bites. Although we could not resist a faint pang of pleasure in seeing her scored off, the general feeling was that Mother MacDowell had shown a very mean spirit. A week later, Mother Lucilla died. As a great privilege, we were allowed to see her as she lay among the lilies in the Lady Chapel that had once been a ballroom and that still had gilt garlands of leaves and little violins on the walls. We filed round the bier on tiptoe, in our black veils and gloves, passing from hand to hand the heavy silver *asperges* and clumsily sprinkling drops of holy water on Mother Lucilla's black habit, that had become sculptured and unreal like a statue's robe. Not one of us doubted, as we looked at her lying there, pale as wax and still smiling, as if she had just been told some holy secret, that we were looking at a saint.

The morning she was buried they dressed us in the white serge uniforms that we wore only on big feast days. Carrying candles that burnt with a faint, nearly invisible flame in the May sunlight, the whole school passed in long ranks under the alley of limes that led to the nuns' cemetery. At the graveside we formed a hollow square, with the younger ones in the centre. Mother Lucilla's four tall brothers, who were all officers in the Irish Guards, carried the coffin; the little boys from the Poor School, transformed into a choir with white surplices, chirped the 'De Profundis' like so many sparrows. We peered with respectful curiosity into the hollow grave. It was lined with spruce boughs that had a solemn, unforgettable smell. Father Kelly was praying, in his rich voice that sounded splendid out of doors, that all the angels might come to meet her at the doors of heaven; the four tall brothers were paying out the bands of the deal coffin that looked like a soldier's, when the wonderful thing happened. As the nuns intoned the Amen, a white butterfly flew up out of the grave, hung for a minute so that we could all see it, then spiralled away, with a flight as purposeful as a bird's, right up into the blue air.

We looked round curiously. Some of the nuns were gazing

after the butterfly. Mother MacDowell, I noticed, was not one of these. Her red face was bowed and impassive, though the sun danced furiously in her spectacles. But Reverend Mother, who had been weeping a little, lifted her head, and, looking straight at the Junior School, gave us a smile that was positively triumphant. Almost giddy with excitement and happiness, we smiled back. It was a sign, if ever there was one.

We were rather subdued for the rest of the day. Even poor Mother MacDowell did not find us quite so impossible as usual. At tea-time recreation we gathered round her in quite a friendly way, while our conversation turned quite naturally on saints. But, today, we were careful to mention no names.

Charlotte, sitting astride a branch of the plane-tree, bent down to ask, very politely:

'How long does it take for a saint to get canonised?'

'Many years, my dear child – centuries sometimes.'

'Like the English martyrs,' put in Laura. 'They've only just been done, haven't they, Mother?'

There was a murmur of disappointment. Then someone had a bright thought.

'But what about the Blessed Marie Madeleine Pérot?' said a voice falling over itself with excitement. 'She's not just Blessed, she's Saint now, and I know a girl whose grandmother was at the Sacred Heart when Mother Pérot was Mistress-General, and the grandmother's still alive.'

We sighed with relief.

'But it's awfully difficult, isn't it, Mother?' said Laura the pessimist. 'There's the Devil's Advocate, and they've got to prove major miracles worked by direct intercession and all that, haven't they?'

Mother MacDowell gave a small, dour smile at this – very different from the angelic smile of Mother Lucilla.

'It's not the miracles that matter so much, my dear. They're only outward signs. There have been big saints who worked no miracles and little saints who worked many. No, what matters is that the person should have attained heroic sanctity on this earth.'

Heroic sanctity? It sounded very difficult indeed. We were quiet for a minute, knitting our brows. Then one by one we remembered Mother Lucilla's severed finger. If that was not heroic sanctity, what was? But suddenly our thoughts were turned violently back to earth. There was a noise of breaking wood, a shrill scream and a crash. Charlotte had fallen off her perch in the plane-tree and was lying on the stones. We drew back, frightened. Mother MacDowell hesitated for a second before she advanced and picked Charlotte up. Then she sat down with Charlotte on her lap while the rest of us stood in a gaping circle. Charlotte's knee bled in streams; Mother MacDowell's habit was already wet and shining. But it was at the nun's face and not at Charlotte's cut knee that we were all looking. For Mother MacDowell had turned from red to a dreadful greenish white. We knew what it was – she was one of those people who cannot bear the sight of blood. But there was no pity in us that day; we all remembered Mother Lucilla, who never flinched at the sight of blood, not even her own. But, to do justice to Mother MacDowell, she managed to control herself. Her lips were trembling, she could not speak, but she produced her coarse white handkerchief as big as a table napkin, and began to wipe away the dirt from the cut knee. Finally, having roughly bandaged Charlotte, who behaved with a stoicism worthy of Mother Lucilla herself, she told off four of us to take our wounded friend to the infirmary. We waited in interested silence while the infirmary sister unwound the handkerchief. The bleeding had entirely stopped. The sister examined the leg carefully; then she began to laugh. 'Why, you little sillies, there's not even a cut. Run along, Charlotte. There's nothing the matter with you – nothing except a *dirty* knee, that is.'

It was perfectly true. There were specks of brown gravel on Charlotte's knee, and that was all. There was not even a spot of blood on the handkerchief.

But when the five of us were in the garden again, Charlotte beckoned us round her, with an air of great solemnity.

'Swear you won't tell – or, rather, don't swear – promise,

because it's something holy.'

We promised eagerly.

'Well, you know there *was* a cut on my knee – you all saw how it bled. And it hurt awfully.'

We nodded.

'Well, when Mother MacDowell began to wipe it with her handkerchief, there was suddenly an awful pain in it, as if it had been burnt or something – and then I just *knew* the cut wasn't there any more.'

'But, Charlotte,' I gasped, 'if that really happened – it was a—'

She seized my hand.

'I know,' she said feverishly, 'it was – a miracle.'

We stared at her with awe-struck admiration.

But Laura, the rationalist, said:

'Who worked it then? Someone's got to work a miracle. Did you pray to anyone?'

'Well – not exactly. But I had my rosary – the one that touched Her – in my pocket.'

It was quite enough for us. Mother Lucilla was as good as canonised in our eyes.

'Promise not to tell yet,' implored Charlotte.

We promised. And we certainly kept the letter of our promise. But, back on the playground, someone asked Mother MacDowell in an off-hand kind of way:

'How big does a major miracle have to be. Would it be a major miracle if a broken arm got set by itself? Or if an awfully deep cut suddenly healed up of its own accord?'

But Mother MacDowell turned fiery red and snapped out: 'That is enough talk about miracles, children. You are all thoroughly over-excited. You will talk French at supper and go to bed half an hour earlier if this goes on.'

We hastily quitted the subject of miracles. Just as we were forming into file to go back to the house, one of the Senior School came running towards Mother MacDowell. She stopped, fumbled in her pocket, and produced a rosary.

'I found this in the Junior School benches, Mother. Does it

belong to any of your children?'

The rosary was of the kind rich parents give their children for First Communion presents; carved amethyst beads threaded on a gold chain. Mother MacDowell held it up by the tip of her fingers; had it been any secular object, one would have said she held it disdainfully.

'And whose is this?' she asked. 'I seem to have seen—'

But Charlotte was already skipping forward to claim her property.

I suppose it must be thirty or forty years since it all happened. Laura is a Carmelite nun, and Charlotte, who married a millionaire, and a Protestant at that, is a grandmother. I might even have forgotten all about it if I had not read in my *Universe* yesterday that the Canonisation of the Blessed Keziah MacDowell had just been ratified by the Holy See.

(Joanna McCallum read this story on *Woman's Hour* in April 1986.)

TEENAGERS

CLARA'S DAY

◆

Penelope Lively

When Clara Tilling was fifteen and a half she took off all her clothes one morning in school assembly. She walked naked through the lines of girls, past the Headmistress at her lectern and the other staff ranged behind her, and out into the entrance lobby. She had left off her bra and pants already, so that all she had to do was unbutton her blouse, remove it and drop it to the floor, and then undo the zipper of her skirt and let that fall. She slipped her feet out of her shoes at the same time and so walked barefoot as well as naked. It all happened very quickly. One or two people giggled and a sort of rustling noise ran through the assembly hall, like a sudden wind among trees. The Head hesitated for a moment – she was reading out the tennis team list – and then went on again, firmly. Clara opened the big glass doors and let herself out.

The entrance lobby was empty. The floor was highly polished and she could see her own reflection, a foreshortened pink blur. There was a big bright modern painting on one wall and several comfortable chairs for waiting parents, arranged round an enormous rubber plant and ashtrays on chrome stalks. Clara had sat there herself once, with her mother, waiting for an interview with the Head.

She walked along the corridor to her form-room, which was also quite empty, with thick gold bars of sunlight falling on the desks and a peaceful feeling, as though no one had been here for a long time nor ever would come. Clara opened the cupboard in the corner, took out one of the science overalls and put it on, and then sat down at her desk. After about a minute Mrs Mayhew came in carrying her clothes and her shoes. She said, 'I should put these on now, Clara,' and stood beside her while she did so. 'Would you like to go home?' she asked, and when Clara said that she wouldn't, thank you, Mrs Mayhew went on briskly. 'Right you are, then, Clara. You'd better get on with some prep, then, till the first period.'

All morning people kept coming up to her to say, 'Well done!' or just to pat her on the back. She was a celebrity right up till dinner-time but after that it tailed off a bit. Half-way through the morning one of the prefects came in and told her the Head wanted to see her straight after school.

The Head's study was more like a sitting-room, except for the big paper-strewn desk that she sat behind. There were squashy chairs and nice pictures on the walls and photos of the Head's husband and her children on the mantelpiece and a Marks & Spencer carrier bag dumped down in one corner. The window was open on to the playing-fields from which came the cheerful incomprehensible noise, like birds singing, of people calling to each other. Except for the distant rumble of traffic you wouldn't think you were in London.

The Head was busy writing when Clara came in; she just looked up to say, 'Hello, Clara. Sit down. Do you mind if I just finish these reports off? I won't be a minute.' She went on writing and Clara sat and looked at the photo of her husband, who had square sensible-looking glasses and her three boys who were all the same but different sizes. Then the Head slapped the pile of reports together and pushed her chair back. 'There . . . Well now . . . So what was all that about, this morning?'

'I don't know,' said Clara.

The Head looked at her, thoughtfully, and Clara looked back. Just before the silence became really embarrassing the Head pushed a hand through her short untidy fair hair, making it even untidier, and said, 'I daresay you don't. Were you trying to attract attention?'

Clara considered. 'Well, I would, wouldn't I? Doing a thing like that. I mean – you'd be bound to.'

The Head nodded. 'Quite. Silly question.'

'Oh no,' said Clara hastily. 'I meant you'd be bound to attract attention, not be bound to be trying to.'

The Head, a linguist, also considered. 'Well . . . That's a fine point, I think. How do you feel about it now?'

Clara tried to examine her feelings which slithered away like fish. In the end she said, 'I don't really feel anything,' which was, in a way, truthful.

The Head nodded again. She looked at her husband on the mantelpiece, almost as though asking for advice. 'Everything all right at home?'

'Oh fine,' Clara assured her. 'Absolutely fine.'

'Good,' said the Head. 'Of course . . . I was thinking, there are quite a lot of people in Four B with separated parents, aren't there? Bryony and Susie Tallance and Rachel.'

'And Midge,' said Clara. 'And Lucy Potter.'

'Yes. Five. Six, with you.'

'Twenty-five per cent,' said Clara. 'Just about.'

'Quite. As a matter of fact that's the national average, did you know? One marriage in four.'

'No I didn't actually,' said Clara.

'Well, it is, I'm afraid. Anyway . . .' She looked over at her husband again. 'You're not fussing about O-levels, are you?'

'Not really,' said Clara. 'I don't *like* exams, but I don't mind as much as some people.'

'Your mocks were fine,' said the Head. 'Physics and chemistry could have been a bit better. But there shouldn't be any great problems there. So . . . Are you still going around with Liz Raymond?'

'Mostly,' said Clara. 'And Stephanie.'

'I want people to come and talk to me if there's anything they're worried about,' said the Head. 'Even things that may seem silly. You know. It doesn't have to be large obvious things. Exams and stuff. Anything.'

'Yes,' said Clara.

The phone rang. The Head picked it up and said no, she hadn't, and yes, she'd be along as soon as she could and tell them to wait.

She put the receiver down and said, 'It wasn't like you, Clara, was it? I mean – there are a few people one wouldn't be *all* that surprised, if they suddenly did something idiotic or unexpected. But you aren't really like that, are you?'

Clara agreed that she wasn't, really.

'I'll be writing a note to your mother. And if you have an urge to do something like that again come and have a talk to me first, right?' The Head smiled and Clara smiled back. That was all, evidently. Clara got up and left. As she was closing the door she saw the Head looking after her, not smiling now, her expression rather bleak.

Most of the school had gone home but all those in Clara's form who had boyfriends at St Benet's, which was practically everyone, were hanging around the bus station deliberately not catching buses because St Benet's came out half an hour later. Clara hung around for a bit too, just to be sociable, and then got on to her bus. She sat on the top deck by herself and looked down on to the pavements. It was very hot; everyone young had bare legs, roadmenders were stripped to the waist, everywhere there was flesh – brown backs and white knees and glimpses of the hair under people's arms and the clefts between breasts and buttocks. In the park, the grass was strewn with sunbathers; there were girls in bikinis sprawled like starfish face down with a rag of material between their legs and the strings of the top half undone. Clara, with no bra or pants on, could feel warm air washing around between her skin and her clothes. Coming down the stairs as the bus approached her stop she had to hold her skirt in case it blew up.

Her mother was already home. She worked part-time as a dentist's receptionist and had what were called flexible hours, which meant more or less that she worked when it suited her. Afternoons, nowadays, often didn't suit because Stan, her friend, who was an actor, was only free in the afternoons.

Stan wasn't there today, though. Clara came into the kitchen where her mother was drinking tea and looking at a magazine. 'Hi!' she said. 'Any news?' which was what she said most days.

Clara said that there was no news and her mother went on reading an article in the magazine called, Clara could see upside down across the table, 'Orgasm – Fact or Fantasy?' Presently she yawned, pushed the magazine over to Clara and went upstairs to have a bath. Clara had another cup of tea and leafed through the magazine, which was mostly advertisements for tampons and deodorants, and then began to do her prep.

The Head's letter came a couple of days later. Clara heard the post flop on to the doormat and when she looked over the banister she knew at once what the typed envelope must be. At the same moment Stan, who had stayed the night, came out of her mother's room on the way to the bathroom. He wore underpants and had a towel slung round his neck like a football scarf, and was humming to himself. When he saw her he said, 'Wotcha! How's tricks, then?' and Clara pulled her dressing-gown more closely round her and said, 'Fine, thanks.'

'That's the stuff,' said Stan vaguely. 'Hey – I got you a couple of tickets for the show. Bring a friend, OK?' He was a stocky muscular man with a lot of black hair on his chest. The smell of him, across the landing, was powerful – a huge inescapable wave of man smell: sweat and aftershave and something you could not put your finger on. Clara always knew when he was in the house before she opened the sitting-room door because whiffs of him gushed about the place. She said, 'Thanks very much. That would be super,' and edged into her room.

When she came down they were both having breakfast. Her mother was just opening the post. She said, 'Coffee on the stove, lovey. Oh goody – my tax rebate's come.' She opened the Head's letter and began to read. First she stared at it with a puzzled look and then she began to laugh. She clapped her hand over her mouth, spluttering. 'I don't *believe* it!' she cried. 'Clara, I simply do not believe it! Stan, just listen to this . . . Isn't she the most incredible girl! Guess what she did! She took off all her clothes in school assembly and walked out starkers!' She handed the letter to Stan and went on laughing.

Stan read the letter. Grinning hugely, he looked up at Clara

'She'll have done it for a dare, I bet. Good on yer, Clara. Terrific! God – I wish I'd been there!' He patted Clara's arm and Clara froze. She went completely rigid, as though she had turned to cement, and when eventually she moved a leg it seemed as though it should make a cracking noise.

Her mother had stopped laughing and was talking again. '. . . the last thing anyone would have expected of you, lovey. You've always been such a prude. Ever since you were a toddler. Talk about modest! Honestly, Stan, she was hilarious, as a little kid – I can see her now, sitting on the beach at Camber clutching a towel around her in case anyone got a glimpse of her bum when she was changing. Aged ten. And when her bust grew she used to sit hunched over like a spoon so no one would notice it, and if she had to strip off for the doctor you'd have thought he'd been about to rape her, from her expression. Even now I can't get her out of the Victorian one-piece school regulation bathing costume – and it's not as though she's not got a nice shape . . .' – 'Smashing!' said Stan, slurping coffee – '. . . spot of puppy fat still but that's going, good hips, my legs if I may say so. Which is what makes this such an absolute scream. Honestly, sweetie, I wouldn't have thought you had it in you. I mean, I've not been allowed to see her in the buff myself since she was twelve. Honestly, I've wondered once or twice if there was something *wrong* with the girl.' Her mother beamed across the breakfast table. 'Anyway, old Mrs Whatsit doesn't seem to be making a fuss. She just thinks I ought to know. More coffee, anyone? God – look at the time! And I said I'd be in early today . . . I'm off. Leave the breakfast things, lovey – we'll do them later. Coming, Stan?'

Clara went on sitting at the table. She ate a piece of toast and drank her coffee. Her mother and Stan bustled about collecting her purse and his jacket and banged out of the house, shouting goodbye. The front gate clicked, the car door slammed, and then Clara began to cry, the tears dripping from her chin on to her folded arms and her face screwed up like a small child's.

(Fiona Mathieson read this story on *Woman's Hour* in March 1987.)

A MODEL DAUGHTER

◆

Clare Boylan

'Think!' said my friend Tilly one day when we were deep into a bottle of lunchtime Meursault; 'if we had had children when we ceased to be impervious virgins they would be seventeen by now. Seventeen or thereabouts. Lovely girls!'

For a moment before her words misted into grapey vapours I could see them sitting opposite us with shiny hair and loose frocks of Laura Ashley prints.

In her early youth Tilly had been very fast and a famous mistress. She was slower now and more faithful and our friendship was occasionally shadowed by a creeping sentimentality that made me fear she would one day rush away from me and into the arms of Jesus.

'Do you regret not having had children?' I said briskly.

'I would like a girl.' She was stubborn: 'Seventeen or so.'

'You could have one. You still could.' She was forty-five but friendship entitled her to lay claim to my age, which was not quite forty.

'Have one what, darling?' Her beautiful blue eyes always had the attractive daze of myopia but after lunch and wine they shimmered under a sea haze.

'A baby!'

'A baby?' She recoiled as if someone had just thrust a seeping member of the species on to her silk knee. 'Don't be revolting!'

'Babies are where children come from,' I pointed out; a little shortly, for I had a worry of my own.

'Not necessarily,' Tilly said. 'It seems to be absurd to go to such lengths. There are young girls everywhere. In primitive countries people drown them at birth. Still they outnumber the men.' She seized the bottle and shook the dregs, very fairly, into either glass. 'If I feel the need of a daughter, I daresay I can get one somewhere.'

'But where?'

Her confidence was shaken but only for a moment. 'A model agency!'

I had a daughter. It was my one secret from Tilly. Her name was Hester and she was seventeen. My daughter was born not of love, not even of sex, but of necessity. I married Victor when I was twenty and we were both pretending to be actors, knowing perfectly well that one day we would have to grow up and get ourselves proper jobs. Six months later, to everyone's surprise, he got a break and was summoned to America. He fell in love, to no one's surprise, with his leading lady. The divorce was quick and uncontested. Shamed by my failure I kept my mouth shut and my head down. I got a small settlement and descended into that curious widowhood of the heart which an early broken marriage brings.

I was too lethargic to work and faced a frugal living on my mean allowance. 'If you had a child,' my mother scolded, 'he would have to pay a proper maintenance.' Even in this I had failed. 'Well, I can't just manufacture a child!' I cried. Mother made a face, as if tasting some invisible treat inside her mouth. 'Pity,' she said.

'Dear Vic,' I wrote, alone in my little room by the gas fire. He no longer seemed dear to me. I had grown sullen and immune to attachments. 'I did not want to tell you this earlier as I had no desire to destroy your happiness as you have mine, but I am expecting our child. I am letting you know now only because money is short and it will be so difficult to work.'

Vic was generous. He was a successful actor now and relieved by my faint-heartedness. A card arrived, offering congratulations and a decent-sized cheque which was to be repeated monthly.

I didn't bother Vic much after that except in due course to announce that Hester had been born and from time to time when I badly needed a bit of extra money (for a furry coat in a really dreadful winter; for a Greek cruise because Tilly was urging me to accompany her) and then I would say that Hester had a little illness or needed her teeth straightened or that she was plaguing me for pony lessons. Once, after his second marriage had broken up, he wrote and asked if he could come and meet Hester. After a momentary panic I answered with a very firm 'no'. I had never asked him to come to her side when she was ill, I pointed out. It would be unfair of him to disturb our peaceful lives.

He accepted this, with a sort of written sigh. 'Just send me a picture of her,' he said. I was shaken, but underneath the dismay there grew a kind of excitement. I said earlier that I had grown immune to attachments. In fact it was merely romantic attachments to which I was resistant, and my friend Tilly consumed enough sexual adventure for both of us. I had a deep secret attachment to my Hester. As soon as Vic asked for her picture I realised that I too had longed to know what she looked like.

I began to carry a camera around. I sought Hester in restaurants, outside schools, in bus queues. One day I was seated in the park in the shade when a child came and looked at me; a solemn dark-eyed girl with pink dress and a little shoulder bag of white crochet work. I snapped the child and smiled at her. She stood quite still and graceful, fulfilling her role. I closed the shutter on my camera and closed my eyes too, to carry the moment past its limits so that she came right up to me and called me Mama. When I looked again, the girl was gone.

I wonder how often Victor looked at the picture I sent him, if he kept it in his breast pocket close to his heart; if he placed some of his hopes on that unknown child. I know I did. It helped to pass a decade swiftly and quite sweetly. Soon I was heading up to forty, the extremes of my youth gone (but not regretted) and I found myself thinking idly that Hester would be leaving school by now and we might be planning her college years. I liked this fantasy, for the placing of Hester in Oxford or Cambridge would make her actual absence more plausible and allow me to enjoy my dreams with no disturbance from the dull utilities of fact.

'Dear Vic,' I wrote, 'It is some time since I have been in touch but the years have flown and we were so busy, Hester and I, with work and school, that we had no time to consider the world outside our own little one. However, the news now is too big to keep to myself. Our girl has won a First to Oxford. I want you to know that I sustain no bitterness in regard to our marriage, for Hester has been a true compensation. I only wish I could indulge her with all the silly clothes students love and a little flat of her own where she could invite her grown-up friends for coffee.'

It would have been a better letter (I would have been a better person) without the embellishment of that final sentence but the truth is I got carried away and there really was a nice little flat which Tilly had been urging me to snap up.

Vic wrote back immediately. 'Wonderful news! Of course my daughter shall have everything she wants but this time I am determined to deliver it (and my congratulations!) in person.' He announced a date when he would arrive and named the restaurant where we would meet for a celebration dinner.

I suffered several moments of deep shock before my brain broke into demented activity. How should I forestall him? My first thought was a death. Hester dead in a tragic horseback accident! But he would want to see her burial place. Besides, I could not bear that loss myself. I could say she had gone abroad with friends for the summer. Vic was rich. He would insist on following her there.

Nothing I could think of was any use. All my little plans fell apart in the face of Victor's strength of purpose and superior cash flow. Besides, I did not entirely want to put him off for there was the bait of Hester's pocket money. I felt it was a point of honour to collect it safely.

On several occasions I was tempted to confide in Tilly but Tilly is like a viper on the subject of superficial friendships and I knew she would find it impossible to forgive my years of concealment. However, I stuck close to her in those worrying weeks, hoping that I might find the courage to blurt it all out or that she might inadvertently produce an anecdote or experience which would prove the solution to my dilemma. It was exactly four days before Vic's arrival that Tilly, in vino, produced her unlikely veritas of maternal regret and provided me with an answer.

A model agency! I had often glanced through fashion magazines when goaded by Tilly into visiting a hairdresser and I knew those purveyors of fantasy by sight. I was not especially interested in clothes so I gave my attention to the girls who showed them. Unlike Tilly, I did not envy them their taut busts and tiny backsides, their perfect skin and carefully arranged clouds of careless hair. It was their determination that made me wistful.

Their qualification, apart from beauty, which can be used or abused in so many ways, was epitomised by an enduring personality which helped them adhere to a diet regime of meagre, proteinous scraps, to drink prickly Perrier instead of easeful gin, to go to bed at ten o'clock rather than allow themselves to be lured on some exciting, promiscuous prowl. It was more or less how I had pictured Hester.

All I needed was a sweet young girl to help me through a single evening. I know Victor. His passions are burning but brief. Once he had met his daughter, he could peacefully forget all about her.

'I want a girl,' I told the telephone of the Modern Beauties Agency and I gave it the date; 'just for an evening.'

'Daywear, beach or evening?' said a voice.

'Just a simple dinner dress.' I was slightly taken aback.

'Own shoes or shoes supplied?'

'One was rather hoping she might have a pair of her own.'

'Size and colouring?'

I could be confident about this, at least. I described Hester as seventeen or thereabouts, tall but slim, with dark hair and a lily-pale skin.

'It's Carmen Miranda you want,' the telephone decided. 'Will you require a hairdresser and make-up artiste?'

'Carmen Miranda? Now wait a minute!'

'Thirty-five pounds an hour and VAT. To whom shall I make out the invoice?'

'Thirty-five pounds? But . . . ! Heavens!' I had anticipated that beauty might be remunerable at about four times the rate of skilled professional housework. I had put aside £50 for the evening. At this price it would cost about £200 – an impossible sum.

'Do you want to confirm that booking or make it provisional? Miss Carmen Miranda is our top professional model. She is very much in demand.'

'No! I mean, yes, I'm sure she is. The thing is, I don't think I have made myself quite clear.' I explained that I did not really require the services of their top professional model. What I wanted – *needed*, was an ingénue, an unspoilt young girl with little or no experience. And cheaper.

'The rate is standard,' said the voice, with a new, steely edge. 'Unless, of course, you want one of our new girls who have not yet completed their training.' She mentioned something that sounded like Poisoned Personality Course and added that these incomplete models could be rented hourly at a reduced rate of twelve pounds, for experience.

'Yes, yes,' I said eagerly. 'That's just right. A young girl, barely out of school. That sounds lovely.'

'All our girls are lovely.'

'I'm sure they are. Thank you so very much. You've got the description?'

'Yes, that's no problem.'

'You've been very kind. Can you tell me who to expect?'

'I'll have to see who's free.'

On the evening of our meeting I felt more excited than on my first date with Victor. Acquiring Hester's childhood photograph had been a rewarding experience. Now I was to meet her in the flesh.

I was looking forward to seeing Victor too. I had often watched him on the television and was intrigued that his face, with its strange orange American tan, had not aged at all while his eyes had, so that he looked like a spaniel with a bulldog's gaze. 'Tricky Vicky', Tilly called my ex-husband but his unreliability did not bother me now; I wanted to hear about his exploits and to be praised for my achievement – Hester – and I was looking forward to getting some of his money. The evening had acquired an additional significance. We would meet as a successful family, untouched by the tension, the sacrifice, the quelling of self that normally accompanies family life. We had got off scot free and yet would not be exposed in loneliness.

I checked with the agency to make sure that my surrogate daughter was still available and they, wearily, assured me that Angela or Hazel or Patricia would meet me in the lounge at the appointed hour. Such nice names! Nothing could no wrong. All my little Angela or Hazel had to remember was to answer to Hester. There were no shared memories to rehearse. Vic had no experience of academic life so she would not be quizzed on that. In any case I had taken the precaution of booking the girl half an hour in advance of Vic's arrival time so that I could give her a little briefing.

It was almost that time when I was startled by the arrival in the lounge of a sort of human sunburst. Women started to wriggle and whisper. 'Good Lord,' I said ungraciously. It was Vic, thirty-five minutes early.

He cast his gaze over the women in the lounge, not really looking for me but allowing each female present to melt and open to his boyish charm. Perhaps he would not recognise me. I could slip out and wait at the exit for Hester to prime herself on her role. I rose, face half averted – and drew attention to myself.

'Barbara!' His voice had gained boom and timbre. He put a little kiss on the air and flopped down casually beside me, fastidiously raising the knees of his trousers.

'Hello, Vic.'

'Sorry I'm so early. First-night nerves,' he said, his nose wincing appealingly under his drooping eyes. He had developed an American accent.

'That's all right. Have a drink.'

'You look good,' he said. 'How's life been treating you? What a time I had, getting here! You would think, since we were shooting in Europe . . .' And he launched, as I had imagined he would, into a story about himself.

When Hester comes, I shall rush to the door to greet her, I thought. I gave Victor my smiling mouth and my nodding head but my attention was elsewhere. I shall see a tall, pale, beautiful girl – probably shy – in the entrance and I shall run to her and put my arms around her and if she doesn't cry out for help I shall just have time to explain before we get back to the table.

Something Victor said brought my mind right back. '. . . Anyway, I'm glad I got here early so we could talk about money before Hester gets here.'

'Money?'

'A sort of financial plan. I thought, twenty thousand dollars now, or five thousand a year until she's twenty-one. If you take the lump sum now you could invest it but there's less risk with an annuity.'

'Twenty thousand dollars?' My head spun as I tried out a string of noughts against the little digit and attempted to perform a dollar conversion.

'Well, I guess that's not a lot these days. What the heck – make it pounds.'

'Oh, Vic. I'm very – she'll be very grateful.'

'Say, what's she like?' Vic leaned forward and touched my knee.

'Quiet. More like me than you, I'm afraid. I hope you won't be disappointed.'

'I've been disappointed since.' The bulldog eyes attempted bashfulness. 'I wasn't disappointed then.'

We were getting along quite nicely when a wretched autograph hunter recognised Vic and hovered at his chair. She just hovered but her presence sapped one.

'Look, dear, if you don't mind . . . !' I said.

The girl glared at me. I flinched in the dull light of those purple-ringed eyes set in a yellowish face and crowned with gluey horns of hair. She wore a cheap Indian cotton anorak and an extraordinary satin dress from which her uncooked-looking breasts popped unpleasingly. Quite suddenly, tears bubbled up in her eyes. 'Aw, shit,' she said and she tottered off. She did not leave the room. Her perambulation took her in the opposite direction where she paused, glancing back. Vic and I laughed uneasily and he called a waiter for champagne. He was appraising the label when the girl returned and crouched beside me, breathing wetly and heavily in my ear: 'Look, are you Mrs Marshall?'

'I am.'

'Well, I'm Araminta.'

Victor was staring.

'Look here, dear . . .'

'From the agency.'

'What?'

'My real name's Angela. Araminta's my professional name – going to be.'

'No!'

'What's the matter?' Victor said.

'I think she's sick or something,' said Araminta.

'Sick!' I echoed faintly. It was not a lie. I rose and bundled my arms around the repellent Araminta. 'Please excuse us.'

Araminta and I faced each other in the uneasy pinkness of the ladies' washroom. 'You must leave immediately,' I said. 'There has been a dreadful mistake.'

'Who says? Whose mistake?' Her voice was a whine.

'You were brought here tonight to represent my daughter Hester, to celebrate with her famous father – whom she has never met before – her scholarship entrance to Oxford University.'

'That's beautiful. Like an episode from "Dallas".'

'If you think, for one instant, that you are fit to stand in the shoes of my daughter then you are even more deranged than you look. Now go away!'

'Here!' Her wail was like a suffering violin string. 'I want my money.'

'Not a penny!'

Araminta's mouth opened into a grille shape and a loud gurgle of grief issued therefrom. 'It's not my fault. No one told me I was to be your frigging daughter. I borrowed money to have me hair done an' all. What am I going to do?'

I was pondering the same question when the door opened, and Vic came in, looking confused. 'Is everything all right? Who's this?' he said of the screaming, streaming Araminta.

My soothing utterances were lost in the noise that Araminta made, of a train reversing, to sniff back her sobs. Her face was striped with purple but erased of tears. 'Hello, Dad,' she said. 'I'm Hester.'

We were all congealed like the victims of Pompeii. After an eternity of seconds Vic showed signs of recovery. 'Hester?' he whispered. 'Barbara . . . ?'

I closed my eyes. I could not look at him. 'She is going through . . . a phase.'

I heard a tap running, a tiny strange bark of dismay as, presumably, some woman attempted to enter and found her path blocked by a famous heartthrob. When I could bear to look I saw Hester calmly splashing her face, applying fresh scribbles of purple to her eyes and daubing her lips with mauve gloss that resembled scar tissue. Poor Vic looked badly shaken. On an impulse I seized the girl and ducked her beneath the tap again, washing every trace of colour from her skin. I scrubbed her dry on a roller towel and then patted her complexion with my own powder puff and a smear of my blusher. Her eyes, even without their purple tracing, resembled Mary Pickford's in their worse excesses of unreasoned terror. 'You some kind of frigging maniac?' she hissed. 'Shut up!' I wielded a hairbrush which I used to remove the glue from her head, and some of her hair. When I had finished there stood a tall, pale girl with wild dark hair, a little overweight, quite pretty, although her eyes and her breasts still popped nastily.

Whatever Vic was feeling he used his actor's training to conceal it. 'Come along, girls,' he said. 'It doesn't do for an actor to get himself arrested in the ladies' loo!'

Hester cawed with mirth.

Back in the restaurant there was a period of peace while Hester ate and Vic brooded. The girl appeared to be ravenously hungry. She did not pay any attention to us until a first course and several glasses of wine had scuttled down her throat and her cheeks were nicely padded with roast beef and then, with a coy, sideways look at Vic, she produced a classic line:

'Where have you been all my life?'

Vic eyed her gloomily. 'Hasn't your mother explained?'

'Not bloody much.'

Odd that I had not noticed before that they both had the same pessimistically protruding eye.

'I think your mother has rather a lot of explaining to do,' Vic said.

'Pardon?' I was so startled I could only squeak.

'Barbara, I am disappointed.' He put up a hand to swat a second squeak of protest which was escaping. 'Yes! I have been let down. Over seventeen years I have given unstintingly to the support of my daughter, trusting that you would bring her up as I would wish. You denied me access to her. I did not attempt to use the force of law in my favour. You did not want your lives disturbed, you said. What life? I ask you, what life have you given this girl? It is clear from her speech that she has been allowed to run wild in the streets. She's even hungry. Look how she eats! Have you anything to say?'

Very little, really. It was true the girl was appalling. 'Just be glad you haven't had to put up with her,' I snapped.

'She won't give me my money,' Hester complained. She shoved another roast potato into her mouth and seized Victor's sleeve. 'You'll give me my money, won't you?'

Victor retrieved his garment. 'Young lady, I'll give you something more valuable than money. I will give you advice. Reach for the moon – not its reflection in some puddle in the gutter. Look beyond the superficial values of youth and fashion. Stand up proud – alone if needs be. You'll have self-respect. You'll have *my* respect. What do you say, dear?'

'Vic,' I interjected, lost in our improvised drama; 'it is you who must look beyond the superficial. She has won a First to Oxford.'

'I'm not talking to you, Barbara. I'm speaking to my daughter. You know I don't believe the academic world equips you for real life. Now, Hester, what do you say?'

'Why don't you ride off into the sunset on your high horse, you big ballocks?' Hester said, and she importuned a waiter for profiteroles.

Victor looked so stunned, so *dis*armed, I was almost sorry for him. 'She is overwrought,' I said. 'Think what she has achieved! She has been locked up with her books all year and now she is in . . . revolt.'

Underneath I had begun to warm to Hester. Victor was not used to challenge. My once-husband seemed quite broken by her reproach. 'You know I don't expect much,' he sighed. 'It's the simple things I like in women – feminine grace, charm and wit.'

'I'm with you, mate!' Hester spoke up through a mouthful of gunge. 'This university lark was all her idea. Personally I've always thought women would be better off burning their brains than their bras. Could I have a liqueur?'

'You mean you don't want to go to university?' I was quite hurt.

'Too bloody right. I'm really a model, you know,' she confided to Vic. 'Although what I'd like best in all the world . . .' (her eyes glittered greedily) '. . . is to be an actress.'

'You'd like to be an actress?' Vic threw me a tiny look of triumph. His expression began to brighten.

'Dearest Dad . . . !' She leaned across the table so that her breasts rested on her pudding plate like a second, uncoated help-ing of dessert and it began to dawn on me that she might be a little bit drunk: 'All my life I have worshipped you from afar. My one dream has been to emul— follow in your hallowed footsteps.'

Vic smiled. His bulldog's gaze flickered with warmth and interest. Their eyes, inches apart, wobbled glassily. The child's look grew positively rakish and I had to kick her under the table to remind her of her filial role.

'Chip off the old block!' Vic said in admiration and he patted her pudgy hand.

'Thank you, Daddy.' Hester wrinkled her nose in exactly the way he often does.

'Would you really like to go on the stage?' he said.

'More than anything – except, of course, the movies.'

'Then the movies it's going to be. I'm bringing you back with me.'

'No!' I moaned.

'You mean it?' Hester said.

'I can get you a small part in the film I'm working on. Just a walk-on but it will be a start. Come back to America with me and we'll get you into stage school. I'll make Hollywood sit up and take notice of my beautiful daughter.'

Hester glowed so that, in the flattering candlelight, she did look rather beautiful. I felt depressed. Vic was taking my daughter away. There would be no more secret dreams for me; and no more money.

'Of course we'll have to tidy you up a bit!' Victor had advanced to practical planning. 'You're going to have to learn to speak properly and I'm afraid, darling, you'll have to lose some of those curves. First thing tomorrow you're going on a diet. I want you as skinny as a stalk of celery before we go back.'

At this Hester's face began to alter shape, the jaw extending, the eyes receding into pink slits, the mouth widening and lengthening. We watched in awe until a horrible howl came out. 'I can't!' she wailed. 'I'm pregnant!'

It was some time before I saw my friend Tilly again. There was such a lot to do with the baby coming and poor Vic in such a state. 'I insist that you tell me everything. Everything!' he had said in the restaurant after Hester dropped her bombshell, and of course the wretched girl did.

She has gone now. I think it's for the best. She ate such a lot and would answer only to Araminta. In any case now that the baby is born it would be confusing to have two Hesters in the house.

In the end Araminta did go back to America with Vic. No longer father and daughter, they had found a new role which seemed to suit both of them much better. And Vic left me really a very generous allowance for the child.

I hope I have explained my story clearly to you, for I simply cannot seem to make Tilly understand. 'Good God, darling,' she said, peering with fascinated horror into the pram on the day I introduced her to the infant. 'Did I never tell you about the Pill?''

And there was Hester, so sweet and solemn in her frills, her hands waving like pink sugar stars; her life stretched out before us, its mysterious curves and dazzling prospects, its sunlit patches and shadows, like the carriage drive to some enchanting manor.

I tried once more to tell my friend about my daughter's coming, but Tilly, fearing tales of childbed, waved a dainty hand burdened with costly mineral rocks, and said: 'What matter the source of life so long as it is lived happily ever after.'

She is right of course, for which of us anyway ever truly understands where babies come from?

(Kate Binchy read this story on *Woman's Hour* in May 1990.)

MARIA

— ♦ —

Elizabeth Bowen

'We have girls of our own, you see,' Mrs Dosely said, smiling warmly.

That seemed to settle it. Maria's aunt Lady Rimlade relaxed at last in Mrs Dosely's armchair, and, glancing round once more at the Rectory drawing-room's fluttery white curtains, alert-looking photographs, and silver cornets spuming out pink sweet-pea, consigned Maria to these pleasant influences.

'Then that will be delightful,' she said in that blandly conclusive tone in which she declared open so many bazaars. 'Thursday *next*, then, Mrs Dosely, about tea-time?'

'That will be delightful.'

'It is *most* kind,' Lady Rimlade concluded.

Maria could not agree with them. She sat scowling under her hat-brim, tying her gloves into knots. Evidently, she thought, I *am* being paid for.

Maria thought a good deal about money; she had no patience with other people's affectations about it, for she enjoyed being a rich little girl. She was only sorry not to know how much they considered her worth; having been sent out to walk in the garden while her aunt had just a short chat, dear, with the Rector's wife. The first phase of the chat, about her own character, she had been able to follow perfectly as she wound her way in and out of some crescent-shaped lobelia beds under the drawing-room window. But just as the two voices changed – one going unconcerned, one very, very diffident – Mrs Dosely approached the window and with an air of immense unconsciousness, shut it. Maria was baulked.

Maria was at one of those comfortable schools where everything is attended to. She was (as she had just heard her Aunt Ena explaining to Mrs Dosely) a motherless girl, sensitive, sometimes difficult, deeply reserved. At school they took all this, with her slight tendency to curvature and her dislike of all puddings, into loving consideration. She was having her character 'done' for her – later on, when she came out, would be time for hair and complexion. In addition to this, she learnt swimming, dancing, some French, the more innocent aspects of history, and *noblesse oblige*. It was a really nice school. All the same, when Maria came home for the holidays they could not do enough to console her for being a motherless girl who had been sent away.

Then, late last summer term, with inconceivable selfishness, her Uncle Philip fell ill and, in fact, nearly died. Aunt Ena had written less often and very distractedly, and when Maria came home she was told, with complete disregard for her motherlessness, that her uncle and aunt would be starting at once for a cruise, and that she was 'to be arranged for'.

This was not so easy. All the relations and all the family friends (who declared when Sir Philip was ill they'd do anything in the world) wrote back their deep disappointment at being unable to have Maria just now, though there was nothing, had things been otherwise, that they would have enjoyed more. One to his farm in fact, said Mr MacRobert, the Vicar, when he was consulted, another to his merchandise. Then he suggested his neighbours, a Mr and Mrs Dosely, of Malton Peele. He came over to preach in Lent; Lady Rimlade had met him; he seemed such a nice man, frank, cheerful and earnest. *She* was exceedingly motherly, everyone said, and sometimes took in Indian children to make ends meet. The Doselys would be suitable, Maria's aunt felt at once. When Maria raged, she drew down urbane pink eyelids and said she did wish Maria would not be rude. So she drove Maria and the two little griffons over the next afternoon to call upon Mrs

Dosely. If Mrs Dosely really seemed sympathetic, she thought she might leave the two little dogs with her too.

'And Mrs Dosely has girls of her own, she tells me,' said Lady Rimlade on the way home. 'I should not wonder if you made quite friends with them. I thought the flowers were done very nicely; I noticed them. Of course, I do not care myself for small silver vases like that, shaped like cornets, but I thought the effect in the Rectory drawing-room very cheerful and homelike.'

Maria took up the word skilfully. 'I suppose no one,' she said, 'who has not been in my position can be expected to realise what it feels like to have no home.'

'Oh, Maria darling . . .'

'I can't tell you what I think of this place you're sending me to,' said Maria. 'I bounced on the bed in that attic they're giving me and it's like iron. I suppose you realise that rectories are always full of diseases? Of course, I shall make the best of it, Aunt Ena. I shouldn't like you to feel I'd complained. But of course you don't realise a bit, do you, what I may be exposed to? So often carelessness about a girl at my age just ruins her life.'

Aunt Ena said nothing; she settled herself a little further down in the rugs and lowered her eyelids as though a strong wind were blowing.

That evening, on her way down to shut up the chickens, Mrs Dosely came upon Mr Hammond, the curate, rolling the cricket pitch in the Rectory field. He was indefatigable, and, though more High Church than they cared for, had outdoor tastes. He came in to meals with them regularly, 'as an arrangement', because his present landlady could not cook and a young man needs to be built up, and her girls were still so young that no one could possibly call Mrs Dosely designing. So she felt she ought to tell him.

'We shall be one more now in the house,' she said, 'till the end of the holidays. Lady Rimlade's little niece Maria – about fifteen – is coming to us while her uncle and aunt are away.'

'Jolly,' said Mr Hammond sombrely, hating girls.

'We *shall* be a party, shan't we?'

'The more the merrier, I daresay,' said Mr Hammond. He was a tall young man with a jaw, rather saturnine; he never said much, but Mrs Dosely expected family life was good for him. 'Let 'em all come,' said Mr Hammond, and went on rolling. Mrs Dosely, with a tin bowl under one arm and a basket hooked on the other, stood at the edge of the pitch and watched him.

'She seemed a dear little thing – not pretty, but such a serious little face, full of character. An only child, you see. I said to her when they were going away that I expected she and Dilly and Doris would soon be inseparable, and her face quite lit up. She has no mother; it seems so sad.'

'*I* never had a mother,' said Mr Hammond, tugging the roller grimly.

'Oh, I do *know*. But for a young girl I do think it still sadder . . . I thought Lady Rimlade charming; so unaffected. I said to her that we all lived quite simply here, and that if Maria came we should treat her as one of ourselves, and she said that was just what Maria would love . . . In age, you see, Maria comes just between Dilly and Doris.'

She broke off; she couldn't help thinking how three years hence Maria might well be having a coming-out dance. Then she imagined herself telling her friend Mrs Brotherhood: 'It's terrible, I never seem to see anything of my girls nowadays. They seem always to be over at Lady Rimlade's.'

'We must make the poor child feel at home here,' she told Mr Hammond brightly.

The Doselys were accustomed to making the best of Anglo-Indian children, so they continued to be optimistic about Maria. 'One must make allowance for character', had become the watchword of this warm-hearted household, through which passed a constant stream of curates with tendencies, servants with tempers, unrealised lady visitors, and yellow-faced children with no morale. Maria was forbearingly swamped by the family; she felt as though she were trying to box an eiderdown. Doris and Dilly had indelibly creased cheeks: they kept on smiling and smiling. Maria couldn't decide how best to be rude to them; they taxed her resourcefulness. She could not know Dilly had thought, 'Her face is like a sick monkey's,' or that Doris who went to one of those sensible schools, decided as soon that a girl in a diamond bracelet was shocking bad form. Dilly had repented at once of her unkind thought (though she had not resisted noting it in her diary), and Doris had simply said: 'What a pretty bangle. Aren't you afraid of losing it?' Mr Dosely thought Maria striking-looking (she had a pale, square-jawed little face, with a straight fringe cut above scowling brows), striking but disagreeable – here he gave a kind of cough in his thoughts and, leaning forward, asked Maria if she were a Girl Guide.

Maria said she hated the Girl Guides, and Mr Dosely laughed heartily and said that this was a pity, because, if so, she must hate the sight of Doris and Dilly. The supper-table rocked with merriment. Shivering in her red *crêpe* frock (it was a rainy August evening, the room was fireless, a window stood open, and outside the trees streamed coldly), Maria looked across at the unmoved Mr Hammond, square-faced, set and concentrated over his helping of macaroni cheese. He was not amused. Maria had always thought curates giggled; she despised curates because they giggled, but was furious with Mr Hammond for not giggling at all. She studied him for some time, and, as he did not look up, at last said: 'Are you a Jesuit?'

Mr Hammond (who had been thinking about the cricket pitch) started violently; his ears went crimson; he sucked in one last streamer of macaroni. 'No,' he said, 'I am not a Jesuit. Why?'

'Oh, nothing,' said Maria. 'I just wondered. As a matter of fact, I don't know what Jesuits are.'

Nobody felt quite comfortable. It was a most unfortunate thing, in view of the nature of Mr Hammond's tendencies, for poor little Maria, in innocence, to have said. Mr Hammond's tendencies were so marked, and, knowing how marked the Doselys thought his tendencies were, he was touchy. Mrs Dosely said she expected Maria must be very fond of dogs. Maria replied that she did not care for any dogs but Alsatians. Mrs Dosely was glad to be able to ask Mr Hammond if it were not he who had told her that he had a cousin who bred Alsatians. Mr Hammond said that this was the case. 'But unfortunately,' he added, looking across at Maria, 'I dislike Alsatians intensely.'

Maria now realised with gratification that she had incurred the hatred of Mr Hammond. This was not bad for one evening. She swished her plateful of maraconi round with her fork, then put the fork down pointedly. Undisguised wholesomeness was, in food as in personalities, repellent to Maria. 'This is the last supper but three – no, two,' she said to herself, 'that I shall eat at this Rectory.'

It had all seemed so simple, it seemed so simple still, yet five nights afterwards found her going to bed once again in what Mrs Dosely called the little white nest that we keep for our girl friends. Really, if one came to look at it one way, the Doselys were an experience for Maria, who had never till now found anybody who could stand her when she didn't mean to be stood. French maids, governesses, highly paid, almost bribed into service, had melted away. There was something marvellously, memorably unwinning about Maria . . . Yet here she still was. She had written twice to her aunt that she couldn't sleep and couldn't eat here, and feared she must be unwell, and Lady Rimlade wrote back advising her to have a little talk about all this with Mrs Dosely. Mrs Dosely, Lady Rimlade pointed out, was motherly. Maria told Mrs Dosely she was afraid she was unhappy and couldn't be well. Mrs Dosely exclaimed at the pity this was, but at all costs – Maria would see? – Lady Rimlade must not be worried. She had so expressly asked not to be worried at all.

'And she's so *kind*,' said Mrs Dosely, patting Maria's hand.

Maria simply thought, 'This woman is mad.' She said with a wan smile that she was sorry, but having her hand patted gave her pins and needles. But rudeness to Mrs Dosely was like dropping a pat of butter on to a hot plate – it slid and melted away.

In fact, all this last week Maria's sole consolation had been Mr Hammond. Her pleasure in Mr Hammond was so intense that three days after her coming he told Mrs Dosely he didn't think he'd come in for meals any more, thank you, as his landlady had by

now learned to cook. Even so, Maria had managed to see quite a
lot of him. She rode round the village after him, about ten yards
behind, on Doris's bicycle; she was there when he offered a prayer
with the Mothers' Union; she never forgot to come out when he
was at work on the cricket pitch ('Don't you seem to get rather
hot' she would ask him feelingly, as he mopped inside his collar.
'Or are you really not as hot as you seem?'), and, having discovered that at six every evening he tugged a bell, then read Even-
song in the church to two ladies, she came in alone every evening
and sat in the front pew, looking up at him. She led the responses,
waiting courteously for Mr Hammond when he lost his place.

But tonight Maria came briskly, mysteriously, up to the little
white nest, locking the door for fear Mrs Dosely might come in to
kiss her good night. She could now agree that music was inspiring.
For they had taken her to the Choral Society's gala, and the effect
it had had on Maria's ideas was stupendous. Half-way through a
rondo called '*Off to the Hills*' it occurred to her that when she got
clear of the Rectory she would go off to Switzerland, stay in a
Palace Hotel, and do a little climbing. She would take, she
thought, a hospital nurse, in case she hurt herself climbing, and an
Alsatian to bother the visitors in the hotel. She had glowed –
but towards the end of '*Hey, nonny, nonny*' a finer and far more
constructive idea came along, eclipsing the other. She clapped
her handkerchief to her mouth and, conveying to watchful Dilly
that she might easily be sick at any moment, quitted the school-
house hurriedly. Safe in her white nest, she put her candlestick
down with a bump, got her notepaper out, and sweeping her
hairbrushes off the dressing-table, sat down at it to write thus:

Dearest Aunt Ena: You must wonder why I have not written
for so long. The fact is, all else had been swept from my mind
by one great experience. I hardly know how to put it all into
words. The fact is I love a Mr Hammond, who is the curate
here, and am loved by him, we are engaged really and hope to
be married quite shortly. He is a fascinating man, extremely
High Church, he has no money but I am quite content to live

with him as a poor man's wife as I shall have to do if you and Uncle Philip are angry, though you may be sorry when I bring my little children to your door to see you. If you do not give your consent we shall elope but I am sure, dear Aunt Ena, that you will sympathise with your little niece in her great happiness. All I beseech is that you will not take me away from the Rectory; I do not think I could live without seeing Wilfred every day – or every night rather, as we meet in the churchyard and sit on a grave with our arms round each other in the moonlight. The Doselys do not know as I felt it my duty to tell you first, but I expect the village people may have noticed as unfortunately there is a right of way through the chucrhyard but we cannot think of anywhere else to sit. Is it not curious to think how true it was when I said at the time when you sent me to the Rectory, that you did not realise what you might be exposing me to? But now I am so thankful that you did expose me, as I have found my great happiness here, and am so truly happy in a good man's love. Goodbye, I must stop now as the moon has risen and I am just going out to meet Wilfred.

    Your loving, full-hearted little niece,

MARIA

Maria, pleased on the whole with this letter, copied it out twice, addressed the neater copy with a flourish, and went to bed. The muslin frills of the nest moved gently on the night air; the moon rose beaming over the churchyard and the pale evening primroses ringing the garden path. No daughter of Mrs Dosely's could have smiled more tenderly in the dark or fallen asleep more innocently.

Mr Hammond had no calendar in his rooms: he was sent so many at Christmas that he threw them all away and was left with none, so he ticked off the days mentally. Three weeks and six long days had still to elapse before the end of Maria's visit. He remained shut up in his rooms for mornings together, to the neglect of the

parish, and was supposed to be writing a book on Cardinal New
man. Postcards of arch white kittens stepping through ros
wreaths arrived for him daily; once he had come in to find a cauli
flower labelled 'From an admirer' on his sitting-room table. Mr
Higgins, the landlady, said the admirer must have come in by th
window, as *she* had admitted no one, so recently Mr Hammon
lived with his window hasped. This morning, the Saturday afte
the Choral Society's gala, as he sat humped over his table writin,
his sermon, a shadow blotted the lower window-panes. Maria
obscuring what light there was in the room with her body, coul
see in only with difficulty; her nose appeared white and flattened
she rolled her eyes ferociously round the gloom. Then she bega
trying to push the window up.

'*Go away!*' shouted Mr Hammond, waving his arms explosivel
as at a cat.

'You must let me in, I have something awful to tell you,
shouted Maria, lips close to the pane. He didn't, so she wen
round to the front door and was admitted by Mrs Higgins wit
due ceremony. Mrs Higgins, beaming, ushered in the little lad
from the Rectory who had come, she said, with an urgent messag
from Mrs Dosely.

Maria came in, her scarlet beret tipped up, with the jaunt
and gallant air of some young lady intriguing for Bonny Princ
Charlie.

'Are we alone?' she said loudly, then waited for Mrs Higgins t
shut the door. 'I thought of writing to you,' she continued, 'bu
your coldness to me lately led me to think that was hopeless.' Sh
hooked her heels on his fender and stood rocking backwards an
forwards. 'Mr Hammond, I warn you: you must leave Malto
Peele at once.'

'I wish *you* would,' said Mr Hammond, who, seated, looked pas
her left ear with a calm concentration of loathing.

'I daresay I may,' said Maria, 'but I don't want you to b
involved in my downfall. You have your future to think of; yo
may be a bishop; I am only a woman. You see, the fact is, M
Hammond, from the way we have been going about together

many people think we must be engaged. I don't want to embarrass you, Mr Hammond.'

Mr Hammond was not embarrassed. 'I always have thought you a horrid little girl, but I never knew you were quite so silly,' he said.

'We've been indiscreet. I don't know what my uncle will say. I only hope you won't be compelled to marry me.'

'Get off that fender,' said Mr Hammond; 'you're ruining it . . . Well then, stay there; I want to look at you. I must say you're something quite new.'

'Yes, aren't I?' said Maria, complacently.

'Yes. Any other ugly, insignificant-looking girls I've known did something to redeem themselves from absolute unattractiveness by being pleasant, say, or a little helpful, or sometimes they were well bred, or had good table manners, or were clever and amusing to talk to. If it were not for the consideration of the Doselys for your unfortunate aunt – who is, I understand from Mr Dosely, so stupid as to be almost mentally deficient – they would keep you – since they really have guaranteed to keep you – in some kind of shed or loose-box at the bottom of the yard . . . I don't want to speak in anger,' went on Mr Hammond, 'I hope I'm not angry; I'm simply sorry for you. I always knew the Doselys took in Anglo-Indian children, but if I'd known they dealt in . . . cases . . . of your sort, I doubt if I'd have ever come to Malton Peele— Shut up, you little hell-cat! I'll teach you to pull my hair—'

She was on top of him all at once, tweaking his hair with science.

'You beastly Bolshevik!' exclaimed Maria, tugging. He caught her wrists and held them. 'Oh! Shut up – you hurt me, you beastly bully, you! Oh! how could you hurt a girl!' She kicked at his shin, weeping. 'I – only came,' she said, 'because I was sorry for you. I needn't have come.' And then you go and start beating me up like this — *Ow!'*

'It's your only hope,' said Mr Hammond with a vehement, grave, but very detached expression, twisting her wrist round further. 'Yes, go on, yell – I'm not hurting you. You may be jolly thankful I *am* a curate . . . As a matter of fact, I got sacked from my prep school for bullying . . . Odd how these things come back . . .'

They scuffled. Maria yelped sharply and bit his wrist. 'Ha, you would, would you? . . . Oh, yes, I know you're a little girl – and a jolly nasty one. The only reason I've ever seen why one wasn't supposed to knock little girls about is that they're generally supposed to be nicer – pleasanter – prettier – than little boys.' He parried a kick and held her at arm's length by her wrists. They glared at each other, both crimson with indignation.

'And you supposed to be a curate!'

'And you supposed to be a lady, you little parasite! This'll teach you – Oh!' said Mr Hammond, sighing luxuriously, 'how pleased the Doselys would be if they knew!'

'Big brute! You great hulking brute!'

'If you'd been my little sister,' said Mr Hammond, regretful, 'this would have happened before. But by this time, of course, you wouldn't be nearly so nasty . . . I should chivvy you round the garden and send you up a tree every day.'

'*Socialist!*'

'Well, get along now.' Mr Hammond let go of her wrists. 'You can't go out of the door with a face like that; if you don't want a crowd you'd better go through the window . . . Now you run home and snivel to Mrs Dosely.'

'*This* will undo your career,' Maria said, nursing wrists balefully. 'I shall have it put in the papers: "*Baronet's niece tortured by demon curate.*" That will undo your career for you, Mr Hammond.'

'I know, I *know*, but it's worth it!' Mr Hammond exclaimed exaltedly. He was twenty-four, and intensely meant what he said. He pushed up the window. 'Now get out,' he stormed, 'or I'll certainly kick you through it.'

'You are in a kind of a way like a brother to me, aren't you?' remarked Maria, lingering on the sill.

'I am not. Get out!'

'But oh, Mr Hammond, I came here to make a confession. I didn't expect violence, as no one's attacked me before. But forgive you because it was righteous anger. I'm afraid we *are* rather compromised. You must read this. I posted one just the same to Aunt Ena three days ago.'

Maria handed over the copy of her letter.

'I may be depraved and ugly and bad, but you must admit, Mr Hammond, I'm not stupid.' She watched him read.

Half an hour later Mr Hammond, like a set of walking fire-irons, with Maria, limp as a rag, approached the Rectory. Maria hiccupped and hiccupped; she'd found Mr Hammond had no sense of humour at all. She was afraid he was full of vanity. 'You miserable little liar,' he'd said quite distantly, as though to a slug, and here she was being positively bundled along. If there'd been a scruff to her neck he would have grasped it. Maria had really enjoyed being bullied, but she did hate being despised. Now they were both going into the study to have yet another scene with Mr and Mrs Dosely. She was billed, it appeared, for yet another confession, and she had been so much shaken about that her technique faltered and she couldn't think where to begin. She wondered in a dim way what was going to happen next, and whether Uncle Philip would be coming to find Mr Hammond with a horse-whip.

Mr Hammond was all jaw; he wore a really disagreeable expression. Doris Dosely, up in the drawing-room window, gazed with awe for a moment, then disappeared.

'Doris!' yelled Mr Hammond. 'Where is your father? Maria has something to tell him.'

'Dunno,' said Doris and reappeared in the door. 'But here's a telegram for Maria – mother has opened it: something about a letter.'

'It would be,' said Mr Hammond. 'Give it me here.'

'I can't, I won't,' said Maria, backing away from the telegram. Mr Hammond, gritting his teeth audibly, received the paper from Doris.

YOUR LETTER BLOWN FROM MY HAND OVERBOARD [he

read out] AFTER HAD READ FIRST SENTENCE WILD WITH ANXIETY PLEASE REPEAT CONTENTS BY TELEGRAM YOUR UNCLE PHILIP WISHES YOU JOIN US MARSEILLES WEDNESDAY AM WRITING DOSELYS AUNT ENA.

'How highly strung poor Lady Rimlade must be,' said Dori kindly.

'She is a better aunt than many people deserve,' said Mr Ham mond.

'I think I may feel dull on that dreary old cruise after the sisterly, brotherly family life I've had here,' said Maria wistfully

(Patricia Hodge read this story on *Woman's Hour* in Decembe 1986.)

WIGTIME

—————— ◆ ——————

Alice Munro

When her mother was dying in the Walley Hospital, Anita came home to take care of her – though nursing was not what she did anymore. She was stopped one day in the corridor by a short, broad-shouldered, broad-hipped woman with clipped greyish-brown hair.

'I heard you were here, Anita,' this woman said, with a laugh that seemed both aggressive and embarrassed. 'Don't look so dumbfounded!'

It was Margot, whom Anita had not seen for more than thirty years.

'I want you to come out to the house,' Margot said. 'Give yourself a break. Come out soon.'

Anita took a day off and went to see her. Margot and her husband had built a new house overlooking the harbour, on a spot where there used to be nothing but scrubby bushes and children's secret paths. It was built of grey brick and was long and low. But high enough at that, Anita suggested – high enough to put some noses out of joint across the street, in the handsome hundred-year-old houses with their prize view.

'Bugger them,' said Margot. 'They took up a petition against us. They went to the Committee.'

But Margot's husband already had the Committee sewn up.

Margot's husband had done well. Anita had already heard that. He owned a fleet of buses that took children to school and senior citizens to see the blossoms in Niagara and the fall leaves in Haliburton. Sometimes they carried singles clubs and other holidayers on more adventurous trips – to Nashville or Las Vegas.

Margot showed her around. The kitchen was done in almond – Anita made a mistake – calling it cream – with teal-green and butter-yellow trim. Margot said that all that natural wood look was passé. They did not enter the living-room, with its rose carpet, striped silk chairs, and yards and yards of swooping pale-green figured curtains. They admired it from the doorway – all exquisite, shadowy, inviolate. The master bedroom and its bath were done in white and gold and poppy red. There was a jacuzzi and a sauna.

'I might have liked something not so bright myself,' said Margot. 'But you can't ask a man to sleep in pastels.'

Anita asked her if she ever thought about getting a job.

Margot flung back her head and snorted with laughter. 'Are you kidding? Anyway, I do have a job. Wait till you see the big lunks I have to feed. Plus this place doesn't exactly run itself on magic horsepower.'

She took a pitcher of sangria out of the refrigerator and put it on a tray, with two matching glasses. 'You like this stuff? Good. We'll sit out on the deck.'

Margot was wearing green flowered shorts and a matching top. Her legs were thick and marked with swollen veins, the flesh of her upper arms was dented, her skin was brown, mole-spotted, leathery from lots of sun. 'How come you're still thin?' she asked with amusement. She flipped Anita's hair. 'How come you're not grey? Any help from the drugstore? You look pretty.' She said this without envy, as if speaking to somebody younger than herself, still untried and unseasoned.

It looked as if all her care, all her vanity, went into the house.

Margot and Anita both grew up on farms in Ashfield Township. Anita lived in a draughty shell of a brick house that hadn't had any new wallpaper or linoleum for twenty years, but there was a stove in the parlour that could be lit, and she sat in there in peace and comfort to do her homework. Margot often did her homework sitting up in the bed she had to share with two little sisters. Anita seldom went to Margot's house, because of the crowdedness and confusion, and the terrible temper of Margot's father. Once, she had gone there when they were getting ducks ready for market. Feathers floated everywhere. There were feathers in the milk jug and a horrible smell of feathers burning on the stove. Blood was puddled on the oilclothed table and dripping on to the floor.

Margot seldom went to Anita's house, because without exactly saying so Anita's mother disapproved of the friendship. When Anita's mother looked at Margot, she seemed to be totting things up – the blood and feathers, the stovepipe sticking through the kitchen roof, Margot's father yelling that he'd tan somebody's arse.

But they met every morning, struggling head down against the snow that blew off Lake Huron, or walking as fast as they could through a predawn world of white fields, icy swamps, pink sky, and fading stars and murderous cold. Away beyond the ice on the lake they could see a ribbon of open water, ink-blue or robin's-egg, depending upon the light. Pressed against their chests were notebooks, textbooks, homework. They wore the skirts, blouses, and sweaters that had been acquired with difficulty (in Margot's case there had been subterfuge and blows) and were kept decent with great effort. They bore the stamp of Walley High School, where they were bound, and they greeted each other with relief. They had got up in the dark in cold rooms with frost-whitened windows and pulled underwear on under their nightclothes, while stove lids banged in the kitchen, dampers were shut, younger brothers and sisters scurried to dress themselves downstairs. Margot and her mother took turns going out to the barn to milk cows and fork down hay. The father drove them all hard, and Margot said they'd think he was sick if he didn't hit somebody before breakfast. Anita could count herself lucky, having brothers to do the barn work and a father who did not usually hit anybody. But she still felt, these mornings, as if she'd come up through deep dark water.

'Think of the coffee,' they told each other, battling on towards the store on the highway, a ramshackle haven. Strong tea, steeped black in the country way, was the drink in both their houses.

Teresa Gault unlocked the store before eight o'clock, to let them in. Pressed against the door, they saw the fluorescent lights come on, blue spurts darting from the ends of the tubes, wavering, almost losing heart, then blazing white. Teresa came smiling like a hostess, edging around the cash register, holding a cherry-red quilted satin dressing gown tight at the throat, as if that could protect her from the freezing air when she opened the door. Her eyebrows were black wings made with a pencil, and she used another pencil – a red one – to outline her mouth. The bow in the upper lip looked as if it had been cut with scissors.

What a relief, what a joy, then, to get inside, into the light, to smell the oil heater and set their books on the counter and take their hands out of their mittens and rub the pain from their fingers. Then they bent over and rubbed their legs – the bare inch or so that was numb and in danger of freezing. They did not wear stockings, because it wasn't the style. They wore ankle socks inside their boots (their saddle shoes were left at school). Their skirts were long – this was the winter of 1948–9 – but there was still a crucial bit of leg left unprotected. Some country girls wore stockings under their socks. Some even wore ski pants pulled up bulkily under their skirts. Margot and Anita would never do that. They would risk freezing rather than risk getting themselves laughed at for such countrified contrivances.

Teresa brought them cups of coffee, hot black coffee, very sweet and strong. She marvelled at their courage. She touched a finger to their cheeks or their hands and gave a little shriek and a shudder. 'Like ice! Like ice!' To her it was amazing that anybody would go out in the Canadian winter, let alone walk a mile in it. What they did every day to get to school made them heroic and strange in her eyes, and a bit grotesque.

This seemed to be particularly so because they were girls. She wanted to know if such exposure interfered with their periods. 'Will it not freeze the eggs?' was what she actually said. Margot and Anita figured this out and made a point, thereafter, of warning each other not to get their eggs frozen. Teresa was not vulgar – she was just foreign. Reuel had met and married her overseas, in Alsace-Lorraine, and after he went home she followed on the boat with all the other war brides. It was Reuel who ran the school bus, this year when Margot and Anita were seventeen and in grade twelve. Its run started here at the store and gas station that the Gaults had bought on the Kincardine highway, within sight of the lake.

Teresa told about her two miscarriages. The first one took place in Walley, before they moved out here and before they owned a car. Reuel scooped her up in his arms and carried her to the hospital. (The thought of being scooped up in Reuel's arms caused such a pleasant commotion in Anita's body that in order to experience it she was almost ready to put up with the agony that Teresa said she had undergone.) The second time happened here in the store. Reuel, working in the garage, could not hear her weak cries as she lay on the floor in her blood. A customer came in and found her. Thank God, said Teresa, for Reuel's sake even more than her own. Reuel would not have forgiven himself. Her eyelids fluttered, her eyes did a devout downward swoop, when she referred to Reuel and their intimate life together.

While Teresa talked, Reuel would be passing in and out of the store. He went out and got the engine running, then left the bus to warm up and went back into the living quarters, without acknowledging any of them, or even answering Teresa, who interrupted herself to ask if he had forgotten his cigarettes, or did he want more coffee, or perhaps he should have warmer gloves. He stomped the snow from his boots in a way that was more an announcement of his presence than a sign of any concern for floors. His tall, striding body brought a fan of cold air behind it, and the tail of his open parka usually managed to knock something down – Jell-O boxes or tins of corn, arranged in a fancy way by Teresa. He didn't turn around to look.

Teresa gave her age as twenty-eight – the same age as Reuel's. Everybody believed she was older – up to ten years older. Margot and Anita examined her close up and decided that she looked burned. Something about her skin, particularly at the hairline and around the mouth and eyes, made you think of a pie left too long in the oven, so that it was not charred but dark brown around the edges. Her hair was thin, as if affected by the same drought or fever, and it was too black – they were certain it was dyed. She was short, and small-boned, with tiny wrists and feet, but her body seemed puffed out below the waist, as if it had never recovered from those brief, dire pregnancies. Her smell was like something sweet cooking – spicy jam.

She would ask anything, just as she would tell anything. She asked Margot and Anita if they were going out with boys yet.

'Oh, why not?' Does your fathers not let you? I was attracted to boys by the time I was fourteen, but my father would not let me. They come and whistle under my window, he chases them away. You should pluck your eyebrows. You both. That would make you look nicer. Boys like a girl when she makes herself all nice. That is something I never forget. When I was on the boat coming across the Atlantic Ocean with all the other wives, I spend my time preparing myself for my husband. Some of those wives, they just sat and played cards. Not me! I was washing my hair and putting on a beautiful oil to soften my skin, and I rubbed and rubbed with a stone to get the rough spots off my feet. I forget what you call them – the rough spots on the feet's skin? And polish my nails and pluck my eyebrows and do myself all up like a prize! For my husband to meet me in Halifax. While all those others do is sit and play cards and gossiping, gossiping with each other.'

They had heard a different story about Teresa's second miscarriage. They had heard that it happened because Reuel told her he was sick of her and wanted her to go back to Europe, and in her despair she had thrown herself against a table and dislodged the baby.

At side roads and at farm gates Reuel stopped to pick up students who were waiting, stomping their feet to keep warm or scuffling in the snowbanks. Margot and Anita were the only girls of their age riding the bus that year. Most of the others were boys in grades nine and ten. They could have been hard to handle, but Reuel quelled them even as they came up the steps.

'Cut it out. Hurry up. On board if you're coming on board.'

And if there was any start of a fracas on the bus, any hooting or grabbing or punching, or even any moving from seat to seat or too much laughing and loud talk, Reuel would call out, 'Smarten up if you don't want to walk! Yes, you there – I mean you!' Once he had put a boy out for smoking, miles from Walley. Reuel himself smoked all the time. He had the lid of a mayonnaise jar sitting on the dashoard for an ashtray. Nobody challenged him, ever, about anything he did. His temper was well known. It was thought to go naturally with his red hair.

People said he had red hair, but Margot and Anita remarked that only his moustache and the hair right above his ears was red. The rest of it, the hair receding from the temples but thick and wavy elsewhere, especially on the back, which was the part they most often got to see – the rest was a tawny colour like the pelt of a fox they had seen one morning crossing the white road. And the hair of his heavy eyebrows, the hair along his arms and on the backs of his hands, was still more faded, though it glinted in any light. How had his moustache kept its fire? They spoke of this. They discussed in detail, coolly, everything about him. Was he good-looking or was he not? He had a redhead's flushed and spotty skin, a high, shining forehead, light-coloured eyes that seemed ferocious but indifferent. Not good-looking, they decided. Queer-looking, actually.

But when Anita was anywhere near him she had a feeling of controlled desperation along the surface of her skin. It was something like the far-off beginning of a sneeze. This feeling was at its worst when she had to get off the bus and he was standing beside the step. The tension flitted from her front to her back as she went past him. She never spoke of this to Margot, whose contempt for men seemed to her firmer than her own. Margot's mother dreaded Margot's father's lovemaking as much as the children dreaded his cuffs and kicks, and once slept all night in the granary, with the door bolted, to avoid it. Margot called lovemaking 'carrying on'. She spoke disparagingly of Teresa's 'carrying on' with Reuel. But it had occurred to Anita that this very scorn of Margot's, her sullenness and disdain, might be a thing that men could find attractive. Margot might be attractive in a way that she herself was not. It had nothing to do with prettiness. Anita thought that she was prettier, though it was plain that Teresa wouldn't give high marks to either of them. It had to do with a bold lassitude that Margot showed sometimes in movement, with the serious breadth of her hips and the already womanly curve of her stomach, and a look that would come over her large brown eyes – a look both defiant and helpless, not matching up with anything Anita had ever heard her say.

By the time they reached Walley, the day had started. Not a star to be seen anymore, nor a hint of pink in the sky. The town, with its buildings, streets, and interposing routines, was set up like a barricade against the stormy or frozen-still world they'd woken up in. Of course their houses were barricades, too, and so was the store, but those were nothing compared to town. A block inside town, it was as if the countryside didn't exist. The great drifts of snow on the roads and the wind tearing and howling through the trees – that didn't exist. In town, you had to behave as if you'd always been in town. Town students, now thronging the streets around the high school, led lives of privilege and ease. They got up at eight o'clock in houses with heated bedrooms and bathrooms. (This was not always the case, but Margot and Anita believed it was.) They were apt not to know your name. They expected you to know theirs, and you did.

The high school was like a fortress, with its narrow windows and decorative ramparts of dark-red brick, its long flight of steps and daunting doors, and the Latin words cut in stone: *Scientia Atque Probitas*. When they got inside those doors, at about a quarter to nine, they had come all the way from home, and home and all stages of the journey seemed improbable. The effects of the coffee had worn off. Nervous yawns overtook them, under the harsh lights of the assembly hall. Ranged ahead were the demands of the day: Latin, English, geometry, chemistry, history, French, geography, physical training. Bells rang at ten to the hour, briefly releasing them. Upstairs, downstairs, clutching books and ink bottles, they made their anxious way, under the hanging lights and the pictures of royalty and dead educators. The wainscoting, varnished every summer, had the same merciless gleam as the principal's glasses. Humiliation was imminent. Their stomachs ached and threatened to growl as the morning wore on. They feared sweat under their arms and blood on their skirts. They shivered going into English or geometry classes, not because they did badly in those classes (the fact was that they did quite well in almost everything) but because of the danger of being asked to get up and read something, say a poem off by heart or write the solution to a problem on the blackboard in front of the class. *In front of the class* – those were dreadful words to them.

Then, three times a week, came physical training – a special problem for Margot, who had not been able to get the money out of her father to buy a gym suit. She had to say that she had left her suit at home, or borrow one from some girl who was being excused. But once she did get a suit on she was able to loosen up and run around the gym, enjoying herself, yelling for the basketball to be thrown to her, while Anita went into such rigours of self-consciousness that she allowed the ball to hit her on the head.

Better moments intervened. At noon hour they walked downtown and looked in the windows of a beautiful carpeted store that sold only wedding and evening clothes. Anita planned a springtime wedding, with bridesmaids in pink-and-green silk and overskirts of white organza. Margot's wedding was to take place in the fall, with the bridesmaids wearing apricot velvet. In Woolworth's they looked at lipsticks and earrings. They dashed into the drugstore and sprayed themselves with sample cologne. If they had any money to buy some necessity for their mothers, they spent some of the change on cherry Cokes or sponge toffee. They could never be deeply unhappy, because they believed that something remarkable was bound to happen to them. They could become heroines; love and power of some sort were surely waiting.

Teresa welcomed them, when they got back, with coffee, or hot chocolate with cream. She dug into a package of store cookies and gave them Fig Newtons or marshmallow puffs dusted with coloured coconut. She took a look at their books and asked what homework they had. Whatever they mentioned, she, too, had studied. In every class, she had been a star.

'English – perfect marks in my English! But I never knew then that I would fall in love and come to Canada. Canada! I think it is only polar bears living in Canada!'

Reuel wouldn't have come in. He'd be fooling around with the bus or with something in the garage. His mood was usually fairly good as they got on the bus. 'All aboard that's coming aboard!' he would call. 'Fasten your seat belts! Adjust your oxygen masks! Say your prayers! We're takin' to the highway!' Then he'd sing to himself, just under the racket of the bus, as they got clear of town. Nearer home his mood of the morning took over, with its aloofness and unspecific contempt. He might say, 'Here you are, ladies – end of a perfect day,' as they got off. Or he might say nothing. But indoors Teresa was full of chat. Those school days she talked about led into wartime adventures: a German soldier hiding in the garden, to whom she had taken a little cabbage soup; then the first Americans she saw – black Americans – arriving on tanks and creating a foolish and wonderful impression that the tanks and the men were all somehow joined together. Then her little wartime wedding dress being made out of her mother's lace tablecloth. Pink roses pinned in her hair. Unfortunately, the dress had been torn up for rags to use in the garage. How could Reuel know?

Sometimes Teresa was deep in conversation with a customer. No treats or hot drinks then – all they got was a flutter of her hand, as if she were being borne past in a ceremonial carriage. They heard bits of the same stories. The German soldier, the black Americans, another German blown to pieces, his leg, in its boot, ending up at the church door, where it remained, everybody walking by to look at it. The brides on the boat. Teresa's amazement at the length of time it took to get from Halifax to here on the train. The miscarriages.

They heard her say that Reuel was afraid for her to have another baby.

'So now he always uses protections.'

There were people who said they never went into that store anymore, because you never knew what you'd have to listen to, or when you'd get out.

In all but the worst weather Margot and Anita lingered at the spot where they had to separate. They spun the day out a little longer, talking. Any subject would do. Did the geography teacher look better with or without his moustache? Did Teresa and Reuel still actually carry on, as Teresa implied? They talked so easily and endlessly that it seemed they talked about everything. But there were things they held back.

Anita held back two ambitions of hers, which she did not reveal to anybody. One of them – to be an archaeologist – was too odd, and the other – to be a fashion model – was too conceited. Margot told her ambition, which was to be a nurse. You didn't need any money to get into it – not like university – and once you graduated you could go anywhere and get a job. New York City, Hawaii – you could get as far away as you liked.

The thing that Margot kept back, Anita thought, was how it must really be at home, with her father. According to her, it was all like some movie comedy. Her father beside himself, a hapless comedian, racing around in vain pursuit (of fleet, mocking Margot) and rattling locked doors (the granary) and shouting monstrous threats and waving over his head whatever weapon he could get hold of – a chair or a hatchet or a stick of firewood. He tripped over his own feet and got mixed up in his own accusations. And no matter what he did, Margot laughed. She laughed, she despised him, she forestalled him. Never, never did she shed a tear or cry out in terror. Not like her mother. So she said.

After Anita graduated as a nurse, she went to work in the Yukon. There she met and married a doctor. This should have been the end of her story, and a good end, too, as things were reckoned in

Walley. But she got a divorce, she moved on. She worked again and saved money and went to the University of British Columbia, where she studied anthropology. When she came home to look after her mother, she had just completed her PhD. She did not have any children.

'So what will you do, now you're through?' said Margot.

People who approved of the course Anita had taken in life usually told her so. Often an older woman would say, 'Good for you!' or, 'I wish I'd had the nerve to do that, when I was still young enough for it to make any difference.' Approval came sometimes from unlikely quarters. It was not to be found everywhere, of course. Anita's mother did not feel it, and that was why, for many years, Anita had not come home. Even in her present shrunken, hallucinatory state, her mother had recognised her, and gathered her strength to mutter, 'Down the drain.'

Anita bent closer.

'*Life*,' her mother said. 'Down the *drain*.'

But another time, after Anita had dressed her sores, she said, 'So glad. So glad to have – a *daughter*.'

Margot didn't seem to approve or disapprove. She seemed puzzled, in an indolent way. Anita began talking to her about some things she might do, but they kept being interrupted. Margot's sons had come in, bringing friends. The sons were tall, with hair of varying redness. Two of them were in high school and one was home from college. There was one even older, who was married and living in the West. Margot was a grandmother. Her sons carried on shouted conversations with her about the whereabouts of their clothes, and what supplies of food, beer and soft drinks there were in the house, also which cars would be going where at what times. Then they all went out to swim in the pool beside the house, and Margot called, 'Don't anybody dare go in the pool that's got suntan lotion on!'

One of the sons called back, 'Nobody's *got* it on,' with a great show of weariness and patience.

'Well, somebody had it on yesterday, and they went in the pool, all right,' replied Margot. 'So I guess it was just somebody that snuck up from the beach, eh?'

Her daughter Debbie arrived home from dancing class and showed them the costume she was going to wear when her dancing school put on a programme at the shopping mall. She was to impersonate a dragonfly. She was ten years old, brown-haired, and stocky, like Margot.

'Pretty hefty dragonfly,' said Margot, lolling back in the deck chair. Her daughter did not arouse in her the warring energy that her sons did. Debbie tried for a sip of the sangria, and Margot batted her away.

'Go get yourself a drink out of the fridge,' she said. 'Listen. This is our visit. OK? Why don't you go phone up Rosalie?'

Debbie left, trailing an automatic complaint. 'I wish it wasn't *pink* lemonade. Why do you always make *pink* lemonade?'

Margot got up and shut the sliding doors to the kitchen. 'Peace,' she said. 'Drink up. After a while I'll get us some sandwiches.'

Spring in that part of Ontario comes in a rush. The ice breaks up into grinding, jostling chunks on the rivers and along the lakeshore; it slides underwater in the pond and turns the water green. The snow melts and the creeks flood, and in no time comes a day when you open your coat and stuff your scarf and mittens in your pockets. There is still snow in the woods when the blackflies are out and the spring wheat showing.

Teresa didn't like spring any better than winter. The lake was too big and the fields too wide and the traffic went by too fast on the highway. Now that the mornings had turned balmy, Margot and Anita didn't need the store's shelter. They were tired of Teresa. Anita read in a magazine that coffee discoloured your skin. They talked about whether miscarriages could cause chemical changes in your brain. They stood outside the store, wondering whether they should go in, just to be polite. Teresa came to the door and waved at them, peekaboo. They waved back with a little flap of their hands the way Reuel waved back every morning – just lifting a hand from the steering wheel at the last moment before he turned onto the highway.

Reuel was singing in the bus one afternoon when he had dropped off all the other passengers. 'He knew the world was round-o,' he sang. 'And uh-uhm could be found-o.'

He was singing a word in the second line so softly they couldn't catch it. He was doing it on purpose, teasing. Then he sang it again, loud and clear so that there was no mistake.

> 'He knew the world was round-o,
> And tail-o could be found-o.'

They didn't look at each other or say anything till they were walking down the highway. Then Margot said, 'Big fat nerve he's got, singing that song in front of us. Big fat *nerve*,' she said, spitting the word out like the worm in an apple.

But only the next day, shortly before the bus reached the end of its run, Margot started humming. She invited Anita to join, poking her in the side and rolling her eyes. They hummed the tune of Reuel's song; then they started working words into the humming, muffling one word, then clearly singing the next, until they finally got their courage up and sang the whole two lines, bland and sweet as 'Jesus Loves Me'.

> 'He knew the world was round-o,
> And tail-o could be found-o.'

Reuel did not say a word. He didn't look at them. He got off the bus ahead of them and didn't wait by the door. Yet less than an hour before, in the school driveway, he had been most genial. One of the other drivers looked at Margot and Anita and said, 'Nice load you got there,' and Reuel said, 'Eyes front, Buster,' moving so that the other driver could not watch them stepping onto the bus.

Next morning before he pulled away from the store, he delivered a lecture. 'I hope I'm going to have a couple of ladies on my bus today and not like yesterday. A girl saying certain things is not like a man saying them. Same thing as a woman getting drunk. A girl gets drunk or talks dirty, first thing you know she's in trouble. Give that some thought.'

Anita wondered if they had been stupid. Had they gone too far? they had displeased Reuel and perhaps disgusted him, made him sick at the sight of them, just as he was sick of Teresa. She was ashamed and regretful and at the same time she thought Reuel wasn't fair. She made a face at Margot to indicate this, turning down the corners of her mouth. But Margot took no notice. She was tapping her fingertips together, looking demurely and cynically at the back of Reuel's head.

Anita woke up in the night with an amazing pain. She thought at first she's been wakened by some calamity, such as a tree falling on the house or flames shooting up through the floorboards. This was shortly before the end of the school year. She had felt sick the evening before, but everybody in the family was complaining of feeling sick, and blaming it on the smell of paint and turpentine. Anita's mother was painting the linoleum, as she did every year at this time.

Anita had cried out with pain before she was fully awake, so that everybody was roused. Her father did not think it proper to phone the doctor before daybreak, but her mother phoned him anyway. The doctor said to bring Anita in to Walley, to the hospital. There he operated on her and removed a burst appendix, which in a few hours might have killed her. She was very sick for several days after the operation, and had to stay nearly three weeks in the hospital. Until the last few days, she could not have any visitors but her mother.

This was a drama for the family. Anita's father did not have the money to pay for the operation and the stay in the hospital – he was going to have to sell a stand of hard-maple trees. Her mother took the credit, rightly, for saving Anita's life, and as long as she lived she would mention this, often adding that she had gone against her husband's orders. (It was really only against his advice.) In a flurry of independence and self-esteem she began to drive the car, a thing she had not done for years. She visited Anita every afternoon and brought news from home. She had finished painting the linoleum, in a design of white and yellow done with a sponge on a dark-green ground. It gave the impression of a distant meadow sprinkled with tiny flowers. The milk inspector had complimented her on it, when he stayed for dinner. A late calf had been born across the creek and nobody could figure out how the cow had got there. The honeysuckle was in bloom in the hedge, and she brought a bouquet and commandeered a vase from the nurses. Anita had never seen her sociability turned on like this before for anybody in the family.

Anita was happy, in spite of weakness and lingering pain. Such a fuss had been made to prevent her dying. Even the sale of the maple trees pleased her, made her feel unique and treasured. People were kind and asked nothing of her, and she took up that kindness and extended it to everything around her. She forgave everyone she could think of – the principal with his glittery glasses, the smelly boys on the bus, unfair Reuel and chattering Teresa and rich girls with lamb's-wool sweaters and her own family and Margot's father, who must suffer in his rampages. She didn't tire all day of looking at the thin yellowish curtains at the window and the limb and trunk of a tree visible to her. It was an ash tree, with strict-looking corduroy lines of bark and thin petal leaves that were losing their fragility and sharp spring green, toughening and darkening as they took on summer maturity. Everything made or growing in the world seemed to her to deserve congratulations.

She thought later that this mood of hers might have come from the pills they gave her for the pain. But perhaps not entirely.

She had been put in a single room because she was so sick. (Her father had told her mother to ask how much extra this was costing, but her mother didn't think they would be charged, since they hadn't asked for it.) The nurses brought her magazines, which she looked at but could not read, being too dazzled and comfortably distracted. She couldn't tell whether time passed quickly or slowly, and she didn't care. Sometimes she dreamed or imagined that Reuel visited her. He showed a sombre tenderness, a muted passion. He loved but relinquished her, caressing her hair.

A couple of days before she was due to go home, her mother came in shiny-faced from the heat of summer, which was now upon them, and from some other disruption. She stood at the end of Anita's bed and said, 'I always knew you thought it wasn't fair of me.'

By this time Anita had had a few holes punched in her happiness. She had been visited by her brothers, who banged against the bed, and her father, who seemed surprised that she expected to kiss him, and by her aunt, who said that after an operation like this a person always got fat. Now her mother's face, her mother's voice came pushing at her like a fist through gauze.

Her mother was talking about Margot. Anita knew that immediately by a twitch of her mouth.

'You always thought I wasn't fair to your friend Margot. I was never fussy about that girl and you thought I wasn't fair. I know you did. So now it turns out. It turns out I wasn't so wrong after all. I could see it in her from an early age. I could see what you couldn't. That she had a sneaky streak and she was oversexed.'

Her mother delivered each sentence separately, in a reckless loud voice. Anita did not look at her eyes. She looked at the little brown mole beneath one nostril. It seemed increasingly loathsome.

Her mother calmed down a little, and said that Reuel had taken Margot to Kincardine on the school bus at the end of the day's run on the very last day of school. Of course they had been alone in the bus at the beginning and the end of the run, ever since Anita got sick. All they did in Kincardine, they said, was eat French-fried potatoes. What nerve! Using a school bus for their jaunts and misbehaving. They drove back that evening, but Margot did not go home. She had not gone home yet. Her father had come to the store and beat on the gas pumps and broken them, scattering glass as far as the highway. He phoned the police about Margot, and Reuel phoned them about the pumps. The police were friends of Reuel's, and now Margot's father was bound over to keep the peace. Margot stayed on at the store, supposedly to escape a beating.

'That's all it is, then,' Anita said. 'Stupid God-damned gossip.'
But no. But no. And don't swear at me, young lady.

Her mother said that she had kept Anita in ignorance. All this
had happened and she had said nothing. She had given Margot the
benefit of the doubt. But now there was no doubt. The news was
that Teresa had tried to poison herself. She had recovered. The
store was closed. Teresa was still living there, but Reuel had taken
Margot with him and they were living here, in Walley. In a back
room somewhere, in the house of friends of his. They were living
together. Reuel was going out to work at the garage every day, so
you could say that he was living with them both. Would he be
allowed to drive the school bus in future? Not likely. Everybody
was saying Margot must be pregnant. Javex, was what Teresa
took.

'And Margot never confided in you,' Anita's mother said. 'She
never sent you a note or one thing all the time you've been in here.
Supposed to be your friend.'

Anita had a feeling that her mother was angry with her not only
because she'd been friends with Margot, a girl who had disgraced
herself, but for another reason as well. She had the feeling that
her mother was seeing the same thing that she herself could see –
Anita unfit, passed over, disregarded, not just by Margot but by
life. Didn't her mother feel an angry disappointment that Anita
was not the one chosen, the one enfolded by drama and turned
into a woman and swept out on such a surge of life? She would
never admit that. And Anita could not admit that she felt a great
failure. She was a child, a know-nothing, betrayed by Margot,
who had turned out to know a lot. She said sulkily, 'I'm tired talking.' She pretended to fall asleep, so that her mother would leave.

Then she lay awake. She lay awake all night. The nurse who
came in the next morning said, 'Well, don't you look like the last
show on earth! Is that incision bothering you? Should I see if I can
get you back on the pills?'

'I hate it here,' Anita said.

'Do you? Well, you only have one more day till you can go
home.'

'I don't mean the hospital,' Anita said. 'I mean *here*. I want to go and live somewhere else.'

The nurse did not seem to be surprised. 'You got your grade twelve?' she said. 'OK. You can go in training. Be a nurse. All it costs is to buy your stuff. Because they can work you for nothing while you're training. Then you can go and get a job anyplace. You can go all over the world.'

That was what Margot had said. And now Anita was the one who would become a nurse, not Margot. She made up her mind that day. But she felt that it was second best. She would rather have been chosen. She would rather have been pinned down by a man and his desire and the destiny that he arranged for her. She would rather have been the subject of scandal.

'Do you want to know?' said Margot. 'Do you want to know really how I got this house? I mean, I didn't go after it till we could afford it. But you know with men – something else can always come first? I put in my time living in dumps. We lived one place, there was just that stuff, you know that under-carpeting stuff, on the floor? That brown hairy stuff looks like the skin off some beast? Just look at it and you can feel things crawling on you. I was sick all the time anyway. I was pregnant with Joe. This was in behind the Toyota place, only it wasn't the Toyota then. Reuel knew the landlord. Of course. We got it cheap.'

But there came a day, Margot said. There came a day about five years ago. Debbie wasn't going to school yet. It was in June. Reuel was going away for the weekend, on a fishing trip up to northern Ontario. Up to the French River, in northern Ontario. Margot had got a phone call that she didn't tell anybody about.

'Is that Mrs Gault?'

Margot said yes.

'Is that Mrs Reuel Gault?'

Yes, said Margot, and the voice – it was a woman's or maybe a young girl's voice, muffled and giggling – asked her if she wanted to know where her husband might be found next weekend.

'You tell me,' said Margot.

'Why don't you check out the Georgian Pines?'

'Fine,' said Margot. 'Where is that?'

'Oh, it's a campground,' the voice said. 'It's a real nice place Don't you know it? It's up on Wasaga Beach. You just check i out.'

That was about a hundred miles to drive. Margot mad arrangements for Sunday. She had to get a sitter for Debbie. Sh couldn't get her regular sitter, Lana, because Lana was going t Toronto on a weekend jaunt with members of the high-school band. She was able to get a friend of Lana's who wasn't in th band. She was just as glad that it turned out that way, because i was Lana's mother, Dorothy Slote, that she was afraid she migh find with Reuel. Dorothy Slote did Reuel's bookkeeping. She wa divorced, and so well known in Walley for her numerous affair that high-school boys would call to her from their cars, on th street, 'Dorothy Slot, she's hot to trot!' Sometimes she wa referred to as Dorothy Slut. Margot felt sorry for Lana – that wa why she had started hiring her to take care of Debbie. Lana wa not going to be as good-looking as her mother, and she was sh and not too bright. Margot always got her a little present a Christmas-time.

On Saturday afternoon Margot drove to Kincardine. She wa gone only a couple of hours, so she let Joe and his girlfriend tak Debbie to the beach. In Kincardine she rented another car – a van as it happened, an old blue crock pot of a thing like what th hippies drove. She also bought a few cheap clothes and a rathe expensive, real-looking wig. She left them in the van, parked in lot behind a supermarket. On Sunday morning she drove her ca that far, parked it in the lot, got into the van, and changed he clothes and donned the wig, as well as some extra makeup. The she continued driving north.

The wig was a nice light-brown colour, ruffled up on top an long and straight in the back. The clothes were tight pink denin pants and a pink-and-white striped top. Margot was thinner then though not *thin*. Also, buffalo sandals, dangly earrings, big pinl sunglasses. The works.

'I didn't miss a trick,' said Margot. 'I did my eyes up kind of Cleopatra-ish. I don't believe my own kids could've recognised me. The mistake I made was those pants – they were too tight and too hot. Them and the wig just about killed me. Because it was a blazing hot day. And I was kind of awkward at parking the van, because I'd never driven one before. Otherwise, no problems.'

She drove up Highway 21, the Bluewater, with the window down to get a breeze off the lake, and her long hair blowing and the van radio tuned to a rock station, just to get her in the mood. In the mood for what? She had no idea. She smoked one cigarette after another, trying to steady her nerves. Men driving along kept honking at her. Of course the highway was busy, of course Wasaga Beach was jammed, a bright, hot Sunday like this, in June. Around the beach the traffic was just crawling, and the smell of French fries and noon-hour barbecues pressed down like a blanket. It took her a while just to find the campground, but she did, and paid her day fee, and drove in. Round and round the parking lot she drove, trying to spot Reuel's car. She didn't see it. Then it occurred to her that the lot would be just for day visitors. She found a parking place.

Now she had to reconnoitre the entire grounds, on foot. She walked first all through the campground part. Trailer hookups, tents, people sitting out beside the trailers and tents drinking beer and playing cards and barbecuing lunch – more or less just what they would have been doing at home. There was a central playground, with swings and slides kept busy, and kids throwing Frisbees, and babies in the sandbox. A refreshment stand, where Margot got a Coke. She was too nervous to eat anything. It was strange to her to be in a family place yet not part of any family.

Nobody whistled or made remarks to her. There were lots of long-haired girls around showing off more than she did. And you had to admit that what they had was in better condition to be shown.

She walked the sandy paths under the pines, away from the trailers. She came to a part of the grounds that looked like an old resort, probably there long before anybody ever thought of trailer hookups. The shade of the big pines was a relief to her. The ground underneath was brown with their needles – hard dirt had turned to a soft and furry dust. There were double cabins and single cabins, painted dark green. Picnic tables beside them. Stone fireplaces. Tubs of flowers in bloom. It was nice.

There were cars parked by some of the cabins, but Reuel's wasn't there. She didn't see anybody around – maybe the people who stayed in cabins were the sort who went down to the beach. Across the road was a place with a bench and a drinking fountain and a trash can. She sat down on the bench to rest.

And out he came. Reuel. He came out of the cabin right across from where she was sitting. Right in front of her nose. He was wearing his bathing trunks and he had a couple of towels slung over his shoulders. He walked in a lazy, slouching way. A roll of white fat sloped over the waistband of his trunks. 'Straighten up, at least!' Margot wanted to yell at him. Was he slouching like that because he felt sneaky and ashamed? Or just worn out with happy exercise? Or had he been slouching for a long time and she hadn't noticed? His big strong body turning into something like custard.

He reached into the car parked beside the cabin, and she knew he was reaching for his cigarettes. She knew, because at the same moment she was fumbling in her bag for hers. If this was a movie, she thought – if this was only a movie, he'd come springing across the road with a light, keen to assist the stray pretty girl. Never recognising her, while the audience held its breath. Then recognition dawning, and horror – incredulity and horror. While she, the wife, sat there cool and satisfied, drawing deep on her cigarette. But none of this happened, of course none of it happened; he didn't even look across the road. She sat sweating in her denim pants, and her hands shook so that she had to put her cigarette away.

The car wasn't his. What kind of car did Dorothy Slut drive?

Maybe he was with somebody else, somebody totally unknown to Margot, a stranger. Some stranger who figured she knew him as well as his wife.

No. No. Not unknown. Not a stranger. Not in the least a stranger. The door of the cabin opened again, and there was Lana Slote. Lana, who was supposed to be in Toronto with the band. Couldn't baby-sit Debbie. Lana, whom Margot had always felt sorry for and been kind to because she thought the girl was slightly lonesome, or unlucky. Because she thought it showed, that Lana was brought up mostly by old grandparents. Lana seemed old-fashioned, prematurely serious without being clever, and not very healthy, as if she were allowed to live on soft drinks and sugared cereal and whatever mush of canned corn and fried potatoes and maraconi-and-cheese loaf those old people dished up for supper. She got bad colds with asthmatic complications, her complexion was dull and pale. But she did have a chunky, appealing little figure, well developed front and back, and chipmunk cheeks when she smiled, and silky flat, naturally blonde hair. She was so meek that even Debbie could boss her around, and the boys thought she was a joke.

Lana was wearing a bathing suit that her grandmother might have chosen for her. A shirred top over her bunchy little breasts and a flowered skirt. Her legs were stumpy, untanned. She stood there on the step as if she was afraid to come out – afraid to appear in a bathing suit or afraid to appear at all. Reuel had to go over and give her a loving little spank to get her moving. With numerous lingering pats he arranged one of the towels around her shoulders. He touched his cheek to her flat blonde head, then rubbed his nose in her hair, no doubt to inhale its baby fragrance. Margot watched it all.

They walked away, down the road to the beach, respectably keeping their distance. Father and child.

Margot observed now that the car was a rented one. From a place in Walkerton. How funny, she thought, if it had been rented in Kincardine, at the same place where she rented the van. She wanted to put a note under the windshield wiper, but she didn't have anything to write on. She had a pen but no paper. But on the grass beside the trash can she spied a Kentucky Fried Chicken bag. Hardly a grease spot on it. She tore it into pieces, and on the

pieces she wrote – or printed, actually, in capital letters – these
messages:

YOU BETTER WATCH YOURSELF,
YOU COULD END UP IN JAIL.

·

THE VICE SQUAD WILL GET YOU IF
YOU DON'T WATCH OUT.

·

PERVERTS NEVER PROSPER.

·

LIKE MOTHER LIKE DAUGHTER.

·

BETTER THROW THAT ONE BACK IN
THE FRENCH RIVER, IT'S NOT FULL GROWN.

·

SHAME.

·

SHAME.

She wrote another that said 'BIG FAT SLOB WITH YOUR BABY
FACED MORON,' but tore that up – she didn't like the tone of it.
Hysterical. She stuck the notes where she was sure they would be
found – under the windshield wiper, in the crack of the door,
weighed down by stones on the picnic table. Then she hurried
away with her heart racing. She drove so badly, at first, that she
almost killed a dog before she got out of the parking lot. She did
not trust herself on the highway, so she drove on back roads,
gravel roads, and kept reminding herself to keep her speed down.
She wanted to go fast. She wanted to take off. She felt right on the
edge of blowing up, blowing to smithereens. Was it good or was it
terrible, the way she felt? She couldn't say. She felt that she had
been cut loose, nothing mattered to her, she was as light as a blade
of grass.

But she ended up in Kincardine. She changed her clothes and
took off the wig and rubbed the makeup off her eyes. She put the

clothes and the wig in the supermarket trash bin – not without
thinking what a pity – and she turned in the van. She wanted to go
into the hotel bar and have a drink, but she was afraid of what she
might do if any man saw her alone and came up with the least
remark to her. Even if he just said, 'Hot day,' she might yelp at
him, she might try to claw his face off.

Home. The children. Pay the sitter. A friend of Lana's. Could she
be the one who had phoned? Get takeout for supper. Pizza – not
Kentucky Fried, which she would never be able to think of again
without being reminded. Then she sat up late, waiting. She had
some drinks. Certain notions kept banging about in her head.
Lawyer. Divorce. Punishment. These notions hit her like gongs,
then died away without giving her any idea about how to proceed.
What should she do first, what should she do next, how should
her life go on? The children all had appointments of one kind or
another, the boys had summer jobs, Debbie was about to have a
minor operation on her ear. She couldn't take them away; she'd
have to do it all herself, right in the middle of everybody's gossip
– which she'd had enough of once before. Also, she and Reuel
were invited to a big anniversary party next weekend; she had to
get the present. A man was coming to look at the drains.

Reuel was so late getting home that she began to be afraid he'd
had an accident. He'd had to go around by Orangeville, to deliver
Lana to the home of her aunt. He'd pretended to be a high-school
teacher transporting a member of the band. (The real teacher had
been told, meanwhile, that Lana's aunt was sick and Lana was in
Orangeville looking after her.) Reuel's stomach was upset,
naturally, after those notes. He sat at the kitchen table chewing
tablets and drinking milk. Margot made coffee, to sober herself
for the fray.

Reuel said it was all innocent. An outing for the girl. Like
Margot, he'd felt sorry for her. Innocent.

Margot laughed at that. She laughed, telling about it.

'I said to him, "Innocent! I know your innocent! Who do you
think you're talking to," I said, "Teresa?" And he said, "*Who?*"

No, really. Just for a minute he looked blank, before he remembered. He said, "*Who?*"

Margot thought then, what punishment? Who for? She thought, he'll probably marry that girl and there'll be babies for sure and pretty soon not enough money to go around.

Before they went to bed at some awful hour in the morning, she had the promise of her house.

'Because there comes a time with men, they really don't want the hassle. They'd rather weasel out. I bargained him down to the wire, and I got pretty near everything I wanted. If he got balky about something later on, all I'd have to say was "Wigtime!" I'd told him the whole thing – the wig and the van and where I sat and everything. I'd say that in front of the kids or anybody, and none of them would know what I was talking about. But he'd know! Reuel would know. *Wigtime!* I still say it once in a while, whenever I think it's appropriate.'

She fished a slice of orange out of her glass and sucked, then chewed on it. 'I put a little something else in this besides the wine,' she said. 'I put a little vodka, too. Notice?'

She stretched her arms and legs out in the sun.

'Whenever I think it's – appropriate.'

Anita thought that Margot might have given up on vanity but she probably hadn't given up on sex. Margot might be able to contemplate sex without fine-looking bodies or kindly sentiments. A healthy battering.

And what about Reuel – what had he given up on? Whatever he did, it wouldn't be till he was ready. That was what all Margot's hard bargaining would really be coming up against – whether Reuel was ready or not. That was something he'd never feel obliged to tell her. So a woman like Margot can still be fooled – this was what Anita thought, with a momentary pleasure, a completely comfortable treachery – by a man like Reuel.

'Now you,' said Margot, with an ample satisfaction. 'I told you something. Time for you to tell me. Tell me how you decided to leave your husband.'

Anita told her what had happened in a restaurant in British

Columbia. Anita and her husband, on a holiday, went into a roadside restaurant, and Anita saw a man who reminded her of a man she had been in love with – no, perhaps she had better say infatuated with – years and years ago. The man in the restaurant had a pale-skinned, heavy face, with a scornful and evasive expression, which could have been a dull copy of the face of the man she loved, and his long-legged body could have been a copy of that man's body if it had been struck by lethargy. Anita could hardly tear herself away when it came time to leave the restaurant. She understood that expression – she felt that she was tearing herself away, she got loose in strips and tatters. All the way up the Island Highway, between the dark enclosing rows of tall fir and spruce trees, and on the ferry to Prince Rupert, she felt an absurd pain of separation. She decided that if she could feel such a pain, if she could feel more for a phantom than she could ever feel in her marriage, she had better go.

So she told Margot. It was more difficult than that, of course, and it was not so clear.

'Then did you go and find that other man?' said Margot.

'No. It was one-sided. I couldn't.'

'Somebody else, then?'

'And somebody else, and somebody else,' said Anita, smiling. The other night when she had been sitting beside her mother's bed, waiting to give her mother an injection, she had thought about men, putting names one upon another as if to pass the time, just as you'd name great rivers of the world, or capital cities, or the children of Queen Victoria. She felt regret about some of them but no repentance. Warmth, in fact, spread from the tidy buildup. An accumulating satisfaction.

'Well, that's one way,' said Margot staunchly. 'But it seems weird to me. It does. I mean – I can't see the use of it, if you don't marry them.' She paused. 'Do you know what I do, sometimes?' She got up quickly and went to the sliding doors. She listened, then opened the door and stuck her head inside. She came back and sat down.

'Just checking to see Debbie's not getting an earful,' she said.

'Boys, you can tell any horrific personal stuff in front of them and you might as well be speaking Hindu, for all they ever listen. But girls listen. Debbie listens . . .

'I'll tell you what I do,' she said. 'I go out and see Teresa.'

'Is she still there?' said Anita with great surprise. 'Is Teresa still out at the store?'

'What store?' said Margot. 'Oh, no! No, no. The store's gone. The gas station's gone. Torn down years ago. Teresa's in the County Home. They have this what they call the Psychiatric Wing out there now. The weird thing is, she worked out there for years and years, just handing round trays and tidying up and doing this and that for them. Then she started having funny spells herself. So now she's sometimes sort of working there and she's sometimes just *there*, if you know what I mean. When she goes off, she's never any trouble. She's just pretty mixed up. Talk-talk-talk-talk-talk. The way she always did, only more so. All she has any idea of is talk-talk-talk, and fix herself up. If you come and see her, she always wants you to bring her some bath oil or perfume or makeup. Last time I went out, I took her some of that highlight stuff for her hair. I thought that was taking a chance, it was kind of complicated for her to use. But she read the directions, she made out fine. She didn't make a mess. What I mean by mixed up is, she figures she's on the boat. The boat with the war brides. Bringing them all out to Canada.'

'War brides,' Anita said. She saw them crowned with white feathers, fierce and unsullied. She was thinking of war bonnets.

She didn't need to see him, for years she hadn't the least wish to see him. A man undermines your life for an uncontrollable time, and then one day there's nothing, just a hollow where he was, it's unaccountable.

'You know what just flashed on my mind this minute?' said Margot. 'Just how the store used to look in the morning. And us coming in half froze.'

Then she said in a flattened, disbelieving voice, 'She used to come and beat on the door. Out there. Out there, when Reuel was with me in the room. It was awful. I don't know. I don't know –

do you think it was love?'

From up here on the deck the two long arms of the breakwater look like matchsticks. The towers and pyramids and conveyor belts of the salt mine look like large solid toys. The lake is glinting like foil. Everything seems bright and distinct and harmless. Spellbound.

'We're all on the boat,' says Margot. 'She thinks we're all on the boat.' But she's the one Reuel's going to meet in Halifax, lucky her.'

Margot and Anita have got this far. They are not ready to stop talking. They are fairly happy.

(Margaret Robertson read this story on *Woman's Hour* in October 1990.)

SOMEWHERE
MORE CENTRAL

◆

Beryl Bainbridge

I never took all that much notice of Grandma when she was alive. She was just there. I mean, I saw her at Christmas and things – I played cards with her to keep her occupied, and sometimes I let her take me out to tea in a café. She had a certain style, but the trouble was that she didn't look old enough to be downright eccentric. She wore fur coats mostly and a lot of jewellery, and hats with flowers flopping over the brim; she even painted her fingernails red. I was surprised that she'd died and even more surprised to hear that she was over seventy. I didn't cry or anything. My mother made enough fuss for both of us, moaning and pulling weird faces. I hadn't realised she was all that attached to her either. Whenever that advert came on the telly, the one about 'Make someone happy this weekend – give them a telephone call', Mother rolled her eyes and said 'My God!' When she rang Grandma, Grandma picked up the receiver and said 'Hallo, stranger.'

The night before the funeral there were the usual threats about how I needn't think I was going to wear my jeans and duffle coat. I didn't argue. My Mum knew perfectly well that I was going to wear them. I don't know why she wastes her breath. In the morning we had to get up at six o'clock, because we were travelling on the early train from Euston. It was February and mild, but just as we were sitting down to breakfast Mother said 'Oh, look Alice,' and outside the window snow was falling on the privet hedge.

When we set off for the station, the pavements were covered over. Mother had to cling onto the railings in case she slipped going down the steps. The bottoms of my jeans were all slushy in no time, so it was just as well she hadn't succeeded in making me wear those ghastly tights and high-heeled shoes. I thought maybe the trains would be delayed by the snow, but almost before we reached the station it was melting, and when we left London and the suburbs behind the snow had gone, even from the hedges and the trees. The sky turned blue. I was sorry on Mother's behalf. You can't really have a sad funeral with the sun shining. She looked terrible. She looked like that poster for 'Keep death off the roads'. She'd borrowed a black coat with a fur collar from the woman next door. She had black stockings and shoes to match. She doesn't wear make-up, and her mouth seemed to have been cut out of white paper. She never said much either. She didn't keep pointing things out as if I was still at primary school, like she usually does – 'Oh look, Alice, cows . . . Oh, Alice, look at the baa lambs.' She just stared out at the flying fields with a forlorn droop to her mouth.

Just as I'm a disappointment to Mother, she'd been a disappointment to Grandma. Only difference is, I couldn't care less. Whenever I have what they call 'problems' at school, I'm sent to the clinic to be understood by some psychologist with a nervous twitch, and he tells me it's perfectly natural to steal from the cloakroom and cheat at French, and anyway it's all my mother's fault. They didn't have a clinic in Mother's day, so she's riddled with guilt. Apparently Grandma was very hurt when Mother got married and even more hurt when she got divorced. First Grandma had to go round pretending I was a premature baby and then later she had to keep her mouth shut about my father running off with another woman. She didn't tell anyone about the divorce for three years, not until everybody started doing the same thing, even the people in Grandma's road. Actually I don't think Grandma minded, not deep down; it was more likely that she just didn't care for the sound of it. There were a lot of things Grandma didn't like the sound of: my record player for one, and the mattress in the spare room for another. If we went down town for tea, she used to peer at the menu outside the café for ages before making up her mind. It drove Mother wild. 'I don't think we'll stop,' Grandma would say, and Mother would ask irritably, 'Why ever not, Grandma?' and Grandma would toss her head and say firmly, 'I don't like the sound of it.' And off she'd trot down the road, swaying a little under the weight of her fur coat, the rain pattering on the cloth roses on her hat, with me and Mother trailing behind.

Once I went on my own with Grandma to a restaurant on the top floor of a large shopping store. We were going to have a proper meal with chips and bread and butter. The manager came forward to show us where to sit and we began to walk across this huge room to the far side, towards a table half-hidden behind a pillar. My mother always moves as if she's anxious to catch a bus, but Grandma took her time. She walked as if she was coming down a flight of stairs in one of those old movies. She looked to right and left, one hand raised slightly and arched at the wrist, as though she dangled a fan. I always felt she was waiting to be recognised by somebody or expecting to be asked to dance. She went slowly past all these tables, and then suddenly she stopped and said quite loudly, 'I don't like the sound of it.' She turned and looked at me; her mouth wobbled the way it did when she'd run out of peppermints or I'd beaten her at cards. I was sure everybody was looking at us, but I wasn't too embarrassed, not the way I am when Mother shows herself up – after all Grandma had nothing to do with me. The manager stopped too and came back to ask what was wrong. 'You're never putting me there?' said Grandma, as though he'd intended sending her to Siberia. She got her own way, of course, 'somewhere more central', as she put it. Before we had tea we smoked a cigarette. When she flipped her lighter it played a little tune. 'I don't like being shoved into a corner,' she said. 'There's no point my light being hid under a bushel.'

I wasn't really looking forward to the funeral. I'd been in a church once before and I didn't think much of it. I couldn't have been the only one either, because the next time I passed it they'd turned it into a Bingo hall.

When we were nearly at Liverpool my mother said if I behaved myself I could go to the graveside. 'You mustn't ask damn fool questions,' she warned. 'And you mustn't laugh at the vicar.'

'Are they going to put Grandma in with Grandpa?' I asked. I knew Grandma hadn't liked him when he was alive. They hadn't slept in the same bed.

My mother said, Yes, they were. They had to – there was a shortage of space.

'Do you know,' she said, 'your Grandma was madly in love with a man called Walter. He played tennis on the Isle of Wight. He married somebody else.'

I wanted to know more about Walter, but the train was coming into Lime Street station and Mother was doing her usual business of jumping round like a ferret in a box and telling me to comb my hair and pull myself together. She led me at a run up the platform because she said we had to be first in the queue for a taxi. We had a connexion to catch at another station.

It turned out that there was a new one-way system for traffic that Mother hadn't known about. If we'd walked, all we'd have had to do, she said, was to sprint past Blacklers and through Williamson Square, and then up Stanley Street and we'd have been there. As it was we went on a sort of flyover and then a motorway and it took twenty minutes to reach Exchange Station. She was breathless with anxiety when she paid the cab driver. We hadn't bought tickets for the next train and the man at the barrier wouldn't let us through without them.

'But they're burying my flesh and blood,' shouted Mother, 'at this very moment,' as though she could hear in her head the sound of spades digging into the earth.

'Can't help that, luv,' said the porter, waving her aside.

Then Mother did a frantic little tap-dance on the spot and screamed out, 'God damn you, may you roast in hell', and on the platform, echoing Mother's thin blast of malice, the guard blew a shrill note on his whistle, and the train went. I kept well out of it. The only good it did, Mother making such a spectacle of herself, was to bring some colour back to her cheeks. When the next train came we had to slink through the barrier without looking at the porter. On the journey Mother never opened her mouth, not even to tell me to sit up straight.

We weren't really late. My Uncle George was waiting for us at the other end, in his new Rover, and he said the cars weren't due for another half hour. 'Mildred's done all the sandwiches for after,' he said, 'and the sausage rolls are ready to pop into the oven.'

'That's nice,' said Mother, in a subdued tone of voice, and she leaned against me in the back of the car and held on to my arm, as if she was desperately ill. I couldn't very well shake her off, but it made me feel a bit stupid.

My Uncle George is an idiot. He said I was a bonny girl and hadn't I grown. The last time he'd seen me I was only six so you can tell he isn't exactly Brain of Britain.

It was funny being in Grandma's house without her there. She was very house-proud and usually she made you take your shoes off in the hall so as not to mess the carpet. My Auntie Mildred was dropping crumbs all over the place and she'd put a milk bottle on the dining-room table. There was dust on the face of the grandfather clock. Grandma was a great one for dusting and polishing. She wore a turban to do it, and an old satin slip with a cardigan over it. She never wore her good clothes when she was in the house. My mother and her used to have arguments about it. Mother said it wasn't right to look slovenly just because one was indoors, and Grandma said Mother was a fine one to talk. She said Mother looked a mess whether she was indoors or out.

I wasn't sure where Grandma was, and I didn't like to ask. When the cars came I was amazed to find that Grandma had come in one of them and was waiting outside. There were only two bunches of flowers on the coffin lid.

'Why aren't there more flowers?' asked my mother. 'Surely everyone sent flowers?'

'I thought it best,' explained my Uncle George, 'to request no flowers but donations to the Heart Diseases Foundation. Mother would have preferred that, I think. She always said flowers at a funeral were a waste of good money.'

Mother didn't say anything, but her lips tightened. She knew that Grandma would be livid at so few flowers in the hearse. Grandma *did* say that flowers were a waste of money, but she'd been talking about other people's funerals, not her own.

I don't remember much about the service, except that there were a lot of people in the church. I thought only old ladies went to church, but there were a dozen men as well. At the back of the pews there was an odd-looking bloke with a grey beard, holding a spotted handkerchief in his hand. He seemed quite upset and emotional. He kept trying to sing the hymns and swallowing and going quiet. I know because I turned round several times to stare at him. I kept wondering if it was Walter from the Isle of Wight.

For some reason they weren't burying Grandma at that church. There wasn't the soil. Instead we followed her to another place at the other end of the village. The vicar had to get there first to meet Grandma, so we went a longer route round by the coal yards and the Council offices.

It was a big graveyard. There were trees, black ones without leaves, and holly bushes, and marble angels set on plinths over-grown with ivy. Four men carried Grandma to her resting place. Ahead of her went some little choirboys in knee-socks and white frilly smocks. They sang a very sad song about fast falls the even-tide. It wasn't even late afternoon, but the sky was grey now and nothing moved, not a branch, not a fold of material, not a leaf on the holly bushes.

The vicar followed directly behind Grandma, and after him came my Uncle George, supporting Mother at the elbow, and lastly me and my Auntie Mildred. We went up the path from the gate and round the side of the church and up another path through a great field of grey stones and tablets and those angels with marble wings. But we didn't stop. The small boys went on singing and the men went on carrying Grandma and we reached a hedge and turned right and then left, until we came to a new plot of ground, so out of the way and unimportant that they'd left bricks and rubble lying on the path. And still we kept on walking. I don't know why someone didn't cry out 'Wait', why some great voice from out of the sky didn't tell us to stop. I thought of Grandma in the restaurant, standing her ground, refusing to budge from her central position.

After she was put in the earth, before they hid her light under a bushel, we threw bits of soil on top of the coffin.

I didn't like the sound of it.

(Beryl Bainbridge read this story on *Woman's Hour* in May 1992.)

FLOWN
THE NEST

HER MOTHER

◆

Anjana Appachana

When she got her daughter's first letter from America, the mother had a good cry. Everything was fine, the daughter said. The plane journey was fine, her professor who met her at the airport was nice, her university was very nice, the house she shared with two American girls (nice girls) was fine, her classes were OK and her teaching was surprisingly fine. She ended the letter saying she was fine and hoping her mother and father were too. The mother let out a moan she could barely control and wept in an agony of longing and pain and frustration. Who would have dreamt that her daughter was doing a PhD in Comparative Literature, she thought, wiping her eyes with her sari palla, when all the words at her command were 'fine', 'nice', and 'OK'? Who would have imagined that she was a gold medallist from Delhi University? Who would know from the blandness of her letter, its vapidity, the monotony of its tone and the indifference of its adjectives that it came from a girl so intense and articulate? Her daughter had written promptly, as she had said she would, the mother thought, cleaning her smudged spectacles and beginning to reread the letter. It had taken only ten days to arrive. She examined her daughter's handwriting. There seemed to be no trace of loneliness there, or discomfort, or insecurity – the writing was firm, rounded and clear. She hadn't mentioned if that overfriendly man at the airport had sat next to her on the plane. The mother hoped not. Once Indian men boarded the plane for a new country, the anonymity drove them crazy. They got drunk and made life hell for the air-hostesses and everyone else nearby, but of course, they thought they were flirting with finesse. Her daughter, for all her arguments with her parents, didn't know how to deal with such men. Most men. Her brows furrowed, the mother took out a letter writing pad from her folder on the dining table and began to write. Eat properly, she wrote. Have plenty of milk, cheese and cereal. Eating badly makes you age fast. That's why western women look so haggard. They might be pencil slim, but look at the lines on their faces. At thirty they start look- ing faded. So don't start these stupid, western dieting fads. Oil your hair every week and avoid shampoos. Chemicals ruin the hair. (You can get almond oil easily if coconut oil isn't available.) With all the hundreds of shampoos in America, American women's hair isn't a patch on Indian women's. Your grandmother had thick, black hair till the day she died.

One day, two months earlier, her daughter had cut off her long thick hair, just like that. The abruptness and sacrilege of this act still haunted the mother. That evening, when she opened the door for her daughter, her hair reached just below her ears. The daughter stood there, not looking at either her mother or father, but almost, it seemed, beyond them, her face a strange mixture of relief and defiance and anger, as her father, his face twisted, said, why, why. I like it short, she said. Fifteen years of growing it below her knees, of oiling it every week, and washing it so lovingly, the mother thought as she touched her daughter's cheek and said, you are angry with us . . . is this your revenge? Her daughter had removed her hand and moved past her parents, past her brother-in-law who was behind them, and into her room. For the father it was as though a limb had been amputated. For days he brooded in his chair in the corner of the sitting-room, almost in mourning, avoiding even looking at her, while the mother murmured, you have perfected the art of hurting us.

Your brother-in-law has finally been allotted his three-bed-roomed house, she wrote, and he moved into it last week. I think he was quite relieved to, after living with us these few months. So there he is, living all alone in that big house with two servants while your sister continues working in Bombay. Your sister says that commuting marriages are inevitable, and like you, is not interested in hearing her mother's opinion on the subject. I suppose they will go on like this for years, postponing having children, postponing being together, until one day when they're as old as your father and me, they'll have nothing to look forward to. Tell me, where would we have been without you both? Of course, you will only support your sister and your brother-in-law and their strange, selfish marriage. Perhaps that is your dream too. Nobody seems to have normal dreams any more.

The mother had once dreamt of love and a large home, silk saris and sapphires. The love she had got, but as her husband struggled in his job and the children came and as they took loans to marry off her husband's sisters, the rest she did not. In the next fifteen years she had collected a nice selection of silk saris and jewellery for her daughters, but by that time, they showed no inclination for either. The older daughter and her husband had had a registered marriage, refused to have even a reception and did not accept so much as a handkerchief from their respective parents. And the younger one had said quite firmly before she left, that she wasn't even thinking of marriage.

The mother looked at her husband's back in the verandah. That's all he did after he came back from the office – sit in the verandah and think of his precious daughters, while she cooked and cleaned, attended to visitors and wrote to all her sisters and his sisters. Solitude to think – what a luxury! She had never thought in solitude. Her thoughts jumped to and fro and up and down and in and out as she dusted, cooked, cleaned, rearranged cupboards, polished the brass, put buttons on shirts and falls on saris, as she sympathised with her neighbour's problems and scolded the dhobi for not putting enough starch on the saris, as she reprimanded the milkman for watering the milk and lit the kerosene stove because the gas had finished, as she took the dry clothes from the clothes line and couldn't press them because the electricity had failed and realised that the cake in the oven would now never rise. The daughter was like her father, the mother thought – she too had wanted the escape of solitude, which meant, of course, that in the process she neither made her bed nor tidied up her room.

How will you look after yourself, my Rani Beti? she wrote. You have always had your mother to look after your comforts. I'm your mother and I don't mind doing all this, but some day you'll have to do it for the man you marry and how will you, when you can't even thread a needle?

But of course, her daughter didn't want marriage. She had been saying so, vehemently, in the last few months. The father blamed the mother. The mother had not taught her how to cook or sew and had only encouraged her and her sister to think and act with an independence quite uncalled for in daughters. How then, he asked her, could she expect her daughters to be suddenly amenable? How could she complain that she had no grandchildren and lose herself in self-pity when it was all her doing? Sometimes the mother fought with the father when he said such things, at other times she cried or brooded. But she was not much of a brooder, and losing her temper or crying helped her cope better.

The mother laid aside her pen. She had vowed not to lecture her daughter, and there she was, filling pages of rubbish when all she wanted to do was cry out, why did you leave us in such anger? what did we not do for you? why, why? No, she would not ask. She wasn't one to get after the poor child like that.

How far away you are, my pet, she wrote. How could you go away like that, so angry with the world? Why, my love, why? Your father says that I taught you to be so independent that all you hankered for was to get away from us. He says it's all my fault. I have heard that refrain enough in my married life. After all that I did for you, tutoring you, disciplining you, indulging you, caring for you, he says he understands you better because you are like him. And I can't even deny that because it's true. I must say it's very unfair, considering that all he did for you and your sister was give you chocolates and books.

When her daughter was six, the mother recalled, the teacher

had asked the class to make a sentence with the word 'good'. She had written, my father is a good man. The mother sighed as she recalled asking her, isn't your mother a good woman? And the daughter's reply, daddy is gooder. The mother wrote, no, I don't understand – you talk like him, look like him, are as obstinate and as stupidly honest. It is as though he conceived you and gave birth to you entirely on his own. She was an ayah, the mother thought, putting her pen aside, that was all she was; she did all the dirty work and her husband got all the love.

The next day, after her husband had left for the office, the mother continued her letter. She wrote in a tinier handwriting now, squeezing as much as possible into the thin air-mail sheet. Write a longer letter to me next time, my Rani, she wrote. Try and write as though you were talking to me. Describe the trees, the buildings, the people. Try not to be your usual perfunctory self. Let your mother experience America through your eyes. Also, before I forget, you must bathe every day, regardless of how cold it gets. People there can be quite dirty. But no, if I recall correctly, it is the English and other Europeans who hate to bathe. Your Naina Aunty, after her trip to Europe, said that they smelled all the time. Americans are almost as clean as Indians. And don't get into the dirty habit of using toilet paper, all right?

The mother blew her nose and wiped her cheek. Two years, she wrote, or even more for you to come back. I can't even begin to count the days for two years. How we worry, how we worry. Had you gone abroad with a husband, we would have been at peace, but now? If you fall ill who will look after you? You can't even make dal. You can't live on bread and cheese forever, but knowing you, you will. You will lose your complexion, your health, your hair. But why should I concern myself with your hair? You cut it off, just like that.

The mother laid her cheek on her hand and gazed at the door where her daughter had stood with her cropped hair, while she, her husband and her son-in-law stood like three figures in a tableau. The short hair made her face look even thinner. Suddenly she looked ordinary, like all the thousands of short-haired, western-looking Delhi girls one saw, all ordinarily attractive like the others, all the same. Her husband saying, why, why? his hands up in the air, his lazy grin suddenly wiped off his face; she recalled it all, like a film in slow motion.

I always thought I understood you, she wrote, your dreams, your problems, but suddenly it seems there is nothing that I understand. No, nothing, she thought, the tiredness weighing down her eyes. She was ranting – the child could do without it. But how, how could she not think of this daughter of hers, who in the last few months, had rushed from her usual, settled quietness to such unsettled stillness that it seemed the very house would begin to balloon outwards, unable to contain her straining.

Enough, she wrote. Let me give you the news before I make you angry with my grief. The day after you left, Mrs Gupta from next door dropped in to comfort me, bless her. She said she had full faith you would come back, that only boys didn't. She says a daughter will always regard her parents' home as her only home, unlike sons who attach themselves to their wives. As you know, she has four sons, all married, and all, she says, under their wives' thumbs. But it was true, the mother thought. Her own husband fell to pieces every time she visited her parents without him. When he accompanied her there he needed so much looking after that she couldn't talk to her mother, so she preferred to go without him. With her parents she felt indulged and irresponsible. Who indulged her now? And when she came back from her parents the ayah would complain that her husband could never find his clothes, slept on the bedcover, constantly misplaced his spectacles, didn't know how to get himself a glass of water and kept waiting for the postman.

With all your talk about women's rights, she wrote, you refuse to see that your father has given me none. And on top of that he says that I am a nag. If I am a nag, it is because he's made me one. And talking of women's rights, some women take it too far. Mrs Parekh is having, as the books say, a torrid affair with a married man. This man's wife is presently with her parents and when Mrs Parekh's husband is on tour, she spends the night with him, and comes back early in the morning to get her children ready for school. Everyone has seen her car parked in the middle of the night outside his flat. Today our ayah said, memsahib, people like us do it for money. Why do memsahibs like her do it? But of course, you will launch into a tirade of how this is none of my business and sum it up with your famous phrase, each to her own. But my child, they're both married. Surely you won't defend it? Sometimes I don't understand how your strong principles co-exist with such strange values for what society says is wrong. Each to her own, you have often told me angrily, never seeming to realise that it is never one's own when one takes such a reckless step, that entire families disintegrate, that children bear scars forever. Each to her own, indeed.

Yes, she was a straightforward girl, the mother thought, and so loyal to those she loved. When the older daughter had got married five years ago, and this one was only seventeen, how staunchly she had supported her sister and brother-in-law's decision to do without all the frills of an Indian wedding. How she had later defended her sister's decision to continue with her job in Bombay, when her husband came on a transfer to Delhi. She had lost her temper with her parents for writing reproachful letters to the older daughter, and scolded them when they expressed their worry to the son-in-law, saying that as long as he was living with them, they should say nothing.

The mother was fond of her son-in-law in her own way. But deep inside she felt that he was irresponsible, uncaring and lazy. Yes, he had infinite charm, but he didn't write regularly to his wife, didn't save a paisa of his salary (he didn't even have a life insurance policy and no thoughts at all of buying a house), and instead of spending his evenings in the house as befitted a married man, went on a binge of plays and other cultural programmes, often taking her younger daughter with him, spending huge amounts on petrol and eating out. His wife was too practical, he told the mother, especially about money. She believed in saving, he believed in spending. She wanted security, he wanted fun. He laughed as he said this, and gave her a huge box of the most expensive barfis. The mother had to smile. She wanted him to pine for her daughter. Instead, he joked about her passion for her work and how he was waiting for the day when she would be earning twice as much as him, so that he could resign from his job and live luxuriously off her, reading, trekking and sleeping. At such times the mother would laugh and say that his priorities were clear. And the older daughter would write and urge the mother not to hound her sister about marriage, to let her pursue her interests. The sisters supported each other, the mother thought, irritated but happy.

Yesterday, the mother wrote, we got a letter from Naina Aunty. Her friend's son, a boy of twenty-six, is doing his PhD in Stanford. He is tall, fair and very handsome. He is also supposed to be very intellectual, so don't get on your high horse. His family background is very cultured. Both his parents are lawyers. They are looking for a suitable match for him and Naina Aunty, who loves you so much, immediately thought of you and mentioned to them that you are also in the States. Now, before losing your temper with me, listen properly. This is just a suggestion. We are *not* forcing you into a marriage you don't want. But you must keep an open mind. At least meet him. Rather, *he* will come to the university to meet you. Talk, go out together, see how much you like each other. *Just* meet him and try and look pleasant and smile for a change. Give your father and me the pleasure of saying, there is *someone* who will look after our child. If something happens to us, who will look after you? I know what a romantic you are, but believe me, arranged marriages work very well. Firstly, the bride is readily accepted by the family. Now look at me. Ours was a love marriage and his parents disliked me and disapproved of our marriage because my *sister* had married out of the community. They thought I was fast because in *those* days I played tennis with other men, wore lipstick and bras. I wonder why I bore it. I should have been as cold and as distant as them. But I was ingratiating and accommodating. Then your father and I had to marry off his sisters. Now in an arranged marriage you can choose not to have such liabilities. I am not materialistic, but I am not a fool either. I know you want to be economically independent, and you must be that, but it will also help if your husband isn't burdened with debts. I am not blaming your father. Responsibilities are responsibilities. But if you can help it, why begin married life with them? Now don't write back and say you're sick of my nagging. You think I am a nag because it is I who wield the stick and your father who gives those wonderful, idealistic lectures. Perhaps when you marry you will realise that fathers and husbands are two very different things. In an arranged marriage you will not be disillusioned because you will not have any illusions to begin with. That is why arranged marriages work. Of course, we will not put any pressure on you. Let us know if it is all right for the boy to meet you and I will write to Naina Aunty accordingly. Each day I pray that you will not marry an American. That would be very hard on us. Now, look at your father and me. Whatever your father's faults, infidelity isn't one of them. Now these Americans, they will divorce you at the drop of a hat. They don't know the meaning of the phrase, 'sanctity of marriage'. My love, if you marry an American and he divorces you and we are no longer in this world, what will you do?

When the milkman came early this morning, he enquired about you. I told him how far away you are. He sighed and said that it was indeed very far. I think he feels for us because he hasn't watered the milk since you left. I'm making the most of it and setting aside lots of thick malai for butter. When the postman came, he said, how is the baby? I replied, now only you will bear her news for us. He immediately asked for baksheesh. I said, nothing doing, what do you mean, baksheesh, it isn't Diwali. He replied, when I got your baby's first letter, wasn't it like Diwali? So I tipped him. Our bai has had a fight with her husband because he got drunk again and spent his entire salary gambling it away. She is in a fury and has left the house saying she won't go back to him unless he swears in the temple that he will never drink again. Your father says, hats off to her. Your father is always enraptured by other women who stand up for themselves. If I stood up for myself he would think he was betrayed.

Betrayal, betrayal, the mother mulled. His job had betrayed him, his strict father had, by a lack of tenderness, betrayed him, India herself had betrayed him after Independence, and this betrayal he raved against every evening, every night. He told her that sometimes he felt glad that his daughter had left a country where brides were burnt for dowry, where everyone was corrupt, where people killed each other in the name of religion and where so many still discriminated against Harijans. At least, he said, his daughter was in a more civilised country. At this the mother got very angry. She said, in America fathers molested their own children. Wives were abused and beaten up, just like the servant classes in India. Friends raped other friends. No one looked after the old. In India, the mother said, every woman got equal pay for equal work. In America they were still fighting for it. Could America ever have a woman president? Never. Could it ever have a black president? Never. Americans were as foolish about religion as Indians, willing to give millions to charlatans who said that the Lord had asked for the money. She was also well read, the mother told her husband, and she knew that no Indian would part with his money so easily. As for discrimination against untouchables in India – it only happened among the uneducated, whereas discrimination against blacks was rampant even among educated Americans. Blacks were the American untouchables. The mother was now in her element. She too had read *Time* and *Newsweek*, she told her husband, and she knew that in India there had never been any question of having segregation in buses where Harijans were concerned, as was the case in America, not so long ago.

Don't rant, her husband told her, and lower your voice, I can hear you without your shrieking. The mother got into a terrible fury and the father left the room.

The mother wrote, you had better give us your views about that country – you can give us a more balanced picture. Your father thinks I'm the proverbial frog in the well. Well, perhaps that is true, but he is another frog in another well and Americans are all frogs in one large, rich well. Imagine, when your aunt was in America, several educated Americans asked her whether India had roads and if people lived in trees. They thought our aunt had learnt all the English she knew in America.

The mother made herself a cup of tea and sipped it slowly. Her son-in-law hadn't even been at home the night her daughter had left. It upset the mother deeply. He could have offered to drive them to the airport at least, comforted them in their sorrow. But he had gone off for one of his plays and arrived a few minutes after they returned from the airport, his hair tousled, his eyes bright. He stopped briefly in the living-room where the mother and father sat quietly, at opposite ends, opened his mouth to say something, then shrugged slightly and went to his room.

Selfish, the mother thought. Thoughtless. The daughter hadn't even enquired about him when she left. Had she recognised that her fun-loving brother-in-law had not an ounce of consideration in him?

The two months before her daughter had left had been the worst. Not only had she stopped talking to her parents, but to him. It frightened the mother. One can say and do what one likes with parents, she told her silent child once, parents will take any-thing. Don't cold-shoulder him too. If he takes a dislike to you and your moods, then you will be alienated even from your sister. Remember, marriage bonds are ultimately stronger than ties between sisters. The daughter had continued reading her book. And soon after, she had cut off her hair. Rapunzel, her brother-in-law had said once, as he watched her dry her hair in the court-yard and it fell like black silk below her knees. Rapunzel, he said again, as the mother smiled and watched her child comb it with her fingers. Rapunzel, Rapunzel, let down your hair. Oh she won't do that, the mother had said, proud that she understood, she is too quiet and withdrawn, and her daughter had gone back to her room and the next day she had cut it off, just like that.

The mother finished her tea and continued her letter. Let me end with some advice, she wrote, and don't groan now. Firstly, keep your distance from American men. You are innocent and have no idea what men are like. Men have more physical feelings than women. I'm sure you understand. Platonic friendships between the two sexes does not exist. In America they do not even pretend that it does. There kissing is as casual as holding hands. And after that you know what happens. One thing can lead to another and the next thing we know you will bring us an American son-in-law. You know we will accept even that if we have to, but it will make us most unhappy.

Secondly, if there is an Indian association in your university, please join it. You might meet some nice Indian men there with the same interests that you have. For get-togethers there, always wear a sari and try to look pleasant. Your father doesn't believe in joining such associations, but I feel it is a must.

The mother was tired of giving advice. What changed you so much the last few months before you left? she wanted to cry, why was going abroad no longer an adventure but an escape? At the airport, when the mother hugged the daughter, she had felt with a mother's instinct that the daughter would not return.

There had been a brief period when her child had seemed suddenly happy, which was strange, considering her final exams were drawing closer. She would work late into the night and the mother would sometimes awaken at night to hear the sounds of her making coffee in the kitchen. Once, on the way to the bathroom she heard sounds of laughter in the kitchen and stepped in to see her daughter and son-in-law cooking a monstrous omelette. He had just returned from one of his late night jaunts. An omelette at 1 a.m., the mother grunted sleepily and the two laughed even more as the toast emerged burnt and the omelette stuck to the pan. Silly children, the mother said and went back to bed.

And then, a few weeks later, that peculiar, turbulent stillness as her daughter continued studying for her exams and stopped talking to all of them, her face pale and shadows under her eyes, emanating a tension that gripped the mother like tentacles and left the father hurt and confused. She snapped at them when they questioned her, so they stopped. I'll talk to her after the exams, the mother told herself. She even stopped having dinner with them, eating either before they all sat at the table, or much after, and then only in her room.

And that pinched look on her face . . . the mother jerked up. It was pain, not anger. Her daughter had been in pain, in pain. She was hiding something. Twelve years ago, when the child was ten, the mother had seen the same pinched, strained look on her face. The child bore her secret for three days, avoiding her parents and her sister, spending long hours in the bathroom and moving almost furtively around the house. The mother noticed that two rolls of cotton had disappeared from her dressing table drawer and that an old bedsheet she had left in the cupboard to cut up and use as dusters had also disappeared. On the third day she saw her daughter go to the bathroom with a suspicious lump in her shirt. She stopped her, her hands on the trembling child's arms, put her fingers into her shirt and took out a large roll of cotton. She guided the child to the bathroom, raised her skirt and pulled down her panties. The daughter watched her mother's face, her eyes filled with terror, waiting for the same terror to reflect on her face, as her mother saw the blood flowing from this unmentionable part of her body and recognised her daughter's imminent death. The mother said, my love, why didn't you tell me, and the child, seeing only compassion, knew she would live, and wept.

The omniscience of motherhood could last only so long, the mother thought, and she could no longer guess her daughter's secrets. Twelve years ago there had been the disappearing cotton and sheet, but now? The mother closed her eyes and her daughter's face swam before her, her eyes dark, that delicate nose and long plaited hair – no, no, it was gone now and she could never picture her with her new face. After her daughter had cut her hair, the mother temporarily lost her vivacity. And the daughter became uncharacteristically tidy – her room spick and span, her desk always in order, every corner dusted, even her cupboard neatly arranged. The mother's daily scoldings to her, which were equally her daily declarations of love, ceased, and she thought she would burst with sadness. So one day, when the mother saw her daughter standing in her room, looking out of the window, a large white handkerchief held to her face, the mother said, don't cry, my love, don't cry, and then, don't you know it's unhygienic to use someone else's hanky, does nothing I tell you register, my Rani? And her daughter, her face flushed, saying, it's clean, and the mother taking it out of her hand and smelling it and snorting, clean what rubbish, and it isn't even your father's, it's your brother-in-law's, it smells of him, and it did, of cigarettes and after shave and God knows what else and the mother had put it for a wash.

The mother's face jerked up. Her finger's grip on the pen loosened and her eyes dilated. Her daughter had not been crying. Her eyes, as they turned to her mother, had that pinched look, but they were clear as she removed the handkerchief from her nose. It had smelled of him as she held it there and she wasn't wiping her tears.

The mother moaned. If God was omniscient, it didn't seem to hurt Him. Why hadn't He denied her the omniscience of motherhood? Oh my love, my love, the mother thought. She held her hand to her aching throat. Oh my love. The tears weren't coming now. She began to write. Sometimes when one is troubled, she wrote, and there is no solution for the trouble, prayer helps. It gives you the strength to carry on. I know you don't believe in rituals, but all I'm asking you to do is to light the lamp in the morning, light an agarbatti, fold your hands, close your eyes and think of truth and correct actions. That's all. Keep these items and the silver idol of Ganesha which I put into your suitcase, in a corner in your cupboard or on your desk. For the mother, who had prayed all her life, prayer was like bathing or brushing her teeth or chopping onions. She had found some strength in the patterns these created, and sometimes, some peace. Once, when her husband reprimanded her for cooking only eight dishes for a dinner party, she had wanted to break all the crockery in the kitchen, but after five minutes in her corner with the Gods, she didn't break them. She couldn't explain this to her child. She couldn't say, it's all right, it happens; or say, you'll forget, knowing her daughter wouldn't. If you don't come back next year, she wrote, knowing her daughter wouldn't, I'll come and get you. She would pretend to have a heart attack, the mother said to herself, her heart beating very fast, her tears falling very rapidly, holding her head in her hands, she would phone her daughter and say, I have to see you before I die, and then her daughter would come home, yes, she would come home, and she would grow her hair again.

(Souad Faress read this story on *Woman's Hour* in May 1992.)

THE
OLDER/YOUNGER
GENERATION

THE KISS

———— ◆ ————

Winifred Beechey

Some families are more given to kissing than others; one sees them at railway stations kissing a whole carriage-full of friends as they prepare to say goodbye. Ours is not a kissing family – that is, what one might call social kissing; but there was one person I always kissed, my husband's Aunt Nesta.

I kissed her for the last time as she lay in her hospital bed: the bedclothes were crisp and undisturbed, and she looked very clean, just as she would have wanted to; and very small, because she was so old, and having started life none too big had ended up, at the age of ninety-one, not much bigger than a child.

Her face was still something of the colour of a ripe apple, and her silvery hair shone with cleanliness as did the pink scalp beneath it.

Two people sat at her bedside in the little cubicle contained by the screens. I had never seen them before; relatives summoned from the north of the country, perhaps. They greeted me without enthusiasm – even with suspicion, I thought – and the woman said, 'She's well away, as you can see.'

Yes, I could tell from Aunt Nessy's breathing that she would not recover consciousness; nevertheless, before I crept out I did kiss her, just in case some little part of her, still aware, should feel it.

In fact, in this moment of her departing I was irrelevant, the couple sitting beside her even more so. The one person who should have been with her was absent, having (as Aunt Nessy had old me some years before in bewilderment, and with a valiantly suppressed trembling of the lip) written to say that she never wanted to see her again.

'Could Aunt Beatrice perhaps be getting a bit old in herself,' I had suggested, 'or could it perhaps be something to do with the accident she had as a child?'

Aunt Nessy had been one of those children who, in the days of large families, had been given away to elderly childless relatives to be brought up as a kind of maid-of-all-work and as an insurance against old age; and what had upset her most when the parting came was having to leave her youngest sister, Beatrice, on whom she had lavished the mother-love within her – birthright of the children she was destined never to conceive.

'She was such a beautiful little baby; and because things were a bit easier by the time she came along she was always dressed in pretty clothes, not second-hand things and hand-me-downs as we were.

'Then one day my mother dropped her! She fell on her head and was unconscious for a long time. My mother was beside herself and after that, although she still almost worshipped her, she was afraid even to hold her up or lift her, so I had all the care of her.

'She was a beautiful child, too, and tall – not like the rest of us. She was like a little princess in the family; my mother gave in to her in everything and she had whatever she fancied. People thought her spoilt, I know, but it was not her fault.'

In the course of time Aunt Nessy, having looked after her adoptive parents until they died, was left a small sum of money. She rented shop premises – run-down, and modest in size, but in a handy position – and opened a sweet shop.

Unable at first to afford even a bed, she slept behind the shop on a sack filled with paper straw from the empty sweet boxes.

Perhaps because she was a bright, good-hearted little peson, her business prospered. Once a year she went to Scarborough for a week. 'I was so tired by that time that all I could do was sit in a deck-chair on the sea-front and sleep all day, but it was enough.'

After the First World War she added ice-cream to her stock-in-trade, and soon she was able to buy the shop outright. Later she branched out, taking on another carefully chosen establishment with two assistants, and a penny-in-the-slot music machine – forerunner of the juke box.

By the time she was fifty she was in a position to fulfil her life's ambition: to sell up, go south, and buy a little house about ten miles from Beatrice ('near, but not too near'). Beatrice was married now, with a family of her own, and because times were hard her sister helped her with surreptitious gifts of money; and with clothes, toys, and treats for the children.

Meanwhile she lived the life of which she had dreamed. She went to church, and cultivated herbs among the vegetables in her garden. She planted the fruit trees and bushes she had always wanted, made her own bread, and experimented with such things as parsley jelly and mint tea, all to her heart's content.

Sometimes Beatrice would come to see her, bringing the children; and afterwards, when they had grown up, they would visit her still. Later, my husband had taken me with him.

Then I went to see her alone. Her house was always freezing cold in winter, although she did not seem to notice it.

She moved very lightly, and was always cheerful and very clean, with a rosy, deeply wrinkled face and big brown eyes. One day as she tripped forward to greet me I had, without pausing to wonder if my embrace would be acceptable to her, bent down and kissed her. I need not have worried. Her response – such a lighting up of her face – made me remember how few times it was likely she had been kissed in her whole life: not as a child, by the parents who had given her away; not by her old foster parents; not often, I guessed, even by Beatrice and her boys.

So it was that every time I went to see her, she would run forward and stand, head on one side, looking like a little robin, waiting for her kiss.

Sometimes she would be invited to her sister's house, but not too often now, because it must be admitted that with the passing of the years Aunt Nessy had come to look a little eccentric.

Indoors she wore a long black pinafore-like garment, sleeveless and reaching almost to the ground, which she had made from a cotton material used later during the war for black-out curtains and called, I think, sateen. The folds of this pinafore fell amply from a short yoke, and beneath it she wore a succession of woollen jumpers. Her coat, also, was black and very long, and winter and summer she wore the same comfortable black straw hat. Her shoes were of the kind then called ward shoes, with low heels, one strap, and a little metal star on the front for ornamentation.

Then, as in the nature of things Beatrice's lot had improved, so Aunt Nessy's had declined, and her little house had come to look very small and pinched.

It happened that I called at Beatrice's house the last time Aunt Nessy visited there – the time before she was banished. I had always found visiting my mother-in-law difficult; it had never been an easy relationship. Perhaps I could have tried harder to be what she wanted in a daughter-in-law. She had been a mother of sons only and I think now that she would have liked me to call her mother; but then, such an idea never entered my head. Again, although I visited her regularly, taking little presents; remembered her birthday and saw to it that her sons did the same; looked after her once when she was ill; and respected my husband's love for her, I did not take much notice of her suggestions: 'My mother seems to think . . .', 'My mother would like . . .', 'My mother would prefer the name to be . . .'. I listened, looking vague, I expect, but did nothing – not from ill-will but because it just did not occur to me to change.

Sometimes she would compare me unfavourably with her ideal daughter-in-law: 'So-and-so asks her husband's mother for recipes.' Again I listened but said nothing. I did not like recipes; in any case I knew how to cook what my husband liked perfectly well without them.

One's mind is occupied so much when one is young, but I wonder now if I could not have thought more about Beatrice. (Only now do I realise how strong the desire in her for a daughter must have been to cause her to dress her youngest son as a little girl almost until the day he went to school, his fair hair nearly reaching his waist; yet he had grown up a man.) Perhaps then I might have come to understand her, and instead of just doing my duty (as I thought), to love her . . .

Perhaps *now*, but not then with my mind brim-full of other more immediate concerns.

Then I could not forgive how (she said) she would often hit my husband when he was a little boy and naughty, on his bare bottom, with the bristles of a hairbrush. (What a thing to do to a loving little boy! He adored her.) Worse, he had helped the baker in some way (held his horse?) every Saturday morning, although he wanted to play football or marbles so much, being gifted in that direction. ('He wanted more to earn enough money to buy me a present,' she said.) Every day on his way to school he had seen a brooch in the jeweller's window, the price showing on a card beside it. It was the sort of brooch only a very little boy could admire. 'You don't think I am going to wear that trash, do you?' she had said when the great day came; and wondered why he had 'got into one of his passionate tempers' (*poor little disappointed boy!*). In the end she had taken the brooch back to the shop and exchanged it for a plain silver cross on a chain.

For these things I did not forgive her.

Aunt Nessy had been upstairs, but hearing voices she came down, and seeing me ran towards me, as lightly and softly as a little bouncing ball, her eyes full of love and welcome.

Only now have I come to understand what it was my sixth sense was trying to tell me then; in any case it would have been too late, Aunt Nessy was waiting, and bending down, I put my arms round her, and kissed her.

(Pauline Letts read this story on *Woman's Hour* in May 1992.)

HOW SLATTERY
TRICKED HIS MOTHER
INTO TOUCHING HIM

◆

Nina Fitzpatrick

This time it wasn't a woman that was the cause of Slattery's trouble. It was the fall of the People's Republics in Eastern Europe. Poland, Hungary, Czechoslovakia, Bulgaria, Rumania – one after another they deserted him. Such betrayal, such exposure! All the reactionary arseholes in Galway crowed over his embarrassment. They shook their fat heads in mock sympathy and quoted Havel at him.

Slattery passed off their gibes in dignified silence and in expensive Einhorn shirts which he wore as an act of defiance. All his life he had been loyal to the causes of socialism and transcendence. Both made him shockproof against anything that happened outside his own head.

In January 1990 he began to crack. He went through a series of rapid transformations. At first he bore himself like a Cabbalist, haughty and waspish in the conviction that he alone possessed the secret of the true socialism. Then he was a wounded *commandante* in a beleaguered city. He staggered through desolate streets, barely able to stay on his feet as blow after blow rained down on him. Finally he was just a cranky old hen from the Legion of Mary. He repeated old phrases, rummaged for old icons, squeaked his big 'No' through pursed lips, forever virtuous.

With the fall of the Sandinistas in Nicaragua he collapsed entirely and went to visit his mother in Kells. She was the only one that loved him.

One last fit of fervour struck him on the bus home. He threw back his shoulders, raised his chin and displayed a dauntless profile to his fellow passengers. He was a Hero of the Retreat. All over the world, on buses, trains and bicycles, on camel-back, horse-back and mule-back, there were comrades like him who had lost a battle but not the war. But then the Abyss opened and the air went out of him. It was neither the Abyss of Pascal nor the Abyss of Dostoevsky. It was neither bottomless nor infinite nor majestic. Rather, it was bothersome, like anal itch, and too shallow to fling oneself into. It was Slattery's Abyss.

He almost cried when he found that his mother wasn't at home. He was desperate to talk to her, to feel her fussing around him, to have her make him a cup of cocoa, put a hot water bottle into the spare bed and say, accusingly as always, 'You haven't said the rosary.' Tonight he promised himself he would say a decade of the Sorrowful Mysteries.

He couldn't bear being alone. He had to find her immediately. She never visited the neighbours so she could only be in town doing the messages. Off to town then.

He walked briskly from shop to shop in search of her. Wary that anybody would stop him and ask questions he adopted an air of I'm-in-a-hurry-so-don't-delay-me. Then he saw her through the window of the Royal Meath Café, sitting alone at a table and eating a cake. As simple as that. Why then did he feel such terror?

She could be any old woman with nobody to talk to, spending the leftovers of her pension on a little treat for herself. She had raised five children, she was eating her mangy doughnut at a dead, tubular steel table, and she would soon die. And then there would be nothing left for him to connect to when all the lines were down. It was the first time he had seen her like that: alone, anonymous, redundant. He shivered. Through the glass he could feel the air around her frozen solid.

When he stood in front of her, she was at first puzzled and then, he thought, ashamed. He wasn't sure if she was ashamed of being caught unawares or if she was ashamed of being seen with him. Nobody in *her* family, she used to say, ever needed psychiatric help. Or mixed with communists, for that matter.

'Seamus, is that you? Have you come all the way from Galway?'

'Right place, wrong son. It's Bernard.'

'To be sure. Here, have a cup of tea. You must be tired out of your wits. All that journey!'

She still had a 1920s sense of the distance between Galway and Kells.

She waved to the waitress but the girl deliberately turned her back.

'That slut wouldn't sell sovereigns. She's such a sourpuss.'

'It's OK, Mother. I'll have something later.'

He was confused. His mother was completely oblivious to the pain she should have felt at being slighted like that. It seemed he had to suffer it for her.

He wished that they were at home and that he could hug her. Up till now he had always lived in a luminous place in his head which fed all his cravings. Now that the light had gone out he felt an abysmal need to touch and to be touched. But she sat there rambling on about Seamus, the two little girls and the sheepdog and how she couldn't stand that dog. Slattery unscrewed his ears and waited till her litany of venom petered out. The crisis in Rumania meant as much as last year's snow. No doubt she would regard his own crisis as a just punishment for his sins.

He walked her home, carrying her bags and trying to comply with her unspoken command that he make himself as invisible as possible. Occasionally she grabbed at him for support, fastening on the sleeve of his coat. 'Here, Mother,' he said, again and again, 'take my arm.' But she pretended not to hear.

The house had the old familiar warm smell of decaying vegetation. Slattery filled his lungs with it and felt home at last. He couldn't wait, he simply had to hug her. He followed her like a dog from the stove to the sink and back again, chatting idiotically of this and that. His whole being, deprived now of the warm fraternity of struggling humanity and a sense of purpose, demanded this hug. Oh, how simple and natural it had been to embrace the comrades in Managua, Bratislava, Addis Abbaba. How many embraces, kisses, mutual toasts, impassioned speeches joined him to the proletariat of three continents! The revolution was sensuous, it was real. It was 1988 with Commandante Philippe in Las Palomas Nightclub, Havana! And now?

She avoided him as if she knew instinctively what he was after. Finally she stood in front of the gas cooker frying his favourite Lorenzen's sausages.

'It's great to be home, Mother,' he said, putting his arm around her shoulders. She stiffened on the spot like a patient in a dentist's chair.

'Set the table,' she said and moved quickly to the sink.

Slattery howled inside and set the table for four. Blindly he followed the old routine: a plate for himself, a plate for the wife, two plates for the boys. His mother looked at him accusingly.

'What do you think you're doing? Have you gone soft in the head on top of everything else?'

The years of revolutionary struggle stood to him. He was determined to get this hug. He kept watching her, waiting for a weak moment. Over tea he tried to soften her calcified soul by subterfuge. He talked about Daddy, about her skill with plants, about himself when he won the scholarship to St Finian's. Once or twice she seemed ductile, but a premature move earned him an elbow in the ribs.

A horrible realisation slowly dawned on Slattery. His own mother was untouchable. Worse, she had never touched *him*. It struck him now that he could not ever recall being kissed or hugged by her, not even patted on the shoulder with a good boy yourself! All her feelings were invested in plants. She was gentle with sweet williams, lupins, dahlias, daffodils and tea roses. Her devotion to thyme, lemon balm and rosemary was almost maternal.

'Look,' she would say softly, 'look at this little one!' and point to some nameless bit of greenery trying to push its way up through the John Innes mixture. Her eyes would fill with an affection she could never muster for an animal or human being. Only the drab sparrows she fed on the windowsill inspired the same tenderness. At last he knew why. She could minister to them without touching.

Now that he saw her frigidity in all its glacial bleakness he was determined to save her. He would humanise his mother! He would beguile her into touching him! That much he would do for her before she died.

He watched her carefully. Her routine was very simple. She got up at six o'clock in the morning, checked the weather and the sky, made herself a cup of tea and went back to bed. Now that there was a man in the house she felt safe and slept until ten. When she rose again she complained that the day was half gone and set to work in the garden. He could never see any traces of her labour except a small pile of weeds or a few twigs. But she always returned to the kitchen fresh and full of affectionate reproaches.

'You read too much, Bernard. Throw away them books and newspapers. Get out into the fresh air. Take deep breaths.'

And she would demonstrate, inhaling and exhaling, at the open door.

Occasionally he felt guilty about spending his days listening to the news and reading newspapers. But when he offered to do something round the house, even so simple a thing as washing the dishes, she would protest.

'You have other things to do, Bernard. Sit down there and go on with your reading.'

But the pages were pure torment. Slattery couldn't tolerate a sentence with more than five words. Complex and compound structures were the façades of megalomania. Long paragraphs were Potemkin villages. His faith could stretch to subject, verb and object, no more.

In the afternoon she watched children's TV programmes. She sat in front of the set with greedy attention, chortling and smiling happily to herself. She was so used to being on her own that she forgot all about Slattery's presence in the room. The screen was blurred and hazy but she made no effort to sharpen the focus. When Slattery tried to correct the picture she got angry and told him to leave her things alone. Watching TV with a blurred screen was a bribe to whatever mad God she believed in. It was the price she paid for indulging herself.

After tea she said the rosary, offering it up for her dead parents and old neighbours, her children, wherever they were, and her grandchildren, the Pope's Intentions, for all that we have and all that we are, to help Bernard find peace of mind and Daddy find eternal peace. Then she read *The Irish Independent*, usually three or four days out of date, and invariably fell asleep over it. She would wake with a start, make herself a mug of hot milk and ginger, and go to bed. Her last words were always the same: 'Say your prayers, Bernard, and we'll hang that door tomorrow.'

As the days passed she grew more and more remote from him. She got used to having him round the house. The indifference that followed her initial excitement at his homecoming made the hug even less likely. In the evenings Slattery slumped in the armchair where his father had slumped before him. He sat there mute and full of grief until he too fell asleep.

One such evening they were watching 'The Late Late Show'. As usual she was cutting the women guests to ribbons: 'Will you look at the gimp and get-up of that one.' Or: 'I'd put manners on that scut if I had my hands on her.' Then, all of a sudden, she grew quiet and intent. A woman healer was being interviewed. The camera showed a close-up of her hands. She had four well-defined bosses where the fingers joined the palm. These, she said, were the marks of the true healer.

Slattery saw his mother looking furtively at her own palm.

'I think I have it too,' she announced.

'Show me,' he demanded.

She bent back her palms and held them up to the light.

'Look at that! I always knew I had a gift!'

She said it in a way that suggested she had been fighting the gift all her life. And yet, at the same time, she seemed deeply moved by her discovery, as if her life made sense after all.

Now, at the eleventh hour, his chance had come.

'Fantastic! Why don't we try it?'

She glanced at him apprehensively.

'No.'

'Look. It's dead simple. I've got an awful headache. Who knows, maybe you can cure it? Let's have a shot at it!'

'Don't be silly! Do you have any mending?'

'Come on! Let's try it.'

'I hope the Lord gives me mending at the Gates. I like mending.'

His father's voice rang in his ears: *Bitch out of Hell.*

'Stop that rubbish about mending. Remember how good you were with Daddy when he was sick?'

She hesitated. It was true.

'And with me when I had the meningitis. Most kids suffer with brain damage after it. And me? I'm as sane as – Slattery looked for a comparison that would appeal to her – as a parish priest.'

She began to withdraw again.

'It's not right to meddle with these things.'

'Look. I don't want you to restore my missing teeth or anything like that. I have a headache. You can cure with your hands. It's as simple as that.'

'Go away.'

But she was weakening. Throw the Gospel at her now.

'Remember the man in the Gospel who buried his talent in the ground?'

She looked at her hands again. God, but she was slow.

'All right. Just this once.'

Slattery set himself low in the couch. For a moment she stood in confusion, as if wondering how to start. Then she picked up her shawl and drew it around her shoulders like a stole. Hieratically, she approached her son with her arms outstretched and held her hands an inch above his head. He could hear her muttering prayers to the Virgin Mary on his behalf. Will she or won't she?

Her bony old hand rested on his head impersonally, with a professional assurance. He felt a glow of heat on the top of his skull. He tightened up inside. His heart was thumping in his chest and his throat went dry. He was a boy again, kneeling in front of the priest, about to receive Holy Communion.

'Did it work?' she asked matter of factly, stepping aside.

'A bit.'

Slattery's voice quavered as if he were about to burst into tears.

'Only a bit. You didn't hold it long enough.'

Next day Slattery stayed on in bed. At two o'clock his mother brought him beef tea and toast and an express letter. She was happy to have somebody to look after again and spoke to him tenderly.

'Keep yourself well wrapped up, Bernard,' she said. 'And call me if you need anything.'

Slattery opened the letter. It was a leaflet from the Communist Party of Ireland inviting him to a public meeting. It read: *In the light of the collapse of the Revisionist Traitor Regimes throughout Eastern Europe we hail the success of genuine communism in Albania! Communist Party of Ireland (Marxist-Leninist). Join us Monday 15 January, 8 p.m., beside the Cathedral.*

Slattery folded the letter pedantically and stuffed it in the pocket of his pyjamas.

'The lectures are starting,' he said. 'I have to be back.'

She nodded.

He decided to take the night bus to Galway. He couldn't bear to look out on the cold, psychotic fields of Meath, Offaly and Roscommon.

(Sean Barrett read this story on *Woman's Hour* in June 1991.)

UNEARTHING SUITE

———— ◆ ————

Margaret Atwood

My parents have something to tell me: something apart from the ordinary course of conversation. I can guess this from the way they sit down first, both on the same chair, my mother on the arm, and turn their heads a little to one side, regarding me with their ultra-blue eyes.

As they have grown older their eyes have become lighter and lighter and more and more bright, as if time is leeching them of darkness, experience clarifying them until they have reached the transparency of stream water. Possibly this is an illusion caused by the whitening of their hair. In any case their eyes are now round and shiny, like the glass-bead eyes of stuffed animals. Not for the first time it occurs to me that I could not have been born, like other people, but must have been hatched out of an egg. My parents' occasional dismay over me was not like the dismay of other parents. It was less dismay than perplexity, the bewilderment of two birds who have found a human child in their nest and have no idea what to do with it.

My father takes a black leather folder from the desk. They both have an air of suppressed excitement, like children waiting for a grown-up friend to open a present they have wrapped; which will contain a joke.

'We went down and bought our urns today,' my father says.

'You what?' I say, shocked. There is nothing wrong with my parents. They are in perfect health. I on the other hand have a cold.

'It's best to be prepared,' my mother says. 'We looked at plots but they're so expensive.'

'They take up too much space,' says my father, who has always been conscious of the uses to which the earth is wrongly in his opinion put. Conversation around the dinner table when I was growing up concerned itself more than once with how many weeks it would take a pair of fruit flies breeding unchecked to cover the earth to a depth of thirty-two feet. Not many, as I recall. He feels much the same about corpses.

'They give you a little niche too,' says my mother.

'It's in here,' says my father, indicating the folder as if I am supposed to remember about all this and deal with it at the right time. I am appalled: surely they aren't leaving something, finally, up to me?

'We want to be sprinkled,' says my mother. 'But they told us it's now illegal.'

'That's ridiculous,' I say. 'Why can't you be sprinkled if you want to?'

'The funeral-parlour lobby,' says my father, who has been known to be cynical about government decisions. My mother concedes that things might get a bit dusty if everyone were to be sprinkled.

'I'll sprinkle you,' I say bravely. 'Don't worry about a thing.'

This is a rash decision and I've made it on the spur of the moment, as I make all my rash decisions. But I fully intend to carry it out, even though it will mean action, a thing I avoid when possible. Under pretence of a pious visit I will steal my parents from their niche, substituting sand if necessary, and smuggle them away. The ashes part doesn't bother me; in fact I approve of it. Much better than waiting, like the Christians, for God to grow them once more instantaneously from the bone outward, sealed meanwhile rouged and waxed and wired, veins filled with formaldehyde, in cement and bronze vaults, a prey to mould and anaerobic bacteria. If God wants to make my parents again the molecules will do just as well to start with, same as before. It is not a question of matter, which turns over completely every seven years anyway, but of form.

We sit for a minute, considering implications. We are way beyond funerals and mourning, or possibly we have by-passed them. I am thinking about the chase, and being arrested, and how I will foil the authorities: already I am concocting fictions. My father is thinking about fertiliser, in the same tone in which other people think about union with the Infinite. My mother is thinking about the wind.

Photographs have never done justice to my mother. This is because they stop time; to really reflect her they would have to show her as a blur. When I think of her she is often on skis. Her only discoverable ambition as a child was to be able to fly, and much of her subsequent life has been spent in various attempts to take off. Stories of her youth involve scenes in trees and on barn roofs, breakneck dashes on frothy-mouthed runaway horses, speedskating races, and, when she was older, climbs out of windows onto forbidden fire escapes, done more for the height and adventure than for the end result, an after-hours college date with some young man or other who had been knocked over by her, perhaps literally. For my mother, despite her daunting athleticism and lack of interest in frilly skirts, was much sought after. Possibly men saw her as a challenge: it would be an accomplishment to get her to pause long enough to pay even a fleeting amount of attention to them.

My father first saw her sliding down a banister – I imagine, in the 1920s, that she would have done this sidesaddle – and resolved then and there to marry her; though it took him a while to track her down, stalking her from tree to tree, crouching behind bushes, butterfly net at the ready. This is a metaphor but not unjustified.

One of their neighbours recently took me to task about her.

'Your poor mother,' she said. 'Married to your father.'

'What?' I said.

'I see her dragging her groceries back from the supermarket,' she said. (True enough, my mother does this. She has a little cart with which she whizzes along the sidewalk, hair wisping out from her head, scarf streaming, exhausting anyone foolhardy enough to make the trip with her; by that I mean myself.) 'Your father won't even drive her.'

When I told her this story, my mother laughed.

My father said the unfortunate woman obviously didn't know that there was more to him than met the eye.

In recent years my mother has taken up a new winter exercise. Twice a week she goes dancing on figure skates: waltzes, tangos, fox trots. On Tuesday and Thursday mornings she can be observed whirring around the local arena to the tune of 'A Bicycle Built For Two' played over the scratchy sound system, speed undiminished, in mittens which do not match her skirt, keeping perfect time.

My father did what he did because it allows him to do what he does. There he goes now, in among the trees, battered grey felt hat – with or without a couple of trout flies stuck in the band, depending on what year we're talking about – on his head to keep things from falling into his hair, things that are invisible to others but which he knows all too well are lurking up there among the innocent-looking leaves, one or two or a clutch of children of any age tagging along after him, his own or his grandchildren or children attracted at random, as a parade attracts followers, as the sun attracts meteors, their eyes getting larger and larger as wonder after wonder is revealed to them: a sacred white larva that will pupate and fly only after seven years, a miraculous beetle that eats wood, a two-sexed worm, a fungus that crawls. No freak show can hold a candle to my father expounding Nature.

He leaves no stone unturned; but having turned it, to see what may be underneath – and at this point no squeals or expressions of disgust are permitted, on pain of his disfavour – he puts everything carefully back: the grub into its hollow, the woodborer beneath its rotting bark, the worm into its burrow, unless needed of course for fishing. He is not a sentimentalist.

Now he spreads a tarpaulin beneath a likely-looking tree, striped maple let us say, and taps the tree trunk with the pole of his axe. Heaven rewards him with a shower of green caterpillars, which he gathers tenderly in, to carry home with him and feed on leafy branches of the appropriate kind stuck into quart jars of water. These he will forget to replace, and soon the caterpillars will go crawling over our walls and ceiling in search of fodder, to drop as if on cue into the soup. My mother is used to this by now and thinks nothing of it.

Meanwhile the children follow him to the next tree: he is better than magicians, since he explains everything. This is indeed one of his purposes: to explain everything, when possible. He wants to see, he wants to know, only to see and know. I'm aware that it is this mentality, this curiosity, which is responsible for the hydrogen bomb and the imminent demise of civilisation and that we would all be better off if we were still at the stone-worshipping stage. Though surely it is not this affable inquisitive-ness that should be blamed.

Look, my father has unearthed a marvel: a slug perhaps, a snake, a spider complete with her sack of eggs? Something educational at any rate. You can't see it from here: only the backs of the children's heads as they peer down into his cupped hands.

My parents do not have houses, like other people. Instead they have earths. These look like houses but are not thought of as houses, exactly. Instead they are more like stopping places, sea-sonal dens, watering holes on some caravan route which my nomadic parents are always following, or about to follow, or have just come back from following. Much of my mother's time is spent packing and unpacking.

Unlocking the door of one of their earths – and unlike foxes they get rid of the bones, not by burial but by burning, the right thing to do unless you want skunks – I am greeted first by dark-ness, then by a profusion of objects heaped apparently at random but actually following some arcane scheme of order: stacks of lumber, cans of paintbrush cleaner with paintbrushes soaking in them, some of these dry and stiff or glued to the insides of the cans by the sticky residue left by evaporation, boxes of four-inch spikes, six-quart baskets filled with an assortment of screws, hinges, staples, and roofing-nails, rolls of roofing, axes, saws, brace-and-bits, levels, peevees, spokeshaves, rasps, drills, post-hole diggers, shovels, mattocks, and crowbars. (Not all of these things are in the same place at the same time: this is a collective memory.) I know what each of these tools is for and may even at some time have used it, which may go part way towards explaining my adult slothfulness. The smell is the smell of my childhood: wood, canvas, tar, kerosene, soil.

This is my father's section of the house. In my mother's, things are arranged, on hooks and shelves, in inviolable order: cups, pots, plates, pans. This is not because my mother makes a fetish of housekeeping but because she doesn't want to waste time on it. All her favourite recipes begin with the word *quick*. Less is more, as far as she is concerned, and this means everything in its place. She has never been interested, luckily, in the house beautiful, but she does insist on the house convenient.

Her space is filled. She does not wish it altered. We used to give her cooking pots for Christmas until we realised that she would much rather have something else.

My father likes projects. My mother likes projects to be finished. Thus you see her, in heavy work gloves, carting cement blocks, one by one, or stacks of wood, from one location to another, dragging underbrush which my father has slashed, hauling buckets of gravel and dumping them out, all in aid of my father's constructionism.

Right now they are digging a large hole in the ground. This will eventually be another earth. My mother has already moved a load of cement blocks to the site, for lining it with; in the mornings she goes to see what animal tracks she can find on the fresh sand, and perhaps to rescue any toads and mice that may have tumbled in.

Although he is never finished, my father does finish things. Last summer a back step suddenly appeared on our log house up north. For twenty years my mother and I had been leaping into space whenever we wanted to reach the clothesline, using biceps and good luck to get ourselves back up and in. Now we descend normally. And there is a sink in the kitchen, so that dirty dishwater no longer has to be carried down the hill in an enamel pail, slopping over onto one's legs, and buried in the garden. It now goes down a drainhole in the approved manner. My mother has added her completing touch: a small printed sign Scotch-taped to the counter, which reads:

PUT NO FAT DOWN SINK.

A jar of dried bacteria stands nearby: one teaspoonful is poured down at intervals, so the stray tea leaves will be devoured. This prevents clogging.

Meanwhile my father is hard at work, erecting cedar logs into vertical walls for the new outhouse, which will contain a chemical toilet, unlike the old one. He is also building a fireplace out of selected pink granite boulders which my mother steps over and around as she sweeps the leaves off the floor.

Where will it all end? I cannot say. As a child I wrote small books which I began with the words *The End*. I needed to know the end was guaranteed.

My own house is divided in two: a room full of paper, constantly in flux, where process, organicism, and fermentation rule and dustballs breed; and another room, formal in design, rigid in content, which is spotlessly clean and to which nothing is ever added.

As for me, I will die no doubt of inertia. Though witness to my parents' exhausting vitality, I spent my childhood learning to equate goodness with immobility. Sitting in the bottoms of canoes that would tip if you lurched, crouching in tents that would leak if you touched them in rainstorms, used for ballast in motorboats stacked precariously high with lumber, I was told not to move, and I did not. I was thought of as being well-behaved.

At intervals my father would bundle the family and the necessary provisions into the current car – *Studebaker* is a name I remember – and make a pilgrimage of one kind or another, a thousand miles here, a thousand miles there. Sometimes we were in search of saw-flies; at other times, of grandparents. We would drive as long as possible along the almost empty post-war highways, through the melancholy small towns of Quebec or northern Ontario, sometimes down into the States, where there were more roadside billboards. Long after the minor-key sunsets late at night, when even the White Rose gasoline stations were closed, we would look for a motel; in those days, a string of homemade cottages beside a sign that read FOLDED WINGS, or, more sombrely, VALHALLA, the tiny clapboard office festooned with Christmas-tree lights. Ever since then, *vacancy* has been a magic word for me: it means there is room. If we did not find a vacancy my father would simply pull over to the side of the road in some likely-looking spot and put up a tent. There were few campgrounds, no motorcycle gangs; there was more emptiness than there is now. Tents were not so portable then; they were heavy and canvas, and sleeping bags were dank and filled with kapok. Everything was grey or khaki.

During these trips my father would drive as fast as he could, hurling the car forward it seemed by strength of will, pursued by all the unpulled weeds in his gardens, all the caterpillars uncollected in his forests, all the nails that needed to be hammered in, all the loads of dirt that had to be shifted from one place to another. I, meanwhile, would lie on a carefully stowed pile of baggage in the back seat, wedged into a small place beneath the roof. I could see out of the window, and I would watch the landscape, which consisted of many dark trees and of the telephone poles and their curves of wire, which looked as if they were moving up and down. Perhaps it was then that I began the translation of the world into words. It was something you could do without moving.

Sometimes, when we were stationary, I held the ends of logs while my father sawed them, or pulled out designated weeds, but most of the time I lived a life of contemplation. In so far as possible I sneaked off into the woods to read books and evade tasks, taking with me supplies filched from my mother's tin of cooking raisins and stash of crackers. In theory I can do almost anything; certainly I have been told how. In practice I do as little as possible. I pretend to myself that I would be quite happy in a hermit's cave, living on gruel, if someone else would make the gruel. Gruel, like so many other things, is beyond me.

What is my mother's secret? For of course she must have one. No one can have a life so apparently cheerful, so seemingly lacking in avalanches and swamps, without having also a secret. By *secret* I mean the price she had to pay. What was the trade-off, what did she sign over to the Devil, for this limpid tranquillity?

She maintains that she once had a quick temper, but no one knows where it has gone. When she was forced to take piano lessons as part of a young lady's battery of accomplishments, she memorised the pieces and played them by rote while reading novels concealed on her lap. 'More *feeling*,' her teacher would say to her. Pictures of her at four show a shy-looking ringleted girl bedecked in the lacy lampshade dresses inflicted on girls before the First World War, but in fact she was inquisitive, inventive, always getting into trouble. One of her first memories is of sliding down a red clay bank in her delicate white post-Victorian pantaloons. She remembers the punishment, true, but she remembers better the lovely feeling of the mud.

Her marriage was an escape from its alternatives. Instead of becoming the wife of some local small-town professional and settling down, in skirts and proper surroundings, to do charity work for the church as would have befitted her status, she married my father and took off down the St John's River in a canoe, never having slept in a tent before; except once, just before the wedding, when she and her sisters spent a weekend practising. My father knew how to light fires in the rain and what to do about rapids, which alarmed my mother's friends. Some of them thought of her as having been kidnapped and dragged off to the wilderness, where she was imprisoned and forced to contend with no electricity, no indoor plumbing, and hordes of ravening bears.

She on the other hand must have felt that she had been rescued from a fate worse than death: antimacassars on the chairs.

Even when we lived in real houses it was something like camping out. There was an improvisational quality to my mother's cooking, as if the ingredients were not bought but scavenged: what we ate depended on what was at hand. She made things out of other things and never threw anything out. Although she did not like dirt, she could never take housecleaning seriously as an end in itself. She polished the hardwood floors by dragging her children over them on an old flannelette blanket. This sounds like fun until I reflect: they were too poor for floor polishers, maids, or babysitters.

After my birth she developed warts, all over both her hands. Her explanation was the ammonia: there were no disposable diapers then. In those days babies wore knitted woollen sweaters, woollen booties, woollen bonnets, and woollen soakers, in which they must have steamed like puddings. My parents did not own a wringer washer; my mother washed everything by hand. During this period she did not get out much to play. In the photographs, she is always posed with a sled or a carriage and one or two suspicious-looking infants. She is never alone.

Possibly she got the warts from being grounded; or, more particularly, from me. It's a burden, this responsibility for the warts of one's mother, but since I missed out on the usual guilts this one will have to do. The warts point towards my mother's secret but do not reveal it. In any case they went away.

My mother lived for two years in the red-light district of Montreal without knowing what it was. She was informed only afterwards, by an older woman who told her she ought not to have done it. 'I don't know why not,' said my mother. That is her secret.

My father studies history. He has been told by Poles that he knows more Polish history than most Poles, by Greeks that he knows more Greek history than most Greeks, by Spaniards that he knows more Spanish history than most Spaniards. Taking the sum total of worldwide *per capita* knowledge into consideration this is probably so. He alone, among my acquaintances, successfully predicted the war in Afghanistan, on the basis of past examples. Who else was paying any attention?

It is his theory that both Hiroshima and the discovery of America were entomological events (the clue is the silkworm) and that fleas have been responsible for more massacres and population depletions than have religions (the clue is the bubonic plague). His overview is dire, though supported, he would hasten to point out, by the facts. Wastefulness, stupidity, arrogance, greed, and brutishness unroll themselves in Technicolor panorama across our dinner table as my father genially carves the roast.

Should civilisation as we know it destroy itself, he informs us, ladling the gravy – as is likely, he adds – it will never be able to rebuild itself in its present form, since all available surface metals have long since been exhausted and the extraction of deeper ones is dependent upon metal technologies, which, as you will remember, will have been demolished. There can never be another iron age, another bronze age; we will be stuck – if there is any *we*, which he doubts – with stone and bone, no good for aeroplanes and computers.

He has scant interest in surviving into the twenty-first century. He knows it will be awful. Any person of sense will agree with him (and lest you make the mistake of thinking him merely quaint, let me remind you that many do).

My mother, however, pouring out the tea and forgetting as usual who takes milk, says she wants to live as long as possible. She wants to see what happens.

My father finds this naïve of her, but lets it pass and goes on to discuss the situation in Poland. He recalls to our memories (paying his listeners the compliment, always, of pretending he is merely reminding them of something they have of course already known, long and well) the Second World War Polish cavalry charge against the German tanks: foolishness and bravery. But foolish. But brave. He helps himself to more mashed potato, shaking his head in wonder. Then, changing the subject, he delivers himself of one of those intricate and reprehensible puns he's so fond of.

How to reconcile his grim vision of life on earth with his undoubted enjoyment of it? Neither is a pose. Both are real. I can't remember – though my father could, without question, ferreting among his books to locate the exact reference – which saint it was who, when asked what he would do if the end of the world were due tomorrow, said he would continue to cultivate his garden. The proper study of mankind may be man, but the proper activity is digging.

My parents have three gardens: one in the city, which produces raspberries, eggplants, irises, and beans; another halfway up, which specialises in peas, potatoes, squash, onions, beets, carrots, broccoli, and cauliflower; and the one up north, small but lovingly cherished, developed from sand, compost, and rations of sheep and horse manure carefully doled out, which yields cabbages, spinach, lettuce, long-lasting rhubarb, and Swiss chard, cool-weather crops.

All spring and summer my parents ricochet from garden to garden, mulching, watering, pulling up the polyphiloprogenitive weeds, 'until,' my mother says, 'I'm bent over like a coat hanger.' In the fall they harvest, usually much more than they can possibly eat. They preserve, store, chill, and freeze. They give away the surplus, to friends and family, and to the occasional stranger whom my father has selected as worthy. These are sometimes women who work in bookstores and have demonstrated their discernment and intelligence by recognising the titles of books my father asks for. On these he will occasionally bestow a cabbage of superior size and delightfulness, a choice clutch of tomatoes, or, if it is fall and he has been chopping and sawing, an elegant piece of wood.

In the winter my parents dutifully chew their way through the end products of their summer's labour, since it would be a shame to waste anything. In the spring, fortified with ever newer and more fertile and rust-resistant varieties from the Stokes Seed

Catalogue, they begin again.

My back aches merely thinking about them as I creep out to some sinful junk-food outlet or phone up Pizza Pizza. But in truth the point of all this gardening is not vitaminisation or self-sufficiency or the production of food, though these count for something. Gardening is not a rational act. What matters is the immersion of the hands in the earth, that ancient ceremony of which the Pope kissing the tarmac is merely a pallid vestigial remnant.

In the spring, at the end of the day, you should smell like dirt.

Here is a fit subject for meditation: the dock. I myself use it, naturally, to lie down on. From it I can see the outlines of the shore, which function for me like a memory. At night I sit on it, in a darkness which is like no other, watching stars if there are any. At dusk there are bats; in the mornings, ducks. Underneath it there are leeches, minnows, and the occasional crayfish. This dock, like Nature, is permanently crumbling away and is always the same.

It is built on cribs of logs weighted down by granite boulders, which are much easier to move around underwater than they are on land. For this venture my father immersed himself in the lake, which he otherwise prefers to stay out of. No wonder; even on good days, at the height of summer, it is not what you would call warm. Scars go purple in it, toes go white, lips go blue. The lake is one of those countless pot-holes left by the retreating glaciers, which had previously scraped off all the topsoil and pushed it south. What remained is bedrock, and when you dip yourself into this lake you know that if you stay in it long enough or even very long at all you will soon get down to the essentials.

My father looks at this dock (his eyes narrowing in calculation, his fingers twitching) and sees mainly that it needs to be repaired. The winter ice has been at it, the sun, the rain; it is patched and treacherous, threads of rot are spreading through it. Sometime soon he will take his crowbar to it, rip apart its punky and dangerous boards and the logs excavated by nesting yellow-jackets, and rebuild the whole thing new.

My mother sees it as a place from which to launch canoes, and as a handy repository for soap and towel when, about three in the afternoon, in the lull between the lunch dishes and reactivating the fire for supper, she goes swimming. Into the gelid, heart-stoppingly cold water she wades, over the blackened pine needles lying on the sand and the waterlogged branches, over the shells of clams and the carapaces of crayfish, splashing the tops of her arms, until she finally plunges in and speeds outward, on her back, her neck coming straight up out of the water like an otter's, her head in its white bathing cap encircled by an aureole of black flies, kicking up a small wake behind her and uttering cries of:

Refreshing! Refreshing!

Today I pry myself loose from my own entropy and lead two children single-file through the woods. We are looking for anything. On the way we gather pieces of fallen birch bark, placing them in paper bags after first shaking them to get out the spiders. They will be useful for lighting the fire. We talk about fires and where they should not be lit. There are charcoal-sided trunks crumbling here and there in the forest, *mementi mori* of an ancient burnout.

The trail we follow is an old one, blazed by my brother during his trail-making phase thirty years ago and brushed out by him routinely since. The blazes are now weathered and grey; hardened tree blood stands out in welts around them. I teach the children to look on both sides of the trees, to turn once in a while and see where they have come from, so that they will learn how to find their way back, always. They stand under the huge trees in their raincoats, space echoing silently around them; a folklore motif, these children in the woods, potentially lost. They sense it and are hushed.

The Indians did that, I tell them, pointing to an old tree bent when young into knees and elbows. Which, like most history, may or may not be true.

Real ones? they want to know.

Real, I say.

Were they alive? they ask.

We go forward, clambering up a hill, over boulders, past a fallen log ripped open by a bear in search of grubs. They have more orders: they are to keep their eyes open for mushrooms, and especially for puffballs, which even they like to eat. Around here there is no such thing as just a walk. I feel genetics stealing over me: in a minute I will be turning over stones for them, and in fact I am soon on my hands and knees, grubbing a gigantic toad out from under a fallen cedar so old it is almost earth, burnt orange. We discuss the fact that toads will not give you warts but will pee on you when frightened. The toad does this, proving my reliability. For its own good I put it into my pocket and the expedition moves forward.

At right angles there's a smaller trail, a recent one, marked not by blazes but by snapped branches and pieces of fluorescent pink tape tied to bushes. It leads to a yellow birch blown down by the wind – you can tell by the roots, topsoil and leaf-mould still matted on them – now neatly sawn and stacked, ready for splitting. Another earthwork.

On the way back we circle the burn-heap, the garden, going as quietly as we can. The trick, I whisper, is to see things before they see you. Not for the first time I feel that this place is haunted, by the ghosts of those not yet dead, my own included.

Nothing goes on forever. Sooner or later I will have to renounce my motionlessness, give up those habits of reverie, speculation, and lethargy by which I currently subsist. I will have to come to grips with the real world, which is composed, I know, not of words but of drainpipes, holes in the ground, furiously multiplying weeds, hunks of granite, stacks of more or less heavy matter which must be moved from one point to the other, usually uphill.

How will I handle it? Only time, which does not by any means tell everything, will tell.

This is another evening, later in the year. My parents have returned yet once again from the north. It is fall, the closing-down season. Like the sun my parents have their annual rhythms, which, come to think of it, are not unrelated to that simile. This is the time of the withering of the last bean plants, the faltering of the cabbages, when the final carrot must be prised from the earth, tough and whiskered and forked like a mandrake; when my parents make great altars of rubbish, old cardboard boxes, excess branches lopped from trees, egg cartons, who knows? – and ignite them to salute the fading sun.

But they have done all that and have made a safe journey. Now they have another revelation to make: something portentous, something momentous. Something has happened that does not happen every day.

'I was up on the roof, sweeping off the leaves—' says my mother.

'As she does every fall—' says my father.

It does not alarm me to picture my seventy-three-year-old mother clambering nimbly about on a roof, a roof with a pitch so steep that I myself would go gingerly, toes and fingers suctioned to the asphalt roofing like a tree-frog's, adrenalin hazing the sky, through which I can see myself hurtling earthward after a moment of forgetfulness, a misstep, one of those countless slips of the mind and therefore of the body about which I ought to have known better. My mother does these things all the time. She has never fallen off. She will never fall.

'Otherwise trees will grow on it,' says my mother.

'And guess what she found?' says my father.

I try to guess, but I cannot. What would my mother have found on the roof? Not a pine cone, not a fungus, not a dead bird. It would not be what anyone else would find there.

In fact it turns out to be a dropping. Now I have to guess what kind of dropping.

'Flying squirrel,' I hazard lamely.

No, no. Nothing so ordinary.

'It was about this big,' says my father, indicating the length and circumference. It is not an owl then.

'Brown?' I say, stalling for time.

'Black,' says my father. They both regard me, heads a little on one side, eyes shining with the glee of playing this ancient game, the game of riddles, scarcely able to contain the right answer.

'And it had hair in it,' says my father, hinting, waiting. Then he lowers his voice a little. 'Fisher,' he says.

'Really?' I say.

'Must be,' says my father, and we all pause to savour the rarity of this event. There are not many fishers left, not many of those beautiful arboreal voracious predators, and we have never before found the signs of one in our area. For my father, this dropping is an interesting biological phenomenon. He has noted it and filed it, along with all the other scraps of fascinating data he notes and files.

For my mother, however, this is something else. For her this dropping – this hand-long, two-fingers-thick, black, hairy dropping – not to put too fine a point on it, this deposit of animal shit – is a miraculous token, a sign of divine grace; as if their mundane, familiar, much-patched but at times still-leaking roof has been visited and made momentarily radiant by an unknown but by no means minor god.

(Shelley Thompson read this story on *Woman's Hour* in April 1992.)

Short Story Index
<u>1989-1993</u>